MW01713235

Debut for a Spy

HARRY CURRIE

Debut for a Spy

Rivercrest
PUBLISHERS
Cambridge, Ontario

RIVERCREST PUBLISHERS
1150 Langs Circle
Cambridge, Ontario
Canada N3H 5E6

Published 1995. First edition

Printed in Canada by University of Toronto Press, Inc.
Bound by TRI-GRAPHIC Printing (Ottawa) Limited
Typeset by Aztext Electronic Publishing Limited

02 01 00 99 98 97 96 95 5 4 3 2 1

Publisher's note: This book is a work of fiction. Names, characters, places, and events are either a product of the author's imagination or are used ficticiously. Any other similarities to actual persons or incidents are entirely coincidental.

Canadian Cataloguing-in-Publication Data

Currie, Harry, 1931-
Debut for a Spy

ISBN 0-9680009-0-8

1. Title

PS8555.U77D4 1995 C813'.54 C95-932312-0
PR9199.3.C87D4 1995

Printed on acid free recycled paper

To Gabriella

my dear wife, my sharpest editor, my wisest critic, my best friend

To George

a son for all seasons, who understood while I wrote

and

In Memory of Tony Kershaw

the second Concord, who shared Kneller Hall and a life in music

Acknowledgements

A first novel is a daunting task. When an idea for a short story began to expand beyond its original concept, it actually frightened me. But with encouragement, cooperation, and assistance from so many people on both sides of the Atlantic it has finally crept into print.

I would be remiss not to acknowledge some of the people who helped along the way:

Greg Ferguson of British Aerospace for an invitation to visit England and learn about the P1127/Harrier first-hand, and being my guide while I was there.

British Aerospace pilots and technicians at Dunsfold who gave me the experience of a lifetime, and documents I couldn't believe.

Bill Bedford, former Chief Test Pilot of Hawker Aviation and the first pilot of XP831, who shared his experiences and memories, and consented to appear in my novel as himself.

My dear friend and former classmate Major Don Pryce and his wife Ann, for facilitating my stay in England, and introducing me to 'Death by Chocolate'.

The Soviet diplomat (best unnamed) who shouldn't have taken me on a tour of the Soviet Embassy in London, and didn't confiscate the photos.

The British Secret Intelligence Service for being there.

The United States Navy Department for research and data on the *USS Enterprise.*

Canadian Pacific Archives, for re-acquainting me with the *Empress of Britain* on which I sailed in 1959, and which still sails for Carnival Lines as the *Carnivale.*

Mienke Atadan of the University of Waterloo for the Russian dialogue.

David Ignatius, author and foreign editor of the Washington Post, for all the information the CIA wouldn't give me.

Dudley Moore for smiling his acquiescence when I told him he was in the novel.

Ronnie Scott for a great evening at his jazz club in London.

Susan Daminato for an early edit which paved the way to the final version.

All those students in schools of the Waterloo County Board of Education who listened to the excerpts-in-progress of their English supply teacher and offered many suggestions.

Rita Jefferies, author of *Out Of Control*, for her insights and advice on the publishing process.

Will Dixon who built the model of XP831 used for the jacket.

All my friends and acquaintances who were models for my characters, albeit unknown to them.

Dana Schiebel, my new partner in Rivercrest, and without whom this never would have been possible.

There are countless others, but the list would grow to the size of a telephone directory.

To all of you, my heartfelt thanks.

Permission to reprint lyrics from the following is gratefully acknowledged:

"Guanabara Bay", music by Andrée Bernard, lyrics by Elisa Amsterdam, Andrée Bernard, and Shirley Eikhard, ©1993 by SGM—Sleeping Giant Music Inc. and B.C. Fiedler Publishing (SOCAN). All Rights Reserved. Used by Permission.

"Let's Get Away From It All", music and lyrics by Matt Dennis and Tom Adair, ©1940 (Renewed) by Music Sales Corporation (ASCAP). International Copyright Secured. All Rights Reserved. Reprinted by permission.

"Love of My Life", music by Roger Kellaway, ©1990 by Castle Music (ASCAP), lyrics by Harry Currie, ©1991 by CurrEnt Productions. All Rights Reserved. Used by Permission.

"You Are Here", lyrics and music by Harry Currie, ©1995 by Riverside Publishers. All Rights Reserved. Used by Permission.

I cannot forecast to you the action of Russia. It is a riddle wrapped in a mystery inside an enigma.

—Winston Churchill

Whoever fights monsters should see to it that in the process he does not become a monster.

—Friederich Wilhelm Nietzsche

Debut for a Spy

PROLOGUE

Cambridge, Ontario—May, 1995

He turned into the driveway of the house on Caledonia Road, weary from a tiring day. This secluded corner of Cambridge had become his sanctuary, not only from daily routine, but from the intrusion of the past.

The house itself was old by Canadian standards, built somewhere around 1830 by one of the original group of Scots settlers. Grey fieldstone construction, it had been added to and modernized over the years with varying degrees of success.

Thanks to a previous owner a board and batten attached garage had been turned into a recreation room with a stone fireplace. Now it was a spacious and comfortable living room.

It was here he chose to sit on this unusually warm spring day, sun-drenched windows open wide, sipping a drambuie, listening to Rob McConnell and 'The Boss Brass' on a new compact disc, the music punctuated by the periodic snap of the flag flying near the just-opened swimming pool.

His wife was out—a note left to say she was doing research at the public library, home around five-thirty. He glanced at his Rolex. Half an hour.

The front door opened and closed—perhaps it was she, home early. No. A blonde fifteen-year-old youth popped into the room with a bright grin on his face. The man pressed the remote mute switch.

"Hi, Dad," the young man called cheerily.

"Hi, Son," he replied with a smile, "how was school?"

"Okay. I got my math test back today—86."

"Hey, not bad. You still like math a lot, don't you?"

"Yeah, it's pretty good. But I have to do a make-up history project on the Falklands Conflict. I won't do very well."

"Anything I can do to help?"

"I dunno, Dad. Maybe. We each had to come up with our own way to write about the war, and I decided to use an airplane. I don't think Miss Stevens'll like it."

"An airplane?"

"Yeah, it's called the Harrier Jump Jet. It got started in England, but now they're made in the States, too. The U.S. Marines had them in the Persian Gulf. They even used one in an Arnold Schwarzenegger movie last year. 'True Lies'."

His pulse raced. He took a deep breath for control.

"How are you using the Harrier and the Falklands Conflict?"

"It hovers, Dad, and doesn't need airfields, so the British used it both as a fighter and for ground support with the troops. It's pretty awesome. I think it's the main reason why the British won the war. But you probably don't know much about VTOL jets like the Harrier, do you, Dad? Your generation was into Spitfires and planes from World War II."

They often joked about the 49-year gap.

"Come on, now, don't sell your old dad short. I know a little about the Harrier and where it came from."

Just a little, he thought, just a little. The pulse again.

"Cool. I'm gonna hit some balls with the guys. Later, Old One," the boy grinned, heading out the door and waving at his father through the window.

He waved back, smiling, but the coincidence of his son researching the Harrier had opened the floodgates of memory, a process which had begun with a trickle upon the disintegration of the Soviet Union.

While the decline of the Communist Party and the failed coup against Gorbachev had been surprising enough, it was the purging of the KGB which had been the key to hidden recesses of his past. Was it all just a ploy? It would be like them, he contemplated. *Perestroika* and *glasnost* sounded idealistic, certainly, but were the realities of the Russian mind-set more deeply rooted in economic and strategic necessity?

Instinctively, he knew it wasn't over. Just last year a CIA analyst named Ames and his wife had been arrested for supplying intelligence to the Russians. As long as there are political boundaries, he mused, there will be spies.

Despite himself, misty, forgotten pictures began to form in his mind, most of the scenes from his own experience, some reconstructed after the fact. Perhaps now, once and for all, he can confront it and finally put it to rest.

When had it begun? There were many strands in the weave, but one in particular stood out as the catalyst. . . .

ONE

Paris, France—Monday, June 11, 1962

The man stood with the shadow of his broad frame blending into that of the statue of Henri IV. Several steps down toward the Square du Vert-Galant, he was completely inconspicuous were anyone to look across Pont Neuf from either side.

It was a cool night, but his shiver was one of anticipation, not of chill. He was about to do what he was good at—what he was paid for—what he enjoyed.

He kept looking toward the Right Bank, for some sign of the approach of his assignment. Over several days he had checked on the movements of his quarry, a senior curator at the Louvre. At midnight on those days when he had night duty, the curator would leave the museum by a private door, walk along the Seine on the Quai du Louvre, and cross Pont Neuf over Île de la Cité to the Left Bank. His apartment was near the end of the bridge.

The time. Seven minutes past midnight. Not long now.

The night was clear, the visibility good, but the watcher removed his thick glasses and gave them a quick polish.

There. Movement at the end of the bridge. Perhaps it was he. The time was right. Shrinking deeper into the shadow, the watcher observed the approaching figure.

A slight stoop, a shuffling gait. It had to be. Still, one must make sure, he thought. Might as well be paid for the right one. He pulled his hat lower on his head.

Timing it exactly, he walked up the few steps on a perfect intercept with the smaller man. Surprised by the sudden appearance, the curator hesitated.

"Excuse me," said the watcher in French, "I wonder if I might trouble you for a match. I dropped my lighter into the Seine."

He held a cigarette in his hand as the older man fumbled nervously in his pocket.

"Yes, of course. . . a moment, please. I myself smoke a pipe."

I know you do, thought the watcher. Found and struck, the match flared, the watcher satisfied by what he saw in the glow.

"Thank you, *m'sieu*, you are most kind."

The watcher turned as if to depart.

"My pleasure," murmured the curator, relief in his voice, taking a step toward the Left Bank.

He heard nothing, but his head was snapped backward by a hand under his chin, and a white-hot pain in his back brought tears to his eyes as he stumbled to his knees.

"Please, please!" he begged through clenched teeth, "take my money! Don't hurt me!"

"I don't want your money, old man," the watcher whispered, crouching behind him. "You have one chance to remain alive. The pain in your back is from a stiletto long enough to reach your heart. Tell me what I want to know and you are free to go."

"Wh-what do you want?"

"A name, old man. We know how you get the information. We know all about your pretty boy at the embassy. Now, who do you pass it to? Tell me, and you live."

There was a hesitation, and the fire in his back raged as the point was pushed in, scraping a rib.

"*Mon Dieu, Mon Dieu*!" he sobbed. "All right! Please! I'll tell you! He is Armand Cantero!"

"Where does he live?"

"Rue Saint-Laurent near Gare de l'Est!"

"The number."

"I don't know!" he gasped. "Black double doors! Third floor!"

"And how do you make the transfer?"

There was a pause. The point moved in.

"No! Have mercy! Oh, God! At the museum! I use the facilities to prepare the material, and the transfer is made at the ticket booth! There is nothing more!"

"Of course. Very ingenious. Are you telling the truth?"

The point moved again.

"Jesus, Mary, and Joseph!" came the choked reply. "Yes, it's the truth! I swear on my mother's grave!"

"Then it's time you went on your way, old man."

The point slid in smoothly, nicking a couple of bones, piercing the lung, entering the heart. For an instant the curator tensed rigidly, then released his life with a rasping sigh.

The watcher, his glasses fogging, held the stiletto in place while he silently counted five, then withdrew it with a steady pull. Wiping it carefully on the old man's coat, he replaced it in a sheath on the inside of his jacket.

He checked several pockets before he found the old man's wallet, then removed his watch and a diamond ring. A smokescreen.

Picking the old man up, he walked to the rail and effortlessly threw the body into the Seine. Glancing both ways, he chose to walk to the Left Bank to avoid people coming from the other side. Striding, he cleansed his glasses of the residue of his victim's fear.

He walked briskly, glancing at his watch. Not bad. Barely 3 minutes from contact. He felt good. Aroused. Ready for a *putain.*

London, England—Tuesday, June 12, 1962

"Secrets—take two!"

The band kicked in with a driving beat, setting up my entry after four bars of intro. I relaxed on the stool and sang from the heart. This take went well—much better than the first. My voice was warmed up, and Don Lusher's trombone solo really swung.

My main worry was the high note at the end. This time it held strong and firm—on the first take I'd sounded like a strangling duck. The band hit the last shot. We froze 'til the reverb died.

"Bang on, David," piped the thin voice over the intercom. "Come into the booth and listen."

A new tune I'd written, HMV were recording it since it was in the running as the theme for the spy movie filming at Pinewood.

The playback was fine, and once the electronic boys got through with it even the notes I winced at would be perfect. As the last sounds faded I grabbed my coat.

"I've gotta run, George. I'm meeting House Paynter near Charing Cross, and I didn't bring the car. Too much bother to park, especially in the rain."

"I'm going to the Strand, David. Why don't I drop you?"

"Thanks. No bother?"

"Not a bit."

We left EMI's Abbey Road studios a few minutes later in George's Rover. This would definitely save me some time.

"You met House Paynter during your army days, David?"

"Yeah, in 1956. He was already Director of the Coldstream Guards Band and I a lowly Student Bandmaster at Kneller Hall, but it didn't bother him a bit. We became good friends."

The difference in our status never mattered to House—rank was not his criterion for measuring people. He did as he pleased, and seemed to lead a charmed life with neither censure nor reprimand from a normally inflexible social system.

"Didn't you have a commission in the Canadian Army at the time? I remember someone telling me about the subterfuge."

"The Brits wouldn't let me attend the course as an officer, so on paper I became a Warrant Officer Class I for the three years I was at the school. Then I was reinstated in my rank as though the time had never happened. Ironically my pay went up with both moves, so I was far better off."

"What a lot of cod's wallop. The services never change, do they? All that bullshit baffling the few brains they have."

"I can't complain, George. Nearly ten years in the Regulars and four in the Reserves and I figure I've come out way ahead."

"But you didn't want to make it a career?"

"Nope—I'd had enough. And musically it was very limiting in the Canadian Army. My appetite had been whetted by London when I was a student, so back I came. I've been very lucky."

In the previous year I had done rather well—some recording work, a little conducting, a few commercials, a fair amount of arranging, and what was most surprising, a lot of singing in clubs and on the BBC. I had two records out, and now I was on the brink of the leading role in a major West End musical.

"Damn," muttered George. "Look at the traffic around Trafalgar Square."

"I'll jump out here, George, and walk across. Then you can cut to the Embankment. Thanks!" I called, slamming the door.

I hummed the new tune as I walked. It seemed to fit the day—one of those for which London was famous—grey, overcast, and drizzling incessantly. The perfect setting for murder and espionage, I grumbled, as I sloshed past Nelson's Column. That thought, however frivolous it seemed at the time, was far more prophetic than I could ever have imagined.

'House' Paynter's real name was Howes, but no one had called him that since he had joined the army as a boy-soldier in 1936. A major now, we had resumed our close friendship on my return to London, and occasionally his contacts opened some musical doors for me. I was indebted to him, but he expected nothing in return.

Until now.

This call had been strange. Normally he was boisterous and full of gags, but not this time. I sensed a strain in his voice.

"Got anything on this afternoon, David?" he had asked, and when I replied nothing special, he continued, "Will you meet me at the Sherlock Holmes in Northumberland Street? I have a friend who would like to propose something that he hopes may interest you."

Why the Sherlock Holmes, I thought. We never went there, and House was almost fanatic about his pet pub in Chelsea. Then there was the way he had spoken—that was not like House. No jokes, no 'Goon Show' voices, not even a knock-knock or a riddle. But I had agreed, and now I walked over to Northumberland Street and the Sherlock Holmes, arriving there damp and curious.

The Sherlock Holmes pub was once called the Northumberland Arms Hotel, and as such it was mentioned in *The Hound of the Baskervilles*. Small wonder, then, about its present name, its decor, and its collection of Holmesiana.

House was sitting comfortably in a corner. Shooting Sherry was his favourite drink, and he had a schooner of it in front of him. He was alone, which surprised me, as I thought he was bringing someone to meet me. He was also in guards officers' undress uniform—dark blue suit, shirt, tie, and bowler hat. This was not like House at all.

"David, over here!" he beckoned, as I threaded my way through the crowd, and when I sat down, "What kept you, old son? I'm two up on you already." His cherubic face beamed. He was more like himself than he had been earlier.

"Well, you didn't tell me it was a pub crawl, 'old bean', did you?" I retorted. "I thought you wanted me to meet someone. What did you mean? Who is it? Where are they? What's going on?"

"All in good time, old son, all in good time. Now, what are you drinking?" We chatted as we sipped—about our army colleagues and their misdemeanors, the state of music in the country, and, of course, the fairer sex. But my curiosity was piqued.

"Come on, House, cut the B.S. This is all very nice, but it's not why you called, is it? What's up?"

He hesitated for a moment, as befuddled as a leprechaun who had misplaced his pot of gold. Once again he was tense.

"I have this friend—an acquaintance, actually—at the War Office. He's a colonel in some kind of nebulous job—I've never been sure of what he actually does. The only thing I really know is that he asks a lot of questions everytime we meet."

"What kind of questions?"

"You know, everything in general, but mostly about people I meet and know. Always seems fairly innocent, but I can never shake off the feeling that he's probing. Well, I mentioned your name a few times and what you've been up to, and he seemed really interested. Then, yesterday, I had lunch at the mess after the changing-of-the-guard, and he asked if I could introduce you."

"What's he want?" I grinned. "An autograph, or a ticket to my new show?"

House looked suddenly serious.

"I really don't know, David, but do me a favour. Don't commit yourself to anything without thinking it over very carefully."

"What on earth are you talking about, House? I'm a civilian musician chasing a career in London. I wasn't even in the British Army. What could he want from me?"

"Well," he paused, "it's just that I've heard rumours about some of his activities. I know I agreed to introduce you, and I really had no choice in the matter, but I couldn't throw you to the lions without a friendly word of warning."

I sipped my drink, reflecting on what House had told me, then tried a shot in the dark.

"Your colonel wouldn't be a cloak-and-dagger type, would he, House? You know, MI5 and all that stuff?"

House just looked at me.

"Oh, for Christ's sake," I laughed, "do you know how funny this is? British stiff-upper nonsense! You're all nuts!"

"David," he began.

"No, House, listen to me. I'll meet your phantom colonel for a few minutes, but what the hell do I know to interest him?"

"Okay," he said, downing his sherry. "I hope you're not annoyed that I said I'd introduce you."

I was amused at his discomfiture.

"Not a bit, House," I replied. "In fact, it'll be a chuckle to see what he wants and then disappoint him, because that's what's going to happen. Where do we meet him?"

Paris, France—the same day

Still savouring his assignment of the night before, the broad man let himself in to the safe house, a nondescript apartment in a rundown building off Boulevard de Clichy in Montmartre.

It was raining in Paris. He wiped the precipitation from his glasses as he climbed the stairs.

As usual it had been a circuitous route using buses and the metro. When he was certain there was no tail he came in.

The Russian was already there. They spoke in that language.

"Ah, Dragon. I read in *Le Monde* that you were successful."

"Of course. Isn't that why you use me?"

"To be sure, to be sure," the Russian purred. "Have a vodka with me while you relate the details."

Over several vodkas the tale was told, the Russian nodding and clucking approval during the telling.

"Splendid, splendid," he chortled. "Now for the next step."

"You wish me to remove this Cantero?"

"He will be only a cut-out. What happens to him is no concern of ours. But we do want the British agent who meets Cantero, and we want him alive. Can you accommodate us? I know it's a little tame for you."

The Russian laughed at his own joke. His companion did not.

"Of course. Cantero will tell me what I need to know. That will be sport enough for this job."

The eyes glinted behind the thick lenses. The coldest eyes I have ever seen, thought the Russian. He hated dealing with this man, in fact, he hated this man, but he did his work thoroughly, and since he was not a Soviet citizen he was *persona non grata,* which suited them well if things were to go wrong.

"Another assignment must have priority. We close in on an American who causes much trouble with the Middle East oil countries. He eludes us because of the way he moves around, but this afternoon we set a little trap for him in London, and then we pounce. There will be a large bonus for this one, my friend."

He paused for effect. There was none. Miffed, he continued.

"For the next few days you must remain by your telephone. This means 24 hours a day. When we find out what we need in England it may be necessary to move with lightning speed. We can't take the chance of missing you—even minutes may count. I apologize for this inconvenience."

"No matter. It is permissible to sleep?"

"Will the telephone awaken you?"

"A whisper would awaken me."

"Then sleep, by all means. But be dressed and ready to move."

The Russian continued, ignoring the look of disdain.

"We have also commenced a major operation in England concerning an aircraft presently under research and development. We may need you there next week. You will be available?"

The eyes stared through the lenses, unblinking.

"That is the arrangement with my government, and you pay me well for each commission. Of course I will be available." He paused briefly. "Is the blonde bitch still there?"

The Russian stiffened.

"There will be no repetition of that incident. It could have been your undoing, and mine as well. You were lucky to walk away with a reprimand. Remember that, my friend. Now I must go. Stay, and finish the vodka."

The Russian handed over an envelope which was received contemptuously and stuffed into a pocket. Not another word was spoken as the Russian walked to the door and let himself out. Glancing at the wide shoulders and back of the mercenary, he wondered for a moment when the time would come that this one would have to be taken out.

Pity the man who draws that assignment, he reflected.

Adjusting the flower in his buttonhole, he stepped out, closing the door firmly behind him.

Inside, the mercenary downed another shot of vodka.

One of these days, he thought, I'll have to remove him.

Another slug.

What a world, he pondered.

There are no good people left.

London, England—the same day

On Whitehall we entered a gateway guarded by mounted troopers of the Royal Horse Guards, crossing a courtyard to a door beneath an arch. A sergeant of the Scots Guards saluted House and asked politely who we wanted to see.

"Colonel Hammond," said House, producing his identity, "and tell him I've brought a guest."

After duly signing in and placing visitors' tags on our coats, we were ushered up a narrow stairway to the second floor by a duty corporal. He knocked on a door part way down the corridor, opening it when a voice called "Come!"

House entered first, standing briefly to attention as he did—the civilian clothes salute. I didn't feel the necessity of saluting—I wasn't in the army—and yet the tug of habit and training was hard to ignore.

The colonel rose as we entered, partially closing the door of a small safe as he did so. He was tall, slender, and wore a neatly trimmed moustache. He was immaculately dressed in a navy blue pin-stripe suit, gold watch chain across his vest, a white starched collar attached to a blue-and-white-striped shirt, and, of course, the regimental tie.

"Ah, Major Paynter," he said, "it was good of you to come."

He swung his eyes to me. He had a steady, direct gaze which didn't waver—not even a blink. The look was so intense it was hard to return. I sensed a very resolute man.

House performed the civilities.

"Sir, may I introduce David Baird? Late of the Canadian Army, and presently working in London as a musician and singer. David, this is Colonel Hammond."

"A pleasure, Captain Baird," said the colonel, taking my hand. "I'm pleased you could spend a few minutes with me."

"Not 'captain' any longer, sir," I replied. "I've been out of the army over a year now, and I never use my former rank as a title. It would be a terrible affectation in show business."

I smiled as I said this, hoping for a glimmer of understanding from this career officer. I was disappointed.

"A military officer is a little like a priest, Captain Baird. Once you've taken the vow you are considered to be in for life, whatever your status. I happen to know you are on the Supplementary List of Officers in the Canadian Army, and so you are technically still an officer holding Her Majesty's commission, and subject to recall to active duty during a national emergency."

The frost melted a bit, a ghost of a smile appearing as he continued.

"Now, I didn't ask to meet you to discuss protocol. Will you sit down, and may I offer you some tea?"

As though on cue House spoke up.

"Sir, if you don't mind, I'll be off. I have some paperwork to tidy up in my office."

This I knew to be a flagrant lie. House detested paperwork and had his band clerk handle everything for him except his signature, and I think he was trying to remedy that oversight.

"Very well, Major," said the colonel, "and thank you for bringing Captain Baird along."

House had departed, tea had appeared in moments brought in by an orderly, and we settled down in our chairs. We chatted as we sipped—about the weather, London traffic, and the musical *Bye Bye Birdie*, one of the few musicals which the colonel had seen.

"Not a patch on *My Fair Lady*, of course," he commented, "but then, how can one compete with Shaw?"

I murmured some words of agreement, wishing he would get on

with it. And then he did.

"Did Major Paynter comment at all on my line of work?" he queried.

"Only that he wasn't sure what it was you did, sir."

"Quite. Well, suffice it to say that I deal in intelligence matters, and it's along these lines I wished to speak with you."

"Perhaps I could save you some time, sir," I interjected. "Are you aware that I was a Director of Music in the army, and that I've never done any intelligence work?"

He studied me for a moment.

"Captain Baird, let me relate what I know about you."

He leaned back in his chair, staring at the ceiling.

"You're 31 years old. You attended McGill and Mount Allison Universities, and hold graduate diplomas from three British colleges of music. You were an athlete in swimming and track, running the hundred-yard-dash in 10 seconds flat.

"Before becoming a Director of Music you held a regular commission in the Royal Canadian Army Service Corps. You are a small arms expert, holding the bronze, silver and gold medallions of the Dominion of Canada Rifle Association. For two years you held the Canadian Forces championship trophy for small arms, using a whole variety of weapons at various distances. Your aggregate score has never been equalled.

"You qualified in all types of service vehicles, both wheeled and tracked. You excelled in hand-to-hand combat, and completed a special flying course, qualifying as a pilot."

Hammond sat back in his chair with a rather pleased look on his face. "Shall I continue?"

I contemplated my reply, drawing in a large breath.

"Sir," I began, "your facts are basically correct, but you must look at them in context. I haven't fired a weapon in over ten years—that was all done when I was an officer cadet. The same is true for driving anything but my own car." I hesitated. "During a practice bout of hand-to-hand combat there was a tragic accident. I flipped my partner too hard. His neck was broken. He died."

The dreadful memory resurfaced.

"I never continued with it. As far as flying is concerned, I took a special *ad hoc* course which the authorities turned a blind eye to. I have barely a hundred hours both dual and solo in Harvards, and

I've never taken a civilian licence. It was even placed on my personnel file that I should never fly operationally—I don't have enough training or experience. With all these skills you've mentioned I'm stale and out of date."

I finished speaking, and for a few moments we regarded each other in silence.

SMASH!

The window shattered, spraying us with shards of glass. I leapt to my feet as the cause landed with a heavy clump on the floor, inches from my right foot.

"Grenade!" I yelled.

I knew we were both dead.

TWO

Self-preservation caused me to react.
Grabbing the grenade I yelled to Hammond.
"The safe!"

He pulled the handle as I threw the grenade, ricocheting it off the desk and barely making it through the door. Hammond slammed it shut and we both dived flat onto the floor. I stuffed fingers into my ears and opened my mouth.

The explosion lifted the safe off the floor, blowing the door clear across the room. But it had contained the blast and the shrapnel, saving our lives. Thank God it had been a delayed fuse.

Despite the ringing in my ears I heard shouts from outside and shots being fired—two singles, then a burst from a sub-machine-gun. More shouts.

"Look alive! There's another!"

A longer burst from the SMG. Silence.

The door flew open and a squad of regulars hurtled to the window, weapons ready. The sergeant knelt by Colonel Hammond.

"You all right, sir?"

"Yes, I think so. A bit cut, but nothing serious. That was close. Captain Baird, how are you?"

"A couple of nicks and my ears are ringing, but that seems to be all. What happened? Who threw it?"

"I expect we'll have some answers shortly. Is the situation in hand, Sergeant?"

The NCO looked toward the window.

"Wot's 'appening, Corporal Miles?"

"There were two of 'em, Sergeant, from what I can see I think they've got 'em both."

"Then let's get out of here and down to the first-aid detachment," said Hammond.

* * *

Twenty minutes later I was holding another cup of tea, but this time laced with brandy.

"For medicinal purposes only," winked the medical orderly when he handed it to me.

Alone in a small sitting room, I sipped with a trembling hand, spilling much of it into the saucer. The grenade incident had left me shaken, and the brandy wasn't working.

Hammond and I had been cleaned off and patched up before he left me to find out what had occurred. He wasn't gone long. Subdued when he returned, he sat down wearily.

"We've been having some roof repairs done. It's a contract with a carefully vetted firm. The two roofers who have been here all week didn't arrive today, and two other characters showed up instead. They were checked out, and the contractor confirmed he'd taken them on as temporary labour. He didn't know they were IRA."

I considered this.

"Were they after you, Colonel?"

"I expect so. I've been responsible for a good number of them being caught and sent up, and they would like to pay me back, I'm sure. I must tell you that that was the closest I've ever come. Quick thinking on your part, Captain Baird."

"I didn't think at all, sir, I just reacted. We were both lucky the safe was there. I don't understand why the damned thing didn't go off sooner. Most grenades in my experience have a four second pyrotechnic train. That one had to be longer, or we wouldn't be here talking about it."

"Fortune smiled, Captain Baird. The grenade was an old one of ours, a type 36. Several weeks ago a box of these disappeared in an ammunition depot break-in. But the fuses they took were 7-second delay, normally used when the grenade is rifle-projected. It's not like the IRA to make mistakes like that."

"What happened to the roofers, sir?"

"Both dead, unfortunately. The security detail kept a sharp eye on them. They only had time for one grenade. They were carrying four more in their tool kits, and two hand guns."

A long period of silence ensued before Hammond spoke again.

"This rather precipitates what I wanted to talk with you about. I said these two chaps were IRA. Much of the funding and the covert direction of the IRA's activities in Britain comes from the Soviets. Are you aware of the KGB?"

"Yes, sir. Isn't it the Soviet counterpart of the CIA?"

"Roughly speaking, yes. But much larger, and completely ruthless and unscrupulous."

I figured they were all like that, but thought better of saying it.

"I don't see how any of this concerns me, sir."

He regarded me blankly.

"We need your help because of someone you've met."

My mind raced to come up with a name that might activate a synapse and make some sense of this. It failed.

"I can't think of anyone you'd be interested in."

He looked at me searchingly.

"Does the name 'Vladimir Nalishkin' mean anything to you?"

The synapse triggered.

"Yes," I answered, "I've met him. I was singing at the Latin Quarter a few weeks ago and he came to see me at the end of my show. In fact, I had a drink with him and his guests, although I don't remember their names. Nalishkin told me that he was the cultural attaché at the Soviet Embassy, and wondered if I would accept an invitation to sing at some embassy 'do' they're planning. Is this significant?"

There was a long hesitation before Hammond continued.

"Captain Baird, I'm going to tell you something which perhaps I should not. But I'm addressing you as a commissioned officer 'On Her Majesty's Service', as the phrase reads, not as a civilian. I trust you will respect what I am about to say as though you were still a regular officer. We were aware of your meeting with Nalishkin because we try to keep track of him twenty-four hours a day. Nalishkin, you see, is the cultural attaché in name only. In reality, he is the head of the KGB section at the Soviet Embassy in London, the *rezident*. He is a very deceptive man, as devious as he is dangerous."

I sat there in amazement as Hammond continued.

"When your name came up I knew we had a chance to get closer to Nalishkin than ever before, if you were willing to co-operate. When we ran a check on you and I discovered your background, I was even more convinced." He stared at me intently. "Are you willing to help us?"

I hesitated, then spoke slowly.

"What would I have to do?"

"Just keep your ears and eyes open. If anything occurs which seems even remotely of interest, let us know. We'll arrange a private contact method to keep in touch."

"And that's all? No tricks—no spy assignments? You won't be asking me to steal documents from Nalishkin's desk or smuggle microfilm into Moscow?"

I said this lightly, but I meant it. Hammond actually laughed, if you can call a couple of throaty grunts a laugh.

"My dear boy, you've been reading too much spy fiction. We're not like the novels at all, you know."

I sat quietly for a moment.

"How do you know I'll have any contact with him worth reporting?"

"We don't, of course. But Nalishkin is well-educated and a very sophisticated man. For all his KGB work, he keeps up an excellent front as the cultural attaché, actually arranging several tours involving the Bolshoi and the Moscow Philharmonic.

"We know he is a great Frank Sinatra fan, and with your similarity in style and material, it would be true to his character to see a lot of you—perhaps even suggest a trip to Russia. Only time will tell, of course, but if it happens I'd like to be a step ahead and not behind. He's done it before, you see, but not with anyone we could have counted on to do us any good. With your background, you're a Godsend."

"Hardly, Colonel. It's all too far behind me."

"The grenade rather disproved that." He paused. "Simply stated,

Captain Baird, we need your help."

I sat still, contemplating in confusion all the information I had been told, and struggling with mixed emotions. On the one hand I felt the call to duty again—the desire to rush to the colours on seeing the poster of Lord Kitchener beckoning 'We Need You!'. I disliked communist regimes, with their secret police and their suppression of human rights and dignity.

On the other hand, I was trying to build a career far removed from this sort of thing. I had even left army music to get away from military regimentation. Did I want this complication in my life? And the greatest fear—would I be drawn deeper into something I'd regret?

Sensing my doubts, Hammond tried to allay them.

"I can understand that this incident has made you extremely wary of accepting my offer, Captain Baird, but let me assure you that nothing like this could happen to you. No one will know about you, not even on our side."

"Colonel, I'd like to think about this before I give you an answer. May I let you know in a couple of days?"

"Of course. I'll give you a number to call."

He wrote one on a piece of paper, handing it to me.

"No matter who answers or how they answer, you must say 'sorry, wrong number—I'll dial again,' and stay on the line. The next person who answers will ask you to state your name, and then you'll be connected to me. Have you got that?"

I said I had, and stood to leave. Hammond stood, too, and offered his hand.

"One more thing, Captain Baird. Nothing about this afternoon should be mentioned to anyone, not even to Major Paynter." He paused. "Opportunities like this don't come that often, you know."

"I'll call you, sir," I said, turning to make my exit.

I walked to the door, subconsciously swinging back to face Hammond, and came briefly to attention.

He smiled, speaking softly.

"Old habits die hard, don't they, David?"

East side of Whitehall, London—a few minutes later

She liked watching from here. Keeping her eye on the door was boring, but the horses standing guard with the mounted troopers in their livery were a helpful distraction. That was only on fine days, of course. With today's rain both horses and troopers wore rain capes and were stuck back in the sentry boxes.

She caught sight of him as he started across the courtyard. Definitely not British. She'd seen him go in with the other one—the guards officer—but she'd never seen this one before. Just under six feet, she guessed. His hair was dark brown, short, with a bit of a wave in it. Nice face, but no Telly star. When he smiled, though, his eyes crinkled and his face came alive. He had an easy walk, looked fit and solid, but very trim. Her libido, never far from the surface, gave her a twinge of desire.

Get behind him, she thought. Should be easy. If he gets in a crowd, lift his wallet. They wanted to know about any strange blokes who came or went. Blimey, this was easy money.

West Side of Whitehall, London—the same time

Walking toward Trafalgar Square I was scarcely aware of the drizzle. My mind was totally pre-occupied with the events of the afternoon and the dilemma I faced.

Entering Charing Cross underground station, I went through the motions of finding the right platform and stood, in a daze, waiting for a Bakerloo train to St. John's Wood.

The crowd grew around me as I heard the rumble of the train approaching through the tunnel. Because of my preoccupation I was totally unaware when the pickpocket removed my wallet.

"Stop! Thief!" jarred me back to the present. A clergyman pointed after a female running for an exit. A quick check of my missing wallet, and reflex took over as I sprinted after her.

She was fast, legging it up the escalator, across the concourse, then the stairs to the street. I knew if she made it into the crowds I'd lose her, but I was closing the gap. With the instinct of street-survival she timed her dash across the Strand, knowing I'd be stopped by the approaching double-decker.

She didn't see the cyclist scooting along the line of parked cars, and the collision with the bike threw her onto the street and under the wheels of the bus.

Her cry ended as life was crushed from her, the terrible images of sight and sound indelibly imprinted in my memory.

Amid the screams and shouts of the onlookers the bus screeched to a halt.

I stared. . . numb. . . unable to move or think.

I'd caused another death.

That made two.

THREE

Whistles were blowing as London Transport personnel and 'Bobbies' arrived, converging on me because of the pointing fingers—after all, I had been chasing her. I was only vaguely aware when a man in a clerical collar handed me my wallet, my bewildered mind hearing a mumbled statement about his seeing it in the street and something about a statement to the police.

Trembling from shock I was led to a bench in the concourse of the underground station which the police had cleared in order to take statements from witnesses. A constable fetched some water which I drank while waiting for the detectives to arrive. I seemed to be in a vacuum, my mind trying to blot out the horror I had caused.

It seemed ages before they got to me. The others had been questioned out of my hearing. Finally, my turn. The senior officer was a large man with a florid face and a shock of sandy hair.

"Now then, sir, sorry to keep you waiting. Might I see some identification?"

I handed him the wallet. Immediately he picked up on an old calling card identifying me as a captain in the army.

"You're a military man, then, sir?"

I explained.

"Ah, yes, I see, sir. Well, this is a very unpleasant thing for you, I'm sure, Mr. Baird. Now, I'm Detective-Inspector Barrow, sir, and I'd like you to tell me in your own words what happened."

I told him as precisely as I could.

"Very good, sir. Did you ever set eyes on this lady before?"

"Not to my knowledge, Inspector. But I didn't really see her face, and under the circumstances I'd prefer not to."

"Not to worry, Mr. Baird. We've recovered a satchel she was carrying, and there was a photo in it. Have a look, please, sir."

He handed me a 5x7 print which took me aback at first glance. It was of a blonde young lady with a pretty but slightly coarse face. She was naked.

"No, Inspector, I don't recognize her. Who was she?"

"Her name was Daphne Boggs, but she worked under the name of Jackie London."

"What kind of work?"

He smiled.

"Rather hard to pin down. She stripped now and then in some of the Soho clubs, posed for men's magazines, and she's even appeared in a couple of pornographic films. She has some unsavoury types as friends, and several run-ins with the law. Not exactly your average garden party guest, you might say."

"What happens now, Inspector?"

"Probably nothing, Mr. Baird. The usual coroner's inquest, but the evidence we've taken today will probably be accepted at face value. Two of the people standing close by actually saw her take your wallet, and one man, a vicar, retrieved it from the street where it had fallen out of her hand."

He paused. "Are you a runner, Mr. Baird?"

"In college."

"That's it, then. She picked the wrong bloke this time. If we need anything further we'll contact you, sir. I'll have one of my men drive you home to St. John's Wood."

We shook hands, and a uniformed constable led me from the concourse to the street and the police Rover. The red double-decker hadn't moved. I shuddered as we drove past it.

* * *

I asked the constable to drop me at the corner of Wellington Road and St. John's Wood Road so that I might walk a bit and clear my head. The events of the afternoon had shaken me badly.

As I sloshed along I wondered at the odd coincidence of the two things happening in the same day.

Then I had a chilling thought. Was it coincidence? It had all begun after I had met Hammond. I knew it didn't make sense—after all, I was a nobody. So why me? I made a conscious effort to push it out of my mind. I couldn't deal with it any more.

I passed Lord's Cricket Ground, that bastion of all the British hold sacred, eventually arriving at my building. The uniformed doorman was quick to usher me in to the warmth.

"Evenin' sir," he greeted, "nawsty out there, init?"

"Yes, Wicks, it is," I replied, "almost bad enough to make me wish I'd stayed in Canada. Is there any post for me?"

"Blimey, sir, I near forgot." He reached for some letters behind his desk. "Beggin' your pardon, Mr. Baird."

"No problem, Wicks. Thank you."

He rang for the lift, opening the cage for me on arrival.

" 'Ave a good evenin' sir," said Wicks as I departed upward.

I had been extremely lucky in finding this flat. The building was not new, but when it had been constructed in 1935 they considered the apartments to be luxury flats for that period, and they had most of the amenities of North American standards. There was a small dining room, a good-sized living room and bedroom, and a modern kitchen and bath. There were even built-in closets and kitchen cupboards—most unusual for Britain at that time.

What made the flat most attractive was the self-contained bed-sitter which was attached. While there was a communicating door off the living-room, this little flat had its own tiny bathroom and kitchenette as well as a separate entrance to the hall. Originally intended as a servant's quarters, most of them were now used as an additional bedroom, an apartment for an elderly family member, or, as in my case, a rental accommodation which helped pay the bills.

I had been able to take over the lease from an American diplomat who was being transferred to the Middle East, and he and his wife were more than willing to sell some of their furniture and appliances for a modest price.

I also inherited their 20-year-old daughter Katherine, a student at the Royal Academy of Dramatic Art.

Kate was one of those people you couldn't take your eyes off. She had that combination of attractiveness and animation which illuminated her personality. What made her more intriguing was that she was not conscious of her appearance or what effect it had on others—especially males.

Well, not conscious of it except for the dimples which appeared when she smiled.

"They make me look like Shirley Temple," she would storm. "How will anyone take me seriously as an actress with those horrid depressions on my face?"

Kate was both intelligent and an extremely natural actress. I knew she could make it to the top with a few lucky breaks, and, Lord knows, in the arts everyone needed those strokes of good fortune and timing regardless of talent and ability.

Kate looked after my flat in return for the modest rent which I charged her. She did my laundry once a week, and occasionally we would share a meal together—sometimes she cooked, sometimes I did, and once in a while we would prepare a meal together.

This arrangement was not without its problems, at least for me. When Kate and her parents had approached me with the proposal, I was understandably reluctant. In a sense I was being asked to be a sort-of foster-parent, and with all my male hormones in place I was afraid it could turn into a 'moth and the flame' scenario with several unpleasant ways of getting burned.

But we had become good friends, and while we were extremely aware of our biological differences we had managed to keep our private lives quite separate.

The flat was an oasis for us both, quite apart from the real world. Kate and I would share our experiences—our triumphs and frustrations—and we would fantasize about our respective futures. I was part father-figure, part confidant; she was part daughter, part house-mother; and we were the best of friends.

* * *

From the moment I stepped inside I sensed something was wrong. I stood still, puzzled. I hadn't noticed anything obviously out of place, and yet I was sure someone had been in the flat.

Then I knew what it was. I have a keen sense of smell, and I recognized an odour which could only be sweat from a human body. It wasn't Kate—I knew her scent only too well—and it certainly wasn't mine. Someone in a hurry had been here, and they had been warmly dressed and nervous. I began to look for obvious signs.

From my days in university residences and in officers' quarters, I had learned to place little traps so that I knew if I had ever had an intruder. I was constantly kidded about being paranoid, and there was probably a grain of truth in the joshing. But in large cities like London you never knew when you might have a break-in. Accordingly, I had placed several strategic things in an apparent random order, but in truth with a careful pattern. I did this in my sock drawer, my desk drawer, and in the way the suitcases were placed in the closet.

All three places had been disturbed, but by an expert. Without the traps I never would have known.

I searched carefully, but as far as I could see nothing had been taken. I had been checked out, but by whom and what for?

I rang Wicks and asked if anyone had been around.

"No one for you, Mr. Baird. The only bloke 'ere today was the one from the Post Office Telephones. 'E 'ad a work order to check the phones in three of the flats."

"Was mine one of them, Wicks?"

"Yes, sir, it was. Is there a problem, Mr. Baird? I can call 'im back if your phone ain't workin' properly."

"Was he in here on his own, Wicks, or were you with him?"

"I'm not allowed to leave the desk, Mr. Baird, except for a few minutes at a time. I let 'im in to each flat when 'e rang down to tell me 'e was ready. 'E was only 'ere about an hour, so 'e couldn't 'ave been in any flat for more than twenty minutes."

"Let me guess, Wicks. All the flats he was in were on my floor, and he was in mine first."

"Blimey, sir, 'ow did you figure that out? That's just the way it 'appened!"

"Just a guess, Wicks, and it really doesn't matter."

I rang off, realizing that my visitor had used the other flats as a cover. Once my door was opened it was simple enough to leave it fixed to gain re-entry, and simply pretend to be in the other two flats. Wicks would not have known.

Now I knew how it was done, but who was behind it and why was still a mystery.

My visit to Colonel Hammond made me wonder if I had been checked out by him, and yet, if what he had told me about Nalishkin was true, I might very well have been visited by the KGB, though Lord knows what for.

I had a sinking feeling, like being sucked down in quicksand. Christ almighty, I thought, what more can happen today?

I heard the door of Kate's flat close. Instinctively I knew I would not tell her of the intrusion, and certainly nothing about my meeting with Hammond. These were my problems, and nothing to trouble her with. Perhaps later I'd tell her about the pickpocket, but not now. I tried to shake off my depression.

If Kate had had a good day she would usually pop in to say hello as she breezed by. If it had been a bad day she would take her time, and when she had decided what to say she would come in to talk, usually over tea.

This had been a good day.

"David," she called, as she opened her door, "guess what!" Her dark eyes flashed.

"I don't know," I responded, "you won a million pounds on the football pools?"

She bounced in, pony tail keeping pace.

"No, even better than a million pounds. I got the lead in *Antigone*, and Olivier's going to direct it for us!"

She was bubbling, and I could hardly believe what I'd heard. "What? You mean Sir Laurence Olivier? How come?"

Despite my traumatic day I became almost as excited as Kate. This was one of those breaks we all dream about—the door opens, all you have to do is step through.

"He and the principal had a bet on the Grand National, and Olivier lost. His forfeit was to direct a play at the Academy. He chose *Antigone*, by Jean Anouilh, and after working with us today in class I was given the lead!"

Her eyes were shining with delight and happiness.

"Kate," I exclaimed, "do you know what this could mean?"

She grabbed my hands. "Of course I do," she beamed. "A chance to be directed by a legend in English theatre."

"Kate, you dope, it's so much more than that. With Olivier involved the critics will all be there, and so will producers and directors. In fact, most of the dramatic community of London will see it, to say nothing of the film people."

I laughed at her startled expression.

"Kate, this could do it for you—it really could!"

A shadow of concern fell over her.

"Oh, God, David, I hadn't thought of all that." She stopped in sudden dismay. "What if I'm not up to it?"

"Dear, dear Kate," I laughed, "if anyone could ever be up to it, it'll be Katherine Fletcher. There isn't a person in the world who can rise to an occasion better than you. You'll be fine—no, take that back—you'll be magnificent. I know you, remember?"

The exhilaration returned, along with an intensity.

"I'll give it everything I've got, David. I'm determined to be the best Antigone there ever was. Will you come to see it?"

"Just try to keep me away! Of course I will—isn't that what 'parents' are supposed to do?"

I smiled at one of our 'in' jokes. Kate had a mercurial swing down to pensive.

"Hah!" she snorted, "parent, my fanny."

She hugged me tenderly, then leaned back, still holding me, and looked at me in a way she had never done before. When she began to speak, her voice was soft.

"David," she began, "I think it's about time we. . . " and at that moment her phone rang.

She stopped, gave me a wry little smile, saying "I guess it'll have to keep," as she ran off to take the call.

Probably just as well, I thought, and yet there was a twinge of disappointment. It was hard playing 'dad' when deep down you really didn't want to.

When she came back the mood was broken, and Kate seemed a little deflated.

"Anything wrong, Kate?" I queried.

"Oh, no, nothing really. It was Mom and Dad, and sometimes I realize just how much I miss them. They were calling from Gibralter. Dad has to attend a meeting in Algeria, and Mom's going with him."

"What's the meeting's about?"

"Oh, probably about oil—that's what he's involved in. They were thrilled about my news of the play. Dad said that they'd get here for it next month. They've been wonderful, David. They've believed in me and encouraged me to follow my instincts. If I make it, it'll be because of them and their faith in me."

"Kate, let me take you out to dinner to celebrate."

She brightened considerably.

"Yes, please, David—I'd like that very much."

Paris, France—the same day

He had been waiting only a few hours, but already he was becoming frustrated with inactivity. He had begun thinking of a way to get one of the streetwalkers in for some diversion, but how to do it without leaving the apartment or placing an incriminating call was the problem. Who knows how he might want to end a sexual encounter with a whore?

The thought was exciting him, causing him to sweat even more. The telephone ring ended his fantasy.

"Yes?"

"I've just heard from our friend in London. You are to fly to Gibralter within the hour. A charter has been arranged with *L'Aviation Petit France* from Le Bourget. You will be met there with full instructions, including the contacts in Gibralter. You must not fail. Do you understand?"

"Perfectly."

Within fifteen seconds he was gone.

London, England—the same day

There was a wonderful Indian restaurant at Notting Hill Gate which we frequented—the food subtle, delicious, and inexpensive.

We shared several dishes—a sag gosht, a beef vindaloo, and a mild vegetable curry, with a saffron-flavoured pulao rice that was out of this world. But what always made the meal were the beautiful puffed puris and the dahl, which was second to none in all of London. This was washed down with cold lager, and topped off with a home-made natural yogurt sprinkled with sugar.

Over the meal we talked about Kate's forthcoming play, about the doors it might open for her, and about her love of the theatre and acting. She was bubbling over, but tonight I was unable to match her enthusiasm. The stress of the day was weighing me down.

I could almost forget about Colonel Hammond and Vladimir Nalishkin, but they refused to go away completely. I sensed them both trying to intrude on my peace of mind.

I made a decision. Let them play their stupid little spy games. I wanted no part of it. I'd call Hammond in the morning and tell him no. Immediately I felt better. I certainly didn't need the problems it would bring, to say nothing of the anxiety. The events of the day proved that.

Daphne Boggs was another story. Eventually Kate asked me what was wrong, and I told her about the pickpocket and the aftermath. She held my hands tightly. Words were superfluous.

Driving home we were quiet—lost in the complexities of our own thoughts.

Neither of us was prepared for the events that were about to overtake us.

FOUR

London, England—Wednesday, June 13, 1962

The best part of driving in London is driving out of it.

That's precisely what I was doing the next morning, and it was one of those perfect days. The sun made the green of England seem even greener, and there was a translucent sheen over the Thames as I criss-crossed it on my way down the Chertsey by-pass near Richmond. This was what I loved about England, and it made the days of drizzle almost bearable.

Kate had left for school early—I hadn't even seen her—and I was to spend the day at the Royal Military School of Music, commonly known all over the world as Kneller Hall.

Since Kneller Hall was in Twickenham, Middlesex, I had decided to drive. Not that I needed much urging to get the Jag out, especially on a day like this. My one real extravagance, it was a Mark II 3.4 automatic in British Racing Green, and I loved handling it. I never ceased to marvel at its engineering or its finish—the soft green leather seats and the burled walnut fascia and trim. I had picked it up barely used from an elderly baronet who had decided to upgrade to a Rolls with a chauffeur. I think I got the better of the deal.

I pondered as I drove, about Kate and her wonderful opportunity, the terrible events of the previous day, and about Colonel Hammond's request and my decision to renege. Strangely, I realized that I was thinking more about Kate's good luck than I was about the intelligence thing. It surprised me that I didn't feel guilty about turning Hammond down.

With much apprehension I had read the papers earlier, afraid of the lurid details I might find about my tragic meeting with Daphne, the pickpocket. To my surprise and relief it had warranted only a small item on a back page, and my name had not been mentioned.

Unusual, I felt. The tabloids liked to have a field day with this sort of thing, and I realized how lucky I was not to be smeared all over the front pages. Thank God for small mercies.

Passing the Twickenham Rugby Grounds I could see the front of the main building of 'KH', with its ornamented red brick. Soaring above the trees were the twin towers, stark against the blue of the sky, standing sentinel for the Union Jack flying between them. It was hard to believe I had spent three years here as a student.

Turning into the main gate from the narrow road I was promptly saluted by the Pupils on guard duty—not because I was recognized as an officer, I realized, but because I was driving a Jaguar. It was safer to salute anything that smelled of status rather than hear about it later with a bollocking.

Parking the car I made my way into the main building—the former country home of Sir Godfrey Kneller, the celebrated court painter during the reign of Queen Anne in the early 1700's.

Lieutenant-Colonel Archibald Mowatt, OBE, LRAM, ARCM, psm, Director of Music, the Royal Military School of Music, and Senior Director of Music for the British Army, was an intimidating figure. Stocky, as many Scots are, his blue eyes pierced out under bushy white eyebrows, and his equally white moustache bristled continuously against a florid complexion.

Many a student bandmaster has wilted under that gaze, and Archie went to great pains to keep up the front, but underneath it all he was a gentleman and even more, a gentle man.

"Good morning, David," he greeted, coming around his desk as I was shown into his office. "It's good to see you again."

"Good morning, Archie," I smiled.

I always smiled when I called him Archie. Just over three years before it would have been unthinkable. As a student, even though

Archie had known about my commission, we both had to play the game for the sake of propriety and protocol. Even so, he had allowed me some licence which the British students had not had, and under the guise of giving me experience I was permitted a great deal of freedom and privilege. But he was still "sir," or "Colonel Mowatt" in those days.

Now, as a retired captain and with my rising status in British music, I was considered an equal—but I still smiled when I called him Archie.

"I'm glad you were able to come today—I know how busy you must be," he said.

"I really don't have a lot on right now. Rehearsals for the show begin in three weeks, and I figured I should have some time off before that grind begins."

"It's good to see you getting on—it's a tough life you've chosen. You've really got to have what it takes."

"Come on, Archie," I replied, "you know how much luck is involved in this business. If I hadn't been in the right place at the right time a lot of these things wouldn't have happened for me. There are lots of guys walking around out there who can do what I do—they just haven't had a chance."

"Not at all, lad," he said with a twinkle in his eye. "It's the wonderful training we gave you here that's made the difference, and don't you forget it." He chuckled as he reached for his cap. "Now let's go down to the rehearsal. Oh, by the way, I hope you're lunching in the mess with us today. There are a couple of people here you should meet."

Every Wednesday night from late May until mid-August, the band at KH presented a public concert on the huge concrete bandstand in the garden behind the main building. These concerts were really part of the training program, not only for the musicians as players, but for the Student Bandmasters to conduct under performance conditions.

As well, there were often guest conductors, both military and civilian, and this served to acquaint the Students and Pupils with personalities in music and a wide variety of styles in conducting. On top of it all, the public were treated to some wonderful concerts, full of military splendour and endless variety.

As Archie stalked into view the rehearsal halted abruptly, and the Band Sergeant-Major brought the band smartly to attention. Archie took up his position at a microphone in the centre of the lawn, and indicated to the Student who was conducting to proceed.

For large outdoor concerts like this, all of the Pupils and Students formed the Kneller Hall band. The Pupils were younger, promising musicians attending a one-year course of intensive instruction on their individual instruments, while the Students were on a three-year course of theory and conducting, designed to prepare them for possible selection as Bandmasters in the British Army. There were also quite a few Commonwealth countries represented, and the mix was both stimulating and interesting.

It didn't take Archie long to get into gear. While the Student struggled valiantly with Vaughan Williams' *The Wasps*, Archie whistled to stop him and give him some 'friendly' advice.

"Don't flap your left arm like that, lad," he bellowed, "you'll take off like a ruddy bird. If you can't do something constructive with it we'll have to tie it down! Start again!"

I sat there, listening to the music and Archie's ravings, remembering my student days in a bit of a daydream, thoroughly enjoying the atmosphere and the sunshine.

I'm not sure when I first noticed her. I think it was a glint of sunshine in a mass of golden hair, but whatever it was it turned my head. She was several rows in front of me and slightly to my right, but with barely a dozen people attending the rehearsal it was surprising I hadn't been aware of her earlier.

I couldn't see her face, but that made it even more alluring, and it fitted perfectly into my daydream. She had on a lovely summer dress, and with that golden crown pulled to one side the view from this angle was fascinating. I kept trying different faces on her in my daydream.

I stopped abruptly when I realized that Archie was calling me to rehearse my piece. Without a chance to put a real face on the lady, I strode to the high, wrought-iron conductor's podium, and picked up the baton.

"Good morning," I smiled at the band, "let's relax and just have fun with this."

I was to conduct a selection of tunes written by Robert Farnon, a Canadian musician who had remained in England after the Second World War. Bob had become the pre-eminent composer of light music in Great Britain, and I had worked with him on occasion. He was a brilliant arranger, and you couldn't know a nicer man.

The band had been well-prepared by the School Bandmaster, and the rehearsal went along smoothly. It felt strange to be back here conducting as a civilian, and I half expected to hear Archie's whistle for me to stop while he admonished me about something, but of course he didn't.

Only once, when I had stopped to explain a different eighth-note treatment that I wanted in a section, did I hear from him.

"What you're asking for is not what's written, is it, David?" he commented, and for Archie it was exceedingly calm.

I took the bull by the horns.

"No, Archie, it's not," I called out, "but these should be played as swing-eighths and not straight-eighths. It's customary in this style of music."

The band became still and silent, expecting a confrontation between the Director and his former student. A lot of them knew I had been something of an upstart.

Archie hesitated, then raised his hat, beaming a smile.

"I bow to your obvious mastery of the genre," he said magnanimously, "please continue at your leisure."

There was a splatter of applause from the 240 band members. "And that'll be enough of that!" roared Archie.

The silence was immediate and deafening. It was not often that Archie gave in so easily.

The remainder of the selection went easily, and when I finished the band applauded. They knew I was one of them, and it made me feel at home to be acknowledged as such.

A break had been called, and I went straight over to Archie.

"I thought you were going to have a 'go' at me for a minute, Archie," I said, laughing.

"Ach, no, lad," he replied, "I was just testin' you out. When you've got the stick in your hand, you're the boss. I just wanted to see if you'd learned that, or if you were still afraid of me."

He was smiling broadly. I replied in my best Scots brogue.

"Ye mus' be daft, Archie. I wasna' afeerd of you, or your prattlin' Scots blaither."

Archie roared with laughter—a rare sight for the astonished army musicians.

"Now come and meet someone, David."

We walked back toward the building, and there she was. This time, though, with her own face. I had a shock when I realized I had done her an injustice. None of the faces I had imagined was the equal of what I saw.

"Miss Templaars," said Archie, saluting out of courtesy, "may I present David Baird? David was once under my control here, but as you can see he has now escaped, though he occasionally returns to torment me."

Before he could complete the introduction she held out her hand and spoke. The accent was European, but a curious mix.

"Already I know many things about Mr. Baird, Colonel Mowatt. In fact, it becomes possible that he will be my next assignment."

She said this with a playful smile at the corners of her mouth, obviously enjoying my confusion.

"I beg your pardon?" I stammered, my face flushing as Archie chuckled heartily.

"Miss Templaars works for the cultural attaché at the Soviet Embassy, David. She's told me about your singing engagement there. It's not often that David gets caught out like that, Miss Templaars. That was a treat to see. Now, if you're not afraid of retaliation, I'll leave you in his care for a wee while."

He strode away, still chuckling. Miss Templaars was still amused, and it was reflected in her blue eyes.

"I hope I don't make anger for you, Mr. Baird. Is it possible to sit with me for some minutes?"

The warm smile made her face radiant. How could I resist?

"I'd be happier if you'd call me David," I said, as I settled beside her, "and I am certainly not angry."

"Then you must call me Marijke," she answered, pronouncing it as Mah-rye-ka.

"Is that a Russian name?"

"Oh, no, no, it is Dutch like my family name," she responded, laughing at my confusion.

"Are you just visiting Kneller Hall?"

"I come in part for curiosity and also for discussion with Colonel Mowatt. I help to arrange a visit for the Kneller Hall band to the Soviet Union. This is in return for the Red Army Band and Chorus visit to United Kingdom."

"So you work for Vladimir Nalishkin?"

"Yes, in cultural affairs."

I thought I'd better leave that one alone.

"Will you really have something to do concerning my performance in your embassy?"

"Yes, this is a possibility. It is agreeable with you?"

She probed me with those wonderful eyes.

"Yes, it is agreeable with me. In fact, I think it would be very nice to have you as my liaison. Who makes the decision?"

"Mr. Nalishkin wants to see if we become—compatible? Is this a good word?"

"That word is fine," I said with a grin. "But it brings up a question, doesn't it? How do we find out if we're compatible?"

"Perhaps we think about it most carefully and we find a way," she bantered. "You are a man good with problems, yes?"

"Sometimes. But I guess it depends on how compatible we're trying to be," I joshed. "The word has different interpretations."

I looked around at the band, still on break, and even though they were out of earshot many were looking our way. I couldn't blame them, with such a beautiful lady in view. I spoke again.

"Considering our surroundings, perhaps we could continue this discussion at a more convenient time and place. Then we can test our compatibility. Can I give you a raincheck?"

"It's possible, if it became in my interest," she teased. "But first, what is this 'raincheck'?"

I explained, unable to keep the smile off my face, and it was returned with that wonderful warmth I had seen earlier.

"Then I am. . . how you say it?. . . letting you. . . ah. . . off the hook, yes? And I am happy for accept your raincheck."

Marijke looked at me, and the gentle smile appeared again.

"I think I like you, David Baird."

Once again I was nonplussed, and thankful when Archie reappeared a moment later.

"How are you two getting along? I hope you haven't done anything to upset Miss Templaars, David, or she's likely to withdraw the invitation for the band to visit Moscow." Archie turned to Marijke with a wicked grin. "Has he been behaving himself, Miss Templaars? You never know with these ruddy colonials."

Archie chuckled, I grinned foolishly, and Marijke smiled that enigmatic smile.

"Oh yes, Colonel Mowatt, David is being a perfect gentlemen. Now I am certain I ask for him."

She turned with that remark, and as she walked away she glanced at me and touched my arm. Archie and I both stared after her for a moment before he spoke.

"Well, lad, you seem to have made quite an impression on the lady. That shouldn't bother you at all, should it?"

"Miss Templaars seems delightful, Archie, but I think I'm going to be up to my ears with the show for quite a while. Unless I'm very mistaken, this is one lady who is deserving of much more consideration than I'll be able to give for some time."

Archie looked at me quizzically.

"That doesn't sound like the David Baird who used to tear up London with House Paynter when he should have been doing his harmony. I mus' be gettin' old. Ach, weel, we've got to get on wi' the rehearsal. I'll see you in a wee while for lunch."

Archie swung in and out of the Scots vernacular as the mood struck him. He could pass for a *Sassenach,* as the Scots referred to the English, without the slightest difficulty. He was about to leave when I remembered Colonel Hammond.

"Archie, I need a favour. I must make a very private call to London. Do you think I could use the phone in your office?"

"Of course, lad. Just go up and see Miss Lanktree and tell her I said it was all right."

I was just reaching the door when I heard the opening chords of *Finlandia* as the rehearsal got under way, and in a few minutes I was safely seated in Archie's chair. I reached for my wallet, extracted the number Hammond had given me, and dialled as I had been directed.

"Selfridge's, good morning," said a voice.

"Sorry, wrong number," I replied, "I'll dial again."

I stayed on the line for several minutes, hearing clicks every now and then. Then a different voice.

"State your name, please."

"David Baird."

A few more clicks. A female voice.

"Captain Baird, where are you calling from?"

"From the office of the Director of Music at Kneller Hall in Twickenham."

"You wanted to speak to Colonel Hammond, sir, but he's been called away on an emergency. I've been instructed to say that he must speak to you personally, and would you be so kind as to ring again tomorrow. He had no way of knowing when he'd be back. And one other thing, sir—you must not call him from any phone in your flat, and that includes Miss Fletcher's. This is a matter of grave importance. Do you understand, sir?"

"I understand what you've told me, all right, but I don't like the implication one little bit. What the hell's going on?"

"I'm afraid I don't know, Captain Baird. I'm sure Colonel Hammond can explain tomorrow."

I hung up with a feeling of unease that lasted all the way back to the bandstand. I had wanted this thing over and done with, and now it would drag on for another day. And that business about the telephones was the last straw. More than ever, I wanted out.

Gibralter—the same day

They sat at a table in a very ordinary café. To outward appearances just a tourist and a local, casually met. They spoke in English, their only common language.

"You hef onderstand everytheeng?"

"Yes, *effendi.* You wish a suitcase flown to Algiers. This is no problem for me. I load cargo for all airlines landing in Gibralter. I myself will place it on the plane."

"You hef right plane? Is meet in Algiers. Mus' be right one."

"Yes, yes. I have the right plane. Today there is only one. I put the case on this plane, don't worry."

"Here ees key for locker een airport. And something for you."

He slid the key and an envelope across the table. The local pocketed the key, then examined the contents of the envelope below the table top. His face registered his surprise.

"So much? This must be very important, *effendi.*"

He smiled at the tourist, whose cold eyes merely glinted behind the glasses.

"You hef problem, perhaps?"

"No, no—no problem. Everything will be perfect, you will see. I personally guarantee it."

"Eef thees go wrong, you are dead man. Thees my guarantee."

Abruptly he departed, leaving the local in a wave of fear.

Twickenham, England—the same day

Lunch in the Officer's Mess at Kneller Hall can be either festive or boring. There are only three dining-in members of the mess—the Commandant of the school, Archie, as Director of Music, and the Adjutant. Trapped there with these three you're in trouble, for the Commandant monopolizes the conversation, and it's invariably about gardening, his real passion in life.

When there are a dozen or so for lunch, as there were that particular Wednesday, it becomes a gala occasion, for the Commandant becomes engrossed with the two people nearest him. Everyone else has a wonderful time, for the food is excellent.

Fortunately, I was seated at the opposite end of the table from the Commandant, and there was no possibility of being drawn into a discourse on rhododendrons and peonies. Marijke Templaars was not so lucky, however, and occasionally she would catch my eye and give me a look that spelled 'help' or 'rescue me', but I could only smile back with pity—there was no way I would have braved the Commandant's lecture on the cross-pollination of hybrid roses.

Sitting opposite me was a flight lieutenant in Royal Air Force uniform, and the wings above his left breast pocket told me that we would have something to talk about.

"Hello, I'm David Baird. What's a pilot doing in the midst of all these musicians?"

"Philip Rideout," he responded, offering his hand. "No longer a pilot. And I've heard tales of your escapades from Archie."

"Now I know I'm in trouble," I grinned, "Archie is not always to be trusted when he talks about me."

"I think you're pretty safe these days, David, but I'd love to hear the details of one or two of your pranks from your point of view. I'll bet Archie doesn't know the whole story."

"Another time, Philip," I whispered, "this is not the place."

I nodded toward the head of the table as we both chuckled.

"How come you're not flying anymore?"

"These things," he said, pointing to his horn-rimmed glasses. "I'd been with my squadron for over a year and then I caught measles, which I had never had as a child. I came out of it with impaired vision which got steadily worse, and I was grounded while they decided what to do with me. I didn't want to leave the air force, and since I had a strong musical background a few strings were pulled and I took the band-master's course. Now I hang on to a baton instead of the control column in a Hawker Hunter."

"Do you miss flying?"

His dark eyes flashed. "I did at first, but I've taken a civilian licence and I fly a small Cessna, so I keep my hand in. But the other day all the old urges came back with a vengeance. I had my band in Dunsfold to play at a commemorative ceremony for Hawker Aircraft. One of my old chums from flying school days is now test flying for Hawker's, and he got permission to give me a close look at a project I would give anything to be involved in."

"Tell me about it."

"I don't see why not. Nothing I was shown is classified, and the public knows of the aircraft's existence. The design details are top secret, but I'm in the dark there, anyway."

Philip ran his hand through his thatch of unruly dark hair, obviously bursting to share what he had seen, and I was just as anxious to hear about it. But before I could encourage him to continue, he plunged on with a worried look.

"Tell me to shut up if this is boring. I tend to forget that other people don't share my passion for flying."

"Are you kidding, Philip? Archie obviously seated us together because he knows how much I like aircraft. I even wangled a flying course despite being an army director of music."

Philip beamed his pleasure.

"A fellow pilot—that's a jolly good bit of luck. I had fears of aspidistras from his nibs down there. Well, have you followed the development of vertical-take-off-and-landing aircraft to any extent?"

"Not much, I'm afraid. I know there've been some experiments with flying bedsteads and planes that sit on their tails, but that's about it. None seems to have been taken seriously."

"That's not the case anymore. Hawker's have a VTOL that works. I've seen it fly, and it's fantastic!"

For the next twenty minutes or so Philip spoke in admiration about this aircraft, the P1127. Still unnamed, it was a jet which took off and landed vertically or with a short run, and then converted to conventional flight as a fighter. Under development by Hawker Aircraft, it promised to revolutionize air warfare, especially in the close support role.

Philip explained that the principle of rotating jet nozzles was called 'vectored thrust', and Hawker was leading the world in VTOL aircraft. The technology was a closely guarded secret.

I thought about it for a moment, throwing out a question.

"What about the Russians? Have they been working on anything similar? If we're this far advanced, I'd be surprised if they weren't watching every step of the way."

"We've heard rumours about a VTOL programme in Russia, but nothing concrete. France is the closest—Dassault has a programme based on one of the Mirage fighters. But they're all trying to use separate engines for the take-off and landing, with a conventional jet for horizontal flying. This way the vertical engines become dead weight during normal flight, and it severely limits the aircraft's performance. We seem to be the only ones who have mastered the 'vectored thrust' principle, and that's why the technology is top secret."

"I hope they're minding the store," I commented. "If the Soviets want something they go after it. All these defectors haven't exactly instilled confidence in British security."

Philip became very defensive. The defections of Burgess, MacLean, and the others had embarrassed Britons to the core, apart from the damage they had done through their espionage.

"Not to worry, old chap. I'm sure as far as the P1127 is concerned they've got it tightly battened down. Ivan will never get his hands on those documents—you mark my words."

We continued talking about flying for the rest of lunch. I hadn't flown in over a year, and I was beginning to realize how much I missed it. Philip offered to take me up in his Cessna, and we parted like old friends, promising to keep in touch.

I was wondering what to do for the afternoon—I had my tux with me, and it seemed pointless to drive home, sit around for a couple of hours, and then drive back for the concert.

Archie settled it for me, appearing at my elbow as I was thanking the Commandant for his hospitality. Marijke was with him.

"David, if you've got nothing pressing this afternoon, I wonder if you could run Miss Templaars back to her embassy and return her here for the concert? There are some papers which I'm going to need sooner than we had anticipated. We've had to move the date of our Moscow visit up considerably. I'd do it myself, but I've got a meeting with the examiners which I can't put off."

I looked at Marijke, receiving a smile of reassurance, and that was enough for me. "Sure, Archie, I'd be happy to."

I smiled at Marijke, and she returned it with warmth.

"I can use your phone, Colonel Mowatt? I make sure these papers are ready so we don't must wait. David, you are sure it doesn't give trouble for you?"

I assured her it did not, and she touched my arm as Archie led her to the phone. I strolled into the museum to look at some of the wonderful collection of ancient instruments while I waited, and, in a short while, Marijke found me there.

"David, I telephone to Vladimir Nalishkin that you drive me to the embassy, and he say he likes to see you for a few minutes when we are there. Is it permissible with you?"

I loved her turn of phrase.

"Of course it is. Are you ready to go?"

"Yes, only for one thing."

With that she leaned over and kissed me—not wanton, but not chaste—it lingered for a moment. She drew back and smiled.

"There," she breathed, "now I claim my raincheck."

"Yes, you have," I quipped with a grin, "and now I'm sorry I didn't give you two rainchecks to claim."

"But you didn't, David Baird," she said softly. "Yes, I think I like you very much." She paused, and the mischievous smile returned. "I am fair. Now I know what are rainchecks, I give you one of these. You must choose when and where you claim it."

"Are there any limitations?"

"I don't make any," she replied softly. "You have an interesting idea, perhaps?"

"As they say in the music business, let's play it by ear."

"I don't know this 'play it by ear.' What does it mean?"

"It means, let's improvise—make it up as we go along."
It was her turn to laugh. "I think I am good at that, yes?"
"I think you are good at that, yes."
Marijke took my arm, and we headed out into the sunlight.
The beautiful day had just become a wonderful day.

FIVE

"Do you know where is the embassy, David?"

"Kensington Palace Gardens off Kensington High Street. But I've never been on the street itself, so I don't know exactly."

"When we come to the security post I get us in. This doesn't become a problem. I thank you for driving me. I hope I don't take you away from something you prefer to do."

I smiled broadly. "Are you kidding?"

Then we lapsed into an expectant silence. It was almost as though we were strangers. Of course, that was the problem—we were strangers, and being alone without the security of social formality put us on our guard with each other. The ice didn't start to break until we crossed the Thames near Mortlake and were heading toward Hammersmith. I thought I'd better start it off.

"How come someone from the Netherlands is working for the Soviets? I thought they would employ only their own people in a foreign posting like this."

"You are right, David, and the answer is simple. I am not born in the Netherlands—I am born in the Soviet Union, and I am a Soviet citizen."

"Oh!" I blurted, sounding more startled than I wanted to. I hadn't anticipated her reply.

"This bothers you, David?"

"No, not at all, but it wasn't the answer I expected. Is your father from Holland?"

"Yes, but he is in Russia since 1937. He meets my mother in Moscow, and they are married in 1939. I am born a year later."

"But your accent isn't completely Russian—I can hear traces of Dutch in there. Did you attend special classes to learn to speak it, or was it just from listening to your father?"

"Neither. When the war is over we live in Holland from 1947 until 1957. Then we go back to Moscow, and I attend university there. Have I such a strange accent when I speak English? Is it so terrible to hear?"

I laughed. "No, of course not. It's just that some words have a Russian sound and some a Dutch sound. You have a lovely blend of both accents. I hope you didn't think I was making fun of you."

"No—I don't think that."

She smiled at me, and briefly rested her hand on my arm.

I navigated around Hammersmith, and shortly we were in Kensington High Street, passing the nearly completed Commonwealth Institute, with it's huge tent-like copper roof.

Just after Kensington Church Street, with the medieval-looking St. Mary Abbots Church on the corner, Marijke squeezed my arm.

"You must turn left very soon, David. You will see iron gates at the end of the street, and I must show my identification to the security guard."

I turned left into Palace Green, which became Kensington Palace Gardens as it proceeded north, and stopped at the barrier. A Royal Borough of Kensington security guard, clad in grey top hat and green frock coat, came out of a kiosk, and Marijke leaned across me to show her embassy identification.

"That's alright, Miss, thank you," he said, stepping back to raise the barrier, and I drove on through.

Kensington Palace Gardens is often referred to as 'Embassy Row' because most of the Victorian mansions on it have been purchased by various governments for diplomatic use. This has ensured their survival. Very few families would have been able to maintain the houses, leading to decay and eventual demolition. Without the foreign purchases these properties would probably have been sold to developers, with the usual disastrous results.

"It's number 13, David, on the right. Drive to the gate and I get us past the attendant."

I pulled in to the entrance, stopping as a man in civilian clothes came to my side of the car. He seemed to recognize Marijke, but was very brusk in his manner.

"Odostoverenia pozalsta," he said to Marijke, and she showed her pass. He continued, *"E muzchyna?"*

"U nivau vstrycha su Palkaunik Nalishkin."

I noticed the stress on Nalishkin's name as Marijke said it, and it had the desired effect.

"Prukudit," he said, stepping back smartly, and we drove in to park the car.

The house itself was very large, but not very pretty to look at. The buff-coloured bricks needed a good cleaning, and this contributed to a forbidding appearance. There were two full stories with a partial story above, the latter probably for the servants when the house had been a residence. A portico with hanging lamps sheltered the heavy, studded oak doors. A flag-staff jutted out from above the portico, but it was not graced by a flag. As we ascended the double entrance stairway I had an uneasy feeling, but I couldn't explain it.

"I take you to Mr. Nalishkin's office, David, and I go to my office and see if papers are ready. Then I come back. Is this agreeable with you?"

"Yes, that's fine. Which floor do you work on, Marijke?"

"I am not so important to work in this building," laughed Marika. "My office is across the street in number 18, which is for administration. This is where I go when I take you inside."

We entered through the heavy doors, stopping by a glass-enclosed security booth on the right-hand side. There was a uniformed guard, but I didn't recognize the uniform. Marijke took a pen and wrote in a large book which lay open on the desk.

"I sign you in," she said, replacing the pen. "Now come. I take you to Mr. Nalishkin."

From the entrance hall, with its black marble columns, she led me into an extremely large two-storied room which reminded me of a banqueting hall in a baronial castle. It was panelled in dark, solid oak, with a huge oak double staircase on our left. As it was in the centre of the house there were no windows, but light poured in through a large, raised, leaded and stained glass skylight which took up most of the area of the ceiling.

Over a landing on the staircase hung a portrait of Lenin, and above us a balcony surrounded the whole room. With the deep maroon carpet, marbled fireplace, leather-upholstered furniture, original paintings, ornate tables with carefully place urns and vases, it was a room worthy of the Czar himself.

"This is magnificent, Marijke. No wonder the Soviets wanted it for their embassy."

"The house is built in 1852 and 1853. When our government buys it in 1930 it is for the Soviet ambassador to live."

"He must have lived in style, even in the 'dirty thirties.' It would take a lot of servants just to keep it tidy."

"Now our ambassadors don't live this way, but most of formal entertaining is here. I hope I hear you sing here soon, David."

She started to walk toward a doorway at the back.

"Come this way," she beckoned.

We walked through into what must have been a formal dining room, with a huge, solid table surrounded by gold brocaded chairs. The brocade was carried into the window drapes, and the chandelier was replicated by heavy, gold lamp standards throughout the room.

"Mr. Nalishkin's office is to the right. The Ambassador and the Minister Counselor are at the front of the building, but this is nicer here to see the gardens."

Marijke indicated one of the chairs near the white-painted double doors. "If you sit here, I go tell Mr. Nalishkin."

Marijke knocked, gave me a quick smile, and went on in. I sat quietly for a moment, allowing the silence to settle, and then the full realization of my circumstance hit me. If Colonel Hammond could see me now, I thought, and nearly laughed out loud as I considered where I was, and alone to boot. I debated doing something daring, like sneaking into an office and looking through the papers on a desk, but I realized that I wouldn't know what I was looking at and the gesture seemed foolish. It was just as well, for Marijke came out almost immediately.

"He is with you in a few minutes, David. He calls on the long distance. I am back for you soon, yes? I must go and get papers for Colonel Mowatt."

"I'll be fine Marijke. Take your time."

She smiled and was gone. I sat quietly for a moment, then my ears became accustomed to the sound of a voice. It was coming from the direction of Nalishkin's office, and on closer inspection I realized that Marijke had not closed his door tightly—it was open just a crack.

There was another chair right beside the door, so I walked softly to it and sat down as nonchalantly as I could. My heart was pounding, which was stupid, for even if I could hear Nalishkin I couldn't understand Russian. But I decided to tune in and try.

At first I could hardly separate the words, which were indeed in Russian, but after a few moments of adjusting to the cadence and timbre of Nalishkin's voice, I began to discern first the syllables and then the words. Unfortunately, it made no sense—the sound of the language was as obscure to me as their alphabet.

Several times Nalishkin had to stop and repeat a word louder and slower, but the only thing I caught was a word that sounded like 'drama', and I presumed he might have been acting in his cultural role concerning theatre. Then he seemed to lose his temper.

"Nyet, nyet, nyet! Pe odinadtsat dvadtsat' sem'!" He paused, then continued louder. *"Pe, odin, odin, dva, sem'! Vy ponimayetye? Dobry!"*

The connection must have improved, for his voice dropped to normal, and it was a strain to hear it. But there had been something vaguely familiar about some of the words I had heard. I took my pen and my engagement book out and wrote down what I could remember phonetically: pay, adeen, adeen, diva, siem.

I must have stared at them for a few minutes, trying to recall the connection, for when I looked up, Vladimir Nalishkin was watching me. I started, nearly panicking, but managed to control the slow closing of my engagement book as I fought to keep my fingers from shaking. I noticed him hesitate as he glanced at the door to his office, and with a look of concern on his face he threw a phrase at me, catching me unawares.

"*Dabry d'ehn*, David."

"I beg your pardon?" I stammered.

"Oh, forgive me, of course you don't speak Russian. I just said 'good afternoon' to you."

Then he was all smiles, coming over to shake my hand. He was a small, elegant man—slender, with thinning dark hair combed back from his forehead. A fastidious dresser, he wore a beautifully cut dark blue serge suit, starched white shirt, and a navy bow tie with very fine white polka dots. The black shoes were polished to a high gloss, but what set it off was the red carnation boutonnière. I had noticed one when I met him at the Latin Quarter, and now I guessed it was his trade mark.

"I would like to welcome you to Soviet territory in the name of the Ambassador. Please come in to my office, and let us celebrate your visit with a drink of vodka."

He held the door for me, and I was not prepared for the elegance of his office, even though it was in a mansion of Victorian decadence. Everything was a work of art—the rugs were Persian, deep pile with exquisite floral patterns, the sofa and matching chairs were aquamarine brocade, the colour picking out and enhancing the exact hue from a subtle trace in the rugs. The coffee table, inlaid with leather, the desk—a masterpiece of carving and inlaid wood, the panelled walls, and the original paintings that were hanging there. Beyond this room were double French doors opening into a glassed conservatory.

If all Soviet citizens are equal and this is an example of that equality, I thought, I wonder who milks the cows?

Nalishkin poured our vodkas from an elegant crystal decanter, and, handing one to me, raised his glass.

"*Za vash'eh zdorov'eh!*" he toasted.

"Cheers!" I responded, and we drank.

"David, I am so glad that you have met Marijke Templaars. It was kind of you to drive her to the embassy. What do you think of her? Do you get along well?"

"Yes, we do. She's a charming lady."

"That is indeed good. I am thinking of making her your liaison for your concert here. You would make all arrangements and details with her, if this is agreeable with you."

I smiled. "You won't hear any objections from me, Mr. Nalishkin. It'll be a pleasure to work with Marijke."

"Then it is settled. But please, David, not 'Mr. Nalishkin'. I would prefer that you are calling me Vladimir, or the familiar, Volodya. Now, the reason I want to speak with you today. The Soviet government is considering to begin a cruise ship service, operating out of Odessa in the Black Sea. To test out the feasibility, we have leased a ship from Canadian Pacific Steamships—the *Empress of Britain*. We have had a crew on board for the past month learning about the ship from the Canadian crew—how would you call it—familiarization? Is that correct?"

"That's the right word, Volodya."

"Good. The ship is scheduled to leave Montreal in two days time with the Soviet crew replacing the Canadian crew. We have flown a group of dignitaries from Russia to Montreal to make the cruise back to Odessa. It is these people we must convince to begin our own service in the Black Sea and the Mediterranean. Now, to get to the point—the ship will dock in Southampton next Tuesday, and then proceed on through the Mediterranean to the Black Sea. We would be very honoured if you would come aboard and perform a concert for us as we continue our journey to Odessa."

I was speechless. On the one hand I didn't want to offend the Soviets, yet I shouldn't be away from London with the show rehearsals imminent. Still, I could use a break before the going got tough. Nalishkin read my silence and carried on.

"I understand why you hesitate, David, with your new show coming. Why don't you consider this a holiday? We ask only one performance of you, and I am authorized to offer you one thousand pounds for your services."

A thousand pounds sterling, I thought. Wow! I'd never been offered that much for a single performance yet, and I knew that the publicity and prestige could only be good for my career. And, sure enough, why not treat it as a well-paid holiday?

"When would I be back in London, Volodya?"

"Only one week after the ship sails from Southampton. Two weeks from today. We fly you here from Moscow. And I promise you, you will be very well looked after. Marijke Templaars will see to that, I am convinced." He laughed loudly.

"Will she be going, too?" I asked, trying not to appear too interested.

"Of course, of course," he chortled. "If I make her your liaison with us that will mean on the high seas as well as on land. You do not object?"

"Not at all, in fact, I think I will enjoy it very much."

"Splendid, splendid! I leave you to work out the details with Marijke. Anything you need you must simply ask her."

There was a tap at the door, and Marijke entered with a radiance that lit the room.

"I don't interrupt?"

"No, no, Marijke. David has just accepted our invitation to sail to Odessa next week. Is that not wonderful?" He was beaming.

"I am happy for me, David, for if you don't agree then I don't go either, and I very much want this. I must thank you to make it possible."

Her smile was warm and sincere.

* * *

We took our leave from Vladimir Nalishkin and the Soviet Embassy, but nothing was said until we had turned into Kensington High Street again—the silence of new acquaintance had descended once more. But this time Marijke broke it.

"What time we are back at Kneller Hall, David?"

"The concert's not 'til eight, but I should be there by seven so I can change." I paused before continuing. "It's only four o'clock now. Would you like a drive and some afternoon tea?"

"Oh, yes, that is very nice. I very much like this English custom of afternoon tea. Where do we go?"

"Leave it to me."

I glanced at her and smiled. It was returned, and her hand touched my arm again. We drove in a contented silence.

I headed out of London as quickly and expeditiously as I could, picking up the Great West Road from Chiswick and then down the A30 past Staines. From then on we were in countryside, and I chose small lanes to meander through as I gradually approached Virginia Water. Reaching this delightful, protected lake, I pulled in to a parking area and stopped the car. The overhanging trees framed our view of the water, and the silence was only broken by the birds and the gentle lapping of waves at the water's edge.

"Oh, David, it is very beautiful here," murmured Marijke. "Is it permissible we can get out?"

"Sure, but you're not exactly dressed for a walk in the woods or along the shore. It's pretty soft ground. I have a blanket in the boot—would you like to sit for a while?"

"Oh, yes, please."

We walked along the path for a hundred yards or so, and settled the blanket under a shady oak with a clear view of the water. We sat quietly, really not knowing what to say. Marijke was close to my shoulder, and her hand found my arm again, but this time it lingered, and in a few minutes it slid down to hold mine, ever so tentatively.

When I felt her head on my shoulder I looked down, and I couldn't resist the urge to kiss the top of her head. We stayed that way for some time, and I felt more content than I could ever remember. Thinking that it was mutual I glanced at Marijke, and I was startled to see a dark, sombre look on her face.

"What's wrong?" I exclaimed. "Have I upset you?"

"No, David, it's not like this," she murmured, shaking her head with a deep sigh. "Sometimes I know there is happiness possible which I don't ever have. Maybe I see it for one minute—like now—and I feel great joy and great sadness both together. When I am with embassy people I don't let myself be like this, but with you I feel safe and show my feelings. I like you very much, David, and I am sorry if I embarrass you."

"I'm not, Marijke. I'm honoured that you would trust me with your feelings. But I don't understand. Why do you think that you may never be happy? Surely even in the Soviet system you have some privacy and the right to choose your friends and live out your life as you wish. I know it may not be as free as you would like it to be, but can it be that bad?"

The consternation showed. I put my arm around her, and she rested her head on my chest. She didn't look up as she spoke.

"There are many things which are not how they look, David. This is very true in the Soviet Union. We are sure about no one, and always we live with fear that something goes wrong and we are destroyed." She hesitated again. "I'm sorry, but I don't speak more about these things. I must ask you don't say anything of this to anyone—not anyone at all. Please?"

"Not a word, Marijke, I promise you. And if you ever wish to talk about it, I want you to know that you can trust me completely, no matter what you tell me."

I hesitated, for I was not sure how she would take what I wanted to say next.

"Please don't misunderstand what I am going to say to you. If things are not right for you in the Soviet Union, why don't you leave? You are out of the country right now, so stay here. I'm sure I could find out who you should talk with, and I would do it without anyone knowing why I was making enquiries."

She shook her head. "This is not possible. Some things I cannot explain. There are many... ah... complicating... yes?... parts of my life which I don't control, and I speak of them to no one. Already I say too much."

She looked up, her eyes beseeching me to keep her confidence. I took her face in my hands, ever so gently.

"You are safe with me, Marijke," I whispered. "I like you so very much, and I would never cause you harm—whatever you might tell me."

I leaned forward and kissed her, gently at first, but a deep hunger in both of us turned it into a passionate, soul-searing revelation that left us trembling and out of breath. As our mouths separated we stared at each other wide-eyed, aware that something mystical had happened in those moments.

"Oh, David," she cried, clutching me tightly.

* * *

We drove away from Virginia Water as if in a dream. I couldn't believe the intensity of emotions which had surfaced, completely without warning. By the time we had reached the tea room on a quiet lane near Sunningdale I had regained my composure, if not my sense of balance. Marijke was almost her old self, but perhaps a little subdued. Over tea, sandwiches and scones, we continued talking.

"Tell me more about your parents, Marijke. What was your father doing in Russia in 1937?"

"In 1937 he is with the Dutch Embassy. When the war begins between the Soviet Union and Germany, he stays in Moscow as liaison officer for the Allies."

"How did he meet your mother?"

"At a reception which she attends with her father. My grandfather is serving with the Soviet Army, and my father has many meetings with him about supplies and munitions. Mother falls in love with the handsome Hollander, and they are married in 1939.

"It is difficult at first for my parents. Stalin signs a treaty with Hitler, and in this way Germany and Soviet Union are allies while the Nazis destroy Europe, including Holland. But my father urges patience—he knows it is only a matter of time before Germany turns on Russia.

"Hitler is afraid of Communism more than anything else and thinks that if Russia becomes too strong he will not be able to conquer it. My father is right, of course, and so begins the Great Patriotic War, as it becomes known in Soviet Union."

"What about after the war? It seems unusual for a diplomat to be left at the same embassy for such a long time."

"This is true, and the Netherlands government wants to move my father, but he resigns and applies for Soviet citizenship. I know my grandfather's influence helps, and also to have him sent to the Soviet Trade Legation in Amsterdam in 1947. It is very smart, for who is better to deal with the Dutch than a Dutchman? And this is where I do my schooling and learn to speak Dutch."

Marijke had become more and more animated as she told me about her parents, and by the time she was finished she was smiling happily again, and the sparkle had returned to her manner.

"That's quite a story, Marijke. I'm sure there's a lot more between the lines."

"What does this mean—'between the lines'?"

"It means that behind many stories there are hidden facts and details which no one will ever know, and yet everyone tries to guess what they are and put their own interpretation on them."

She looked at me strangely, but seemed unable or unwilling to comment further. I felt I was on thin ice here, and that perhaps I should return to 1962 and leave the skeletons in the closet. I reached across the table and took her hand in mine.

"What happens with us, Marijke?"

"Us? How do you mean this, David?"

"Us—you and me. You know that I will want to see you, and not just because of business. But where do we go from here? I mean, will this present difficulties for you with the embassy?"

She reached over with her other hand and covered mine. There was a wistful smile on her face.

"I think we take each day when it comes. I feel for you something very special, and maybe a little frightening. They warn us about personal involvement when we are in other countries, and I am afraid I am sent back if anyone knows about this.

"But two things help us. The first is I become your liaison with our embassy for both cruise ship and concert, and so it looks not strange for us to meet. The second is I pretend to our people that what looks like romance is only to win you over—that it becomes one-sided and I only pretend. And they will believe me."

"Why should they? Won't they suspect something?"

"No. And here you must trust me without question, if you want to see me. You can do this?"

I looked at her intensely.

"Yes."

Her eyes were serious but there was a smile on her lips.

"Then we enjoy what we find, David Baird, and don't look too far for tomorrow. It comes, and who can know what it brings?"

* * *

We drove gradually back to Twickenham, arriving at Kneller Hall just after seven. I left Marijke with Archie while I changed, and I was glad that I was able to escort her to the dignitaries area and sit with her while I waited my turn to conduct.

The concert was splendid, from the opening fanfare played by the Kneller Hall Trumpeters, through the pageantry of a visiting Highland band, and various solos and selections performed and conducted by both visitors and students. My piece went well, and I enjoyed the experience immensely. When I had returned to my seat, Marijke took my hand in the dark and squeezed it, and that was better than a hundred compliments.

When the concert was over there was a reception in the mess, and necessity forced Marijke and me to spend time apart, talking to various guests. Somewhere about 11:30 she managed to extricate herself and find me, only to tell me that the embassy had sent a car for her, and that for appearances she should take it and be driven back to her flat.

"Go to the ladies' room, and then come to the museum," I whispered. "I'll be waiting."

For the second time that day she found me there alone, and for the second time that day we kissed amidst musical history.

"I couldn't let you go without saying good night," I said, holding her close. "When will I see you?"

She handed me a slip of paper with a telephone number on it.

"Please, you call me."

"Is it safe? Are your calls monitored?"

She smiled. "There is no problem. Play the game we talk about, and everybody believes us. I must go now."

She walked to the stairs leading out of the museum, then turned to me. "*Do svidania*, David Baird," she said softly, and then she was gone.

* * *

Driving home later, my mind was full of conflicting thoughts and emotions. Only two days before I had not given the Soviet Union more than a passing thought, and now I was entangled with them like the twinings of a bramble bush. I felt very confused. Turning on the radio, I sought the soothing distraction of music, but nothing seemed to penetrate my fog. Even Mozart has his limitations.

I parked the car, waved at the night porter as I passed, and took the lift up. Stepping into my flat, I had a sense of foreboding. Something was not right. Not again, I thought, remembering my visitor of the day before.

A night light was on in the hall, and I could see that Kate's door was open. Invariably when she was in her own flat the door was closed. What was wrong? I snapped on some lights, walked into the living room, and started as I saw her in a corner on the floor, sitting with her arms around her legs, rocking back and forth.

"Kate, what's the matter? What's happened?" I ran to her.

She appeared to come to, as if in a trance.

"David," she said wildly, "they're. . . gone!"

She was racked with a fit of sobbing. I reached for her and held her, afraid to ask the next question.

"Who's gone, Kate?"

She choked on each word. "The plane. . . Mom. . . Dad. . . everything! No. . . survivors! They're. . . they're. . . both. . . dead!"

Her keening was the sound of an animal in pain.

SIX

Paris, France—Thursday, June 14, 1962

It was after midnight, but his instructions had been to report immediately on his return to Paris. He dialled the special number, let it ring once, hung up, then dialled again.

"Yes?"

The query was in French. He responded in kind.

"It went as planned. There were no problems."

"So we have heard. Well done. The baggage handler has been taken. Does he know anything?"

"Not even where I come from, and names were not used."

"Good. Your honorarium will arrive in the usual manner, plus a generous bonus. You are ready for the next assignment?"

"Yes. I will begin tomorrow."

"You understand there must be no warning to the courier?"

"Leave this to me. I am no amateur who plays at these games."

He put the receiver down before there was a further exchange. Arrogant bastards, he thought. Dismissing them, he prepared to go out. He needed sexual gratification, and where better to find it than on the streets of Paris? He trembled when he thought of how it might end.

His thoughts returned to the woman in London, and it aroused him even more. On his previous visit he had been interrupted. This time I'll finish it, he thought. My way.

London, England—the same night

I held Kate for nearly half an hour before she fell into a fitful sleep. As desperate as I was to find out what had happened, I realized that there was no point in trying to talk to her. It was obvious she had been given a sedative, and this, coupled with her grief, had made her delirious. Eventually I carried her to her room and tucked her in as well as I could. I sat by the bed for a few minutes until I was sure she had settled, then left quietly.

Too agitated to sleep, I made a cup of tea and sat down in the living room, idly fingering the pieces on my chess board as my mind churned. Who could I call at this hour, I wondered, who would be able to tell me what had happened?

A newspaper—of course! I headed for the phone, absent-mindedly carrying a pawn with me, setting it down on the phone stand to look up the number of the *Observer*. I was connected to the newsroom and explained what I wanted.

"We have very little on that crash as yet, sir. The authorities are not releasing much."

"What airline was it?"

"A small charter line called Straitsair. It flies cargo and passengers around the western Mediterranean—some of the islands and Morocco, Algeria, Tunisia and Gibralter."

"Where did the plane go down?"

"We're not sure. We found out from the control tower in Gibralter that the flight plan filed was between Gib and Dar-el-Beida airport in Algiers, which is about five hundred miles. The aircraft was a Fokker F27, which has a range of more than double that distance, and it carried a full load of fuel.

"Forty-two minutes into the flight Gibralter tower lost all voice communication with Flight SA23, and it disappeared from the radar screen. We've tried every which-way, and that's all we can get out of anybody. We don't know whether there has been an air-sea search, we don't know if there was a visual sighting of what happened from ships or other aircraft, and we can't get anyone to talk to us. It's as if an official silence has been drawn over the whole thing, and we don't know why."

"What time did it happen?"

"Flight SA23 departed Gibralter at 1422 hours GMT, and all contact was lost at 1504 hours. I'm sorry I can't tell you more."

"Not at all—you've given me far more than I started with. Thank you for your time and your help."

I rang off and just stood there in neutral. There seemed to be nothing I could do to find out more or to help Kate. I wondered about the veil of silence which the journalist had alluded to. Why would they be trying to hide what had happened? I was about to walk back to the living room when the phone rang, startling me.

"Lords 0-5-8-2," I answered.

"David Baird?"

"Yes."

"This is Barbara Vandenberg. I must apologize for calling at this hour, but I was so worried about Kate I had to. How is she?"

Barbara Vandenburg was the wife of the American Ambassador to the Court of St. James.

"She's asleep now, Mrs. Vandenburg, but she seemed pretty much out of it when I got home about an hour ago."

"When Dwight called me and told me about the Fletchers I went straight over to the Royal Academy to get her. We had her with us at the residence until she insisted on going home about 9:00pm. The embassy doctor gave her a sedative, and I hoped she would fall asleep, but she didn't want to stay here. I've been worrying that I should have insisted."

"Do you know what happened, Mrs. Vandenberg? I only have a sketchy account from the *Observer*."

She told me what she knew but I'd gotten more from the paper.

"Why does there seem to be a blackout on the details surrounding the disaster, Mrs. Vandenberg? Has the Ambassador commented on it?"

"David, I don't know anything. I'm just a private citizen like anybody else, and I think I prefer it that way. If Kate needs anything tomorrow, or if I can help in any way, please call the residence and I'll do everything I can. We knew the Fletchers well, and Kate was very special to them. I feel sick about this." She sighed deeply.

"I'll tell her you called, Mrs. Vandenberg, and I'll certainly get in touch if Kate needs anything. Good night."

Curious, I thought, as I hung up. Cal Fletcher must have been pretty high up on the totem pole to warrant all this attention at the ambassadorial level. I had thought he was just another civil servant doing his routine job, but I was beginning to see it in a different light. I doubted if Kate knew the details of her father's job, and certainly the American Embassy wasn't going to tell me, but I might just know someone who could fill in the blanks. After all, the flight originated from British territory.

I was still holding the pawn, and as I walked over to put it back a light went on in my head. *Holy shit*! I knew what some of the words were that Nalishkin had said on the phone! In fact, I had them in the palm of my hand. The sooner I talked to Hammond the better.

I went to bed, but sleep eluded me. My mind whirled in confusion as I dozed fitfully, awakening every few minutes in a panic. When the door of my bedroom opened and a white-shrouded apparition stood there I thought I had lost all sense of what was real and what was imagined, and for a moment I was terrified.

But it was only Kate in her nightdress. Her voice had a dream-like quality, and I wasn't sure that she was really awake.

"David, I'm sorry, but I can't be alone, and I'm so cold. May I stay with you?"

It wasn't cold in the flat, but she was obviously suffering from shock. I hesitated for a split second, but this was no time for stuffy decorum.

"Sure, Kate. Come here." I pulled the covers back. "Can I get you anything?"

"A drink of water, please. I'm very thirsty."

I got it from the fridge and she drank greedily, then I lay down on top of the covers and we settled as I put out the light.

"I used to come to Mom and Dad's bed when I was little, and we would all cuddle together. I loved them so much, David. When I got older we'd still have family meetings on their bed either late at night or in the morning, and if I had a problem that's where it got sorted out. I'm going to miss that. This was their room, and I just had to come tonight. Will you hold me, please?"

I put my arm around her, and she snuggled up, and not another word was spoken by either of us. The sedative must still have been working, for she was soon fast asleep, and even though I remained wide awake we stayed like that until morning.

* * *

Just after 7:00am I eased my arm from around Kate and got up. She looked as if she would be asleep for quite a long time, and I had some burning matters to attend to. I showered and shaved while the coffee perked, and sat with a cup while I planned what to do in logical sequence. I didn't want to leave Kate alone, so I decided to call one of her student friends from the Royal Academy to spend the day with her, or at least until I could get back. While I pondered, there was a quiet tap at the door.

I approached it a bit apprehensively—too many strange things were happening. Looking through the spy-hole I saw a well- dressed middle-aged lady flanked by two cynical faces in suits, and I opened the door.

"Good morning, Mrs. Vandenberg. Please come in."

"Good morning, David. How did you know who I was?"

"You're wearing Fifth Avenue, not Mayfair, and in view of what's happened I figured you'd be the only American lady knocking on my door at 7:45am surrounded by the CIA."

"They're not CIA, they're Secret Service, but otherwise you're right on." She smiled for a moment, and then the concerned look reappeared. "Is Kate awake? What kind of night did she have?"

I walked them through to the living room. "She's not awake yet, and she had a pretty restless night. I don't expect she'll be up for awhile."

"Do you mind if we wait? I knew Kate's mother well, and the least I can do is be here for her if she needs me. And I'm sure you must have things to do."

"I appreciate your coming, and yes, I have a couple of things I must do, but I wouldn't have left her alone."

"We'll probably be at the residence or the embassy. If Kate is up to it there are going to be some formalities which must be attended to. You can call her if you want to talk to her later."

"Mrs. Vandenberg... Barbara... Kate is in my bedroom. She couldn't be alone last night."

"David," she said softly, "I'm just glad she has someone to be with, especially at a time like this." It was a wan smile.

I told them to make themselves at home, have coffee if they wished, and left the building.

Getting the Jag, I drove down Edgware Road to Marble Arch and parked on a side street, then walked a few feet on Oxford Street and went into the Cumberland Hotel. I wanted to use the phone in a fairly public place where I wouldn't stand out.

I went through the routine, and this time was met with Highland Whiskey Exporters. When I passed my last hurdle I half expected to be told that Colonel Hammond was not in yet, but to my surprise he answered personally.

"Good morning, Captain Baird. You're up and about rather early, aren't you?"

"Yes, sir, I am."

"I hope you've got some good news for me, David. The last couple of days have produced an abundance of the other variety. Are you going to be able to help us? I rather think we need it."

"I can't give you a direct answer yet, sir. I must see you as soon as possible. I have some information for you, and I think it is very important, but I wouldn't want to talk on an open line. And I also need some information which you may be able to provide. And I'm sorry, sir, but it's all rather urgent."

There was an imperceptible pause, and then his usually languid manner became very crisp.

"Do you know the Bank of Montreal in Lower Regent Street?"

"If it's the one in Waterloo Place, then I do."

"That's the one. Be there at 0930. Ask the commissionaire on duty for the Foreign Exchange Officer."

There was a click and he was gone. He didn't mess about.

I had time for some breakfast before heading for the bank, and the Cumberland's was quite good—except for the coffee. No wonder they didn't drink coffee in Britain—they didn't know how to make it. Most places boiled it until it tasted burnt, and then gave you half a cup of this mud topped up with scummy hot milk. I ordered tea instead.

I left the Cumberland just after 9 o'clock. It wasn't far to the bank, but traffic could be a little heavy on Piccadilly and I didn't want to be late.

I went around Eros and his fountain, headed down The Haymarket, and stopped at the bottom before turning right. On my left was Canada House, and it always made me a bit nostalgic to see the huge Canadian Red Ensign hanging over the main entrance. I got lucky with parking along Pall Mall, walking back and around the corner to the Bank of Montreal.

Entering the building I looked about for the blue uniform of the

Corps of Commissionaires, located that worthy, and asked him for the Foreign Exchange Officer. He studied me for a moment, then with a nod of his head bade me to follow him. We went through a gate at the side, along a corridor, and down a flight of stairs, stopping at an office with nothing marked on the door. He knocked, a voice I recognized called "Come!", and he opened the door. I stepped inside, the door closing behind me as Colonel Hammond rose, leaning across a bare desk to take my hand.

"Good morning, David—please sit down." We did so.

"Why here, sir?" I asked.

"The 'neighbours' keep tabs on me when they can pick me up, and I don't want them to have any inkling of your connection with me. I led them a merry chase this morning, and right now they think I'm next door in New Zealand House. I have several places like this which I can get into and out of through accesses they don't know, and I try to keep it that way. The commissionaire is one of ours, by the way. Now, what's come up?"

"What can you tell me about Calvin Fletcher, formerly with the American Embassy here in London? About a year ago he was posted to the Middle East, I know he has something to do with oil, and that's the extent of my information. Can you fill me in?"

Hammond pursed his lips, tapped his fingertips together, and was lost in thought. I waited, impatiently.

"Does this request affect your decision, David?"

"It may, sir, but I can only judge that when I hear it. To be honest with you, I had decided to decline, but I may rescind that decision after this meeting based on some information I have for you, and/or what you are willing to tell me about Cal Fletcher."

"Very well. You don't leave me much option, do you?" The famous frosty smile was back.

"I'm sorry, sir, but I find myself in the middle of something not of my own choosing, and I'm hampered by my lack of knowledge. If you want me to work with you, you should understand right now that I have to know what it's all about—not just an unconnected segment. At our meeting the other day you said that my background would allow me to deal with problems in unique ways. Well, one of the things I must do is make decisions based on what I know related to what I encounter. And now, to use a vulgar North American expression, you're going to have to 'put your money where your mouth is'—sir."

The only sound in the ensuing silence was the clash of our eyes. I knew he had given in when he drew a deep breath.

"Do you know what OPEC stands for, David?"

"No."

"Not many people do—yet. Two years ago, most of the countries which produce oil for export set up an organization to regulate pricing on the world market. OPEC—Organization of Petroleum Exporting Countries. They are going to set a common price for oil, and if they stick together our days of playing one country against the other for better prices are over."

"Where does Cal Fletcher fit in?"

"Nominally, Cal Fletcher works for the State Department, or so you would be told if you enquired. In truth, he is an Ambassador-at-Large who reports directly to the President of the United States on all matters concerning petroleum—production, purchasing, transportation, marketing, world reserves, exploration and development. You name it—if it's about oil, Cal Fletcher knows about it, and everything and everybody concerned with it."

"What's he been up to recently?"

"Now we come to the nub, or as you might say, 'the crunch.' After the formation of OPEC, the U.S. realized that an unfriendly government in power in one of the OPEC countries could have a disastrous effect on the American economy—they are extremely dependant on oil, as you know.

"Over the past twenty years, Cal Fletcher had built up private contacts in all of these countries—people of immense influence—some in government, some in opposition, some in the private sector—but all of whom respected him as a straight shooter and a man of his word. When Cal wanted something, his private network went into operation, and it happened.

"This gave the Americans a real advantage in petroleum negotiations, yet his network remained discreetly in the background. With the threat of OPEC, Cal was quietly visiting and re-establishing his old contacts and setting up new ones, and it would have minimized the influence of OPEC on American petroleum requirements."

"Your use of 'would have' suggests that you are aware of the outcome of this story."

"Certain elements would stop at nothing to keep the Americans out of preferential negotiations for petroleum."

I shivered at the implication.

"What happened to Straitsair Flight SA23 yesterday?"

"A phosphorus bomb in the cargo hold. It was timed to go off approximately forty minutes after departure. The aircraft was virtually incinerated in the air—there was nothing left of it or the 28 passengers and crew when it hit the water, and what was left sank immediately. One of our submarines and a destroyer were on the scene within ten minutes. All they recovered were ashes."

"How do you know about the bomb and where it was located in the aircraft?"

"Because we have the man who did it."

"What? Who was it?"

"A cargo handler for some of the smaller charter lines which fly into Gib. His name is Naheed. One of the ground crew remembered seeing him arrive for work carrying a suitcase, and when the aircraft exploded he was grabbed and his locker searched. No suitcase. Our people were called in, and with a little persuasion he admitted it. Of course he was expendable, and too simple-minded to realize that he would be the prime suspect. All after-the-fact, unfortunately."

"What about security? Surely if Cal Fletcher was this important to the U.S. he would have been better protected."

"Not the case, I'm afraid. This was Cal Fletcher's style. He moved about without fuss or fanfare, and was almost incognito most of the time. That's why he was so successful. He knew the risks that he ran, but this time his luck didn't hold. Regrettably, it was one of the few trips with his wife. Normally he wouldn't take her, but they were to have a holiday at a friend's estate in Algeria after his talks, and this time he broke his own rule."

We were quiet for a moment while I digested what I had been told, but it still wasn't enough.

"Who was behind it, Colonel?"

"Our people have made intensive enquiries in Gibralter since yesterday. We know who Naheed was seen with yesterday morning, and we have been able to establish a pretty definite link to where the order would have originated. There is no doubt in our minds or the CIA's that it was the KGB."

"And where did the order originate?"

"Here in London."

"Nalishkin?"

"Yes."

"Is there any doubt?"

"None whatsoever."

"What's going to be done about it?"

"Nothing."

"Nothing? Why?"

"We can't prove it. And unless we catch the bastard with blood on his hands it's a waste of time trying."

"Isn't all this pointless, sir? Won't someone pick up the torch from Cal Fletcher and carry on from where he left off? Why murder him, and his wife, and all those innocent people? I don't understand. What has it accomplished?"

"It may very well have accomplished exactly what they want. Fletcher took twenty years to establish this rapport, and the lynchpin for this network was his own personal integrity. None of them, Fletcher included, trusted the politicians, and no one knew the names of the people in the various countries. He wanted to protect them, he gave them his word, and that was enough.

"There is supposed to be a list hidden somewhere, to be accessed in case of dire emergency, but as of this morning no one in the State Department or 'the cousins' has come up with it, and they don't know where to look. Even if the list were found it's doubtful that anyone but Cal Fletcher could approach these people. It was his integrity and his charisma which did it.

"What worries us most is that the Soviets are looking for the list, too, and if they should get their hands on it I wouldn't give much chance to individuals in OPEC countries who are part of a secret network in league with the United States. Life is pretty cheap in most of those countries, and death even cheaper."

Silence returned while I pondered. I had received more than I had bargained for. A fierce hatred clutched my heart when I thought of Nalishkin, but I had to control myself, bide my time, and be careful. Hammond interrupted the flow of my thoughts.

"David, I understand your concern for Katherine Fletcher, and I am truly sorry for what has happened. I made a decision to tell you everything—I've held nothing back—but don't let your actions make me regret that decision."

"What can I tell Kate?"

"If I were you—nothing at all. The official story will be that there was probably a leak in the fuel line, and that this caused an explosion which destroyed the aircraft. The public will be shocked and titillated, and then they will forget about it in a few days. And those of us who know the truth will carry on doing what we have to do."

There was a brief hesitation before he continued.

"What I have to tell you now may very well prejudice you against us completely. Yesterday after you left here you were involved in an unfortunate incident at Charing Cross. It concerned a certain Daphne Boggs. Among the lady's unsavoury activities is one which she kept well hidden. Daphne had been recruited by the Soviets, and she had been used by them for various tasks, some of them quite indelicate."

"Are you suggesting that it was all because of my meeting with you, Colonel?"

"Exactly. She tagged you leaving the building, and probably followed you to pick your pocket and tell the Soviets who you were and your proximity to me. She failed, of course."

"Perhaps she had an accomplice, sir."

"No, she was alone yesterday, and she was dead even before she could have described you to anyone."

"How do you know this, Colonel?"

"We had a watcher on her who saw the whole thing. He was the vicar who spoke to the police. When I was informed we pulled some strings and your name was withheld. The press co-operated and played it down."

"I wondered about that."

"I'm being totally frank with you, David. Now it's your turn. What have you got for me?"

It was indeed my turn.

"Are you aware of an aircraft called the P1127 which is under development by Hawker Siddeley?"

"Of course. What have you heard and from whom?"

"I know about its VTOL capability, that the technology of vectored thrust is top secret, and a guess that the Soviets would love to get the information. Who told me is unimportant, because it was no more than what is available in the aircraft magazines."

"Go on."

"Yesterday afternoon I was in the Soviet Embassy, just outside Nalishkin's door while he was on the phone. He spoke in Russian, but a few things sounded familiar and I wrote them down."

I pulled my engagement book out, turning up the page.

"Chess moves," I explained.

"I beg your pardon?"

"Chess moves. When I was attending university we listened to radio broadcasts of chess matches between the Americans and the Soviets. Very often we could hear the Russian commentator in the background giving the moves in Russian, and we became familiar with some of the letters and numbers. Nalishkin used some of them yesterday: pay, adeen, adeen, diva, siem—in English: P, one, one, two, seven. He was talking about that aircraft, the P1127."

Hammond was writing while I spoke.

"Do you remember anything else—anything at all?"

"A little before that I caught a word that sounded like 'drama', and I presumed he must have been talking about the theatre."

Hammond's brow furrowed.

"I'm going to pronounce a word in Russian. Is this what you heard? *Uh-eh-ra-drama. Uh-eh-ra-drama.*"

"Yes, I'm pretty sure that's it. What does it mean?"

"It's Russian for aerodrome or airfield."

He wrote for a moment more, then threw down his pencil.

"This is exactly what I meant, David. You've already given us invaluable information. We know they're interested in this aircraft, but now it looks as if there's a push on, and we'll have to tighten security, especially around Dunsfold."

He regarded me quizzically before continuing.

"A while ago you quoted one of those vulgar Americanisms at me, and now I am about to do the same to you in return. 'You pays your money and you takes your choice'—isn't that it? In other words, my dear fellow, are you with us or not?"

It was hard to say the words—I still had doubts, but now I had a reason to hurt them. It was enough to tip the balance.

"I'm in, sir, for whatever it's worth."

"Good lad!"

"And I should tell you that I'm sailing on a Soviet cruise next week through the Mediterranean and the Black Sea to Odessa. It's at the invitation of the Soviet Government, and I'll be giving a concert aboard to entertain the dignitaries."

"Good God! We knew about the cruise, of course, but never imagined we'd have someone aboard. I'll brief you on what to watch for, but the main thing is to be cautious. They don't know about you, and I want to keep it that way."

"Colonel, who am I working for—MI6?"

"I'd prefer to keep you in the dark, David. You're working for me, and I have a foot in several camps. You're not going to be official—you won't appear in the records. That's for your protection as well as ours.

"We've had some nasty leaks recently, and the last thing I want is for your name to surface when you're somewhere in the middle of a Russian sea. It would be rather a long swim home, especially with an anchor tied to your feet. I'll have some emergency procedures ready before you depart, so we'll meet before you sail. You understood my message about your phone?"

"Yes, sir. . . what's going on?"

"The Soviets—they put bugs in the two phones in your flat, both yours and Miss Fletcher's."

"Why?"

"I've surmised that they wanted to catch anything they could between Katherine Fletcher and her father. What do you think?"

"It's possible. Cal phoned from Gibralter on Tuesday night to tell Kate where they were and where they were going."

"It could very well have been that call which caused their deaths, but I don't think you should mention that hypothesis to Miss Fletcher. Just be careful when you use the phone. We don't want to alert them that we're onto the bug for fear of exposing you in some way. We'll have to live with it for a bit."

Hammond looked down at his scribblings. He was lost in thought, which suited me, for I was wrestling with how to approach a more personal matter without making it sound personal. Hammond reached his decision first.

"I have an idea about the P1127 which I must check out this morning. If I haven't reached you by 1700 hours call me on a public phone. And, by the way, use your new codename from now on."

"What is it, sir?"

"It's 'Minstrel'. Rather appropriate, don't you think?"

He seemed pleased with his choice, but I liked it, too.

"Now, is there anything else you want to discuss, David?"

It was shit or get off the pot. I decided to stay seated.

"There is one more thing, sir. What do you know about Marijke Templaars?"

"Why?"

"She's been made my liaison with the Soviets for the concert and the cruise."

That's all he needed to know, I thought. I hoped he couldn't see my heart pounding.

"Not much about her—she hasn't been here long, and she has only recently begun to work for the Soviet government. I'll do a little digging and see what we come up with. We know a fair bit about her father and grandfather, though."

"Like what, sir?"

"For a while no one seemed to know which side of the fence her father was on. Then in 1957 he was expelled from Holland as a Soviet spy. I expect his father-in-law helped save his neck."

"Marijke Templaars grandfather?"

"Yes, General Josef Dmitrienko."

"Right—she told me that her grandfather was in the army."

"Army!" he snorted. "General Josef Dmitrienko is in charge of Directorate "K" of the First Chief Directorate of the KGB! You watch your ass, lad!"

My world began to crumble.

SEVEN

I left the bank in confusion, my head spinning, jostling several people on the street. I had to sit quietly and think. I headed up Lower Regent Street, skirted Piccadilly Circus, and crossed over to the Lyons Corner House.

One of the few places where coffee was bearable, it wasn't crowded at that time of morning, so I was able to find a private corner to sip my caffeine.

Hammond's disclosures of Marijke's father and grandfather had unsettled me. Rationally, I knew that nothing had changed. Perhaps she hadn't told me everything for fear of spooking me, yet I couldn't be sure. Should I carry on as though I knew nothing, or should I confront her and hope she could explain?

Instinctively I decided to leave things as they were, but be mindful of what I said and did until I gave her a chance to tell me of her own free will. Pictures of her flashed through my mind, and they were accompanied by mixed feelings of desire and uncertainty. As Hammond had put it—I'd better watch my ass.

Shaking clear of my own predicament, I shouldered Kate's tragedy, realizing I had to be circumspect about what I knew and yet comfort her as best I could. It was time to call and see how I could help, so I paid my bill and found a telephone.

Dialling the ambassador's residence, I was put through to a social secretary of some sort.

"I'm sorry, Mr. Baird, they're not here. They're at the embassy sorting through some papers. If you have the time they would like to see you there in the ambassador's office."

"Should I call to tell them I'm coming?"

"Why don't I do that for you? Are you leaving now?"

"Yes, but it'll be half an hour before I get there."

I thanked her and rang off, made my way back to the Jag and headed up New Bond Street, turning left on Grosvenor.

The new U.S. Embassy occupied the whole west side of Grosvenor Square, having moved from its former location just opposite in 1960. Naturally it was a modern building, with more glass showing than anything else. The most imposing feature was the huge golden eagle over the facade of the building, as some critics had said, "ready to swoop on the poor, defenceless London pigeons." It seemed appropriate, though, that the embassy had remained on the square which contained the statue of Franklin D. Roosevelt, erected in 1948 by a grateful British public.

I parked without difficulty, then presented myself to a doorman in a navy blue civilian-type uniform with silver buttons.

I was surprised that he was English and not American, as was his colleague above in the main entrance hall. This was a large, oblong area with a fountain in the centre. Mainly in marble, there were also marble pillars with a golden trim panel, the whole thing having a rather sterile feel about it.

The second doorman called on an intercom, and in a few moments I was being escorted in an elevator, or 'lift' as the British would say, to the second floor.

The corridor here was lined with portraits of former U.S. Ambassadors to the Court of St. James—the only one I recognized instantly was Joe Kennedy.

At the end of the corridor we entered a door to the ambassador's secretary's office, and here the doorman left me.

"Hello, Mr. Baird, I'm Donna Wong, Mr. Vandenberg's secretary." She gave me a pleasant smile. "I've heard you sing on the radio, and I really like what you do."

"I'm very flattered, Donna. Where are you from?"

"San Francisco, but I've been away from there for years. Even so, nowhere else seems like home. I guess my heart's still there."

"That'd be a good lyric for a song."

"Maybe someone will write one and you can sing it for me." She smiled graciously. "I'll tell the ambassador you're here."

She spoke a few words on the intercom, then rose to open the door, giving me a friendly glance.

I entered an office which exuded style and taste. The thick, beige carpet was offset by the most subtle blue wallpaper, the exquisite drapes containing the essence of both colours. They were open, and Grosvenor Square itself was the backdrop for this elegance. The grouping of couches and chairs was in a soft, chocolate brown leather, with a matching coffee table of oak with brass fittings.

The walls contained water colours and oils of American scenes, except for one complete panel displaying photographs of famous personalities, each one with a greeting, and some of the ambassador himself with the star, politician, or sports legend.

I couldn't help but contrast this building with the Soviet Embassy. They were so different, yet in some respects they were identical, for they were each a façade to the world at large, making a statement which they wanted others to believe.

Dwight Vandenberg, his wife Barbara, and Kate, were clustered around a coffee table littered with papers. The ambassador and Kate rose, Kate running into my arms, and the ambassador taking a few steps toward me with a tense smile on his face.

"I'm glad you came," blurted Kate, on the verge of tears.

"How are you doing, Kate?" I spoke softly, holding her.

"Just so-so," she sobbed, burying her face in my jacket.

"I'm sorry I wasn't there when you woke up. There were a couple of things I had to do and they wouldn't wait. I knew you were in good hands when Mrs. Vandenberg showed up."

"It's okay." She got some control back. "You know, none of this seems real—all this paper we're sorting through. It's like being in a play where all the characters are imaginary, and then it hits me that it's Mom and Dad and the tears start again. I thought I had cried it out, but I was wrong."

The ambassador took two more steps and held out his hand. He was tall and slender, dark hair flecked with grey, and had very regular, ruggedly handsome features.

"David, I'm Dwight Vandenberg. We've met before."

"Yes, sir, five years ago at Bushey Park in the Officer's Club. I brought my quintet from Kneller Hall to play for a dance, and you came up to request songs I hadn't sung in years. You out-ranked me a little, so I thought I'd better try to do them."

He had been a lieutenant-general then, and my remark brought a chuckle to both the ambassador and his wife. It was short-lived.

"I'm sorry that we had to get this paper work done at a time like this, but Kate is the sole survivor, and since she is leaving for home this evening we had no choice."

"You're going home?" I said, incredulously.

She nodded. "I have to be with my grandmother for a while—my father's mother. She's my only living grandparent, and this is a terrible shock for her. There's going to be a memorial service for my parents in the church, and I'd like to be there. I spoke to Gram on the phone this morning, and she needs me with her. Quite honestly, I think I need her, too. All of a sudden we're all that's left of our family."

Her eyes welled. Barbara Vandenberg spoke from the couch.

"David, Kate's flight leaves at 8:30pm. I know she'd like you to drive her out, but if you can't, we'll send her in an embassy car. Unfortunately, Dwight and I have to attend a reception this evening, so we won't be able to go."

"But we'd send someone with her," said the ambassador. "I wouldn't want her to be alone."

"It's no problem for me," I responded. "I'll take her. Which airline is it?"

"BOAC, flight 85, to Montreal," he replied.

Again I was surprised. "Montreal? I didn't know your grandmother lived in Canada."

Kate actually gave a little smile. "She doesn't. She lives in Colebrook, New Hampshire. Montreal is the closest international airport, and it'll save some time."

"How will you get to Colebrook from Montreal?"

The ambassador had the answer. "I've arranged a car from the consulate in Montreal. They'll drive Kate right to her grandmother's door."

Barbara rose from the couch. She was a very classy lady, and she and Dwight Vandenberg were well matched. I guessed that she would have had a lot to do with the tasteful style in his office.

"Kate, why don't you come with me for a few minutes to get some air and freshen up. I'm sure Dwight has a few things he'd like to discuss with David."

"Oh. . . sure." She looked at me quizzically, as though she wondered what the ambassador and I would have to talk about without her being present. I wondered, too.

When the door closed he asked me to sit down.

"Would you like something to drink, David?"

"No, sir, I'm fine, thanks."

"Let me get right to the point. We've been going through Cal Fletcher's documents with a fine-tooth comb. I needed Kate here partially as her parents' beneficiary, but also to help me with personal papers I couldn't identify.

"We're trying to find a list of names Cal left which is extremely critical to the to the U.S. government, and it doesn't seem to be here. It's entirely possible that he coded it in some way and left it in plain sight, and that's why I needed Kate."

He stopped talking, looked at me expectantly, and I wasn't sure what to say. Normally I would have responded with curiosity, but since I knew exactly what he was looking for, that element was missing. My comment was hesitant and rather lame.

"Can you be more specific about the list, sir?"

"No, I can't, and it's for security reasons. All I can say is that it would be disastrous for the United States and some of her friends if the list were to be acquired by the wrong parties."

He stared at me for a moment and then continued. "I know you took over the Fletchers' flat about a year ago, and I wondered if you knew of any spot that Cal might have used as a hiding place. He may have felt that he shouldn't keep the list at the embassy."

"No, sir, nothing at all, and in case you're wondering, Cal Fletcher never told me anything about this, nor was anything to be delivered in the event of his death. Did you ask Kate?"

"Yes, of course, but her answer was negative, I'm afraid. You were our only hope."

"Have you read the will? Perhaps that would contain a clue."

"Nothing that we could see. It seems pretty straightforward. There was a letter to be given to Kate if he were to die, but it was all personal, and nothing seemed out of place. Kate handed it to us to read, and there were no instructions to do anything, or retrieve anything, or send anything. We've run into a blank wall, but we simply must find that list."

"Are you sure that it existed, sir? Perhaps he had it committed to memory but never wrote it down."

"That wouldn't be like him. Cal knew if anything happened to him the list had to be passed on. He was the only one with the names. I know he didn't trust the system well enough to document it in the normal way, but he would never have left us high and dry in the event of his death or incapacitation. It's around, but he's hidden it well. I only hope we find it first."

"Could it have been blown up with him in the plane?" Shit! I slipped! Perhaps he wouldn't notice.

There was a long silence, the ambassador staring at me.

"There's been no statement that mentioned an explosion, only that the plane is missing. Why did you say 'blown up'?"

"Only a presumption, sir." I was trying not to get flustered. "The latest reports say that there were no survivors and that nothing of the aircraft has been found. That would be consistent with an explosion rather than a crash into the ocean."

The hesitation was not as pronounced this time.

"You seem particularly well-informed for a layman." A pause. "Have you said anything about this to Kate?"

"No, not a word."

"Then don't, please. Kate has enough to contend with. I wouldn't want her confused with speculation."

"There'll be no speculation from me, sir."

I looked him straight in the eye. His gaze averted first.

"Good. Now, if you should run across something suspicious or strange, or if Kate does, will you contact us? Some of us are not going to rest until that list turns up."

"I'll keep my eyes open, sir, but I'm pretty sure it's not in the flat." I wasn't going to lie—and the truth is, I didn't know what I'd do if I found it. Something wasn't sitting right.

The ladies returned, and though the Vandenbergs invited us to join them for lunch, Kate felt that she should rest for a while and pack for her trip.

"And I'm not feeling very sociable. I hope you understand."

Everyone did.

Kate was very quiet as we walked to the car, but after we had started driving she opened up.

"What did you and Dwight talk about?"

"A list of your father's they're looking for. He wondered if I had come across anything in the flat, but of course I hadn't."

"Did you talk about the accident?"

"A little."

"Do they know what happened?"

"They don't seem to have much to go on. Nothing seems to have been found." I hated to lie to Kate like this.

She sighed. "Why do I get the impression that they're not telling me everything? Do they think I'm stupid? If a plane crashes in a normal way there's going to be something they can find. Bodies float, don't they? Are they trying to pretend that this plane is on the bottom of the Mediterranean with everyone still securely strapped in their seats? I can't believe it. And if I don't believe it, neither do they, and yet they're not talking to me—not even speculating. It really pisses me off."

I felt I should pour oil on the troubled waters.

"What if there were a good reason not to tell you, Kate? What if it were highly classified, something that couldn't be revealed to the public? Your father worked for the U.S. government, and a very sensitive list is missing. You told me that he was involved in oil, but even you might not have known the extent of his responsibilities, and not because he didn't want to tell you, but maybe he couldn't because of the security connected to it."

"I know, I know," she said, impatiently. Then she got angry. "But I'm frustrated because I can't do anything, and I can't blame anybody because I don't know what happened. I'll never see them again, and the horrible part is that I can't even bury them!"

She burst into tears, and I reached over to take her hand. I felt totally useless, and it didn't help that I knew the truth and couldn't tell her.

We continued home in silence. Kate had regained some of her composure by the time we arrived, and once in the flat I made some tea and a couple of sandwiches and insisted that she eat something, even just a few bites. She agreed reluctantly, and we sat at the old refectory table that I used in my dining room. This was the spot where we normally discussed things, and I hoped I could distract her for a while—the setting was right.

"Did your grandparents always live in Colebrook?"

"Yes, their parents both had farms near the town, and they met at school in Colebrook. My grandfather left school to work when he was in ninth grade, but they remained good friends and got married when they were only 18."

"Did your grandfather work on the farm?"

"No, his father was killed in an accident, and they lost the farm. My grandfather got a job at a resort hotel nearby, and eventually became assistant manager before he retired."

"Was this resort called The Balsams?"

Now Kate was surprised. "Yes. Do you know it?"

"I know of it, but I've never been to it. Pretty rich for my blood. Did you spend much time in Colebrook?"

"Quite a few of my summers, and occasional Christmases and Thanksgivings. I loved it there. When my grandfather died four years ago I spent the summer there with my grandmother on my own. It was the first time I had been there without Mom or Dad, and Gram and I got to know each other very well. That's why I have to go to her now." She smiled in recollection. "I even had my first job that summer in Colebrook, working in a restaurant."

"Howard's?"

"David, how did you know that? Are you psychic or something?"

I laughed. "No, it's the only restaurant I know in Colebrook. I stop there for lunch every time I drive back and forth to the Maritime Provinces. They've got the greatest pies."

"This is incredible! I can't believe you know about Colebrook and The Balsams and Howard's, and we've never talked about it."

Kate was actually bubbling for a few minutes, then realized she had forgotten about her parents' deaths, and I watched her face change as she returned to the present.

"I think I know what you were doing, David. You do get over it, don't you?"

"In time, yes. You never forget, but you begin to accept, then you put it into perspective, and you go on with your life. You've already started, and I know your parents would want it."

She reached over to take my hand. "Thank you for that, and for last night, and for being here for me, and for caring."

I made no comment, and we just sat quietly for several minutes. Then Kate seemed to make up her mind about something.

"David, a couple of days ago I tried to say something about us when the phone call interrupted me. I'd like to say it now."

"By 'us', do you mean you and me?"

She nodded.

I sighed. "Kate, I don't think this is the right time. You know how much I care for you, and you can count on me for anything, but to discuss a change in our relationship right now would be wrong. We've got to have the air clear around us for that to happen, and at this moment it's anything but clear. Let's leave things as they are for now. You don't need any more complications, and I have a confusion or two of my own to handle, and I'm not faring very well." I gave her a taut little smile.

"Are you involved with someone? Damn. . . I'm sorry. . . I didn't realize. I've been making a fool of myself."

"No you haven't. It's something that's just happened, and you and I haven't had the opportunity to talk. But as for being involved—I'm so perplexed I don't think I can answer honestly."

Kate was about to reply when my phone rang. She grimaced.

"Saved by the bell again. How do you do it?"

I smiled as I went to the phone, then I remembered that this was a 3-way conversation, and the smile froze as I picked up the receiver. It was the secretary of Giles Mortimer, who was BBC Radio's Head of Light Entertainment.

"Would you be able to pop in to see Mr. Mortimer sometime this afternoon? He would consider it a great favour."

Nothing wrong with being owed a favour by Broadcasting House.

"How about right now? I could leave in a few minutes."

"That would work nicely, Mr. Baird. We'll see you shortly."

I rang off and walked back to the dining room. Kate was clearing the dishes.

"You go on, David. I'll clean up, then I should pack my suitcase, and I think I'll have a nap." She gave me a quick kiss. "We'll get to it someday—provided I cut the phone wire."

Paris, France—the same day

He stood before the black double doors on Rue St. Laurent, package in hand. The number 7 stared back at him. Pushing the button beside the name Cantero, he waited expectantly. There was a crackle as a thin, disembodied voice spoke from a tiny speaker.

"Who is it?"

"I have a package for Cantero."

"I don't expect any package. Go away."

"Wait, *m'sieu*. It is from the Louvre, and I have been told to place it in your hands alone."

That should do it, he thought. There was a hesitation, and the speaker crackled again.

"Very well. Bring it up."

The latch opened with a click, and he walked up the two flights to the third floor. Tapping on the door of the apartment at the front of the building, he held the package up to be visible in the spy-hole. The door clicked and opened.

"Will you sign for it, please?"

He handed the phony receipt and a pen to the small man for a scrawled signature. Shoving the door hard with his shoulder, he bulldozed his way in, knocking the smaller man to the floor. The gun in his hand emerged from under the package, pointing at the prostrate figure.

"Now, *m'sieu*, we will get to know each other better. It may take us some time, but I'm in no hurry."

The eyes glinted with anticipation.

He closed the door.

EIGHT

London, England—the same day

I decided to drive to the BBC. It wasn't far to Portland Place, and not really into city traffic. Through Regent's Park it took me 20 minutes from leaving my flat. Not bad for London.

Giles Mortimer's office was on the third floor. Cramped and cluttered, it overflowed with files, papers, audio tapes and LP's. A florid face betrayed Giles' losing battle with weight, and the trace of Yorkshire in his voice was never hidden for long, as hard as he tried. But he was a genuine soul.

"Thanks for coming by, David. You're not stuck into rehearsals for your show yet, are you?"

"No, I still have a couple of weeks before we start, and even then it'll be mainly chorus and dancers for the first few days."

We continued talking about my show, *Curtain Call*. It was a new concept, especially in the finale, when I would actually perform in front of the curtain with material which could change whenever we wished—even from one day to the next. This and the plot gave the show its title. Giles was very interested.

"It sounds like a winner. The press are already touting it as a 'must see'. Now, we've had a lot of good comment on that *Playhouse* show you did for us which aired last week and some decisions have been made.

I would have waited to set up a meeting with you, but something spurred me on which you'll hear about in due course."

"Now I'm curious, Giles. What have you got up your sleeve?"

To my amazement he offered me a radio series, each programme to be based on one of the great songwriters. I could hire the best bands and groups available for backing and have musical control. I'd M.C. each show, and share the singing with international stars. I was overwhelmed.

"This is a terrific idea, Giles! When are we going to start?"

"October, most likely. Will *Curtain Call* be running smoothly by then?"

"I should think so. We open the last week of August, so we should have all the bugs out by October."

His phone buzzed. Giles picked it up, listened for a moment, then said, "Send him in, Sybil." He looked at me and went on. "I mentioned before that this meeting had a dual purpose, David. I've done my part, and now someone else you know will carry on."

The door opened, and in walked Colonel Hammond.

"Good afternoon, David." He smiled at my surprised look.

"Is there anyone you don't know, Colonel?"

"Giles was one of us during the war. We stay in close touch. It also provides us a useful cover on occasion."

Giles took my hand. "We'll be talking soon, David, and I'll organize a meeting with the producer so we can do some advance planning. Cheerio!"

Hammond sat down in Giles' chair. I was a bit bewildered by the change in management and the apparent shift of topic, but Hammond went right ahead.

"I don't have much time, so listen carefully. Your information about the P1127 has us worried. We've increased security, and I've warned the project leaders to watch where they leave documents. I've alerted their personnel department to double check everyone who has been hired in the last year and to refer any new people directly to us. But I've got to have someone who knows that aircraft thoroughly from first-hand experience.

"I hope you're game for this. On Monday I want you to report to the chief test pilot at Dunsfold. You're to be given some conversion instruction on the P1127. I want you to study the aircraft and its technology so you know exactly what we're dealing with. Only then will you be equipped to listen and observe when you are with the Soviets."

"Won't it look peculiar for a civilian to be in Dunsfold doing a conversion into a VTOL, sir?"

"It would, but I've covered that." He produced a small card, sliding it over to me across the desk. It was a military I-card with my picture on it—the same one which had been on my Canadian Army I-card. Someone had been busy.

"You are now Major David Baird, Royal Corps of Transport, in the Territorial Army, which is about the same as the Canadian Army's Reserve Force, or Militia, I think you call it now. You are on temporary duty, attached to the War Office, and more particularly to the Ground Support (Air) Section. You are being sent to Dunsfold to evaluate the P1127 for the army in both ground support and communications."

I studied the card for a few moments, not sure what to say.

"Is this the real thing or a phony?"

"It's genuine. You're really what it says you are. Now I need your signature on a couple of documents, one of which is to say you understand that you are bound by the Official Secrets Act, and then all of this becomes legal."

He pushed the papers at me, indicated where I had to sign, and I scrawled my name like an automaton, feeling the frustration building inside me like a well about to overflow. And then I blew.

"Jesus Christ, Colonel! I'm still in my diapers when it comes to flying. I can only get a slow, fixed-wing trainer with a piston engine up and down. What the hell am I going to do in a vertical take-off jet, for God's sake? I'm either going to look like a complete asshole or I'm going to kill myself, or maybe both in random order."

The colonel waited patiently through my outburst, allowing a few seconds space before interjecting.

"I rather expected something like this. Now let me explain. You're the closest person we have to the centre of this thing. You know how to fly, which, however basic your skills, puts you streets ahead of anyone else in our organization. You're involved with Ivan for the next week or so in a completely innocent situation—they won't suspect a thing where you're concerned, and yet you'll be practically sitting in the hip pocket of the very man who's trying to make off with the technology of this aircraft.

"I've already spoken to Bill Bedford, the chief test pilot, who'll be the only one who knows the real reason you're there. Bedford won't let you loose in the kite if he thinks you're going to prang it—you'll have to prove yourself to him. You may end up just sitting in the cockpit to get the feel of it and watching others do the actual flying with you on the ground.

"Remember, army pilots only fly Austers and other light aircraft, so there will be no expectation for you to have fighter or jet experience. Can you honestly say that you wouldn't enjoy getting your hands on something that is at the leading edge of the aerospace industry?"

He sat back smugly. I considered his explanations and calmed with each passing thought.

"Okay. That's a little different. I thought I was being shoved into the lion's den without a chair or whip. Of course I'll enjoy the experience, and if Bill Bedford is patient I might even get it right. What time on Monday, and how shall I dress? The only thing I kept was my old flight suit."

"Take that along. You should report in at 0700. Bedford is expecting you, and he'll give you a briefing before you go near the aircraft. I've taken the liberty of accessing your file in Ottawa, and we have your measurements. For Monday you'll have a battledress with the correct badges, and I've ordered a forage cap, shirt, tie and socks from Herbert Johnson's, Cole's of Knightsbridge, et cetera. I have a batman spiffing up a web belt for you, but I wasn't sure what to do about footwear. Do you still have a pair of military-style dark brown shoes?"

"I have a pair of Lotus Veldtschoens which I wore in uniform. They're virtually indestructible."

"Splendid. I'll have a civilian messenger deliver all this to your flat over the weekend. Is there always a porter on duty?"

"Both night and day, and he'll accept and hold anything for me until I collect it."

"Then that seems to take care of that. Now, one other detail. I had lunch with House Paynter today, and he tells me you're going to Paris tomorrow by car. Is this true?"

"God, yes—I'd almost forgotten. So much has happened in the last few days I almost feel as though I'm leading two lives, or is it three? I think I've lost track. Anyway, the answer is yes, I am driving to Paris tomorrow. It's about my car.

"When I bought the Jag a year ago I didn't pay purchase tax. The condition was that I export it within one year, and that year is up on Saturday. I've discovered a loop-hole. If I take the car out of Britain and bring it back in, then I'm eligible for another tax exemption. House is coming along for the ride, and Kate was going to come and bring another friend from RADA, but that'll be off now. Why, sir?"

"We have to make a pick-up in Paris, and our regular courier is down with a bad case of Asian flu. When I heard you were going I thought it might save a lot of fuss if you could attend the rendezvous and bring the material back with you."

There was a long hesitation. I didn't want to do anything like this, and yet I didn't want to appear timid—I'd already balked at the idea of flying the P1127. I probably decided to say yes because of that refusal.

"How do I do it?"

"Good lad. That helps us out enormously. Near Gare de l'Est in Paris there is a sidewalk café. If you come out of the station you would turn immediately right, and it is on the very first corner. At 1600 tomorrow, Paris time, you must sit there sipping coffee, with a copy of the Financial Times and a Fodor's guide to France sitting on top of it. A man will sit at your table, also with coffee, and ask to see your guide. He will examine it, return it to you in a few minutes, and then you will give him a little Union Jack pin as a souvenir. That's it. Any questions?"

"What does this man look like?"

"The usual fellow is small and dapper, with a very thin moustache, but it is not always the same man, so I can't be precise. We've never had a bit of problem with this exchange, so you have nothing to worry about."

"I'll do it, sir, but it's against my better judgment." I paused. "Do you know any more about Marijke Templaars?"

"Not yet, but as soon as I have something I'll let you know. Have a good trip tomorrow, by the way, and let me know when you're back so I can arrange to get the guide from you. Incidentally, here is your newspaper, your guide, the pin, and a bit of information from Dunsfold which should give you some advance preparation for Monday."

He passed me a briefcase, gave me a cheery wave and was gone. Before I could change my mind, I guessed. I looked in the briefcase to find the salmon-coloured Financial Times, the Fodor's guide, an envelope containing the pin, and a tied folder which contained a sheaf of pilot's notes, obviously of the test flights of the P1127. I immediately felt uncomfortable about having them, and wondered where I'd keep them safely, especially since the flat had been visited by the KGB. Under the spare tire in the boot?

I wondered if Marijke had any knowledge of this, indeed, if she worked for the KGB as well. Or was she simply what she said she was, working for the cultural attaché's office? In that instant I knew that whatever she was it didn't matter. I was in love with her, and I wanted to be with her. Impulsively, I reached for Giles' phone and looked up the number of the Soviet embassy. My hands perspired as I dialled, and when the call was answered I could hardly keep the tremor from my voice as I asked for her. When she came on her voice was soft on the line.

"Marijke Templaars."

"Hello, Marijke. How are you?"

"Oh, David, what a nice surprise. I am very fine, I think. How are you?"

We chatted about things in general, ever mindful that the call was probably monitored, but I reasoned that, if what she had told me was true, they would think that she was simply leading me on, and they would approve. I told her about my BBC offer, and she was very excited at the news. I mentioned that I was driving a friend to the airport, but that I would be free from 8:30pm, and that perhaps we could see each other later in the evening.

"Not this evening, David. It would not be convenient for me."

There was a strain in her voice when she said this, and I didn't like the word 'convenient'. After an awkward silence, she spoke, rather hesitantly.

"Tomorrow is my free day. I do not work at all. Is it possible that we can be together sometime tomorrow?"

I explained about the car and Paris, and that I wouldn't be back until sometime Saturday. I almost felt a door closing between us. In an instant she changed all that.

"Is it possible that I come with you tomorrow?"

"To Paris? With me? In the car? Really?"

"Yes, of course," she laughed, "I would like that very much."

"I must pick you up very early, around 4:00am. I want to be on the 6 o'clock crossing from Dover. Is that all right?"

"Yes, that's very fine. Now, I must tell you where I live. I am at 31a Kensington Square. It is in the mews, and my name is on the door, but I look out for you."

I hesitated—I didn't want to let her go.

"You're sure about tonight—that there's no possibility?"

"No, not tonight. It is not possible. I am very sorry."

The strain was back in her voice. I knew I shouldn't push it.

"Okay, I'll see you early tomorrow. 'Til then, Marijke."

"Goodbye, David."

I took a few minutes to phone House to tell him what had happened, and that Kate wouldn't be with us for the Paris trip.

"Oh, you rotten swine," said Bluebottle's hysterical voice, "then I will not have the pleasure of the company of a female of the opposite sex. I don't like this game, my Capitain. I will ask Gladys Cudney of the Luton Girls' Choir if she would like a trip to Paris. Then we can make beautiful music in the back seat. Yi-hi-hi!"

"Well, whatever you decide is fine with me, but be ready to leave your place by 4:30am. Even if we speed we'll just make it."

"I hear you, my Capitain. Have no fear. Ensign Bluebottle of the East Finchley Wolf Cubs will be ready. Yes he will!"

At that point I rang off. When House gets going with a Goon Show character you can't stop him until he runs out of steam, and, fuelled with shooting sherry, that can take a very long time.

* * *

When I got back to St. John's Wood I found tea waiting with crumpets and cakes. Kate had walked down to a little parade of shops for the goodies and had decided to surprise me.

"I had to do something. I couldn't just sit around, thinking. I don't like my thoughts right now—they're not very charitable. They'll probably give me dinner on the plane, but that won't be for hours. Besides, you needed something, too."

We were sitting in our discussion seats.

"How long will you stay with your grandmother?"

"Only about a week. I can't afford to be away from school any longer, especially with the play coming up. I realize that the best tribute I can pay Mom and Dad is to be the finest actress I'm capable of. And that starts with *Antigone* as soon as I return. Will you meet me, David, if I let you know my flight?"

"Sure I will. Just call and tell me when." I looked at my watch. "We'd better go, Kate. I'm never sure about traffic. Do you have everything packed?"

"Yes, it's all by the door. I'm not taking much for a week."

On the way to Heathrow I told Kate about my BBC offer, and she was very happy for me, but I could tell that events were taking their toll, and for the rest of the drive we were quiet.

Paris, France—the same day

He walked down the stairs in good spirits. The little man was tough, much tougher than he would have thought. Silly bastard, he thought, to believe in that loyalty crap. That's why he holds out.

Outside, he breathed deeply. Oh, well, tomorrow is another day. The little fucker can't move, can't call out, can't do anything—except piss and shit and lie in it until I come back. That should soften him up.

And then the real fun begins.

London Airport, Heathrow—the same day

It wasn't difficult to find the ticket for Kate at the BOAC counter, and I waited with her until she could go into the departure lounge. At the last minute she dropped her carry-on bag, put her arms around me and hugged me fiercely.

"I'll miss you very, very much."

"And I'll miss you, Kate. Give my regards to your grandmother. Tell her I'll call in to see her the next time I pass through Colebrook."

Kate gave me a desperate look, then kissed me, long and hard. It was the first time she had ever done that. We held each other for a few moments.

"Oh, Kate," was all I could say.

"I hope she's worth it, David," she whispered in my ear.

And then she was gone.

I drove back to London in the state of confusion which seemed almost normal for me during these last few days. I had thought I had everything under control and in its place, and now nothing seemed to be where it should be, least of all my emotions.

On an impulse I drove to Kensington Square and parked the car. Now I knew I was beyond help. I hadn't done this sort of thing since my first crush in grade 7. Of course, I rationalized that if I knew where her flat was tonight I wouldn't waste time looking in the morning.

I found the mews without difficulty, walking along quietly until I came to 31a. It appeared to be almost a complete mews cottage on its own—much larger than I would have expected. The curtains were drawn, but light spilled from around them, seeping out into the mews along with the sounds of music and laughter. I couldn't see in, but my mind played terrible tricks with me, and it felt as though my heart had been encased in a block of ice.

Shaking, I turned to walk away, scarcely noticing the Facel Vega parked near the door. It was already behind me when I realized that I had seen CD plates on the car, and that it had to belong to someone in the Diplomatic Corps—someone who had money and was undoubtedly in Marijke's flat.

Out of spite I took the number down—MWE 473—and resolved to have it checked out through Hammond.

I was still trembling when I reached my car, and, sliding into the seat, I sat still until I had calmed down. I was irrationally and insanely jealous. I knew I had no right to be, and that knowledge didn't help at all.

I tried not to think as I drove home, and once there I poured myself a Jack Daniels and coke and tried to think sensibly. I had known Marijke for little more than a day, and, except for a few intimate moments, we were virtually strangers. And yet, there was something which had touched me so deeply that it had thrown me completely off balance, unleashing a raw emotion which I had never even suspected was in me. It was terrifying to realize how out-of-control I had almost become outside Marijke's flat.

I knew I couldn't allow these emotions to dominate me, and I determined then and there that no matter what Marijke's present or past was, I would cope with it with logic and understanding.

Perhaps a day of fun in Paris would help.

It's amazing how easily we can delude ourselves.

NINE

London, England—Friday, June 15, 1962

It was still dark when I drove into the mews at Kensington Square. I hadn't slept well, and I hoped I wouldn't be too tired to drive. It was going to be a long day. Marijke was out of her door and at the car before I could turn the engine off. She was subdued, too, and I had a fleeting thought of the night before which immediately I put out of my mind. Let's not spoil it, I reasoned.

"Good morning, David. You are well today?" She smiled as she handed me an overnight case which I dropped into the boot.

"Yes, I am, but a little tired. How are you?"

"Very fine, I think, especially now that I am with you."

I accelerated away—we had no time to dawdle. There was very little traffic, and though I was confident that we could make the run to Dover in time I wouldn't be driving slowly.

On the way to pick up House I told Marijke about him, our friendship, and our crazy escapades.

House lived just outside Croydon on Coombe Road in a little row house which he had bought when his wife had left him some ten years before. He was at the door as we pulled up, and sure enough, he had a young lady with him. I was dying to know if her name was Gladys and if she sang in the Luton Girls' Choir.

"Haa-lo," said Eccles' slow-witted drawl, "it's a be-u-tiful day, my good man."

"Oh, no," I groaned, "not this early. Spare me please!"

He dropped the imitation indignantly.

"The trouble with you colonials is that you have no appreciation for the finer dramatic offerings of the mother country. Well, so be it. Let me introduce Nickola Salvator-Rusher, private secretary to the managing editor of the *Daily Express*, which means that she works for another of those damned Canucks. Nicki, this is David, and don't let him sing to you or you'll end up jumping into bed with him. He has that effect on women—it's something to do with the maple syrup on his vocal chords."

"Oh, shut up, Harpic, and behave yourself. Nickola, I feel sorry for you having to spend the next 24 hours with this lunatic. If you want to bail out now I'll understand."

"This isn't half as bad as working at the *Express*," she smiled, "there I'm surrounded by crazies. I've only got House to deal with here, and I can handle him. But from what I hear, you've got your touch of insanity, too."

"Now what have you been telling her, you incompetent?" I glared at House. "Trying to ruin my reputation, are you, Harpic?"

"No, old chap, you've done well enough in that department all by your lonesome. Anything I might say can only enhance it."

"Before we get completely carried away, let me introduce Marijke Templaars. Marijke works for the Soviet Embassy."

There was a moment's pause after I said that—a beat or two of dead space. If Marijke was aware of it she paid it no heed.

We drove off with the banter continuing.

"What is this 'Harpic' name you call House, David? I only know this as a cleaner for drains," said Marijke.

"You've got it, sweetheart," I replied with Bogie's voice, "because Harpic gets 'right round the bend', just like House is."

"Shut up, you rotten swine," retorted House as Bluebottle.

My speed quickly stilling the giddiness, I utilised several shortcuts to get to the A25, whizzing past Biggin Hill, the famous RAF fighter station of World War II. On the main road the Jag crept up to 100mph with no trouble at all, and I only hoped that nothing unexpected would pop out from a side road.

There was a gradual lightening in the sky, but the overcast made it hard to tell when the sun had come up. This became fog patches along the coast, forcing me to slow down.

Entering Dover, we dashed through the town to the eastern docks. Ahead we could see the black hull and white superstructure of the ferry in the slip, with the distinctive yellow funnel topped with black of the Sealink Line. We drove on board the *Maid of Kent* with 12 minutes to spare.

House, Nickola, and Marijke cheered as I parked and switched off the engine, then we hastened up a companionway to the promenade deck, parking ourselves on the rail to have a good view as we pulled away from the dock.

It was fascinating to see the expanse of the famous White Cliffs of Dover. Unless you see them from the water, it's impossible to sense the impact of their entirety. There was a stillness on the deck, everyone gazing in awe at the chalk formations, and I couldn't help but start to sing softly "There'll Be Bluebirds Over the White Cliffs of Dover," the famous wartime song. I had only got one line out, when passengers on the deck began to sing with me. It was a wonderful experience.

Then, much to my embarrassment, several people recognized me and came for an autograph, which the ladies found exciting, but House just sighed and shook his head, muttering "There 'e goes. Ten minutes from now they'll all be pulling their knickers down. I dunno what the 'ell they sees in 'im. Beats me."

"You're just jealous, you mangy cur," I muttered after the last autograph had left.

"Do you sing also, House?" asked Marijke.

"Of course—anyone can, David proves that," he blustered.

"Oh, I've heard all about it," said Nicki. "His band say it's like a cross between Mel Torme and Louis Armstrong. They call him the 'Velvet Frog'."

We had a good snicker at this, House trying to ignore us.

"I don't like this game," he said in Bluebottle's voice. "If you make fun of me I will spin around in a decreasing circle and disappear up my own bum. *Yes I will!*"

Laughing merrily we purchased some duty-free items, then headed for the restaurant, deciding to have tea but not to eat until we got to Calais. Fresh croissants and pastries would be a welcome change from the usual English fare.

The sun, now peeking through the dispersing clouds, was giving some promise for a pleasant day as we drove off the boat to passport control. I wondered about Marijke's nationality.

"Passports out, everyone," I exclaimed, then softly queried Marijke. "Will this be a problem for you?"

"No," she replied, "if no one speaks about the Soviet Union." She glanced behind at House and Nicki.

"Mum's the word," muttered House.

As I handed over our passports I noticed one that was from the Netherlands. After one or two bored questions, we were on our way. I gave the passports back, and Marijke smiled brightly at me.

"Having dual citizenship is a good thing, yes?" She laughed.

"Would it be difficult with a Soviet passport?" asked Nicki.

"Much trouble and delay, I think. This way is easier."

"I didn't know that Soviet citizens were allowed to hold dual citizenship," commented House.

"Maybe we surprise you in the Soviet Union," Marijke laughed. "Now, please, we forget about it and have a good time."

We had been one of the last cars off the boat, so I hastened to catch the retreating tail-end of an Austin Mini which seemed to know the way out of the dock maze. I followed him blindly, snaking our way over bridges and past sundry docks, thankfully emerging into Place d'Armes. This is the main square, and the heart of what had been mediaeval Calais, though few relics of that period survive. Parking near a massive watch tower, we walked to find a *café* or *boulangerie*.

Moscow, U.S.S.R.—the same day

The office of General Josef Dmitrienko, Chief of Directorate "K" of the First Chief Directorate, KGB, was in the old Comintern headquarters next to the Agricultural Fairgrounds at 1a Tekstilshchikov Street. Spacious, with a view over the fairgrounds, it was sparsely furnished—in keeping with the character of its occupant.

Coffee had been placed before the general and his guest, his son-in-law Bren Templaars, and the steward had left them alone.

"The room is clean, sir?" asked the younger man quietly.

"It's just been swept. I have it done every two hours, and before and after every meeting. I can't afford to take chances, not after all these years."

"What has happened, sir?"

"The American, Fletcher, has been removed. They say he has left a list, one which names his contacts in the Middle-East. No one has found it—yet."

"Will you see this list if it is located?"

"Yes. And I will ensure that a copy is given to the right people. It would be disastrous if it were handled incorrectly." He took a sip of his coffee. "Have you heard from Marijke?"

"Pouch mail only. My daughter seems to be enjoying England."

"I have misgivings about my granddaughter being around Nalishkin. He and his patron would bring me down if they could. We have been rivals for as long as I can remember. It was no coincidence that Marijke was sent to work with him, but I couldn't interfere without the danger of causing an inquiry, and that we dare not risk."

"What about the aircraft project?"

"I can't find out anything. Directorate "S" is running it, and that bastard Rastvorov won't tell me more than he has to. If you have secure communication with Marijke, tell her to be very careful, Bren."

Calais, France—the same day

On Rue Royale we spotted just what we wanted—a little *boulangerie* which had tables and served coffee as well.

Soon we were munching happily on *brioches, croisssants au beurre,* and cups of hot, strong *café au lait*. The bread, still warm from the ovens, was an experience. Baked without additives, it remains fresh for only a few hours, so French bakers prepare a morning and an afternoon batch to ensure the quality for their customers.

Thus fortified we stopped briefly near the town hall so Marijke could see Rodin's famous sculpture *The Six Burghers*.

She explained how these six had offered their lives to prevent the English king from carrying out further reprisals against the townspeople of Calais in the year 1347.

"Did the king really execute them?" asked House.

"No," answered Marijke. "Edward's queen, Phillipa, stops it, and they are spared. But Calais remains in English hands for 211 years more. In 1895 this statue is made to mark the 200 years of war between France and England."

"How do you know all this?" queried Nicki. "I've never even heard the story and it's part of our history."

"Maybe you don't like the answer, Nicki. I say no more."

"No, tell us, love," said House. "We're all friends here."

Marijke hesitated. "In the Soviet Union this becomes an example of imperialistic aggression. The six burghers represent an early attempt by the people to overthrow the capitalistic yoke."

The immediate silence was broken by House's chuckle.

"I love it. These six were probably the biggest capitalists in Calais, and the Russians hold them up as heroes. There's hope for you people yet, Marijke. All is not lost."

We laughed our way back to the car, and in moments we were speeding on *Nationale Un,* known by the cynical locals as *la route des Anglais* because of the Brits' non-stop rush toward Paris.

I drove as fast as I dared, towns and villages flashing past interspersed with stretches of forest and farmland. Everywhere there were splashes of colour—the weathered burnt umber of the roof tiles on houses and barns—gradually giving way to slate as we reached the outskirts of Paris three hours later.

Using the Eiffel Tower as a beacon, I threaded my way to the greatest street in the world, l'Avenue des Champs-Élysées. Before us was the breathtaking sight of l'Arc de Triomphe. We gazed silently at its splendour. Marijke was the first to speak.

"I cannot believe how majestic it is. The photographs are not good for it, I think."

"You mean they don't do it justice," I responded. "I agree. At night, with the floodlights on, it'll be even more impressive."

We parked the car with some difficulty, then walked along toward the arch, finally settling for a sidewalk cafe which gave us a good view. We ate while we planned our afternoon's tour. I telephoned l'Hôtel St. James et d'Albany to tell them we would be there about 5:00pm, then we were off on our whirlwind to the sights of Paris.

Rue St. Laurent, Paris—the same time

He stood by the bed. The smell was overpowering. He placed a surgical mask over his mouth, donning a gown which he tied behind him, and pulling on latex gloves. Finally he picked up the scalpel. He looked down at the helpless man.

"Now, my friend, we will see how brave you really are."

Near Gare de l'Est, Paris—the same time

We had only scheduled two stops, one for Marijke to see the Sainte-Chapelle with its breathtaking stained-glass, and the other for Nicki to see the *Mona Lisa* and *Venus de Milo* at the Louvre.

Even so we were running late. It was nearing 4:00pm, and my nerves were on edge. We weren't far from Gare de l'Est, and I was anxious to get this over with. On the way I explained.

"I have to meet a man near the station and pick up something for a friend in England. Then we'll head for the hotel."

"Anyone I know?" asked House matter-of-factly.

"No, I don't think so," I replied, avoiding his gaze.

We pulled in to the parking area in front of Gare de l'Est, called Place du 11 Novembre 1918. I got out. It was five minutes to four. I retrieved my Financial Times from the boot, checked that I had the Union Jack pin in my pocket, and reached in to grab the Fodor's guide from the dash.

"I'll be as quick as I can. Keep the keys in case you have to move the car."

"Speed it up, old son."

"Hurry back."

"We'll be waiting."

I walked to the corner of Rue d'Alsace and Rue de Strasbourg, crossing the street to the sidewalk cafe. Sitting, I ordered a coffee from the waiter, laid out the paper with the guide on top of it, and waited. By five past four no one had approached me, and I was beginning to wonder how long I should stay. The fringe on the Cinzano umbrella flapped lazily over my head as I looked around at the other patrons, but none seemed interested in me. In fact, they were all in pairs or groups except for one elderly man who was reading a book.

I had almost decided to leave when I noticed a man hurrying across the street. He wasn't very tall, but his breadth made him seem shorter than he actually was. He was dressed in a dark suit and carried a raincoat. As he approached I could see that he was sweating profusely. He had dark hair, and cold eyes covered by horn-rimmed glasses.

Speaking to a waiter, he glanced around until he spotted me, then headed toward my table. Observing my paper and the Fodor's, he came closer.

"Pardon, m'sieu. Est-ce que je peux m'asseoir avec vous?"

"Certainement."

He sat down. I looked away. I figured that if he was the right contact he would have to make the moves. I certainly wasn't going to set it up. He laid his folded raincoat on the table. When his coffee came, so did the small talk.

"Il fait chaud, aujourd'hui."

"Oui, mais aussi il fait beau."

"I belief you are Eenglish, *m'sieu?"*

His accent wasn't French. I decided to play it out.

"Yes, I am."

"Is thet new Fodor's guide you hef?"

"Yes, I got it yesterday."

"May I pliz hef it for looking?"

"Certainly." I handed it over.

He leafed through it for a couple of minutes, then pulled something from his pocket.

"I gif you gift. Now you hef something for marking your plez in book."

"Thank you, that's most kind. And I have something for you."

I fished out the pin, placing it before him on the table.

"Just a small souvenir from England."

"Thenk you. You very generous."

"Well, I must be running along. Nice to have met you."

I started to rise, holding out my hand. He ignored me, putting his right hand inside the folded raincoat.

"I theenk, Mestair English, you hed bettair sitting down."

I froze. "I beg your pardon?"

"Before you moof, looking at coat."

I looked. There was something metallic and round with a hole in it pointed at me. I sat down, my heart pounding.

"You know what ees thees?"

"Yes, I think so. I don't understand. What do you want?"

I was trembling and sweating, all at once.

"You and I, Meestair Eenglish, we takink walk. You weel holt my left arm. Eef you let go, I fire gon. I haf silencer. Nobody hear. They theenk you dronk on strit. I deesappear. Pouf!"

He picked up my Fodor's, slipping it into his left pocket, and the Union Jack followed. He stood up.

"We go now. Pliz."

I stood, moved around the table and took his arm. We walked to the corner, waited for a green light, and stepped across. My terror had lessened, but my heart was pumping hard and the blood was racing through my veins. The adrenalin was running wild. This was not good. I had to get control. I remembered the words of Sergeant Kobayashi, our hand-to-hand combat instructor.

"You must clear your mind," he would admonish. "You must have only focus."

That was it. Focus. I tried, but everything was coming at me like a kaleidoscope. I had to concentrate. *Focus.*

I began to look for an opening. I thought I might get away from him on the street, but if his shots went wild, then innocent people might be wounded or even killed. I ruled this out. I looked up at the street sign. At least I would memorize where I was going. Come on, *focus.*

South on Boulevard de Strasbourg. It was a wide, tree-lined street with a boulevard down the centre strip. Lots of shops, and, unfortunately, lots of people on this beautiful day. Forget it. Not now. Wait for the right opportunity. *Focus.* My heart slowed.

The corner. We turned left, crossed Strasbourg, and walked down Rue St. Laurent. Much narrower, fewer people, but the parked cars restricted movement. I wouldn't make it. *Focus.*

Half-way down the block we crossed the street toward large, black double doors. On either side, at the curb, were slender, cast iron rods, with round balls at the top, embedded in the pavement. They were about 30 inches high. Some sort of sidewalk or curb protector. I considered pushing my captor into one as we passed. Perhaps he would be knocked to the ground, but again, if he weren't, I was finished. No. Not yet. *Focus.*

"You stan' close to door."

As I did this he held the coat toward me with his right hand while he fished out keys with his left.

"You unlock right door, step back. Not try anything."

He knew what he was doing. He went partially in, backwards, and motioned me to follow. The coat was pointing toward me all the way. Indicating that I should start up the stairs, he kicked the door shut and followed four steps behind me.

"All way to top."

We went up two floors. He motioned me to a corner, unlocked a door, threw it wide, and directed I should enter. He was right behind me. Something hard in my back. The door slammed. Be calm. Look around. *Focus.*

The room was quite bare. A heavy oak refectory table, very similar to my own, ran parallel to the two windows. There was a wooden chair on the side opposite the windows, and another to the right of the table by the wall. On a small shelf by this chair was a telephone.

"Sit. Put hands flet on table. Not moof."

I did as I was told. Time was running out. I had to do something. Could I talk him out of it? Try. *Focus.*

"Look, I'm not the person who was supposed to meet you today. He's a friend of mine in England, and just asked me to take his place because he's sick. I don't even know what this is all about, so I can't tell you anything. I was just doing him a favour."

"You theenk I belief you? You crazy. Now not spik."

He picked up the phone, dialling with his left hand. The gun was plainly visible. An automatic pistol, it looked to be about 9mm calibre. The silencer was crude and home-made.

He began speaking rapidly. In Russian. I couldn't follow it, but he did mention the street, St. Laurent, and some numbers. He hung up. Obviously, they were coming for me.

Walking to the door to the adjoining room, he threw it open.

"You not suppose meet me? Is joke! I not who you suppose to meet. You want see courier? Come. You come!"

He beckoned me to the door, indicating I should enter. "You go. Haf good look so you don' forget."

I walked in. The stench made me gag. I hesitated, but I was prodded in the back. There was a bed and a dresser in the room. The curtains were drawn, so the light was dim. I realized there was a man on the bed. He was naked, and his arms and legs were tied to the bedposts. He wasn't moving, and as my eyes became accustomed to the light I realized that there was a hole in the middle of his forehead.

"He is hard man to make talk. Is why I late. But I convince him, yes?"

I looked more closely. My stomach heaved, but I wanted to see what this son-of-a-bitch had done. I wanted to hate him. The Frenchman, or so I believed him to be, was a small man, and in the ruin of his face there was a thin moustache. This poor bastard was the one Hammond had described.

There were welts, burns, and cuts all over his body. His face was slashed and bruised, and his nose had been pulped. One eye, out of the socket, dangled on his cheek. Three fingers were gone from his right hand. Through an incision in his lower abdomen intestines had been pulled. There was a bloody hunk of tissue hanging from his mouth. I didn't know what it was 'til I saw the pool of coagulating blood between his legs. His testicles. I turned away, retching. Now—now I could hate. Steady. *Focus.*

"You come back, sit. They not be long."

Slowly, I walked to the outer room and sat down. He had taken his jacket off, hanging it over the other chair. It was very hot. I was sweating, but he was bathed in perspiration—and he smelled. Tugging on the windows, he opened both sets in turn. They were floor to ceiling casement windows, and they opened inward, lying flat to the inner wall. Outside, there were two iron bars as safety guards, the upper one not much above the knee.

I took stock. If I didn't make an attempt before the others got here, I was finished. Once the Russians had me, there was no way of knowing what would happen. It was possible I might never be heard of again. At best, I would be accused, tried publicly, and used as propaganda. Perhaps I would be exchanged, perhaps not. I could probably expect intimidation and torture, and after what I had seen in the next room, I would rather be dead. Easy, now. Concentrate. *Focus.*

What about the pistol? I got a better look at it. I guessed it was an old Czechoslovakian gun, a CZ Model 39. In my shooting days I had taken an interest in small arms of the world. The CZ Model 39 had distinctive finger grips at the rear of the slide. If this was the right gun the cartridge was underpowered. It also had a heavy trigger pull, making it inaccurate.

The corpse in the next room corroborated my guess, or so I hoped. There was very little blood behind his head. Probably the bullet had not exited—it was still in his skull. The home-made silencer would also affect the muzzle velocity. It all seemed to fit. If I was right, I had a chance. If I was wrong, I was dead.

My heart had slowed to normal, and my breathing was almost negligible. I had picked a spot inside me to concentrate my focus. A pinpoint of white, intense light. My senses were heightened. I was as ready as I could be, given the circumstances.

But still I waited. *Focus.* Easy now. *Focus.*

There was a sudden crash from the street below. He backed to the window, glancing down sideways.

Now!

Yelling involuntarily, with the strength and speed of desperation I grabbed the underside of the table, hoisted it in front of me, and ran at him, holding it like a shield. I heard the gun cough once, twice, and then I hit him full force with the table. There was a scream, and suddenly he was gone. The iron rails had caught him just above the knee, and he went out backward through the open window, crashing to the ground two stories below.

I stood there trembling, looking at the two bulges in the bottom of the table. The flattened tip of a slug was just visible in the centre of one bulge. My guess about the gun had been right.

This was not the time to stand and pat myself on the back. I started for the window, but caught myself. There was shouting from the street, and I didn't want anyone to see a face peering out of the window from which a man had fallen. I reached inside his coat pocket, taking the Fodor's and the pin. I took my handkerchief out, wiping the table where I had touched it, then ran to the door, using the handkerchief again as I wrenched it open.

Taking the stairs two at a time, I stopped at the bottom. The outer door was open. A *gendarme*, running. I ducked under the staircase as he and two other men clomped up the stairs.

Stepping out slowly, I walked to the back of the gathering crowd as calmly as I could. I was not prepared for what I saw.

He had fallen on one of the iron posts, impaling himself through the back. Impacting right to the ground, the bloody rod protruded grotesquely from his abdomen.

I turned away, the bile rising in my throat. I forced myself to walk slowly. It wasn't too hard—my head was spinning. For a moment I thought I would faint, then caught myself. I still had to get away. I couldn't draw attention to myself.

"David! *David!*"

I looked around. Was I hallucinating? Then, there was House.

"How did you get here?" I choked.

"I saw you walking off with that character and didn't like the look of it. Followed in the Jag. It's at the end of the street. I saw him come through the window. Damned sloppy dive. Terrible entry. Only gave him a 3. Figured I'd come and find you, and there you were. Don't tell me, I know. Basil Hammond, isn't it? I warned you. Oh, well, let's get the hell out of here."

We were walking to the corner, when a *gendarme* appeared in front of us. He held up his nightstick.

"Restez ici, s'il vous plaît. Que personne ne parte."

House went into gear.

"Nothing to do with us, old boy. We heard the commotion and went to have a look. I'm British and he's Canadian. Just here as tourists. I think they need you there. Quite a mess. Blighter took a flyer out of the window."

The crowd was getting thicker, and the commotion was getting out of hand, for there had been a minor street accident just before his fall. One of the gendarmes at the scene blew his whistle, and ours was uncertain about what to do.

"I must go zere, but I mus' ask you not to leave until I can return for your names."

"Certainment, monsieur l'agent. Nous restons ici," lied House. The moment his back was turned, we were gone. The ladies saw us coming in a hurry, and got out.

"David, what's wrong? What has happened?" said Marijke anxiously.

"I can't explain right now. Please, we must leave in a hurry. House, you drive. I'll navigate. ladies, please get in the back, and don't ask questions."

As we moved off I grabbed the Paris street guide.

"Don't speed, House, whatever you do."

We drove steadily out of Paris. I directed House as well as I could, for I was feeling progressively cold all over, and shivering despite the heat.

"Marijke, can you pass me the blanket? I don't feel well."

She passed it to me, but said nothing, just gave me a strange look. I wrapped myself in it, but it wasn't helping much. I was also beginning to feel quite ill. I blacked out for a bit, coming to when I heard House say we were on route N2.

"When we get to Le Bourget, N2 veers off right, but we should stay straight and pick up N17."

I blacked out once more, for how long I didn't know. Again, I heard House's voice, this time calling me.

"David, sorry, old son, but how long do we stay on N17?"

I glanced at the map. I was having trouble seeing it.

"I think until we get to Lens. House, you'll have to stop the car. I'm going to be ill."

I barely made it to the trees. I was violently sick. I was so weak both House and Marijke came to help me to the car. I went into the back with Marijke, Nicki into the front with House.

As I fell asleep in Marijke's arms I remembered the looks on their faces.

Nicki's was perplexed. House's was knowing. Marijke's was contemplative. Mine was just sick.

It was death number three.

But this time I was glad.

That scared the hell out of me.

TEN

Vimy, France—the same day

I was flying in a plane. The turbulence of the darkened night sky was buffeting us brutally through the air. The door in the main cabin was open. I was not strapped in. With a violent wrench the port wing dropped and I was flung through the door. Clutching frantically for my parachute I pulled the ring, but it came off in my hand and I was free-falling through the black woollen clouds.

Breaking through the cloud base all I could see in the dim light was forest. I hurtled downward and with rising terror I saw that the treetops were sharpened to needle points. They were waiting for me, reaching for me. I cried out in horror. . . .

I woke up.

"David. . . David," said a soothing voice, "it's all right."

I looked up. Marijke was holding me. I was in the back seat of my Jag. House was driving. For a few moments I couldn't remember what I was doing here, then it all flooded back.

I sat up in a panic.

"Where are we?"

"Still on the N17, and just past Vimy. The sign said the Canadian Cemetery was on our left. I was going to drop you off so we could leave you at rest with your fellow-countrymen, and then you had to go and ruin it by coming back from the dead. Extremely 'inconsoderate' of you. I was all set to do my Scottish mouth-music version of 'The Last Post.' Very touching it would have been. Now you've spoiled it all, you rotting twine."

"Very funny," was all I could mumble.

"Are you feeling any better, David?" asked Nicki.

"Yes, some, thanks. Does anyone have some gum or a mint?"

"Here, love," said Nicki, handing me one of each.

"Do you want to sleep more?" queried Marijke.

"No, not now." I thought for a moment. "I think we should find a place to stop so I can clean up and you can get something to eat. I feel as though I've been dragged through a sewer. Start looking, all of you, and the first likely place should do it. We also have to figure out where we'll cross into Belgium."

"Listen to me, everybody," said House quietly. "I don't want to start a panic, and I don't want anyone to react at all. Got it? Don't turn around! There's a police car approaching from behind. He's moving quickly with flashing lights. What do I do, David?"

"Nothing! Just drive, steady and normally. If he gets on our tail pay no attention. House, put those sunglasses on. Nicki, look like you're reading—grab the Paris guidebook. Marijke, you and I will pretend to be necking."

"Necking? I don't hear this before. What is necking?"

"Kissing and things like that. I'll explain later. Just pretend, and keep your head between mine and the window."

We went into our routines.

"He's on our tail," muttered House, checking the mirror.

"Steady, everyone," I said, putting my arms around Marijke and burying my face in her hair.

We waited, keeping up the charade.

"Beside us," said House through his teeth. "Looking us over."

It was like waiting for the depth charges to explode. We didn't know what would happen next. It seemed like forever.

"He's gone," breathed House.

"Thank God," said Nicki, shaken.

"Keep up the act for a few minutes. We want to make sure he's clear, and that there isn't another car behind in radio contact. And we can't be sure there isn't an unmarked car around."

We waited a few more minutes.

"That copper is away ahead now, David, and speeding."

"Okay. If he was looking for us, seeing the ladies probably convinced him that he had the wrong party. No one knew about them, and they can't stop every car on the road with British plates. I think we got lucky. Let's hope it stays that way."

We were virtually in the outskirts of Lens, a small industrial city that had suffered badly in both world wars. It had a tired, gritty appearance about it, possibly because it was the centre of a large coal mining district.

"If you head for the station, House, we'll probably find a hotel quite near it." Even my voice was weak.

We crossed tracks coming into town. House turned left at an intersection, and very soon the station appeared, and there, on Place de la Gare, was the Hôtel France.

"Park and go in, House, and find out if they can feed you and if I can get a good wash."

"Your wish is my command, my Cap-itan," said Bluebottle's voice. House used his humour to deal with pressures and problems. He parked, jumped out of the car, and went inside.

It was silent for a few minutes, then Marijke spoke softly.

"Is it possible you can tell us what happens in Paris, David? Perhaps it is none of our business, but we are all very concerned. It seems to affect you very much. Can we do anything to help?"

"After I've cleaned up I'll tell you what I can. I'm sorry to have spoiled our night in Paris."

"It doesn't matter."

"Don't worry on my account, David," said Nicki. "I'll work on House to bring me over for a weekend. He owes me, anyway."

House came bounding down the steps.

"Good news, troops. They're more than delighted to have some guests for dinner, and since there is virtually no one in the hotel, they've given us a couple of rooms to use to freshen up. All we have to do is pay a small service charge. I would therefore suggest taking our toiletries in with us."

In minutes we were entering what must have been a small, elegant hotel in its day, but it, too, was showing the weariness of age and hard times. We all wanted to wash first, so the ladies were shown to one room while House and I went to the other.

As soon as we were alone, House started in.

"I don't have to know the details, David, but what the hell were you doing back there? Surely Hammond hasn't sucked you in as a courier. You've got far too much going for you to be involved in that sort of rubbish, and far too much to lose if you get caught. That should be quite apparent after today.

"I've told the ladies nothing, pleading ignorance, but you're going to have to give them something that sounds plausible. Remember, one of them works for a major newspaper, and the other works for the Russians, for Christ's sake! I feel like Oliver Hardy—'another fine mess you've gotten me into'."

"It was a one-off favour, House. Hammond knew about the Paris trip from you, and asked if I would stand in for a guy who was sick. No problems, he said, just a simple little pick-up."

I proceeded to tell House about the meeting and what had happened. Regardless of secrecy, he had already guessed much of it, and since we were all still in jeopardy I needed his counsel. We talked as we washed and shaved. House was concerned.

"If that *gendarme* we ducked told his superiors about us, then you can be sure that Interpol has flashed at least a warning to airports, stations, and what-have-you, to be on the lookout for a Brit and a Canadian with our general descriptions. Perhaps it's only for questioning, but if the Soviet embassy in Paris gets involved, then we might be headed for the high-jump."

"That's why I told you to get on the N17. It's far less travelled. Now I'm going to suggest some tiny roads as we approach the Belgian border. Even if they've contacted some of the major border posts they really don't know which way we headed, and they certainly don't know how we're travelling. If we'd gone straight back to Calais we probably would have been picked up by now. We've got a far better chance through Belgium and a ferry in Ostend."

House was thoughtful for a moment.

"Look, David, as far as I'm concerned, once we're back in the UK I'm forgetting all about this little contretemps. But the ladies out there are a different story. What will you say?"

"I think I know how to handle it. Let's go and join them."

We were shown to a table, and in a few minutes Marijke and Nicki were seated with us. The mood was quiet, and we ordered out of necessity, not festivity. The house wine was pleasant and not very strong, which was a good thing. I didn't want to sleep again, for we had to navigate our way to the border on tricky roads, and I knew it would take all my concentration.

We passed on dessert, but ordered coffee, and then I felt I had to explain as best I could.

"Look, all of you, let me tell you what happened back there. I think I owe it to you, and though I don't know everything I'll tell you what I've pieced together. Before we left England I was asked by a friend who was ill to do a favour for him in Paris. All I had to do was meet a man and exchange a couple of things. That's what I was doing at the café near Gare de l'Est. But it seems that the underworld had become involved, and the man who met me was not the one who should have been there. He held a gun on me, and was taking me to be picked up by his boss. Fortunately for me, he had an accident, and I was able to get away."

"What were you exchanging, David?" asked Nicki, quietly.

"I don't know," I said truthfully, "and I don't want to know. I can't afford to get involved in anything like this. That's why we left in a hurry. I'm sorry to have dragged you all into it. Right now I just want to get us all back to England without being detained. We're looking for an easy way across the Belgian frontier—a crossing which is little used. Once we're out of France there's less chance of being stopped."

"I think it's all rather exciting," whispered Nicki. "Nothing like this ever happens to me. Here we are on the lam from the law, plotting an illegal dash across a border. Do you always give your dates this much fun, David?" She laughed.

Marijke was thoughtful.

"I think this might be much trouble for me, too, if the police hold us. Remember, I am not in France properly. This could make much difficulties for me. So, for me, too, I hope we get away." Then she smiled. "But for me, too, it is exciting. How do you say it? Let's run for it!"

We expressed our gratitude to the concierge, paid our bill, then tanked up with *l'essence* down the street. I asked House to drive again so I could navigate from the passenger seat.

For nearly two hours we twisted and turned through side roads and country lanes, passing close to Armentières, finally entering a little town called Steenwerck. There was hardly a light to be seen. In the town square a signpost indicated *la poste de frontière,* le Seau, and Route D38. We drove on.

I started to get butterflies in my stomach. What if all this were for nought, and we ended up being stopped and arrested?

"House, in le Seau we're only a few hundred yards from the border. Let's park the car and have a quiet walk before we drive up to it. I don't want to get into a point of no return. We can decide what to do after we have a look."

Le Seau was not much more than an intersection of two roads surrounded by four buildings. House parked before the intersection, and he and I got out to reconnoitre. We walked to the corner, then a jog right to start down the road to the border. The signpost said N331. About two hundred yards away we could see the lights of the crossing. We stopped to have a look.

"What do you think, David?"

"I'm not sure. From here it looks like a couple of outhouses about 50 feet apart with a wooden barrier beside each one. I can't see anyone about, can you?"

"No, not a sausage. Let's move a little closer."

We walked slowly and quietly, and had covered about 50 yards when the door of the guardpost on the French side opened, and a man stepped out. We froze. My heart was thumping.

Without a backward glance the guard walked to the Belgian guardpost, calling out as he did so.

"Pierre! Pierre!"

The other door opened, and out stepped his Belgian counterpart.

"Oui, mon ami! Qu'est ce que c'est?"

"House, stay here," I whispered. "I'm going closer to try to hear. If I'm seen, run to the car and get away."

I crouched in the ditch, moving forward as quickly as I could. I stopped about 20 yards from the French barrier, and strained my ears. I was just outside the circle of light cast by the floodlight on the guardpost.

I could make out most of the words, and the laughter of the Belgian guard cut through the night.

"Eh bien! Bon soir, Bruno. Je tu vois demain. Couche bien, mon ami."

The Frenchman was heading back in my direction. I dropped to the ground until I heard the door of the guardhouse slam, then got back to

House as quickly as I could.

"What's up, David?"

"The French guard's had a phone call to stay on duty, otherwise they would have opened the frontier and gone home. The Belgian wasn't ordered to stay, so he's taking off."

"Was the call because of us?"

"I think so, from what I could hear."

"What now, old son?"

"I don't know. We need a diversion. Let's separate. You go through the field to the left, I'll go to the right. Walk about fifty yards, then meet me back here."

"What am I looking for?"

"Anything at all. Just tell me what's there. And be quiet."

We parted, and I went carefully through the weeds but found nothing at all within my 50-yard limit. I returned to meet House.

"Anything?"

"Only a small shed with some farm implements."

"What's it built out of?"

"Boards. Not very sturdy."

"Show me."

We moved silently and quickly. About forty yards from the frontier post stood the shed. I had a quick look around.

"This might do it. Let's get back to the car."

Marijke and Nicki were starting to worry.

"We were afraid you'd been stopped. Can we get through?"

I explained the circumstances.

"I'm going to give the guard something to think about. Nicki, may I have the bottle of cognac you bought? I'll replace it."

"Don't worry about it, love."

I opened the boot and got the survival kit out, slinging it on my shoulder. The blanket I wedged over the bonnet of the car.

"House, drive the car slowly without headlights until you're about a hundred yards from the border. Keep the engine running, the passenger door open. When I arrive we'll make a dash for it."

"What are you up to?"

"I'll tell you later if it works. If I don't show, get the hell out of here and hide."

Before they could respond I was gone. Carefully making my way back toward the frontier post, I walked the last twenty yards in the shadow at the rear. After a few minutes of feeling along the skirting I found what I was looking for—the phone wire. Pulling snippers from my emergency pack I cut it with a gentle snap.

Then I crept off toward the shed. About twenty feet from it I stopped, took the lid off the cognac, and, with a twinge of guilt about wasting such a beautiful beverage, took one small mouthful and let it burn down my throat. I fished out my handkerchief, moistened the end with cognac and stuffed the rest into the bottle. Lighting a match from the waterproof container I set the handkerchief ablaze, and hurled the fiery missile at the shed.

As I turned to run there was an explosion behind me, nearly knocking me down. I glanced back to see the shed engulfed with flame. In seconds I was diving into the passenger seat of the car.

"Jesus, David, won't that attract attention?"

Before I could reply the door of the frontier post slammed open and the guard ran toward the blaze with a fire extinguisher.

"Now, House! Tramp on it!"

He did, but he wasn't happy.

"We're going to hit the barrier!"

"Ram it, House! Hard!"

With a splintering crash it disintegrated.

We hurtled on into the darkness of Belgium.

ELEVEN

London, England—just after midnight, Saturday, June 16, 1962

The telephone jolted him from the soothing effects of Tchaikowsky on the turntable and vodka in his brain. He answered, though his tongue did not wish to co-operate.

"Yes?"

"Scramble."

He pressed the button, waiting a few seconds before speaking.

"Go ahead."

"I have some unfortunate news, Comrade. Dragon is dead."

His mind was instantly clear.

"How?"

"The British agent. Dragon took him and then called us. We left immediately. We found Dragon dead in the street, apparently fallen from a window. His gun was underneath him, and according to our contact with the *Deuxième Bureau* it had been fired. The slugs were dug out of a table in an apartment on the third floor. There was another body there, probably the one Dragon had worked over to snare the Englishman."

"Any sign of the swine?"

"One *gendarme* reported an Englishman leaving the area with another man. In the confusion he wasn't detained. They've alerted all departure points and border crossings, but nothing yet."

"All right. Keep me informed."

He put down the phone, cursing to himself. What kind of man could have turned the tables on that sadist? It didn't seem possible. He must be a savage.

Shit. Where do I find another psychopath at short notice?

Ieper, Belgium—the same night

We had dashed out to the main highway, dropped our speed, and proceeded into Ieper, trying to look like ordinary tourists. I had removed the blanket from the hood and replaced the emergency kit. The only damage from the barrier was the hood ornament, but, fortunately, it got caught in the blanket and wasn't left behind.

"Oh, Jesus," from House.

I looked ahead. A roadblock. There was no way out.

"We can't run—they'll get us for sure. We'll have to bluff. House, you carry it. We'll follow."

We pulled up as a police officer approached with a flashlight, shining it into the car.

"You are from England, *m'sieu?*" he asked in good English.

"Yes, we're on a little tour," said House. "We wanted to see the battlegrounds and pay our respects to our fallen comrades."

"You are *un soldat, m'sieu?*"

"Yes," said House, handing over his I-card. "I'm in the Coldstream Guards."

The policeman examined it carefully, then looked at me. "And you, *m'sieu?* You are in the army also?"

I had a flash of inspiration. "Yes, old chap," I replied with an English accent, "Royal Corps of Transport."

I handed him the I-card which Hammond had given me. House had a look of incredulity on his face and I flashed him a warning glance. The policeman studied the cards, then handed them back.

"I must examine your vehicle. Please accompany me."

We both got out and walked around the car, the officer shining his light all the way around the body. He stopped at the front, carefully examining the grill, the lights and the hood.

"What 'appened to the cat, *m'sieu?* Doesn't the Jaguar usually 'ave an ornament?"

"Paris," I replied. "Some blighter decided he wanted a souvenir. Yanked the ruddy thing right off."

"The French 'ave no manners, *m'sieu*. It would not 'appen in Belgium."

"Can you tell us what the problem is, Officer?"

"About 'alf an hour ago a car ran a small border crossing. We also 'ave an alert for an Englishman and a Canadian. But you are both British officers and there is no damage on the car. I'm sorry to 'ave detain you. Please enjoy your visit."

He saluted, then turned back to his vehicle, signalling to his comrades that we should pass.

"Remind me to ask you about this later," muttered House as we drove away with a wave to the policeman.

"Just forget it, House, along with everything else. Please."

We drove to the town centre in silence. Nicki broke it.

"I don't recall the name 'Ieper' from school."

"Most people know it by it's French name, 'Ypres'," said House. "Pity it's night. Ypres was nothing but rubble at the end of World War I, and it was carefully rebuilt stone by stone by the citizens. Now, navigator, what in hell are we up to?"

"A place to stop for the night, but we mustn't use a normal hotel. We don't want all these bits of information coming together in some bright spark's head, and then make ourselves readily available by being in the nearest four-star hostelry. We'll get back on side roads and look for something smaller."

On we went through darkened villages, looking for a sign that would lead us to a guesthouse or bed-and-breakfast. I hoped I was right in my assumption that anyone looking for us would stick to the main roads and hotels.

"Do the Belgians all speak French, then?" asked Nicki.

"Only in this region," answered House. "But they call it 'Walloon', not French. Some linguists say it's a purer French than Parisian."

"What about the rest of Belgium?"

"The North speak Flemish, almost like Dutch," said Marijke.

"That's right," confirmed House. "Signs are often in both languages all over the country. To compound the problem, the eastern section has many German-speaking people. On top of all that, most Belgians are quite fluent in English. France may have its Eiffel Tower, but Belgium lays honest claim to the Tower of Babel."

We passed a sign to Bikschote. Something caught my eye.

"Hold on! Back up, House! I think I saw a sign on the right."

House backed up carefully.

"Stop, and I'll get out to have a look."

I hopped out, ran part way down a lane, and found the sign which said 'l'Auberge Marique', and underneath, in English, 'Bed and Breakfast.' There was an arrow which pointed to a house partially hidden by a grove of trees. I hurried back to the car.

"This might do, if they have a vacancy. Drive down the lane and we'll ask."

House turned in, and we pulled up at the rear of a pretty little stone two-storey farmhouse. There was a light on inside, so I hoped we wouldn't disturb anyone by at least enquiring. There were no other cars parked there, and that was a good sign.

"Nicki and I'll go ask, David. You and Marijke sit tight."

When they had gone it was awfully quiet. I didn't know what to say to Marijke, nor she to me. It was the first time we had been alone since Croydon, and that seemed like an eternity away. She found the words first.

"I'm sorry for the trouble you have in Paris, David. I see how much it affects you. I think it becomes more serious than you tell us, but we don't interfere. I want that you know if I can help I am here for you."

She reached and took my hand. Suddenly I felt very weary.

"Thank you, Marijke. I don't know what more I can say right now. In fact, I don't know whether I will ever be able to say more about it. I'll have to wait 'til we get back to England. I guess that should be 'if' we get back to England."

It was quiet again, but House and Nicki came bouncing out of the door and ran to the car.

"It's marvellous," gushed Nicki. "She had a reservation for both rooms, but they didn't show. She'd just turned the lights off before we arrived, so she's glad to have us. She's very nice."

"Two rooms? How are we arranging that?" I asked.

"Well, old son, Nicki and I would like to stay together, but if that doesn't suit you we'll do it some other way."

"David, it is all right with me," whispered Marijke. "We mustn't make more difficulty for House and Nicki. Is this agreeable for you?"

"Of course, but I didn't want you to get the wrong idea. It's not expected, you know."

"Shhh," she said, putting her hand on my mouth, then answered House. "This is fine for us, too, House. We all go in."

The car was in a perfect spot at the back of the house, for the trees were a natural screen even for the house. We entered through a large kitchen with a huge table in the centre of the floor. It was full of charm, with an old cooking fireplace on one wall, the whole room decorated in blue and white to match the Delft tiles which lined it.

"Marijke and David, this is Madame Marique," said House.

"Welcome to my house," she smiled. "I am honoured to have you as my guests. I will show you your rooms, and then how would you like a cup of Belgian chocolate before you retire?"

Of course we agreed, and Madame Marique then led us upstairs to a small sitting room with bedrooms on either side.

"You may choose between you," she stated, "and then come down for your chocolate. The bathroom is just there, beside that bedroom. The plumbing is old, but there is plenty of hot water."

"Marijke, you choose for us," I said. Then to Madame Marique, "Is there a telephone I may use to call England? I would place a collect call."

"But of course. Please come with me."

She led the way back downstairs, then turned left at the foot to show me a small sitting room.

"There is a telephone here, and I will close the two doors so you will have privacy." She smiled at me.

"Merci, madame."

"Avec plaisir, monsieur."

When she had gone I took out the number Hammond had given me, picked up the handset to wait for the operator, and hoped she spoke English. I needn't have worried. The call went straight through, and I heard the number ringing.

"'Oo shall I say is calling, *m'sieu?"*

Oh Lord. "Tell them it's Mr. Minstrel, operator, and that it is an emergency."

She did so, and in no time I heard Hammond's voice.

"Hello, Minstrel, I was hoping to hear from you," he said pleasantly. "I understand you had a bit of a problem earlier today. Where are you calling from?"

"Belgium. A little guest house called l'Auberge Marique in a village called Bikschote. The phone number is 49-33-76. I don't know the area code."

"No matter. Do you still have the item you started out with, by any chance? Or did that disappear in the confusion?"

"I have it, and the other one as well."

"You have them both?"

"Yes."

"Minstrel, you have saved us no end of trouble. Now, I've been on to our office in Paris all day, and through our contacts in the SDECE I think the police alert will be cancelled by tomorrow morning. I won't ask how you did it, but getting to Belgium was exactly the right thing to do. What time are you intending to return home?"

"The ferry closest to 0900 Belgian time."

"There's one at that time exactly. After you board I'll have someone meet you. Give him an envelope with both items. It will save you any problem from then on."

"How will I know him?"

"He will say 'Is this your car, sir, or one on hire?', to which you will respond, 'I would never dream of hiring one', and he will countersign, 'Then you are indeed a fortunate man'.

"When you get in to London, call me from a public phone. I must see you tomorrow afternoon. I'll tell you where at that time. I know what you must be thinking, but I can assure you that I had no idea that things would go so wrong. I would never have done that to you if I had had the slightest suspicion." He paused. "A lot of people owe you a tremendous amount for your actions. Please remember that."

"I hear you, sir, but I'm not coping with what happened very well. I don't know whether I can continue with our arrangement. I'll see you tomorrow afternoon, perhaps for the last time. I hope you understand."

There was just a hum on the line for nearly half a minute.

"Sir, are you still there?"

He sounded really weary—about the way I felt.

"Yes, Minstrel, I'm here, and yes, I do understand. I can only say that I am most terribly, terribly, sorry for what I inadvertently put you through. I wish you good night."

"Good night, sir."

I hung up, sat for a moment, then headed for the kitchen where the others were already drinking chocolate. I sat down, and Madame Marique placed a steaming mug in front of me. She had also prepared a little plate of pâté and biscuits, and another of chocolates and truffles.

"Everything all right, David?" asked House, gently. He must have known who I was calling.

"Yes, I think so. By tomorrow morning everything should be taken care of. We should have a trouble-free crossing."

House, Marijke, and Nicki exchanged knowing glances.

"What boat do you intend to catch tomorrow?" queried Madame Marique, to which I replied.

"Then you must be away from here by 7:45 to give you time to get on board. That means breakfast will be at 7 o'clock. So, away with you to bed, and I will see you in the morning. *Allez*, go! You must get your rest. *Bon soir, bon soir!*"

And she shooed us up to bed. I was so tired I could hardly climb the stairs. Marijke and I said good night to House and Nicki, then closed the door of our room. As tired as I was, I felt embarrassed and uncomfortable.

"Marijke, I can sleep in the chair and give you the bed."

"Why you would want that when the bed is big enough for both? Are you afraid I bite, or I pull off the duvet?"

"No, nothing like that. It's just that this is not exactly a romantic evening, and I am so tired that I can hardly keep my eyes open. It's not the way I wanted to spend a night with you."

"Another time comes, David," she whispered. "Now, go to bed."

She turned out the light and opened the curtain. I undressed quickly and slid under the duvet. I looked toward the window. Marijke was undressing on that side of the bed, and I could see her in silhouette against the moonlight—her hair, the line of her body, the curve of her breasts. Then she was beside me, her warmth touching me.

"Go to sleep, David. Only thing that is important is we are together. We don't even must talk. I hold you until you sleep."

I did as she suggested, even as I mumbled my protest.

"I want to talk to you about what happened, but I can't."

"It doesn't matter."

I felt her body curve into mine, the softness and warmth. Her arm came around, enfolding me. I began to relax.

"You can tell me one thing?"

"I don't know," I breathed. "What?"

"What kind of accident does this man have in Paris?"

What the hell, I thought.

"A fall. A very nasty fall."

"Good night, David," she whispered, kissing my shoulder. I thought I heard the word 'love' as I fell into a fitful sleep.

The dreams were confused, fragmented. I was being pursued, and my feet wouldn't move. Nothing had shape. I was being haunted by vague terrors, and I was powerless to escape.

Gradually, there was a change. A feeling of warmth and security began to replace the fear. It grew in intensity, and the anxieties were whisked away. I was being carried on a river of clouds into a pool of softness, and the euphoria was almost too much to bear. Suddenly, the dam burst, and I was swept into peace, tranquillity, and darkness.

Then I slept soundly.

TWELVE

Bikschote, Belgium—early the next morning

David. . . David."

I barely heard it, and yet it was enough to penetrate my subconscious. I opened my eyes and looked up. Marijke's face came into view. She was smiling. What a wonderful sight in the morning.

"Good morning, David. I am afraid you are sleeping all the day. I am sorry I wake you, but we are to be for breakfast soon, and I know we must get to the boat in Oostende." She used the Belgian form.

She leaned over, kissing me on one cheek, then the other, and then on the forehead.

"How are you feeling today? I hope you are better."

"I am better, thanks, but I think I could have slept for a week." I noticed her attire. "You're dressed? What time is it?"

"It is nearly 06:30. House, Nicki and I have finished in the bathroom, and we go for a walk before breakfast. We think we let you sleep longest and then the bathroom is free. We see you at breakfast in one half hour."

She gave me another kiss and then a cheery wave as she went out, shutting the door behind her.

Fine thing, I thought. I spend the night with the girl of my dreams, and I can't remember a thing except sleeping. And yet, I felt strangely relaxed, almost as if... no, that was a ridiculous thought. Surely I would have remembered that! I took my time getting ready, soaking in the old tub, and enjoying the spaciousness of the bathroom. I was even amused by the bidet, a rare sight in North America and Britain.

When I arrived in the kitchen the others were back and seated. I entered to a chorus of "Good morning".

"Did you sleep well?" asked Madame Marique.

"Yes, thank you, surprisingly well."

"Good. Well, I hope you all like eggs for breakfast. I have made them perhaps a little different for you."

Different was right. They were fantastic. Lightly scrambled, flavoured with herbs and spices, they were served in toast shells, and looked and smelled absolutely wonderful.

"I have also some sauce, if you would care to try it over the eggs. Some people prefer it, some do not."

It was like a Hollandaise sauce, but creamier, and with a delicate lemon flavour. We were all enthusiastic in our praise.

"What do you call this, madame?" asked Nicki.

"Oh, the egg dish is just '*Oeufs Brouillés aux Herbes*', and the sauce is my version of '*Sauce Suprême*' with black pepper and lemon. I am happy you enjoy it. There are croissants with fresh cream cheese and strawberry jam as well. Please, do not leave my table hungry. And there is more coffee when you are ready."

When we pulled ourselves away, we were stuffed. It took no time at all to pack the car, say our farewells to Madame Marique, and head for the main road. I was driving, and in a couple of minutes we were back on N369 heading toward Diksmuide.

The questions all came at once.

"Who did you call last night?"

"What happened with the police in France?"

"Are they still looking for us?"

I had my answers ready.

"Hold it! One at a time. I called a friend who is quite high up in the Foreign Office. He informed me that the Paris police had now realized that this whole thing was an internal problem with the Paris underworld, and that by morning the alert to detain a Canadian and a Briton for questioning would be called off. I can only hope he's right."

There were cheers in the car. The mood of the other three was almost as bright as it had been the day before on our drive to Paris. I recognized that I was unable to rationalize the events, ergo: I felt that I was not cut out for this kind of work. I was still resolved that I would see Hammond and withdraw from any future involvement. That determination alone was giving me some of the feeling of relief that the others were sharing.

In what seemed to be a very short time we were near Ostend. The sights of the Belgian countryside had shortened the trip—the villages and hamlets, copses of trees, glimpses of castles and cathedrals, all contributing to an orderly beauty which was part nature and part loving care.

Without any difficulty we followed the signs for the cross-channel ferries, and I took the option of purchasing the tickets on board Sealink's *Princess Josephine Carlotta*, or as everyone called it, the *'PJC'*.

House, Nicki, and Marijke went to find seats on the promenade deck, and I proceeded to the purser's office to pay for our passage. There were only a few people in the queue, so I didn't have to wait long to step up to the wicket. I was being served by the purser himself, as the three rings on his sleeve indicated.

"I'd like to pay for my car and passengers, please."

"How many people are travelling?"

"Four, including the driver."

"What is the make of the car?"

"It's a 1961 Mark II Jaguar 4-door saloon."

"Is this your car, sir, or one on hire?"

"It's mine. Do you need the registration papers?"

There was a pause as we looked at each other. A faint smile appeared at the corners of his mouth as he repeated his question.

"Is this your car, sir, or one on hire?"

"I've already told you, it's m. . . oh!"

I stopped in embarrassment, flushing.

"I beg your pardon. I didn't. . . I mean. . . !"

He just kept looking at me as I floundered. Then I came out of my funk.

"I would never dream of hiring one."

"Then," he smiled broadly, "You are indeed a fortunate man."

I passed over an envelope which I had obtained from Madame

Marique that morning. In it I had placed the Fodor's guide, complete with bookmark, and the Union Jack pin.

We completed this and the ticket transaction, and I left as he wished me a good crossing. He was still smiling, and I was annoyed that he must have thought I was a bumbling fool. Well, what could I expect—I was a rank amateur in the spy business.

I found the other three on deck. They had secured seats for us all, and they were busily munching on a small box of Bruyerre chocolates, one of the best choclatiers in Belgium.

"I've managed to save you a few, David," said Marijke, "but House said we shouldn't in case you weren't feeling well and that they might make you ill. He said it was for your own good."

"Of course, Little Neddie," said he as Grytpype-Thynne, "we wouldn't want you heaving to into the English Channel. Think of the bottlers, lad. I'm told that '62 is going to be a wonderful year. Why, you can already savour the bouquet."

"Which only confirms," I stated, sniffing the air, "that there is definitely something fishy about this. I think I can manage a couple of these without feeding the seagulls. Where did you get them?"

"From Madame Marique," said Nicki. "They were a little gift, she said. Evidently she represents Bruyerre to supplement her Bed and Breakfast. Such a generous, charming lady."

House and Nicki decided to have a stroll around the deck, leaving Marijke and me sitting to hold on to the places. It was very pleasant in the sun, surrounded by the blue of the North Sea, but I sensed we both had things to say which were difficult to put into words.

"I think you are much better today, David, but I also think that in Paris something happens which is very bad for you. I think it makes much problems for you. If you want, I will listen. I like to help you, if I can."

I hesitated, trying to find the words.

"I want to tell you, Marijke, but I am afraid. It's not you—it's who you work for. I feel I can trust you—I want to trust you, and yet there are some things which, if I told you, might put you in a terrible position. I don't want to compromise you, and I don't want you in a position which might make you choose between protecting me or saving yourself. I won't do that to either of us. Do you understand?"

"Yes. . . yes. . . I understand. But it is important that you know you can trust me with anything. Now, we say no more about it."

I put my arm around her and held her close. Even with all of the people about us, it was as if we were alone. We caressed each other with our eyes, and occasionally with our lips, and I felt at the same time the greatest happiness and the deepest despair. On the one hand I was so close to Marijke, and yet, on the other, there was a gulf between us which might never be bridged. I wondered if I were losing my mind.

We docked in Dover after the 2-hour crossing, the time change making it 10:00am in the UK. I had some formalities concerning the car, as I was, in a sense, re-importing it. I had to produce proof of length of ownership, and sign forms indicating that I would export it from Britain within the year, or pay all duties and taxes from which I had been exempt. Everything went smoothly, and, much to my surprise, there was an unexpected bonus: I was presented a road-tax disc for three months at no charge. At least some things went as well or better than anticipated.

The uniformed people at the terminus made me nervous, although no one had looked askance at us when we had gone through customs and immigration. There were several police officers about, but they didn't seem to be looking for anyone. Still, I was relieved when we drove away and got outside Dover.

Both House and Nicki wanted to go into London, so we drove back a different way, this time using the A2 through Canterbury. We had intended driving without a stop, but breakfast had been early, and as we were leaving Canterbury we decided to find a pub and have a sandwich. This was accomplished at the Drover's Arms in Hambledown, and then we pushed on, slowing only for the traffic in the Chatham-Rochester area.

Nicki directed me to her place in East London.

"When you get to Mile End Road just turn left and stop, please, David. I just live on the other side in Trinity Green."

"Do you share, Nicki, or is it your place?" asked Marijke.

"No, it's not mine," she laughed. "I share with three other girls who work in the City or on Fleet Street. We live in a converted almshouse. The owner did a smashing job of fixing it up, but he's away in the Far East for the BBC. He won't be back for at least three years. It's great being this close to work."

I stopped the car, and Nicki and House got out. I did, too, to help get their cases out of the boot. As I handed Nicki hers, I decided to ask for her co-operation.

"Is it too much to ask that you forget about what happened in Paris, Nicki? I know you work for a newspaper, but I'm afraid that this could come back to haunt me someday if there were any publicity about it."

She gave me a smile. "I'm not a reporter, David, and my guess is that it won't even make the London papers. Most local crime stories stay in the city of origin, unless there are national or international implications. From what you've told me, this one will be for Parisians only. Consider it forgotten."

"Thanks," I mumbled, giving her a peck on the cheek. If she only knew, I thought.

"Enough of that, you rotten swine," said Bluebottle's voice. House patted me on the shoulder. "Call me, old son, won't you? Let me know what's going on?"

Marijke and I waved as we pulled away.

"Where to?"

"I must go home to my flat on Kensington Square, David."

"Are you free later? Do you want to go out this evening, or perhaps just be together?"

"That would be nice, but tonight it's not possible. I am on duty at the embassy for twelve hours from 6:00pm."

"What kind of duty? Or are you allowed to tell me?"

"It's just to have an embassy official present. We know where all the important people can be reached, and in an emergency we can contact them. Some routine things we can take care of without disturbing the senior officials. We all take our turn at weekend duty. It's not so bad. I write letters and read, and there is a cot for us so we can sleep some."

"Are you alone in the building?"

She laughed. "Why, do you want to visit me? Unfortunately, there are two security people on duty at all times, and even at night some people come in to work. The minister counsellor is often there, and Mr. Nalishkin spends much time there at night."

I bet he does, I thought.

"What about tomorrow? Do you have any plans?"

She was silent for a moment.

"Yes," she said softly, "I have plans for tomorrow."

"Uh. . . oh," I stammered, my heart sinking like a stone.

"Something is wrong?"

"I guess I was hoping we could spend the day together," I said, trying to keep the disappointment out of my voice.

"Then this is a happy coincidence," she said with a smile, "for these are my plans, too." She saw the look on my face. "I'm sorry if I tease you, David. Do you prefer I don't do this?"

I laughed. "No, love, just be yourself. That's who I'm falling in love with."

She looked at me, startled, and kept looking for the longest time. I couldn't find any more words, so I just kept driving and glancing her way. There was almost a look of fear on her face, and then she relaxed, put her head on my shoulder, and we continued on to Kensington Square.

When we arrived at her flat we stood beside the car for a few minutes, just looking at each other and holding hands.

"You come for me at eleven tomorrow?"

I nodded. "What will we do?"

"I decide. Perhaps we stay overnight." She smiled, shyly. "You are crazy, David Baird. Maybe I start to love you, too."

She kissed me quickly, dashed into her flat, and left me in a complete daze. I stayed there, leaning against the car, and stared at the door for several minutes.

When I had recovered and driven away, I stopped at a call box on Bayswater Road and put through my call to Hammond. I waited for the required procedures, but I was connected immediately.

"Hello, Minstrel. No problems with the crossing, I take it?"

"No, sir, no bother at all."

"Good. Now, about our meeting. Come to the Royal Albert Hall tonight at 2030. Go to the artists' entrance. Do you know it?"

"I sang in the Royal Choral Society for three years, sir."

"Then you know exactly where I mean. Tell the attendant you want dressing room 8. I'll see you there."

"Sir, I haven't changed my mind."

"2030, Minstrel."

He's not happy, I thought, on my way home. Still, I'd been involved in something quite unnecessary, and it tainted the way I felt about the whole affair. I hoped he would understand.

Back at the flat I parked, went in, waved at the week-end man, and walked up to my floor. I opened the door, stopped abruptly, and sniffed the air.

Not again, I raged. This time it was different—not BO, but cologne, and Old Spice at that. It was strong, and that could mean he was still here. I walked softly, scanning the living room. Nothing. Kate's flat? Perhaps. I'd check mine first.

The kitchen opened to the dining room. I could see there was no one there. That left my bathroom and bedroom. The bathroom door was open. There was no place to hide. My bedroom was next. On top of my dresser in the corner there was an antique mirror. Before I walked in I glanced at it.

He was behind the door.

In his hand was a gun.

THIRTEEN

Moscow, U.S.S.R.— the same day

General Josef Dmitrienko answered the light tap on the door of his apartment on Marxa Prospeckt.

"Come in, Bren." They walked through to his study. "What is so urgent?"

"This afternoon I read a signal which reported the death of one of our agents in Paris yesterday. His codename was Dragon."

"That bastard. Good riddance. What happened?"

"Paris station thinks it was a British courier. He was shoved out a window."

"What are they basing it on?"

"Dragon was holding the Englishman for our people, and an Englishman was seen leaving the area in company with a Canadian."

"I don't follow, Bren. What's the significance?"

"I had a call from Marijke. She was in Paris yesterday."

"Did she say anything about Dragon—anything at all?"

"Nothing."

"What's the connection?"

"Marijke was travelling with a singer, her present assignment."

"Well?"

"He's Canadian, and they were accompanied by a British army officer."

"Does anyone else know?"

"Doubtful. It was a personal call from Marijke. Even if it were monitored I don't think anyone would make the connection."

The general was thoughtful.

"Leave it with me, Bren."

London, England—the same day

I stared at his image in the mirror as the anger and frustration of the previous day caught up with me. It was an effort to hold back, fighting for control and focus. What was the word Sergeant Kobayashi had us memorize? SADAI, that was it. Surprise and Disarm and Incapacitate. Thank you, Sergeant.

I hit the door hard with my body. It was solid wood, and went back like a hammer. I grabbed the handle and did it again. Pulling the door as I leapt into the room, I destroyed his cover. There was blood on his face and he was dazed, but still the gun in his right hand came up.

I kicked, catching him on the wrist, and the gun fell. He lunged at me. I let him come, then fell back across the bed as I grasped his lapels, my feet arching him up and over me with his own momentum. I released my hold, giving him a final foot-thrust. He flew over me, landing head first against the wall. His neck might have snapped, but, no, he tried to rise. I jumped onto the bed, and as he came up I kicked, catching him square on the jaw. He went down in a heap and didn't move.

I retrieved his gun. It was a Walther PPK. The kind the pros carried. Well now, I thought, let's see what kind of pro he is.

I kept the gun pointed at him. The safety was off, and the indicator pin was protruding through the top of the slide, so there was a round in the chamber. I approached him warily. If he had so much as stirred I would have fired. I placed the muzzle against his head, waited a moment, then started through his pockets. Bingo. On the first try I found his wallet. I backed around the bed and began flipping through it.

Oh, Jesus! There was a card with the US eagle on it, stating that Anthony Cippola was with the US Department of Agriculture. Not on your fucking life, *paesano.* Then a business card. This one gave the address of the American Embassy—24 Grosvenor Square—and stated that Mr. Cippola was a liaison officer on the Joint Agricultural Review Commission. Balls! The only connection I could see with farming was how high they were piling the shit. I couldn't call anyone—the tap was undoubtedly still on my phone, and until I knew what was going on I didn't want the KGB to become involved in anymore of my business. I decided to wake him up and see what he was doing here.

There were spirits of ammonia in my medicine cabinet. I grabbed a facecloth, then the pitcher of ice water from the refrigerator. Warily I approached him again—I didn't want to find him playing 'possum and jumping me. He didn't move, and as I held the gun on him with my right hand, I wafted the ammonia under his nose with my left. When he started to groan and move a bit, I stepped back, and from a safe distance gave him a splash of icy water in the face.

He was shocked awake, almost jumping up.

"Hold it!" I yelled. "Move slowly or I'll shoot!"

He settled back on the floor, gradually taking in his surroundings. He was very confused, and unable to speak. The blow on his head had been severe. He probably had a concussion.

"Can you hear me?" I asked, loudly.

He focused on me for the first time, then nodded his head, wincing as he did so.

"I'm going to throw you a damp cloth. Wipe your face and neck with it. Don't try anything. Or I'll shoot."

"Not much chance," he croaked. "I can hardly move."

I dipped the cloth and tossed it to him. He began using it.

"Who are you, and why were you in my apartment?"

"Tony Cippola. I work for the U.S. Department of Agriculture. I must have come to the wrong apartment—it's all a mistake."

"Bullshit! How did you get in here without a key, and what was the gun for? I'll call the embassy or Dwight Vandenburg and find out what they've got to say about you. My guess is that you're CIA, and if you don't talk to me I'll call right now."

"Okay, okay... don't call the embassy until you hear me out, at least. Can I get up?"

"Yes, but slowly, and then walk to the living room and sit down. I'm right behind you."

He struggled to get up, but I wouldn't help him—I wasn't taking any chances.

"Jesus, my head," he muttered as he went through the door.

He looked in the bathroom, stopped, then looked back at me.

"I'm sorry! Don't shoot! Please!"

He grabbed for the toilet and threw up. I waited at the door, holding the gun on him in case it was a trick. After the fourth heave I thought he must be a pretty good actor or it was for real.

He cleaned himself up at the sink and came out. I indicated that he should proceed as before, and he walked a few steps, stopping again.

"I know I'm a pain in the ass, but have you got any aspirin? My head's like a sledgehammer."

"Stand still and I'll get it."

I grabbed it from the medicine cabinet, taking the bathroom glass and the ice water with my left hand. We walked slowly to the living room. I handed him the aspirin and the water, and he downed three tablets.

"Lie on the sofa," I said, "and keep your hands in plain sight. I didn't check for another weapon, and if you have one, don't try to get it or you'll get shot. Now, tell me the truth or I'll call Dwight Vandenberg, and I'm not kidding. Are you CIA?"

He hesitated, reluctant to break one of their unwritten rules. I held the gun on him, walking over to pick up the phone.

"Christ, man, hold on. You talk to Vandenberg about me I'm finished."

"Well, what's the answer?"

"Off the record? Yeah, I'm CIA."

I put down the phone. "What's your job?"

"I'm what's called a case officer. I recruit and run agents, collect information any way I can."

"Why are you in my flat?"

"One of my informants tells me something strange. He's an Arab who works for an oil company. It's about Cal Fletcher and a missing list. I do some nosing around and I damn near get my head bitten off. They tell me it's classified, that I better forget about it or I'll end up in Finland countin' reindeer turds.

"But something's really wrong here, so I call this guy at Langley I can trust, and he tells me the official word is that there isn't any fucking list, that it never existed, and the file on it is closed. See, but I know there's this wild hunt going on, and my informant tells me the KGB is in it up to their goddam keesters. I figure I can't let it go."

"So you go on a scouting expedition all by yourself with no official sanction?"

"Yep. I knew Fletcher had lived here, so I wanted to have a snoop around. I know his kid has the apartment next door. I figure I might come up with something."

"Did you?"

"No, and I checked just about everywhere. I was just gonna leave when you got home. Heard you were in France so I thought I had plenty o' time. Shit, I didn't even know it was you until you popped me in the bedroom. Jesus Christ, for a singer you're one mean son-of-a-bitch. Where'd ya learn all that shit?"

"In the army. Now, what am I going to do with you? Should I hand you over to Scotland Yard, or should I call your head of station, or whatever the hell they call him?"

"Either way, I'm finished. Look, I'm sorry the way things went down, but I was only trying to find out what this cover-up is all about. There's something real bad happening, and I dunno who's involved so I couldn't make it official. Maybe I'm outta line, but we got too many questions and not enough answers."

I thought about it for a few minutes. If I turned him in, I would only draw attention to myself again. And there was always the possibility that he was telling the truth. Perhaps he could be an ally, in the event I needed one. Decision.

"Sit up. I'm sorry I hurt you, but you didn't exactly make an appointment. You'd better see a doctor. You probably have a concussion. Here's the deal. If you get anything on that list, or if you hear anything about Cal Fletcher, then I want you to fill me in. I'm responsible for Fletcher's daughter and I wouldn't mind some answers of my own. If you agree, then I forget about your visit."

"Suits me. You coulda flushed me, so I'll play fair with you. If I can help with anything, call me, and we'll meet." He hesitated. "One thing, can I have my piece back? Otherwise I'm in trouble."

I released the clip, emptied it, ejected the cartridge in the chamber, snapped the clip back and tossed him the gun. He stared.

"Shit, I shoulda' taken music," he complained.

"I hope you're not driving, Tony."

"No, I'll get a cab outside."

I retrieved his wallet, kept one of his cards, and opened the door for him. He held out his hand, and I took it.

"Thanks, Dave. I owe you."

He went out, wobbling a little, then turned to me again.

"You ever think of changin' jobs, lemme know."

He gave me a crooked grin, then headed down the stairs.

* * *

I took a long soak in the tub—more to relax than to scrub. What had it been now—five days? Less than a week ago I was leading a relatively simple life—singing, coping with producers, agents, club managers—well, maybe not that simple, after all. But this was ridiculous—phone taps, KGB, CIA, MI whatever, grenades, pickpockets, that disaster in Paris, and now a fight in my own flat. Enough, enough, enough! Even a month at the Chiswick Empire couldn't be this much trouble.

I relaxed in the tub, got a couple of hours of sleep, then cold-showered to re-start the engine. Toad-in-the-hole with coffee in Knightsbridge, and I arrived at the Royal Albert Hall with a few minutes to spare. I presented myself at the artists' entrance.

"Can I help you, sir?" asked the attendant.

"Dressing room 8, please."

I thought he looked at me strangely.

"Take the stairs down one floor, turn right. It's the second door on the left."

As I walked down I could hear the sounds of the Royal Philharmonic Orchestra being led through Vaughan Williams' *London Symphony* by Sir Adrian Boult. Strange, I thought, how certain composers are able to evoke the feelings of their homeland in their music, and become identified with it forever. Vaughan Williams in England, Sibelius in Finland, Wagner in Germany, to think of a few. There is something mystical about it which defies analysis. I wished I were in the hall listening.

Dressing room 8 was open and empty. I sat down in one of the chairs to wait, but within a minute Colonel Hammond had appeared. I stood as he entered.

"David, I'm glad to see you're all right. Sit, please."

We did.

"Before you say anything, Colonel, I think you should know that I can't go on with this. The secrecy stuff is one thing, but yesterday I was involved in the senseless death of a man that'll haunt me the rest of my life, even if he was a sadistic bastard.

"On top of the thing at Charing Cross, it's too much. What am I supposed to do—pretend it didn't happen? Just so much dust that gets swept out by the broom? This could affect my music. My sanity. I don't think I can take any more."

We had another of those long pauses. I had said my piece, and I guess Hammond was looking for the right way to respond.

"His name was Karl Szrubek, at least that's what he called himself. He worked for Bulgaria's State Security Service, the *Darjavna Sugurnost* or DS. The DS is completely dominated by the KGB, and the Soviets are smart enough to use DS agents for their dirtiest jobs. Szrubek's codename was Dragon."

"Have the Soviets or Bulgarians become officially involved because of what happened to Szrubek?"

"Of course not. They're much too smart for that. Szrubek is an orphan. There is nothing official to link him with either the Bulgarian or Soviet governments. No one came forward to identify the body or claim it. They've torn the page out of the book, so to speak. He didn't exist."

"How do you know this?"

"Mainly from the French SDECE. They've got a file on him which goes back several years. They've never been able to pin anything definite on him in France. They couldn't make anything stick. He kept his nose quite clean there, but used it as the base of his not-so-nice activities in other countries."

"What sort of activities?"

"Terrorism, assassinations, arms smuggling, drug trafficking—you name it, and Szrubek has been involved. SDECE says he was a master at torture and extracting information. If you hadn't put an end to him he would have gotten away with the murder of our agent in Paris—there was nothing to incriminate him."

"It doesn't affect my decision, sir. Sorry."

"Tell me the whole sequence, please, David."

I poured it all out—the meeting, the walk, the Frenchman's body, the fall, the flight to Belgium—every facet I could recall. It took time, and

Hammond didn't interrupt once. It was almost a catharsis, in fact, I felt better when it was out. I realized that keeping it inside me for the past day had caused it to fester. Hammond was pensive as I finished.

"Well done, David," he said quietly. "I've been asked to state the appreciation of Her Majesty's Government for salvaging what could have been a disaster on an international scale. That is no word of a lie, please believe me. And the French government is thankful to be rid of a thorn over which they had no control—unofficially, of course."

"I still feel. . . " I began.

"Before you say it again, let me tell you one more thing. Last Tuesday Karl Szrubek travelled to Gibralter. On Wednesday he was seen in a café talking to a man we couldn't identify at the time, but in the follow-up to the Straitsair bombing we now know it was Naheed, the cargo handler who planted the bomb.

"Szrubek paid him, gave him the assignment, and handed him the case with the bomb. David, you killed the man who murdered the Fletchers!"

My mind was in turmoil. I almost felt elated. The Fletchers' deaths had been avenged! My God! What was happening to me? Could I become so callous so quickly? If I continued, could this become second nature, until I didn't give it a second thought?

Hammond sensed my struggle.

"David—it shouldn't have happened. I don't want you put in these situations—it was never my intention. I want you to provide information, but only the information you acquire by happenstance. From here on it's strictly observation. Could you live with that?"

I couldn't answer immediately. I had come here determined to get off the merry-go-round, and now I was faltering. 'The best laid plans,' rhymed Robbie Burns, and mine were 'gang aft aglae.'

"Okay, Colonel. I'll stick it out for now, at least until the end of the cruise."

"Thank you for that," he said, softly. "But let me tell you—you make a damn good agent."

"Funny, if that's an offer then it's the second one today."

"What? What do you mean?"

I told him of my confrontation with Tony Cippola.

"Most peculiar," he mused. "We've wondered if there really were such a list, of course, but what on earth is going on at the American

Embassy? It sounds like a faction row to me—maybe a power struggle between the CIA and NSA. Those things happen, unfortunately—we've had our share. That's one reason I want to keep you out of the mainstream. No one knows who you are, and that's the way I want it left. There's far less chance of being exposed by a casual remark, or even a deliberate remark."

"Deliberate?"

"I'm sure you know about the Burgess-Maclean debacle, George Blake, who is in Wormwood Scrubs for forty-two years, and now Kim Philby. Some of us are not convinced that the cancer has been rooted out. I have some suspicions of my own. It forces many of us to keep our assets to ourselves. You are one asset that I don't intend to compromise."

"Let's hope you're right, sir. I think I've had my fill of the spy business as such. Information-gathering should be a lot easier on the nerves."

I remembered the Facel Vega.

"Since I'm hanging in for another inning, sir, could you find out who owns a dark blue Facel Vega registration number MWE 473? It has diplomatic plates on it."

"Do you want to tell me about it, David?"

"Not yet, sir. If it pans out gold I'll fill you in."

He frowned at that one.

"Rather quaint colonial expression, that."

Hammond stood to leave, then recalled something.

"By the way, the Templaars woman you asked about."

My heart jumped. Steady, I thought.

"What have you heard, Colonel?"

"Not a lot. Seems hard to pick up anything. Almost as if she's been whitewashed from the records. But from the bit we've gleaned about her training in Russia, she's most definitely KGB. Does this help?"

He swept out.

Yessir. Thank you, sir. Three bags full, sir. That helps a bunch.

And the merry-go-round goes 'round.

FOURTEEN

Richmond, England—Sunday, June 17, 1962

He'd been up for an hour, though it was only 7:00am. It was hard to sleep since Daphne's death. He looked out at the green, wondering if he should call this early. Making up his mind, he went to the phone.

"It's me. Did you get a name?"

"Yeah, I got it. But I don't feel right about telling you. There were no charges laid. It wasn't his fault."

"I don't give a monkey's fuck whose fault it was! You owe me, you bastard! There's not a penny more coming your way if you don't give me that name. Now, last chance. 'Oo is 'e?"

"His name is David Baird. He's a singer. He lives on St. John's Wood Road in a block of flats. Drives a green Jag."

"Thank you very much. Very wise of you."

Smiling, he put the receiver down and got ready to go out.

London, England—the same morning

I awoke from a deep sleep with the sound of the door buzzer. Stumbling to the intercom, I answered to hear Wicks' cheery voice.

"Mo'ning, Mr. Baird. I 'ope I didn't wike you up."

"It's all right, Wicks. It isn't Monday, is it? I couldn't have slept through. You're not usually here on week-ends."

"Naow, Mr. Baird," he laughed, "me mite's a bit shovel an' pick, so I told 'im I'd tike 'is shift. There's been a delivery for you, sir. Do you want me to fetch it up the apples and pears?"

Wicks loved throwing Cockney rhyming slang at me, but at least he made it easy by leaving both words in. Cockneys can have a conversation which will leave you dumbfounded.

"Yerss," I said as Mate from the Goons, "just run it up the apples, Mite, while I get me titfer an' a spot of the 'Oly."

Wicks rang off with a wicked laugh. I had barely got my robe before he was at the door. We exchanged a bit more repartee, and he went off chuckling.

The parcel was from British-Lion Export and Import, or so the label read, but I had a pretty good idea that such a company only existed on paper somewhere. I opened it partially, stopping when I saw khaki-coloured clothing. I wasn't in any hurry to put a uniform on again.

Then I remembered. Marijke had said we might stay overnight. Now what? I was due at Dunsfold by 0700 tomorrow. Well, whatever happens, happens. I checked that the uniform was complete, packing it in my carry-all together with my Lotus Veldtschoen military-style shoes. I remembered braces for the trousers, threw in my flight suit, and set my trenchcoat out in case it rained.

I had plenty of time before I was to meet Marijke, so I got ready at my leisure. I knew I was blocking what Hammond had told me about her—in fact, I had shut down on everything connected to the world of espionage since last night. That's probably why I had had a good sleep. Now the uniform was bringing it back, and I resented the intrusion.

I stopped for coffee at a Kona Coffee House in Earl's Court, arriving at Kensington Square just before eleven o'clock. I knocked on the door, and it opened to the object of my anticipation.

"Good morning. How was your duty shift?"

"Good morning, David. Oh, not so bad. Please come in. I am almost ready to go."

I stepped in, closing the door, but I couldn't take my eyes off her. I wanted a sign or signal that things were the way I had thought when I left her last night. She caught the look in my eyes, shook her head in an imperceptible warning, then kissed me hard on the mouth.

"Don't say anything important," she whispered, then hurried off to the kitchen.

"Can you carry this to the car, please, David?"

I followed her to the kitchen where she was indicating a large hamper.

"What's this?"

"Oh, just in case we get hungry later," she laughed, heading back to the living room.

She picked up a navy blue cardigan, draped it around her shoulders, and turned to face me. With a navy and white summer skirt, crisp white blouse and white sandals, she looked like a model from Vanity Fair. The picture was breathtaking.

"Let us go, then," she smiled, taking her white purse and heading for the door.

Stowing the hamper in the boot, we climbed in and I started the engine. Then I just sat, looking at her with a smile.

"What are you doing, David? Are we not going?"

I laughed. "This is your day, remember? I don't even know where to point the car."

"Oh, I forget. Can you drive to Brighton?"

"Sure."

I slipped the car into drive, then hesitated.

"I love you, Marijke," I said softly.

"And I love you, David Baird," she responded, eyes sparkling.

Thus assured, I headed for Brighton.

I had turned the radio on to the BBC Light Programme, and we listened to David Jacobs playing records. Much to my surprise and Marijke's delight, he played one of mine—"Polka Dots and Moonbeams"—and I sang along with it.

The conversation had been light, warm, friendly, and most pleasant, but I had been waiting for an explanation of her warning at the flat. When nothing came after half an hour, I couldn't contain my curiosity.

"Marijke, why did you warn me not to say anything important when we were in your flat?"

"Because I know the flat has listening devices. It really belongs to the embassy—they lease it—and they have given it to me to use."

"Why is it bugged?"

"For some time it was used as a safe-house by the KGB, and they planted hidden cameras and microphones. It is no longer used for this purpose, but the equipment is still there, and it is functional. I can never be sure if it is turned on or not."

"Doesn't this bother you?"

"Not really. In the Soviet Union you expect they watch you. I am careful in the flat, and I don't invite personal friends in case something is said which is dangerous."

I nearly asked what had been going on Thursday night, when I'd stood outside to the sounds of music and laughter, but I caught myself just in time. Forget it, buddy, I admonished myself. I also wanted to query her about the KGB. In a way she had opened the door, but I sensed that this was neither the time nor place.

Passing through the Sussex Downs, we were nearing our destination.

"Do you want to go right into Brighton?"

"Oh, no, not immediately. Can you drive to a village called Rottingdean? It is outside Brighton."

"I know Rottingdean. The English writer Rudyard Kipling lived there. We'll have to go into Brighton first and then take the shore road east to Rottingdean. It won't take long."

The view of the English Channel was quite unobstructed on the right, while on the left the mansions and gardens had continued unabated since we had left Brighton. The sun was occasionally peaking through a high overcast, and this added a lustre of light and shade to the beauty of our surroundings. It was also a warm day, unusual for the south coast of England.

"Can you stop the car, David, just after this corner?" I did as I was asked, then looked at her expectantly.

"Now we get out for a few minutes."

We did, and Marijke indicated that we should walk back the way we had come. She was holding my arm, and she drew back on it, bringing us to a halt.

"You see this house on the right? The one with the stone fence and the iron bars on top?"

"Yes. What about it?"

"The Soviet government rents this house for the ambassador and senior government officials when they want to be out of London for talks or private meetings, or just to have a few days off."

We stood looking at the building, or what we could see of it because of the fence and the shrubbery. I was perplexed.

"Why are you telling me this, Marijke?"

She looked at me with an enigmatic expression which left me bewildered. I didn't know how to read it.

"There are many things which I tell you today. This is only one. Now, I am hungry. Do you know where we can place a blanket and have what is called a picnic?"

I knew the very spot. We went back to the car, continuing east. In a short while I found a convenient lay-by, parked the car, and we got the food and the blanket from the trunk.

"It's a long walk, but it'll be worth it. Do you mind?"

"No, I love to walk. The hamper is too heavy?"

"No, it's not that big, and there is a shoulder strap. I won't even notice it."

So saying, we started out, following the line of the Cuckmere River which had cut into the chalk of the cliff. Gradually the stream dropped farther and farther down, while we stayed on top of the promontory, leaving us a few hundred feet above sea level. It was a shear drop down, so we stayed well back of the edge.

Now, across the water of Cuckmere Haven on our left, was a succession of peaks, seven stark white chalk humps of varying heights stretching for about five miles toward Beachy Head. The cap of green vegetation right up to the chalk face and on the dipping vales between, sometimes right to the water's edge, enhanced the sharp contrast of texture and colour.

"Oh!" exclaimed Marijke. "This is wonderful! So beautiful!"

We walked as far as we could, then stopped about twenty feet from the cliff. Putting down the blanket and hamper, we stood and gazed across the mile of water which separated us from the start of the chalk cliffs. The sun was stronger now, and the water gleamed an irridescent blue, throwing back the sparkling reflections of the brilliant white peaks.

Marijke put her arm around me, leaning back into me. I kissed the top of her head and held her close.

"Have they a name, David?" she whispered.

"They're called the Seven Sisters, and each Sister has a name, though not a very feminine one. This little bay is called Cuckmere Haven, and starting from there they are called Haven Brow, Short Brow, Rough Brow, Bran Point, Flagstaff Point, Baily's Hill, and Went Hill Brow. Not very romantic, are they?"

"Oh, I think they are. The names are real, not just made up. The Seven Sisters stand there for centuries, watching generations of people come and go. They are still there when we are gone. It takes my breath away. Do you feel it, too?"

"Yes, very much. I sometimes think magnificent natural places have a personality—a presence that looks at us poor mortals with pity. We run around like fools, chasing the unattainable all our lives, sometimes causing wars and destruction, and they sit there serene, watching us in our frantic insanity."

Marijke turned suddenly, her arms going around my neck, pulling me to her and kissing me passionately. I responded instantly, and the fire I had experienced on that first day at Virginia Water was rekindled with terrifying abandon. I fought myself, lest I lose control and become the animal I sensed within me. I was frightened of myself for the first time in my life.

Marijke pulled back. There was a wildness in her eyes.

"Now, David! I want you now! Take me! I want you inside me!"

It was a cry of anguish, of longing, of pain.

I threw the blanket out, we fell on it, and virtually tore the clothes off each other. I grasped her breasts, biting her nipples, and she raked my back with her nails. I ran my hand down her body and she spread her legs wide. My fingers went inside to incredible heat and wetness. Grasping my erection, she guided it into her as I thrust forward hard. She cried out, but held me tightly, wrapping her legs around me, matching thrust for thrust.

In the frenzy I lost all sense of being. A white light approached me, blinding in its intensity. I was striving toward it. It was the meaning of life, and I reached for it, but I knew if I grasped it I would become part of it forever, that earthly life would end. Still I strove, and just as I was about to enter immortality I heard Marijke shout *"O Gott! O Gott! O Gott!"* and the light exploded in my face, my body reacting in spasms as the rays danced about, and, gradually, oh, so gradually, ebbed away.

I regained my senses slowly, aware that I was still inside her, and that neither of us had moved. I was still hard, but I moved as though to pull out. She resisted, holding me in her with her heels on my buttocks. I kissed her, gently, and looked at her eyes, as full of wonder as my own.

"Now," she whispered, "now make love to me."

The walls of her vagina contracted around my penis, and desire returned instantly. But this time it was slow, and gentle, and caressing, and the peak arrived gradually, with a tumbling down the other side which left us both shaken and exhausted.

I looked into her eyes, into a depth which passed all understanding. In that instant I knew that there could be no one else for me in this life. Tears filled my eyes.

"I love you, Marijke. I don't understand what has happened, but I know that I will love you forever."

"And I love you, David. You give me a happiness which I never expect to find."

We dressed rather quickly, for we were outdoors on a beautiful day, and it was quite possible that others would come along. So far we had been lucky, and it was just as well, for I think we would have been oblivious even if a commando of Royal Marines had scaled the cliff to sit, cheering us on.

We were both ravenous now, and Marijke pulled salads, sandwiches, and wine, from the hamper, and we ate with gusto and satisfaction. Sipping coffee from a Thermos flask, we sat shoulder to shoulder to regard the Seven Sisters, who looked back, aloof.

"I wonder what they think of us?" pondered Marijke, quietly.

"Probably that we're just another couple of silly humans in the passing parade."

"No, I think not. Somehow I think they understand we discover something wonderful in their presence, and in some strange way we become part of them, and they a part of us forever."

It was an eery statement, and what made it more so was that I understood what Marijke had said, for I felt the same way.

We gathered up our things and began the walk back, stopping for a moment just before the Sisters disappeared from view.

"I shall always think of this place and this time with you in my heart, Marijke."

I held her close, and kissed her.

"Something of mystery happens for us, David, and to me this

becomes always our enchanted place."

We stowed everything in the trunk, getting back in the Jag, and for a few minutes, just sat there holding hands.

"Now where?"

"Turn around, please, and go back through Brighton."

The sun was losing ground now to the clouds. Typical of coastal weather, it was ever-changing. We drove back the way we had come, arriving at the Palace Pier intersection.

"Now, can you drive toward Chichester? I think it is along the coast from here."

"Yes—about 25 miles. Does it matter which road we take?"

"I think not. Why?"

"Then we'll take the A27 and go through Arundel. It'll be quicker than the Marine Drive on a Sunday."

Arundel is like something out of Walt Disney. Houses rise in tiers above the river Arun, toward a fairytale castle on one side and a 19th century Gothic cathedral on the other. The castle is inhabited by the Duke of Norfolk, the premier peer of the realm. What is most striking about Arundel is that the architecture of centuries stands side by side with modern development in reasonable harmony.

Marijke asked about dukes and titles, so I explained the honours system as simply as I could as we drove along. The concept bothered her.

"Is it not better for people to be equal? I think the titles cause some people to think they are better than others."

"That happens. But humans function best on a system of hierarchy. Our social structures demand it. If we don't have a system of honours and titles, we create one. The American president's wife is called 'The First Lady', for example, and some people even refer to the whole mystique of the Kennedy presidency as 'Camelot', likening them to King Arthur and the Knights of the Round Table."

"This does not happen in the Soviet Union. We have no titles or honours."

"Sure you do. Even after the revolution new orders were created like the Orders of Lenin and Suvorov, and some ancient ones continued like the Order of Alexander Nevsky, which was founded in the reign of the Empress Catherine. And if someone becomes a 'Hero' of the Soviet Union, it is both a title and an honour. The only difference is that the British have kept what has evolved over centuries of civilized development, and most of the rest of us, in our ignorance, scrap what we have inherited, then create a substitute, all the while pretending it is something else."

Marijke pondered all of this for a few minutes.

"Why does a Canadian know about all of this?"

"I became interested in heraldry, and it sort of grew from there."

There was a brief pause. "Heraldry? What is heraldry?"

"Enough!" I laughed. "Save that one for our next lesson on obsolescent institutions."

She looked at me seriously.

"I hope you don't mind telling me about these things. I have much to learn about western countries. They tell us in the Soviet Union that much of capitalistic countries is decadent. Now I listen to you explain about titles, and it does not seem so bad to me. It would seem highly structured, but, at the same time, adding colour and variety to society." A pause. "When will you be honoured with a title? Will you be Lord Baird of Canada, or just a simple knight like Sir David Baird?"

I looked over. Marijke was smiling broadly—teasing me as usual.

"Why not some good Canadian names? I could be 'the Earl of Moose Jaw', or 'the Marquess of Buctouche', or even 'His Grace, the Duke of Wa-Wa'."

We laughed, our giddiness a mark of the ease we felt in each other's company. There was warmth, there was understanding, there was love, and it was wonderful.

But I broke the bubble when I told her that we were entering Chichester. Suddenly she was sober.

"Can you go toward Wittering, please?"

"West Wittering or East Wittering?" I kidded.

"It doesn't matter. We branch off soon."

I decided to drive through the centre of this old town to let Marijke see it. The spire of the cathedral dominated the horizon, and it fascinated me because the composer Gustav Holst was buried there, as I held him in awe.

Eventually we came to a fork in the road.

"Take the left road, David. We come to a village called Bracklesham Bay."

It took another few minutes.

"Here we are. We can't go any further or we'll be in the water. Now what?"

"Turn left on the street just before the beach. Now, stop by the house on the right with the fence."

It was a large property, about three acres, the Victorian house set almost in the centre and covered by trees. A six-foot stone fence surrounded the property, and there was a massive double gate for cars with a single one for pedestrians. Both were locked with a heavy chain and padlock.

"What is this, Marijke?"

"I will explain later. Now we go in."

She extracted a ring of keys from her purse, locating one which fitted the single gate's lock, and we entered the property. It was a fair distance to the house, and I remarked to myself how secluded it was. At the door Marijke found another key, and we entered to the musty odour of a closed-up house.

"Are you going to tell me where we are, or are we playing games and I must guess?"

I tried to be light-hearted, but Marijke's mood had changed drastically from the bantering in the car. She looked at me with a desperation in her eyes, and then spoke to me in a low voice.

"This house is leased by the KGB. Only six people know about it, all KGB. Even the ambassador has no knowledge. It is leased through cut-outs, and the people who sign the contracts don't know who they lease for. They are paid well, and they are gone."

"Why are you telling me this? What are we doing here?"

She ignored my question.

"The house is used as a safe house for interviews with agents, and very often as a trap for people they are trying to blackmail or force into co-operating. Each of the bedrooms upstairs has equipment for sound and film recording, and also this large living room. There is a central control room through this door, and it monitors everything in the house, including the 'playroom' downstairs."

"The 'playroom'?"

"It is a torture chamber from Middle Ages, with a rack, manacles and chains on walls and table, pulleys with ropes, and all torture equipment you imagine."

I felt a lump in my stomach.

"What's the 'playroom' for?"

"It will surprise you how many people express hidden desire to control someone in a place like this. KGB is very good finding out people who work for different governments and who have these desires. When they find out they can have these fantasies with no limits, they become pawns in the hands of KGB. They come here, maybe once a month, and their victim is supplied, and they do what they wish.

"KGB makes film of everything, and with each visit people sink deeper and deeper, for when they begin on these fantasies they get more sick with each visit." Her voice was choked. "At least once that I know the victim dies in the 'playroom', and if I know of one there are others."

The immensity of this was weighing me down. I felt I was drowning in a morass of human degradation.

"Where do their victims come from?"

"Mainly they are prostitutes hired by the KGB. Sometimes the client brings his own." Her voice dropped. "And sometimes there are special considerations."

"And they supply information in return for this?"

"It is price for admission. Better the information, better the fantasy. Do you want to see 'playroom'? I show you the door."

She walked across the living room into the hall, indicating a door near the kitchen. I followed her.

"No, thanks. I get the picture. But I'd like to know why you brought me here, and why you're telling me all this. Surely it's not safe for us to be here if what you say is true."

"Of the six people who know about this house, four are away in Moscow until tomorrow. One is on duty at the embassy. He must not leave his post for any reason. The other is me."

"Does that mean you are in the KGB?"

"Yes. And so is Vladimir Nalishkin. He is a KGB colonel, and the *rezident* or chief of station in London. You are shocked?"

I considered my answer carefully as I walked to the back of the kitchen and looked out the window to the waterfront.

"I'm not shocked, Marijke. I think I know you. I may not know everything about you, but I know what kind of person you are. You must have a good reason to be in the KGB, and I don't think I should know what it is. But you haven't answered my question. Why are we here?"

"There is secret operation being planned of which I know nothing. Four who have gone to Moscow are involved. In some way they use this house, but I don't know how. I must not ask questions, I only listen. But I know it is very big, and it is very soon."

I feared the answer to the next question.

"Marijke, why me?"

She looked at me, then sighed in resignation.

"I know about you, David. Last night, when I am on duty, I read all the signals which come in. On Friday, a man who works for us in Paris, a Bulgarian, is pushed from a window. It is near Gare de l'Est. He is holding a British agent for KGB in Paris. When they arrive, he is dead. Not one person knows who the British agent is who pushes him. No one but me. You, my darling, are this agent, and one KGB would give anything to find."

I was stunned. I didn't know how to answer her. If I tried to deny it, I would look a fool. Marijke had been with me in Paris, and it was easy for her to piece it together. But to admit to it? I wasn't so sure.

"Let's get outside. This place depresses me."

"We can walk on the beach?"

"Sure, as long as its away from here."

We walked through the hall toward the front door. I jumped when a voice spoke quietly from the living room.

"I think you'd better stop right there, lovebirds."

We both froze and looked wildly into the room. A man in a rather flashy suit stood there, gun in hand. I presumed he was one of the Soviets until Marijke spoke.

"Who are you? Why are you here?"

"My name doesn't matter." There was a trace of cockney inflection. "I'm here to keep an appointment with Mr. David Baird."

"I don't know you. We haven't any appointment. What the hell are you playing at?"

"I hope you 'aven't forgotten your meeting with a lady last Tuesday in the Charing Cross underground station. Her name was Daphne Boggs, or Jackie London, if you prefer."

Marijke gasped. I looked at her, but she shook her head. I responded to the man.

"I haven't forgotten. It was a terrible accident. I didn't want anything like that to happen. I chased her when I caught her stealing my wallet. Who are you, anyway?"

"Daphne was my old lady. You killed her, mate, no matter 'ow it 'appened. Now you're gonna pay for it."

"Then this is between you and me. Let my friend go. It's got nothing to do with her."

"Not a chance. She's 'ad a good look at me. Besides, she's a large part of your punishment, me old lad."

He gave me a crooked grin.

It sent a chill to my soul.

FIFTEEN

"How can you do this?" I fumed. "I didn't try to hurt Daphne. She came after me, for Christ's sake."

"I don't give a shit one way or the other. You caused it to 'appen. When I set out today I wasn't sure 'ow I was going to 'andle it, then when I saw you on the cliff by the ocean I knew exactly what to do. Comin' 'ere gave me the chance I needed."

"You watched us?"

"Yeah, through binoculars. Fucks like a mink, don't she?"

"You've been watching us all day, you snooping bastard. How did you get in here?"

"Easy. Locks are my stock an' trade."

I stared at him, looking for a way to resolve this without anyone getting hurt. He was quite tall and heavy set, but I thought I could handle him. The gun changed the odds considerably. I hadn't counted on Marijke's intervention.

"I think there are things you must know. You interfere with something very serious, and it will be very bad for you."

"You're trying to bluff me, lady, but it won't work. Shut up, or I'll cut you apart right now."

"You make a big mistake, Mr. Styles."

"What?" He recoiled. "'Ow do you know my name?"

"Roger Styles, I think. Jackie called you 'Rog', didn't she?"

"What the bleedin' 'ell's goin' on?"

"I heard all about you from Jackie. Mr. Styles. I think there are things about her you don't know. I work for the Soviet government in London. Do you know what is the KGB?"

"Yeah, I know about them—spies an' all."

"Then perhaps you will be interested to hear that your Jackie was working for the KGB, and that she is a spy?"

"Not on your bleedin' life!"

"Oh yes, this is true, and I show you. I open this door over here." She indicated one at the back. "You permit me?"

"Go ahead. One wrong move and I kill Baird where he stands."

"I don't try anything, Mr. Styles."

Marijke took the ring of keys out, selected one, and unlocked the door. Throwing several switches, she turned lights on, revealing a box room about ten feet square. It seemed to be full of equipment. She hesitated in the doorway.

"I must get something from a file cabinet, Mr. Styles. You can watch me from there."

She stepped in, Styles watching with a growing bewilderment. A couple of minutes elapsed until she reappeared with papers.

"This is agreement which Jackie signs for working with us, Mr. Styles, and a copy of background information we have about her. You live at Richmond Green, I think. There is also a photograph of Jackie. Please, you look."

She handed him the papers. He was completely distracted, and I was about to make an attempt at him, but Marijke caught my eye and warned me off. Styles threw the papers on the floor.

"I didn't know about this. I'm 'aving a hard time believing it. What would Jackie do this for?"

"Money, Mr. Styles. And there is far worse I can show you about Jackie. Things that will disgust you."

"Fuck off! Why should this make any difference, anyway? You're both gonna pay for what happened."

He produced a pair of handcuffs. Marijke intervened again.

"There is something you had better know, Mr. Styles. Please look in that room. Look at the equipment in there, and see if it is turned on."

"What the 'ell for?"

"Do it, Mr. Styles. Your life depends on it."

He walked over, looked in for a moment, still keeping us covered with the gun.

"What the fuck is all this, then?"

"The mirror on the wall is one-way glass, Mr. Styles. The cameras in there see everything in this room. You look inside now. What do you see?"

He jumped back as though struck.

"Bleedin' hell! 'Ow's my face on that Telly?"

"The camera, Mr. Styles. It sends everything that happens here back to London. Even now agents of the KGB are coming. You are a marked man, Mr. Styles. If something happens to us, they hunt you down, they torture you, then they kill you."

"I don't believe you," he muttered unconvincingly.

"Then you make the biggest mistake of your life. You have one chance. Leave, and I tell them don't harm you. They watch you, and if you talk about this house or what you see today they come after you. You have not much time. We have agents close to here they contact by radio. You only get away if you go now."

He weighed up the situation, becoming more agitated.

"Looks like you're in deep shit, old son," I goaded.

"Fuck!" he exclaimed, running for the door, then down to the gate, which was open, and disappearing. We heard a car start, then burn rubber as it tore away.

I let out a long breath as Marijke turned off switches and lights, then closed and locked everything.

"Let us go out of here, David."

We went out the front way, locking the door and then the gate. We followed a path alongside the property which led to the water. We hadn't said much as we walked, but the fresh air and the waves seemed to change the atmosphere from the evil I felt in the house and our meeting with Roger Styles. I put my arm around Marijke as we scrunched on the pebbled beach.

"I don't think he bothers you again, David. He is afraid."

"What about all the things you told him? The video link back to London, for instance. Is any of that true?"

"No, is not true. I switch on the equipment when I open the door. There is no possibility to have pictures sent to London. It would be necessary to use commercial equipment and lines for transmission, and it becomes not secure."

"You bluffed him."

"I play it by ear, yes?" she laughed.

"Benny Goodman couldn't have done better," I chuckled. "But what about Daphne, or Jackie London, or whatever she called herself? That had to be true."

"Yes, that much is true. She works as an agent, and she is used for sex traps."

"Did you really have more to show him if he'd wanted proof?"

"Yes—photographs from the playroom—terrible pictures."

"Did you know her well? What was she like?"

"I don't really get to know her. I must. . . work with her once, and I organize some things for her. She is person who looks after herself before anyone. She is very hard."

"I didn't mean her to get hurt. It happened before I met you, and I said nothing because I was unaware you knew her."

"And we don't hear who causes this at the tube station. I think this is a good thing, otherwise they suspect about you."

She put her arm about my waist, her head on my shoulder. I kissed the top of her head, then we stopped and kissed properly for a few minutes. Slowly we started back toward the house.

Something caught my eye. Protruding from the roof of the house at the rear, there was a peculiar antenna array—a parabolic dish with an extended grid narrowing to a point about a yard from the dish.

"What's that antenna for, Marijke?"

"I don't know. They have some special radio communications equipment, but they don't tell me what it is for."

I filed it in my memory and we continued walking. I knew I couldn't simply ignore what Marijke had deduced, but I hoped she would believe my explanation.

"I really am a singer and musician, Marijke. I spent some time in the army as a musician, like House and Archie Mowatt. Because of my background I was asked to help out the British intelligence people, but just for a short time and just for a specific reason. Reluctantly, I agreed. That business in Paris was really how I explained it, but I left out the part about the KGB. I was just doing someone a favour, and then I killed that man. I don't feel very good about it regardless of what he was."

"He is a swine, David, and he deserves to die. Someday I tell you why I want to kill him myself if I can do it. But he is a Soviet agent, and I must tolerate him and co-operate with him when they give an order. I'm glad he is dead." Her eyes spilled hatred.

I took it all in, but some things didn't add up.

"I still don't understand why you brought me here."

"I want to tell you I know about Paris, but I think that if I tell you in London, you will be afraid I tell Nalishkin about you. I want to give you something so you know you can trust me. You know about this house, you know about an operation coming soon. Perhaps this will help your people. You must not say how you hear about this. There is a Soviet agent inside MI6, and if they find out I pass information, then I am tortured and killed. My life is in your hands, David. This is what I want. I am KGB, but I love you, and I want that you believe me more than anything else."

I had to ask the next question, but I felt that in so doing I was becoming more and more like 'them'.

"Can you tell me who the Soviet mole is inside MI6?"

"No. I know nothing except his code name."

"What is that?"

A pause.

"You will tell them?"

"Yes, but not the source. I won't compromise you. Not ever."

"He is called 'Amethyst', and that is all I know."

"You've taken a terrible risk in bringing me here. What if someone should find out? Is there any chance that some of the equipment there could record or transmit without your knowledge?"

"No, we are safe. There is no danger—not from the KGB."

"Then let's get out of here before we stretch our luck."

* * *

Five minutes later we headed away from Bracklesham Bay and the most bizarre house I had ever been in.

We drove aimlessly and without speaking for some time. Marijke seemed depressed.

"David, I am sorry I tell you all this. I am afraid it changes your feeling for me. This is true, yes?"

"No, that's not true. Nothing can change my feeling for you. I'm just having a hard time with the ruthlessness of governments trying to discredit each other, and the degradation they sink to just so they can find out what the other guy is up to."

We were entering Chiddingfold, and the large green centreing this secluded village of old houses seemed just right for a stop, especially when I spotted a pub called the Crown Inn.

"What we are doing, David?"

"We need something to help us get into a better mood, and this looks like the right place to find it. Come on."

It was a delightful place, parts of it 14th-century, said the publican, and we found a corner that seemed just right. Marijke had a sherry and I settled for a large drambuie. There were a number of regulars there, yet we felt quite private in our niche by the window.

"I want to tell you about me, David, but it is impossible. Other people are involved, and I can say nothing."

"It doesn't matter. I don't think I should know, anyway. I don't even want to know about what you do in the KGB. As far as I am concerned, you work for the cultural attaché. That's enough for me. If I don't know anything, then I can't hurt you. I wouldn't say anything intentionally, but there is always the chance that something might slip, and that could be disastrous. So," I raised my glass, "here's to culture. It brought us together."

We drank, and Marijke smiled warmly.

"I want to be with you tonight. Is it possible, David?"

"I have a complication tomorrow. I have an appointment at 7:00am which I must keep. By coincidence it's quite near here. But what time do you have to be at work?"

"Not until noon. Is there a place we can stay so I get a train to London in the morning? This way you don't drive me back, and you are closer for your appointment."

"You wouldn't mind?"

"To be with you? You are crazy! Of course I don't mind."

I asked the publican where he could recommend, and 'The Angel' in Guildford seemed to fill the bill. There was a regular service to London by train, and I was only minutes to Dunsfold. We elected to go straight there, as I had telephoned from Chiddingfold and they were holding a room for us.

It only took 15 minutes through Godalming, and the hotel was right on the High Street. There was no parking area at the hotel, but I found a space on the street very near the door.

The Angel was a surprise. Another 14th-century inn, besides the beams it had open fireplaces and a gallery. The menu looked good, too, so we decided to clean up and have dinner in the hotel.

We had been given a very large room with a private bath, and it felt as though we had transported back in time, it was so elegant and tasteful. Marijke decided to lie down for a few minutes while I had a bath, and soon I was soaking in an immense tub. I must have dozed off, for I heard the door creak and opened my eyes to find Marijke there, naked.

"I am afraid perhaps you drown," she smiled.

"Were you going to jump in and rescue me?"

"I think about it."

"Help! Help!" I shouted, sinking beneath the water.

I felt her hands pull me up. She was in the tub.

"I must help you breathe," she laughed, covering my mouth with hers. Then she sat back.

"What is this I see?" she snickered, pointing to something which had broken the surface of the water.

"Up periscope!" I commanded. "Prepare torpedo for launch!"

I'd always loved playing in the bath as a kid.

But this was a lot more fun than Rubber Duckie.

SIXTEEN

Guildford, Surrey—Monday, June 18, 1962

I awoke the next morning at the crack of dawn. I wasn't tired at all, in fact, I felt more at ease and rested than I had for months. The passion which accompanies newly discovered love seems to invigorate in exact proportion to the amount of love-making.

We had eventually dressed and arrived for dinner on the previous evening, but it was patently obvious to both of us that food was not the priority of the night. Rather, it was a voyage of discovery, and in the ensuing hours we set sail on numerous occasions. Sometimes it was fierce, sometimes tender, and, on occasion, full of laughter. Now, I was energetic, totally calm, and completely in love.

I looked at Marijke sleeping peacefully, and couldn't resist leaning over to kiss her lightly. Her eyes opened.

"Oh, good morning," she breathed, "we must get up?"

"No, not yet. I'm sorry I woke you up. I didn't mean to."

She snuggled over.

"It doesn't matter. But now I am awake. . . !"

She kissed me, and our interest in the proceedings increased very quickly. Ah, well. *Un autre voyage.*

A short time later we lay quietly, talking. I had something to broach and now it couldn't wait.

"Marijke, you remember that I said I had been in the army?"

"Yes, like House and Colonel Mowatt, you said. In music."

"That's right. Well, I've been given a reserve commission in the British Army to help them out with a couple of things. That's what I'm doing today. I thought I should tell you because I must report in uniform this morning, and I didn't want it to be a complete surprise when you saw it."

There was a thoughtful silence.

"It connects, doesn't it? I mean to the thing you help with in Paris? No, please don't tell me. I don't want to know about it. It's better for both I don't know."

We both lay quietly without talking. Shortly, Marijke spoke again, very softly.

"We play deadly games, David. I hope on the same side."

I tried to respond, but she put her fingers on my lips, silencing me.

"Come," she brightened, hopping out of bed, "we get ready and have breakfast together."

Heads and eyes turned when we walked into the dining room. Mostly because of Marijke's beauty, I realized, but a uniform does attract attention, and the staff who saw us the night before had not pegged us as a military couple.

It felt both familiar and strange to be wearing khaki again. The British version of the battledress was not quite as green as the Canadian Army's, but in other respects it was exactly what I had worn as working dress for nearly ten years. It fitted well, and the correct badges were in place. The shoulder flash said Royal Corps of Transport, but I couldn't quite accept the major's crowns on my epaulettes—I'd become accustomed to captain's pips. After we had ordered, Marijke looked me over for several minutes. I couldn't tell from her expression whether it was approval or the reverse.

"You look very good in a uniform, David. Very handsome. But the badge with the wings—you are a flyer?"

"Not really. I know how to fly, but I'm not a pilot in the military sense of the word. I was just barely qualified when I left the army."

"And the two ribbons?"

"They don't mean anything significant. One is the Coronation Medal which I got in the reserves in Canada along with thousands of others. I think my name was picked out of a hat. The red and white one is the Canadian Forces Decoration for being in the services for twelve years."

"I thought you were only in the army for ten years?"

"In the regulars I only did nine years and a few months, but I had four years in reserve units which counts, too. The British consider it a bit of a joke. We Canadians can put the letters 'CD' after our names and the Brits figure it's too much fuss for only twelve years. I tend to agree with them."

We had light breakfasts of toasted English muffins with strawberry jam and a touch of Devon cream. I had coffee, but Marijke wanted tea. We had a few minutes to spare, and it felt good to linger over refills.

"Are you busy tonight? Any duties at the embassy or anything? I'd like to take you to a jazz club if you're not busy. I'll probably sing a few tunes. I haven't sung live in nearly two weeks, so I often drop in at Ronnie Scott's if I have to blow the pipes out. It gives me practice with real musicians. Much better than vocalising at home. What do you say—do I have an audience of one?"

The strained look came back—I had seen it before when she was otherwise occupied one night the previous week. Then I'd thought I might be imagining it, but now I knew I wasn't mistaken. The problem was I didn't know how to read it or what to say.

"I am to work tonight, but I try to change it for tomorrow. I will like coming with you very much and hearing you sing. I am at my flat at six o'clock. You can call me?"

"Sure."

"I say one thing more. It means very much to me."

She reached across the table and held my hands.

"You are the first man I love, and you are the first man I give myself to from the heart."

Her eyes were moist, and I knew this statement was meant to convey something to me which I did not fully comprehend. But I recognized where it was coming from.

"You honour me, Marijke. I love you, like I never have loved before. I don't ever want to lose you."

There was a fear in her eyes, as though I had raised a spectre which she had no wish to confront.

"I try for tonight, David. Go soft, what you do today."

I had placed my things in the Jag, came back in to pay the bill at the desk, and Marijke kissed me goodbye as I left the lobby. I turned to wave as she climbed the stairs, then strode out to the car and my appointment with the technological unknown.

* * *

There are two Dunsfolds. One is a quiet little village in the Surrey countryside whose claims to modernity include the leaded stained-glass windows of the cruciform church, and the 16th century timbering in a house called Burningfold.

This Dunsfold lent its name to the other one, an airfield carved from the countryside near the village in 1942. Now, twenty years later, Dunsfold Airfield, or Aerodrome, as some called it, was at the forefront of the most remarkable advance in the history of flight since the development of the jet engine itself.

Leased by Hawker Siddeley Aviation Limited, Dunsfold was the centre for the flight testing and development of the unique aircraft without a name—the P1127.

I had read the notes which Hammond had secured for me, and knew as much as I could from what was written on paper. Just exactly what was to be accomplished by this excursion and charade on my part was eluding me, but I couldn't help but feel excited and nervous about my impending encounter with this mythical beast.

Mythical, yes, just as Pegasus and flying carpets were mythical, until we created our own beasts of the air to provide winged transportation. An aircraft without a propellor was a myth until Frank Whittle proved otherwise, and now this latest in modern mythology—a jet aircraft which could lift straight up off the ground. As I drove south I realized that I had very little idea about what to expect.

Dunsfold wasn't far from Guildford, and my musings almost made me miss my landmarks: shortly after a pub called the Leather Bottle watch for a gravel pit on the left, then take the right fork off the main road. I curved through some pretty copses, and passing a couple of farms I knew I was nearly at the gate.

Suddenly there was a chain-link security fence on my right, with a barrier dead ahead. I came to an abrupt halt.

The security guard came out of his gatehouse, clipboard in hand. Just a performance, I kept reminding myself. Steady now. Ignore the two guys with guns in the gatehouse. Focus. Curtain up.

"Good morning, sir," he said, saluting. "May I 'ave your name, please, sir?"

"Major Baird. Mr. Bedford is expecting me."

"Ah, yes, sir, 'ere it is. Now, if you don't mind, sir, I'd like to see your identification."

I produced my I-card, and he perused it before returning it to me. Then he scribbled on his board, handing me a tag in a plastic case with a clip.

"Wear this on your uniform while you are on the airfield, sir. Do you know where you are going?"

"No, I don't."

"Go straight down to the perimeter track, sir, turn right, travel along the track. At the flight control tower on the right turn in and park near it. Mr. Bedford's office is in that building."

I followed his instructions, and as I drove I realized that the airfield had probably changed very little from its World War II days. I could see quite a few Nissen huts, and apart from the main hangar, which seemed to have had a facelift, most everything else looked wartime issue. At least the flight control centre was solid—concrete with a balcony on the second floor, the control tower itself with its sloped windows making up the third floor.

I decided to leave everything in the Jag until I had scouted the situation, so I headed for the door of the tower building.

There was a man standing just inside, watching me approach. Slightly taller than my 5' 11", he had a spare frame, light brown hair, and was dressed in a hound's-tooth jacket with a bow-tie. As I drew closer I perceived an analytical gaze peering at me out of hazel eyes.

"Hello," he said to me in resonant, measured tones, "I'm Bill Bedford," with a careful separation of his surname into two syllables.

"David Baird," I replied as we shook hands.

"You're the chap Basil Hammond called me about. Let's go up."

He led me inside, down a short hallway, and up a flight of stairs. His office was at the top of the stairs on the left. It was small—barely room for the desk, a filing cabinet, a locker, and a table by the window, with one chair for a visitor. Bill closed the door, and motioned me to sit.

"I didn't realize you were playing the role in costume," he smiled.

"Hammond's idea, Bill. He felt it would look more convincing for an army pilot to be here than a Canadian civilian."

"He's right, of course, but those wings could be dangerous around a group of flyers. You might get caught out with a question which would give it all away."

"I hope not. I think I can handle the basics, if it doesn't get too technical."

"Do you, indeed," he commented, with a slight smile. "Well, then, what makes an aircraft fly?"

I looked at him incredulously.

"You're kidding, aren't you?"

"Not in the slightest, old chap."

"Do you want it text-book or will a brief version suffice?"

"Keep it short, if you like."

"There are four contradictory forces affecting an object in flight—lift, thrust, weight, and drag. The thrust of the engine, overcoming drag, causes air to flow over the wings or airfoil. The airfoil is shaped in cross-section with a longer, curved top, and a shorter, straight bottom. The bisected airstream must move faster across the top of the airfoil in order to reconnect at the rear, and this causes a reduction of pressure on the upper surface which results in an upward load on the airfoil. When thrust and lift are greater than weight and drag, the aircraft flies."

Bill sat there looking at me, then burst out laughing.

"I see you've done your homework. Or is it possible that those wings are not just decoration?"

"Hammond didn't tell you? I qualified on Harvards when I was in the Canadian Army. What you see is what I wore for nearly ten years—even the corps is right. I haven't flown a lot, but I know enough that you don't have to spoon-feed me while I'm here."

"I should have guessed that Basil Hammond had something up his sleeve, and that he wanted me to find out on my own. Well, so be it. That was a bloody good answer, by the way, and if the rest of what you know about flying is just as thorough, then you'll come away from this with a lot of valuable information and a good working knowledge of vertical flight."

He gave me a furtive smile.

"How about the singing part of this? Is that real, too?"

"'Fraid so. I'm just about to open in a show in the West End. I'm still not sure how I got talked into this spy caper, but here I am, and I said I'd see it through."

"Well, don't tell me anything you shouldn't. Let's play it on face value. It'll be far easier with everyone else around."

He tapped the desk with a pencil.

"I've set aside the morning to give you the familiarization tour, and I'm a firm believer in getting hands on as quickly as possible. But before we go down to the hangar, do you understand what we're up against in making a jet take off vertically?"

"I think so. I've read the notes Hammond got for me, and as I understand it, the problem has to do with those old forces of lift, thrust, weight, and drag. In vertical take-off you have no lift from the airfoil, so the engine must generate enough power to overcome dead weight."

"Exactly! Now this engine which Bristol's have developed, the Pegasus, is a marvel. The first one we put in the airframe, however, was barely able to generate enough thrust to get the thing off the ground. We stripped everything from the aircraft we didn't need. They even suggested I go on a diet.

"Ironically, I had broken my leg in an auto accident just before that first attempt at a hover, and the cast weighed almost enough to keep me on the ground. Thank the Lord it didn't. Anyway, we lifted off with an installed thrust of barely 10,000 pounds, and that's about what the aircraft weighs. You can see why we had to strip the extra weight off."

"I'm gathering that this has changed a bit."

"It's changed a lot. In fact, the first prototype, XP831, has just had a new engine installed, the Pegasus 3, and this gives us 13,500 pounds of thrust. It's made a remarkable difference. Now we can fly it like a real aircraft."

He stood up.

"Let's go introduce you to our babies."

We left the building, walking past the parking area toward one of the hangars. The main doors were closed, but we entered through a small door inset into the larger one. The lights were on, and there, centred on the floor, were two P1127's.

At first glance they had a bug-like appearance, similar to huge moths at rest. Compared to the Hawker Hunter fighter which sat nearby, they were not nearly as sleek or streamlined. Instead, they had an almost dumpy look. Bill had been watching my face.

"Don't worry, David. Even I thought it was an ugly brute, and that I'd never be able to make friends with a thing like that. But its grown on me for the past two years, and I've got a lot of respect for it. Remember that it looks like this because of its vertical take-off requirement—the configuration of engine placement, cockpit, type of wing and tailplane, have all contributed to its appearance. But let me tell you something. You see that pretty Hunter over there? This stubby little thing can leave that fighter standing still, and we're years away from the finished product. Just you wait and see what this baby will do."

We went over to the closest aircraft, XP831, and Bill explained details as we walked around.

"I'm sure you've noticed that there is no conventional jet-pipe at the tail. Instead, these rotating nozzles, two on either side, are what provide the lift when they're pointing down and the thrust when they're pointing backward. That's the beauty of this aircraft—simplicity."

"It can't be all that simple if it's been flying for two years and there are still modifications to be made."

"Now, now, old chap," he admonished, "remember that we're in uncharted territory here. It hasn't been done before in this particular form. For example, look at the intake nozzles. They've tried various materials and designs to get it right. Last December one of the damn things came off when I was flying, and I nearly bought the farm.

"It happened in the second prototype, XP836. I was losing control stability at 200 feet, trying to get it down at Yeovilton, and it kept rolling on me. I ejected at a 30-degree roll angle and touched the ground seconds after the 'chute opened. The aircraft crashed into a storage barn and burned. Closest call I've ever had. But the failure of that nozzle brought about the present inflatable rubber intakes, and that's cleared the problem."

"Nice way to find out. I thought research and development was all done in labs these days. I didn't realize that so much of it was done while flying the aircraft. Isn't that dangerous?"

"Of course it can be, old chap. We do try to minimize the odds. But it also makes the job fascinating, don't you think?"

The hazel eyes glinted, and I wondered at the combination of methodical technician and dare-devil flyer which made up a test-pilot like Bill Bedford. The two elements seemed a contradiction, yet without them both the experimental test-pilot could not exist. A special breed indeed, I realized.

"You should have a look in the cockpit, David. Run up those steps and climb in."

I did as I was told, except that I didn't run. The step-ladder arrangement was made of aluminum (the Brits add an 'i' and call it aluminium) and not very secure. The canopy was open, and it was easy to climb in.

It was a relatively small cockpit. I was surprised at the paucity of instruments on the panel—there didn't seem to be many more than there were in the Harvards I had flown. I said so to Bill who was crouched on the top step of the platform beside me.

"You're absolutely right, old chap. The only instrument you wouldn't see in a conventional aircraft is that nozzle angle gauge on the right. But you should have seen the cockpit when we first took her up in 1960. There was nothing in here except the seat, the throttle box and the stick. They wanted us to see if it worked before they put any details into it. Once we got it to hover 12 inches off the ground, they knew they had an aircraft."

He pointed to the throttle box lower down on my left side.

"Now this is where the magic is. The lever on the left is the throttle, of course. The one on the right is the nozzle selection lever. When it's fully back the nozzles point downward at an angle of 82 degrees to the fuselage. That's straight down to the ground. Advance the throttle to full, and she lifts off the ground and continues to rise until you pull the throttle back to maintain height. Then you're in a fairly stable hover."

"What about attitude control? Surely the ailerons and rudder have no effect in the hover."

"Absolutely correct. We've got puffers in the wing tips, the front and rear of the fuselage and crossways in the tail. They get air from the cold side of the engine—the compressor. They're linked to the pedals and stick, so the aircraft will behave in the hover just as it does in conventional flight using the same control motions. There is a measure of autostabilization, but this can be overridden by the controls if necessary."

"You make it sound so easy, Bill."

"It is now, but we had to find this all out by trial and error. We've got the vertical aspects pretty well in-hand, but there are some conventional flight characteristics we're still trying to perfect without compromising VTOL performance. We'll get there."

"How do you shift to conventional flight from the vertical?"

"Simplicity itself, provided you don't rush it. Having achieved the hover at the height selected, move the nozzle selection lever gently forward to about twenty degrees. The aircraft will move forward without losing height. With each successive move forward of both lever and throttle, more and more lift is achieved by the wings. When you have accelerated to 160 knots the aircraft is completely wing-borne, and the nozzle control lever may be pushed fully forward. Then it's a conventional aircraft."

"What about landing?"

"Almost the exact reverse of the procedure. Approach the landing point from a mile's distance, and ease the speed off to 200 knots. Descend to about 200 feet. Move the nozzle control lever back to the stop, then lift it through the gate to the reverse thrust stop. This puts the nozzles about 20 degrees forward of vertical. As the aircraft slows to the hover, increase the power on the throttle to compensate for the loss of wing-lift. Lifting the lever over the gate to the VTOL stop will maintain the hover. If you want to move forward slightly, tilt the nose down a bit and she'll move like a helicopter. When you're over the precise landing spot, ease off the throttle and she'll land gently. On touchdown, throttle back, then push the nozzle lever forward and use the throttle to taxi."

"It sounds too easy, Bill. In fact, it doesn't seem to be as tricky as taking off and landing in a normal aircraft."

"In many ways it isn't. You've got time to think here before you take the next step, and you can correct or even reverse your decision if you've made an error or you simply change your mind. In a conventional take-off and landing you don't have those options—you do it right the first time or you're in trouble."

"What about conventional take-offs and landings? Can you use it this way, and is it harder or easier?"

"One thing at a time, old chap. Let's address that a bit later. Now I see they want to tow XP831 out and down to the engine running pens for a test, so we'd best clear off. Out you get."

We stood outside and watched while they towed the little craft out. I was amused when I saw the badge on the tractor. Massey-Harris, from Brantford in Ontario. I almost felt homesick, and mentioned it to Bill.

"Well, my dear chap, if you really want to feel nostalgic, let me show you something."

He led me along to the area in front of the control tower.

"Do you know anything about Dunsfold Aerodrome, David?"

"No, nothing at all."

We stopped in front of a white, hexagonal obelisk about four feet high.

"Have a look at the side face."

I did so, and to my amazement read:

THIS AERODROME

BUILT BY

THE

ROYAL CANADIAN ENGINEERS

ASSISTED BY

CANADIAN FORESTRY CORPS

RCASC

RCOC

MCMXLII

Above it was the RCAF badge. I was more than surprised. On the front face, below the badge of the Royal Canadian Engineers, was the official opening inscription, stating that on the 16th of October, 1942, Lieut.-General A.G.L. McNaughton, then General Officer Commanding Canadian Forces Overseas, had opened the new airfield and handed it over to the Royal Canadian Air Force. One facet had the Canadian Forestry Corps badge at the top, and the rest were capped by maple leaves.

"I had no idea, Bill," I said, still surprised. "I thought the RCAF had flown from British airfields through the war."

"All except this one," he chuckled. "In fact, this was called 'RCAF Station Dunsfold' until it was handed over to the UK much later in the war."

"What did they fly out of here?"

"In the beginning Mustangs and Tomahawks, but as time went by nearly everything that flew used the field sooner or later. Ernest Hemingway flew out of here as an observer when he was a war correspondent on some 'ops' over Europe."

"I wonder how many Canadians know about all this?"

"Probably only the those who were stationed here. Come on, let's have a 'cuppa' at the canteen and then head to the pens."

We walked the short distance to the canteen, just behind the air traffic control centre. Tea in hand, I was introduced to Bill's deputy, Hugh Merewether, and two American pilots from NASA, Fred Drinkwater and Jack Reeder. It was difficult to skirt the questions, especially from the Americans, and I signalled to Bill that we should escape as quickly as possible.

We drove down to the engine running pens in Bill's Austin.

"Phew," I breathed, "that was tricky."

"My fault, old chap. I should have realized that your fellow North Americans would have been curious. Sorry about that. Do you want to stay out of their way?"

"Not now that they've seen me. But next time I'll be ready for their questions. Why are they here?"

"We had a lot of help from NASA when we were doing wind-tunnel tests on models of the P1127. Merewether and I were actually over there, and we both flew the Bell X-14 to give us the feel of vertical flight. *Ergo: quid pro quo.*"

"Are the Americans developing the X-14?"

"No. The mechanics aren't practical. But it did fly, and it was an important step in vertical flight and thrust-vectoring."

We parked near the pens and walked to the bay. XP831 was backed in, sheet-metal shrouds covering the exhaust nozzles all the way to the ground and to the rear of the aircraft. I noticed chains holding it down to the concrete decking in several places.

"This pen was built just for the P1127. It has steel mesh grids over an underground duct. It carries the discharge from the engines safely out with the nozzles in either position. This way we can run the engine up to test various components without it taxying or taking off."

Bill introduced me to Frank Cross, head of the experimental design office of Hawker's, and I watched while they plugged in the starting trolley of 2000 lb/sq.in. carbon dioxide canisters.

"Eventually we want to have self-starters on board, but to save weight for now we use this kick-start. I've got to climb in for a few minutes. You'll be better off in the observation booth."

I went inside. There were two technicians bent over a panel containing numerous gauges, and they barely said hello. I watched through the tiny window. Bill was in the cockpit, and on his signal Frank Cross activated the starter. There was an instant whine which increased in dynamic and pitch. Cross pulled the starter hose from the engine nacelle and came inside. Picking up a headset and microphone he was soon talking to Bill, but because of the tremendous noise of the Pegasus engine I couldn't hear him.

For about fifteen minutes the Pegasus was run up and down with obvious instructions from Frank Cross. The needles on the gauges danced, and the technicians took note of the variations. Then the noise died away as Bill shut the engine down. He clambered out.

"Everything seems in good order, Bill," said Frank Cross. "If you're flying her this afternoon I'll get her pulled out."

"One minute Frank. David, how would you like to start her up? It'll give you the feel of the thing without flying."

"Sure, I'd love to," I said, surprised. "But I don't know the engine-start sequence."

"I'll guide you through it on the headset. I can tell from the control panel in the booth if you've done the right thing. Here, take my helmet. The microphone is internal. I'll show you where to plug it in."

He handed me a blue-grey cloth helmet with an oxygen mask and microphone built into the flap. I handed him my forage hat, pulled on the cloth helmet, then climbed up the ladder and into the cockpit. In a moment Bill was beside me, kneeling again on the top platform of the ladder. He plugged in the radio lead. My hands were shaking, I was that nervous. I hoped he didn't see it. Expertly he went over the controls and instruments I would use.

"You won't need the oxygen unless you push the throttle completely forward and tear off out of here. If you reach 10,000 feet you'd better get ready to use it. But try to be back just after lunch, there's a good chap."

He was smiling at me, and I gave him a crooked grin back. A quick pat on the shoulder, and he was gone. The ladder followed a moment later. Good God! What if I did something stupid and ripped the aircraft right out of the pen. I started to sweat. The seat harness, which I had done up at Bill's suggestion, was making me feel claustrophobic. His voice on the headset made me jump.

"Right. All set, David?"

"Roger. When you're ready." Could he hear my voice shake?

"Canopy shut."

I pulled it down and locked. "Canopy shut."

"Oil temperature above zero."

I looked. Check. "Oil temperature above zero."

"Master instrumentation switch on."

Click. "Master instrumentation switch on."

"Booster pumps on."

Click. Click. "Booster pumps on."

"Magnetic indicators black."

Check. "Magnetic indicators black."

"Throttle/HP cock at idling."

Set. "Throttle/HP cock at idling."

"Starter trolley connected."

The exchange of 'thumbs up'. "Starter trolley connected."

"Ignition time switch turned clockwise, fully on."

Twist. "Ignition time switch turned clockwise, fully on."

There was a pause. A whine was increasing in intensity.

"That's it, David. Light up in 9 seconds, and idling speed reached in 35 seconds. Just keep your eye on the jet-pipe temperature. It shouldn't go above 350 to 450 degrees Centigrade."

The Pegasus roared to life. What power! But how to stand the noise? Perhaps the 'bone dome', as they called the hard helmet, muffled much of it when it went over the inner cloth helmet.

"I want to take you through some control manoeuvres, David. Are you game?"

"Roger, Bill. Fire away." Such bravado, I thought.

"Nozzle control lever to VTOL stop."

Full back on the stop. "Roger."

"Move throttle slowly forward to mid-quadrant."

Slowly done. The Pegasus rumbled madly behind me. The airframe shifted. It wanted to move. I hoped to hell it didn't.

"Roger. Throttle at mid-quadrant."

"Nozzle control lever slowly forward about 20 degrees."

I could sense a shift in the airframe. Chains, hang on!

"Roger. Twenty degrees."

"Now, smoothly move the nozzle control lever fully forward."

Now it really wanted to fly. I, however, did not.

"You've run through a simulated vertical take-off, David. Now try to bring it back and pretend to land on your own."

"Roger. I'll do my best."

I moved the throttle back to indicate that I was dropping my airspeed to 200 knots. Pausing for a moment, I moved the control lever smoothly back to the VTOL stop, then lifted it over the spring load to reverse thrust. I increased throttle slightly, simulating a hover. Moving the nozzle lever back to the VTOL stop, I began to ease the throttle back, and after a few moments I dropped the power right off to indicate I had landed. I rotated the nozzle control forward, as though I were going to taxi, then moved the throttle slightly to indicate ground movement.

"Jolly good, David! Now, throttle back and shut her down."

Throttle back, ignition time switch off, booster pumps off, master instrumentation switch off. The roaring stopped and was replaced by a reducing whine. I undid the canopy latch and pushed it back. The ladder appeared, so I undid my harness and got out. My legs were wobbling as I went down the ladder, so I held on tightly. I felt a great sense of relief. Bill was waiting for me at the bottom, holding my hat.

"Good show, David. How did it feel?"

"The truth? I was scared shitless. But I wouldn't have missed it for all the tea in China."

"That was a chance for you to get the feeling of the aircraft without actually flying it. We don't have a simulator yet. That won't come until we're sure it's going into production. I thought it was something you should experience."

I was about to answer when there was a roar from the runway.

"Come on!" shouted Bill. "That's 972 about to take off."

We dashed around the corner of the pen, and there, just opposite us on the runway, was the other P1127 prototype, about 200 yards away. With an increased roar it lifted off a grid in the runway, the nose dipping for an instant then correcting. Straight up to about 60 feet, then it hung, suspended on a cushion of air. A little pirouette, and it smoothly flew away from us, accelerating until it disappeared. The silence was deafening.

"Good God! Did I really see what I think I saw?"

Bill laughed at my excitement.

"Nearly two years we've been doing this, and it still moves me to see one of these little wonders doing its bag of tricks. Let's head back, shall we?"

Walking toward the car, Bill asked about my assignment.

"I don't want to pry, old chap, and I realize the need for secrecy and all that, but if I knew what you were looking for I might be able to organize something directed toward your needs."

I decided to be as candid as I could.

"I wish I knew myself, Bill. I stumbled on some information which told us that the Soviets had something up their sleeves concerning this aircraft. That's why security has been increased. In another context, I'm going to be spending some time with the Soviet who seems to be the king-pin in this. He knows nothing about my contact with Hammond—to him I'm just a singer. Hammond thought I should have a first-hand look at the P1127 in case I hit on something which connects—the more I know about the aircraft, then the better chance I have of tying threads together. Here I am, having the thrill of my life."

"Well, now, if it's a thrill you want, wait 'til this afternoon. We'll have some lunch at the Three Compasses, and you can fly XP831 in the hover off the grid. How does that suit you?"

I think I mumbled 'wonderful' or something, hoping that they served cookies at The Three Compasses.

I'd have a head start on chucking them.

SEVENTEEN

Dunsfold, Surrey—the same day

The Three Compasses Pub has been Dunsfold Aerodrome's watering hole from day one. In fact, the southeast gate of the airfield is called 'The Compasses Gate'. No one is quite sure whether this is in honour of the Compasses bridge over the disused Wey & Arun Junction Canal or the pub 200 yards farther along, but as the canal is largely forgotten and the pub is currently in use, most people associate the gate with the pub. So much for folklore.

As pubs go it is an attractive, no nonsense establishment with blackened beams and whitewashed walls, where people can get down to the serious business of supping and imbibing with nary a bit of wasted time. This is probably why it has appealed to the aircraft people from Dunsfold, whether service or civilian.

Bill and I had procured a draft and were sitting in a cheery alcove surrounded by windows. I was on an upholstered bench seat under the window, and the sun from the improved day made the break very pleasant. The pub was filling quickly with a mix of locals and people from the airfield, and business became brisk.

The two American pilots had come in with Hugh Merewether, and were standing near the huge fireplace with its pitch-black mantel. Catching sight of us they came over, and of course we talked flying.

Most of us had ordered sandwiches, and in keeping with tradition we were served quickly and abundantly.

I tried to keep the topics away from me as much as possible. When I had to respond to something I kept it pretty much to the truth—that I had flown briefly in the Canadian Army, that I was a reservist in Britain on a special call-out to examine the P1127 for possible army co-operation duties in the field. It was a position easy to defend, and I didn't have to pretend that I had flown jets or in combat, for army pilots generally fly light aircraft similar to those used in civilian recreational flying.

"I guess what I'm trying to find out is whether it will be easy enough for army pilots to convert to a VTOL jet without having to spend months back in a classroom and retraining."

"What do you think so far, David?" asked Jack Reeder.

"I haven't seen enough to form an opinion yet, but in theory it should work. I'd say the P1127 is more manageable than a regular jet fighter because of its hover capability, and as a close-support weapon it can operate right with forward troops. I guess I'll find out what the reality is this afternoon."

"Is he taking it up, Bill?" asked Fred Drinkwater.

"Just some hovers over the grid. David doesn't come here with bags of fighter and test-pilot experience like you NASA superstars, remember. I'm not going to turn him loose the way you two tore off on your first flights."

Everyone laughed as Bill gently chided the Americans, then Hugh Merewether quietly put it in perspective.

"I think Bill should tell you all about the day that he and XP831 both nearly dropped into the Compasses for lunch."

There was a great hubbub about the table as everyone teased Bill and coaxed him to tell the story.

"There's nothing to it, really. We were trying to induce the yaw effect which occasionally sets in between 30 and 100 knots, searching for a solution. I was in a turn at about 60 knots and 200 feet, suddenly putting full aileron on to counteract a wing drop. I realized I had no control, and one false step would have meant curtains. Luckily I chose the correct rudder pedal, or I would have come right through the roof of the pub—I was bang overhead when it happened."

Everyone joined in the laughter. All pilots have been in a dicey situation at one time or another, and if you didn't laugh at it later you'd never fly again. It also helps to share the moment with people who understand. But I couldn't restrain my quip.

"Is that when they put that sign up over there, Bill? 'No Hawkers?'"

There were groans all round. A few minutes later I was able to get in the question which was puzzling me about the Americans' participation in the flight-testing.

"Since you're both with NASA, are you here to evaluate the P1127 program, or to make recommendations about adopting the aircraft for the U.S.?"

"I guess it's a little of both," said Fred Drinkwater, "but there's also the research aspect. The more we know about VTOL technique the better equipped we are to consult with designers who want assistance from NASA on their own projects."

"Will there be more Americans coming over?"

"Nobody from NASA, but the USAF or the Navy might get interested based on our reports. Of course, there's Joe Stavic, who's already here."

"Who's he with?"

"He just retired as a major in the USAF," answered Reeder. "The rumour is that he's going to be working for McDonnell-Douglas or Boeing, and that he's checking out the P1127 for one of them to study the feasibility of developing a night-fighter version. He's had more experience in night flying than anyone we know."

"Has the P1127 been flown at night?"

"Not up 'til now," answered Bill. "831 has just had a night-flying conversion, and Stavic is going to give her a preliminary flight tomorrow at 2000 hours. I don't think we're ready for this yet, but we're getting pressure from the American ambassador, so the company is going along with it."

"Why is Dwight Vandenberg involved?"

"Stavic worked for him in the air force," replied Reeder. "We're guessing that Vandenberg had a lot to do with Stavic's new job, so the squeeze is on."

"And you can understand Hawker's desire to interest the Americans in this project," commented Bill. "It could mean the difference between success and failure for the whole programme."

It was time to go back to the airfield. The Americans went with Hugh Merewether, and I drove with Bill.

"Did you bring a flying suit, David?"

"Yes, I have my old Canadian Army suit. Actually, it was an air force flying suit. I don't think the army had one of its own."

"You'll need some extra kit for this afternoon, so we'll drop in on the flight safety department and get you fixed up."

We went around the perimeter track, past the hangar and flight control, and turned in to one of the Nissen huts. There I was introduced to the flight safety officer, Harold Duffield, and received a cloth helmet, a 'bone dome', and gloves.

"No parachute, Bill? I'll be at least 2 feet off the ground."

I think I was trying to be funny to alleviate my fears.

"No need, old chap. The Martin-Baker ejector seat could blow you straight through the canopy 200 feet in the air and bring you down safely, even from a height of 2 feet."

"Through the canopy? Isn't that a mite rough on the head?"

"The canopy is designed to blow just before you hit it. Works most of the time, I'm told. If it doesn't, you end up an inch or two shorter than before, otherwise no ill effects."

I caught the glint in his eye and the suppressed smile. He could dish it out as well as take it.

"May I use the phone in your office, Bill?"

"Of course. We're going to change there anyway."

We drove to the parking area near the hangar, and went up to Bill's office. Changing quickly, he excused himself and told me to use the phone at my convenience and just tell the operator the number for her to ring through. I pulled on my flying suit and sat down, then ran the call instructions. Hammond came on the line.

"Yes, Minstrel. How's the day going?"

"Just fine, sir. Bill Bedford has been more than helpful. I'm actually going to lift it off the ground this afternoon."

"I told you it would be worthwhile, didn't I?"

"I hate to admit it, Colonel, but you were right. It's fascinating. I'm still nervous about it, but I'm glad I came. Now, I must tell you something. There's something big in the wind being planned by the KGB, and very soon. Nalishkin is directly involved, and three others at the embassy who are KGB. They've all been out of the country, due back today."

"Good. At least we can check exactly who they are through passport control. Can you tell me how you know?"

"No, sir. Sorry. I might compromise the source. Another thing, sir. I think your fears are well founded. There's a Soviet mole inside MI6. His code name is 'Amethyst'."

"Is there, by God," he breathed. "Well, well. That ties in to something I had already picked up, but we never knew what 'Amethyst' referred to. Now we have to find him. Anything else?"

I deliberately held back about the house in Bracklesham Bay. I was afraid it might be traced to Marijke. But I described the antenna I had seen, and asked Hammond to check it out and tell me what it could be used for.

"Does this have a bearing on something?"

"Playing a hunch, sir. If it ties together I'll tell you."

"Minstrel, about that licence plate you wanted me to check. The car belongs to Kurt Werner, a first secretary in the West German embassy. Is there something about him we should know?"

"Not yet, sir. It's just another hunch. I don't want to give you any false trails. I'm just keeping my eyes and ears open, and I'm definitely going to keep out of trouble."

"Well done again, Minstrel. Good luck this afternoon."

A few minutes later Bill and I were on the way down the perimeter track toward the engine-running pens.

"We'll leave the car and walk over to the grid. 831 is there now, by the look of things."

I looked toward the field and saw the squat outline of the aircraft and several people around it.

"You mentioned the grid before, Bill. What is it?"

"It has several uses. Basically, it's a hole in the runway covered by steel mesh. No one was sure what effect the jet exhaust would have on the tarmac when the nozzles are straight down. We didn't want it all broken up. Then there is the ground effect—buffeting which is caused by the bouncing of the exhaust back up to the aircraft under 20 or 30 feet. Finally, the re-ingestion of hot gases into the intakes—it impedes the efficiency of the engine, and in the early days especially, this was critical."

"Is it still necessary to use the grid?"

"Not so much now, but for a prolonged low-level hover it's still wise."

We parked and began to walk, helmets and gloves in hand.

"I'll lift her off once, David, to see that everything is in order. Oh, yes, you'll have to have a radio call-sign. I'm Hawker Alpha, so you should choose a phonetic alphabet word farther down the list for yourself and I'll inform the tower."

"How about Hawker X-ray? Seems to fit what I'm doing."

"Fair enough. When you get clearance from the tower to hover, then he'll hand you over to me. I'll have a portable radio set and be able to guide you from the ground right beside you. Are you feeling up to this?"

"I won't kid you, Bill. I'm pretty nervous. But I think I can handle it, and I don't panic easily."

"You've already got the feel of the cockpit, the engine and nozzle controls. That's a help. If I'm not comfortable about letting you go farther than a two-foot hover, then we'll stop right there. That's a promise."

We arrived at the grid area. Everything seemed ready. Bill and I did the walk-around the aircraft, checking control surfaces. Then, without more than a word to the technicians, he climbed into the cockpit. I stood well back, but in a spot where I could watch his face. The canopy closed, and more quickly than I expected the starting trolley fired. When the whine crescendo began I popped both helmets on to save my ears from the roar.

After waiting as the seconds counted down, Bill applied throttle, and after a moment's hesitation XP831 lifted into the air. He continued up to about 50 feet, then hovered. He rotated a couple of times, then retracted the undercarriage and gradually accelerated away toward the southwest.

Putting on left bank, he brought the aircraft around the field, approaching from the opposite end of the runway. The speed eased up, and he came into the hover just over the grid. Out popped the undercarriage, and XP831 floated down to bounce slightly and then stop, the engine noise winding down. Bill wasted no time in getting out.

"You make it look too easy, Bill. I almost feel I could do it." I gave him a hopeful grin.

"We'll see, old chap. Now, here's a card with the engine start procedure on it. Clip it on your knee. If you must ask me a question, do it, but try to get this sequence on your own if you can. Off you go."

I walked over on jelly knees. It was hard to navigate the ladder. When I had settled into the cockpit I plugged in the radio cord and switched on. I fastened the harness, glanced out at Bill and he gave me a thumbs up. The ladder was gone. I took a deep breath.

Glancing at the card clipped on my knee, I ran through the sequence that I had done in the morning. I got the signal from the technician on the cart, and in a few moments the whine had turned into the throaty rumble I was beginning to recognize. I waited the 35 seconds, then keyed the mike.

"Dunsfold tower, this is Hawker X-ray."

"Hawker X-ray, this is Dunsfold tower. Pass your message."

"Dunsfold tower, Hawker X-ray requesting permission to hover on the grid."

"Hawker X-ray, you are cleared to hover. Passing you over to Bill Bedford who will monitor. Switch to alternate frequency."

I switched the radio over.

"Bill here, David. We can dispense with the formalities at this level. When you're ready. Check nozzle lever back to stop."

"Nozzle lever back."

"You'll need full throttle to unstick. Then drop it back to catch the hover as quickly as you can. I don't want you in orbit."

"Roger, Bill. Here goes."

I eased the throttle forward. The engine noise increased greatly, but except for a slight shudder nothing happened. More throttle. Careful. I don't want to shoot up in a burst. Throttle nearly at maximum. Suddenly I felt the shift. I was up! Ease back on the throttle. She wobbled a bit, but I didn't want to make corrections at this altitude. Let the auto-stabilizers handle it.

"That's fine, David. You're at five feet. Now ease off the throttle and set her down gently."

I moved the throttle marginally. Nothing happened. I moved it again. I sank down more quickly than I would have liked. My instinct told me to shove the throttle forward, but I refrained. I felt the bump when I touched the ground, and I knew I bounced a bit, but I eased the throttle back to idle.

"Good work, David. You did right. Don't overreact on the throttle. Get used to the bounce—it happens quite often. Now, repeat that procedure several times to get the feel of it."

I did it four times more, each one smoother and easier than the last. I began to feel confident until I realized that this was like a baby's first steps. I had a long way to go to the Olympics.

"Now take it up to 50 feet, hold the hover for a moment, then bring her down."

I did everything the same way, just allowed 831 to climb to 50 feet and held it. I looked around for orientation. I couldn't see the grid under me, so I checked for stability by looking at the buildings nearby. In the trees on the left a house gable. Pens and Nissen huts on the right. I wasn't wandering. Down we went.

"Repeat that a few times."

Four more. The confidence returned, but I realized I wasn't flying. The aircraft was flying itself. I was back on the grid.

"Now take it up to 50 feet, hover, move the stick a little to port, then centre it."

I took it up again, gently pushed the control column left and back. The aircraft wobbled left, then steadied.

"Now try a slight lean to starboard, then fore, then aft. Get the feel of the controls in the air. Good. Now give it a bit of right rudder, and she'll turn around for you. That's it. Now left rudder for the other way. Fine. Now, listen carefully. I want you to drop the nose just a bit and hold the stick there. You'll move forward a little. Go about 20 yards, then hover."

I moved the stick forward carefully. The nose dropped, and I began to move. I gauged where I was in relation to the buildings, then eased the stick back.

"That's good. Now, a little rudder, turn her around, and bring her back to the grid, and land."

A little right rudder, and when I had sighted myself on the buildings I eased up, then nose down until I saw the grid disappear, and stick back. Throttle back, and down we went, this time with hardly a tremor as we touched.

"Jolly good, David. Now, do you want to quit, or do want one more step?"

"Let's go on." My bravado was not mirrored in my intestines.

"Okay. Listen carefully, and you're on your own. When I've finished speaking, switch to the tower frequency, because you'll have to get permission from them. Then, lift to hover at 50 feet, take her down the runway gently at 50 feet, turn around at the end of the runway, bring her back, and land. Any problems?"

"Nope. See you later, alligator."

I switched the radio over as I caught the look on Bill's face, and I laughed in the face mask.

"Dunsfold tower, this is Hawker X-ray."

"Hawker X-ray, this is Dunsfold tower. Pass your message."

"Dunsfold tower, Hawker X-ray requesting permission for a hover pass over runway 25."

"Hawker X-ray, hold for incoming aircraft on runway 25."

"Hawker X-ray. Roger."

I squinted through the heavy perspex to see a Hawker Hunter two-seat trainer land gracefully, then taxi off.

"Hawker X-ray, this is Dunsfold tower."

"Hawker X-ray. Pass your message, Dunsfold tower."

"Hawker X-ray, you are cleared to hover-pass on runway 25."

"Roger, Dunsfold."

I gave Bill a thumbs up, pushed the throttle and rose up. Holding at 50 feet, I dropped the nose and began to move, slowly at first, then I pushed it down a touch more and went a bit faster. As I approached the end of the runway I eased the nose up, applied some left rudder and swung around. I was just dropping the nose for the return pass when the radio crackled to life.

"Mayday! Mayday! Airforce Delta Bravo Tango! Flame-out! Two miles east of Dunsfold. Request emergency landing! ETA 40 seconds!"

The tower jumped in.

"Hawker X-ray abort landing—repeat—abort landing! Clear main runway! Delta Bravo Tango cleared for straight in approach!"

Reflexes overode thought. I banged the undercarriage up, fed on throttle and eased forward on the nozzle control lever. In two seconds I was zipping over the startled heads of the crew around the hover grid, speed increasing rapidly. I remembered about Bill's problem with yaw, so I kept it straight as I held the stick back to gain height. Glancing at the airspeed indicator I was shocked to see I was already over 200 knots. I eased the throttle back, then put the aircraft into a turn and bank left. The altimeter said 2300 feet. My thought processes began to function and I took stock. I was in an experimental jet fighter 2300 feet above the English countryside hurtling along at a cool 240 knots. Let's see—that's about 275mph or 440kph. The fastest I had ever flown in the Harvard IV was about 180mph.

Now what, smartass?

EIGHTEEN

Moscow, U.S.S.R.— the same day

The Zil limousine moved swiftly along Leningradsky Prospekt, travelling northwest out of the city toward the airport. Nalishkin was honoured that the head of the Directorate had accompanied him, though he knew this wily old bird well enough to realize that it was not out of any sense of regard.

When the thick plate glass partition closed, isolating them from the driver, Nalishkin knew the real reason was at hand.

"The truth, Volodya. What are your chances of success?"

"The truth, Comrade General. Excellent. It is planned to the finest degree. We have safeguards and back-up plans in place. They will not expect it, I assure you."

"You understand that failure will be on your head? I will disavow everything connected with the project. It will be your problem and yours alone."

"And if it succeeds?"

"Then promotions, decorations, privileges—for you and for me, Comrade Colonel. I will rise above Dmitrienko, and then I will crush him. What about his bitch of a granddaughter? Is there any sign of weakness?"

"None, Comrade General. She performs her duties with a zeal I find surprising, regardless of how demeaning. I felt sure I would prove that she is just using her grandfather's influence. I can't seem to break her down."

"Pity. I was hoping it would give us a lever—a chink in the bastard's armour. I've always suspected he was up to something, but I can't find it. Worst of all, the prick is in my way. This had better succeed, Volodya."

"Have no fear, Comrade. It will."

General Rastvorov grunted. Nalishkin was reminded of a saying told him by his father.

Stand well back when you let go of the bucket.

Rastvorov knew that one too.

Over Dunsfold, Surrey—the same day

I eased the throttle back as the airspeed touched 240 knots. Looking left through the perspex canopy I could see the triangle of runways at Dunsfold. Two miles away, I guessed. There appeared to be an aircraft on the main runway. Correcting my heading to parallel the airfield, I glanced again. The aircraft was gone. I keyed the mike. Be calm.

"Dunsfold tower, this is Hawker X-ray."

"Hawker X-ray, this is Dunsfold tower! Pass your message!"

Why did he sound so excited?

"Dunsfold tower, Hawker X-ray requesting some talkdown assistance to return aircraft."

"Roger Hawker X-ray. All other aircraft, clear this frequency! Emergency! Repeat, clear this frequency!" A pause. Different voice. "David, it's Bill Bedford. Do you read me?"

"Loud and clear."

"Do you want to eject?"

"Wot, and bang me 'ead on the canopy? Not on your Nellie. Let's get her down."

"Sir Sydney will be relieved. How do you want to do this?"

"I'm about two miles southeast of the airfield. I'll bring her around and line up on the runway. You can talk me down."

"Do you want to attempt a conventional landing?"

"That's a negative. I don't know the landing characteristics. Let's bring her in vertically."

"Roger, David."

"Turning 90 degrees to port. I can still see the airfield."

"Roger."

I watched carefully. I wanted to make the next turn to line up—I didn't want a lot of corrections and I certainly didn't want to go around again. Now.

"Hawker X-ray turning on final."

"Roger. We have you at 2.5 miles from the runway. Decrease speed to 200 knots."

"Roger, Dunsfold."

I eased the throttle back.

"Speed 200 knots."

"Descend to 200 feet."

"Roger."

I inched the stick forward, checking the altimeter and sighting visually. I centred the stick when I reached the height.

"Hawker X-ray, you are over the perimeter track."

"Roger."

Bill spoke very quietly. "Now gently, David. Ease the nozzles back to reverse thrust."

"Roger."

This was the tricky part. My heart was pounding, my hands sweating in the gloves.

I lifted the lever back and through the gate. The forward speed ceased quickly, but the nose went up and the aircraft wobbled unsteadily. It started to sideslip.

I applied more throttle, adjusting the control column. It steadied, holding in a hover. Easing the nozzle lever forward through the gate, I was stationery.

"Well done, David! Undercarriage down, and bring her in."

"Roger."

I lowered the undercarriage and looked out to check my bearings. I was almost over the tower. There was a large, delta-winged RAF aircraft near the hangar. Looked like a Javelin. Must have been the one in trouble.

Tilting the nose forward I inched toward the hover grid, reducing power slightly as I went. Over the grid at 100 feet I held for a moment, then eased the power off and let her settle. When she touched I dropped the throttle back and shut her down. I couldn't move, not even to open the canopy.

I heard the ladder bang as it was placed, then the canopy was popped from the outside, and there was Bill Bedford.

"Good Lord, David! Are you all right?"

I unsnapped the mask.

"I think so. That was some lesson, Bill. Do you do that for all of your first-timers?"

He started to laugh in relief, and so did I. Gingerly I climbed out. I was shaking. I took the helmets off, then grinned as best I could.

"Is that enough for today, or would you like me to try for the world's airspeed record before I go home?"

He had sobered up.

"David, when I heard that Mayday call I didn't know what to tell you to do. I was afraid I'd make you panic, and then you might have gone in. But you're safe, and you saved the aircraft. Do you know how much she's worth?"

"Nope. No idea."

"Give or take a million pounds sterling. But they don't like to insure experimental aircraft. And I hate to think of the set-back to the programme. Come on! Let's change! I'm buying!"

* * *

Half an hour later we were back at the Compasses. We'd parked, and Bill held the door for me. I guess I expected it to be quiet by 4 o'clock, so when a wall of cheering hit me I was taken aback. Then someone started singing 'For he's a jolly good fellow' and I was surrounded by airfield personnel. I was bewildered.

"What on earth for?" I shouted to Bill over the din.

"You brought their aircraft back. They want to thank you in their own way."

A drink was pressed into my left hand, and my right was continually being shaken. Some faces I knew, most I did not. Then there were two fellows in RAF flying coveralls.

"We're the crew from the Javelin you cleared for. Just wanted to add our thanks. Understand it was your first time in the kite. Quite an adventure, what?"

"Nothing compared to yours. Glad you got down in one piece."

Then there were my fellow North Americans.

"That must answer your question, David," grinned Reeder. "You must have had... what... a 20 minute conversion before the shit hit the fan?"

Several other people exchanged good-humoured remarks, and then they began to leave with waves and 'Cheerios'. Bill and I were sitting to have a few quiet minutes before we left. I was feeling pretty drained, but there was something at the back of my mind which had been pushed out by the excitement. It took me a moment to think of it.

"Bill, I caught sight of a gable, obviously on a building at the south of the airfield near the hovergrid. It's partially hidden by the trees. It seems to be all alone over there. Can you tell me anything about it?"

"You must mean the cottage. It was on the land where the runways are, and when they built the airfield they moved it over there rather than knock it down. It's been used from time to time as a residence and for storage, but it hasn't been occupied now for some years. Why do you ask?"

"Just curiosity. Is it possible to have a look at it?"

"By all means," he smiled, "but haven't you had enough for one day?"

"I might forget about it tomorrow, and I have an idea that I should check out."

In five minutes we were back through the gate and around the perimeter track to the old house. We passed several areas back in the trees which had tarmac leading in to them.

"Part of the aircraft dispersal areas from the Second World War. The sort of thing the P1127 would do away with. Won't be necessary to have squadrons all grouped around a highly visible airfield like this. Weapons today would obliterate it."

We parked on the perimeter and walked toward the two-story cottage. The rust-coloured shingling was in a terrible state, which meant rainwater was probably leaking into the house in torrents. There was a small out-building connected to the house on the right, but what I was interested in were the windows in the gable on the second floor. The glass had been broken out, and the attempt at boarding them up looked pretty flimsy.

"What are you looking for, David?"

I took a position on the ground.

"Stand here, Bill. Put your back to the windows, face this line, and tell me what you see."

He did as I had directed.

"Well?"

"Well—nothing. Only the hovergrid. Just a hole in the ground. No buildings, no hangars, no tower. Nothing."

"Now tell me what you'd see from that window up there if XP831 were on the grid and being test-flown."

"Oh! I see what you mean. It would be a ring-side seat for all of the hover trials. But this is inside the security fence and it's patrolled at irregular intervals."

"That wouldn't stop a determined spy. It's a natural—the house has been here for years and yet it supplies the perfect vantage-point and good cover both day and night. Can we get in?"

We walked around to the door. It was latched, but with minimal pressure it gave, and we were in. The smell was awful—years of animal and bird droppings, wood decay and mildew from leaks and moisture. I looked around on the lower level, but I most wanted to see the room with the gable window. We went on up.

One window frame was still in place, and the boarding over that window had been pried back at the left side. Indeed there was a perfect view of the hovergrid, and at this height even the mesh itself could be seen clearly. The remnants of the windowframe masked the opening completely from the outside. I asked Bill to have a look.

"I agree that it's possible, David. But we have nothing tangible to back it up. It's still only a theory."

I was looking through the debris on the floor. Dead leaves, broken glass, twigs, ticking from a long-destroyed mattress. I stirred it around with my foot, moving it here and there. Something caught my eye. I stooped to pick it up with my handkerchief.

"That might do it, Bill."

He examined my find.

"Yes, indeed."

It was a plastic cap from a 35 millimetre film canister.

"Someone's been up here taking pictures. I'll turn this in and see what Hammond can find out from it. Bill, Security should be told to examine the fence around here for marks of entry. If they're careful I'm sure they'll see signs."

"I'll take care of that part. Who do you think it is?"

"Most likely the Soviets. I just wish I knew what they were going to try. It's like trying to plug the holes in the dyke before the water comes through."

"I'll suggest they put more men on guard duty. The inner fence around the hangars, the assembly areas, and the design office are all well-lit and carefully patrolled, but we don't want to take chances."

We left the cottage after a last cursory look around, following the perimeter track back to the hangar. I got out and met Bill behind his car. He stared at me for a long moment.

"Bit more than meets the eye, aren't you, Baird?"

I shook his hand with an embarrassed grin.

"See you in the morning, Bill."

"0930 hours, old chap."

I stepped back and saluted, climbed into the Jag, and drove away. I wondered what the aviation history books would say about Bill Bedford, the pioneer test-pilot of the VTOL era.

Facts, skills, accomplishments—undoubtedly. But the humour and warmth of the real man would be hidden between the lines.

A pity.

NINETEEN

London, England—the same day

I used secondary roads for the drive into London, avoiding Kingston's traffic. Somewhere around Putney Heath I stopped at a call box to telephone Hammond.

"You've just caught me, Minstrel. Problem?"

"I have something for you, sir. It should go to a lab."

"Where are you calling from?"

"Putney Heath."

"Do you know the Coldstreams' mess?"

"Duke of York's Headquarters in Chelsea."

"Right. See you there presently."

It wasn't quite six, so I decided to call Marijke when I got to the mess. Traffic was slow through Putney and over the bridge and my arrival was delayed, but I was ahead of Hammond. Signing in as his guest I was informed that I was welcome to wait for him inside—a concession, I'm sure. The Guards can be a very pompous lot, and while I was wearing a major's rank I was 'only' in the Royal Corps of Transport, and in battle dress at that. As I entered the lounge there was an immediate exclamation.

"Good God! David?"

And there was House, looking astonished.

"What the hell are you doing in that outfit? Have we struck the bottom of the British barrel already? No more hearts-of-oak, is that it? Reduced to the maple tree, all sugar and sap. I knew it would happen one day. And crowns! God save us all! He's a major! Well, Major Disaster, what have you to say for yourself? Come on, explain to these honourable Coldstream gentlemen!"

The assembly of officers gathered around, sensing a lamb being led to the slaughter. I decided to play it out in Bluebottle's falsetto.

"You rotten swine! If you don't shut up I will place milk-loaded exploding-type reeds in your sexyphones and you will become the director of the Cold-cream Guards Band. Yes I will!"

It wasn't very funny, but it was the best I could do under the circumstances, and it produced a ripple of laughter from the honourable gentlemen. They were obviously hoping for more exchanges, but House decided wisely to cut it off.

"Gentlemen, may I introduce my friend and fellow Goon addict David Baird. You will soon see him in the musical *Curtain Call*, though I trust not dressed like a fugitive from the Indian mutiny as he presently is. Please make him welcome, but watch your wallets! Bourbon and coke, old son?"

House got my drink from the mess steward, and I shook hands with one or two officers who introduced themselves. Then House and I withdrew to a couple of chairs with a little more privacy.

"What's up, David? More of the same? I would have thought Paris was lesson enough."

"This is different, House. I can't tell you much, but I'm in on the ground floor of one of the most exciting projects in aviation. There's no danger—at least, not like in France—and I had some time before rehearsals started, so I said I'd help out."

"Why the uniform?"

"It's only a TA commission, and temporary at that. It was the easiest way to get me involved in the project."

"How long will it last?"

"Today and tomorrow. Nothing to get worried about. Now let's change the subject. What are you up to tonight?"

"Nothing much. I wasn't sure whether to call Nicki or just hang around the mess. Any suggestions?"

"I have to see Hammond for a few minutes when he gets here, but if Marijke is free I want to take her to Ronnie Scott's. Are you interested?"

"Oh, yeah, I'd like that," said Eccles' voice.

"Well then, show me where I can use the phone, you nit-wit, and I'll find out if it's a 'go'."

Off the entrance hall there was a small telephone room with a chair and table for making more private calls. Probably to one's banker or broker, I thought, knowing the financial position of most Guards officers. I sat, sipped my drink, and called Marijke.

"Oh, David. I am glad to hear from you. I think perhaps you are held up with your meeting."

She was being circumspect, which was natural after what she had said about her flat.

"What about tonight? Are you free, or do you have to work?"

"No, I don't work tonight. It is changed for tomorrow. Is it still possible that we go out?"

"Yes. And I missed you today. I'll be glad to see you. What time shall I come for you?"

"Is half-of-eight too late?"

"No, that's fine. Do you mind if House and Nicki come, too?"

"No, they are nice. I look to see you later. I miss you, too, David."

I hung up and just sat for a moment, sensing her warmth and her body. I was completely captivated, and while it felt exhilarating and exciting it was also frightening, for I knew I had lost a control over myself which I thought was unassailable. I stepped from the telephone room as Colonel Hammond came through the door.

"Well, Major Baird. Good to see you. Let me get a drink and we'll chat."

House saw us come in together, nodded at Hammond, but decided to keep his distance. The colonel began talking as we sat down.

"I was held up by a call from Sir Sydney Camm. You know who he is, of course."

"Chief Engineer of Hawker's. He was responsible for those wonderful biplanes in the Hart/Fury class, and the Hawker Hurricane which became a legend in World War II. Why, Colonel?"

"He rang through to me shortly after you did. Bill Bedford told him of your little episode this afternoon. He had a few comments to make."

I couldn't fathom his look.

"Good or bad, Colonel?"

"Favourable, I'd say."

The frosty smile had appeared.

"Evidently your reactions averted what could have been a set-back for the whole program. If you had crashed this afternoon, no matter what the reason, the Air Ministry would have demanded a review of the P1127. They've already lost one, as you well know, and the second prang might have been the straw to the camel's back. He wanted me to know that you had done good work."

"I didn't do anything, Colonel. Just got the hell out of there because I had to."

"Not according to Bill Bedford." The focus changed abruptly. "Well, what have you brought me?"

I handed over an envelope containing the film container cap, and explained how we had found it.

"I didn't touch it, sir. There could be a fingerprint on it."

"I'll get it analyzed this evening. Now, I've made some enquiries to our communications people and they say what you saw was probably a microwave antenna."

"How do they work?"

"On an extremely narrow beam. If the transmitter and receiver are not precisely lined up, then there would be no communication."

"What about someone else just picking it up?"

"Virtually impossible. The beam is so confined that it travels in one precise direction. Even the most powerful receiver in the world wouldn't catch it if it weren't aimed exactly right. And if there is any obstruction, the signal is lost. There can be nothing in the way."

"What's the range?"

"It depends on the height of the two antennae and the amplification of the signal. From what you described, they estimate a maximum range of 60 miles. Is all this connected?"

"I'm not sure, sir. So far it doesn't make sense. But any further action could compromise my source. I can't take that chance. I hope you understand."

"David, in this business we learn to protect our assets. That's the cardinal rule. But if circumstances force us to place an asset in jeopardy we try to warn and not leave him out in the cold. Defection and protective custody is not out of the question. Remember this when you are weighing things in the balance. I trust your judgement."

He stood. I was beginning to realize that this was his way of ending a meeting.

"I must go. I have a dinner engagement with a field marshal and two admirals. Once again, well done, and good luck tomorrow."

We shook hands and he strode away. House waited until he had disappeared into the dining room, then sauntered over.

"I'm beginning to wonder if I did the right thing by introducing you, old son. Your whole world seems turned around."

"Not really, House. This is temporary. A week from now I'll have forgotten all about it."

He gave me a strange look.

"I doubt that, old son, I really doubt that."

"Mark my words. Well, are you coming? I'm picking Marijke up at 8:30."

"I'll call Nicki, but even if she can't make it I'll come along, provided you don't mind the odd man out."

"Of course we won't mind, Harpic. I've got to change, so I'll nip back to the flat, pick Marijke up, then stop here for you. Will you be in the bandroom or the mess?"

"The mess, I guess. Good Lord, I'm bored. That rhyme's a crime!"

"Do you ever stop?"

"I'd cry or die to end, my friend."

"Enough! I'll see you later."

I grabbed my hat and belt and tore through the door with my fingers in my ears. House was incorrigible, but I couldn't imagine not having him as a friend. How dull life would be.

* * *

Arriving at my flat I caught Wicks completely off guard.

"'S'truth Mr. Baird! 'Ave you been called up or sumfing?"

I gave him the story about the Territorial Army, but I could see that he was staring at the uniform, the ribbons and the wings. Wicks had been in the desert with Montgomery and the British 8th Army, so he had seen his share of action.

I showered and changed quickly into a pair of white duck trousers, open necked shirt, and summer-weight royal blue blazer. As I dressed, my mind was working overtime. There were so many loose ends to think about.

I left the flat early. I wanted to make a telephone call, and obviously I couldn't use my own. The Cumberland was convenient, so I parked in a spot on Quebec Street and went in. Then I called the American embassy, and asked for Tony Cippola. He was there, which didn't surprise me, but had he really worked for the Department of Agriculture I'm sure it would have been nine-to-five.

"Tony Cippola," he said, tentatively.

"Tony, I don't know if this call is monitored or not, so I won't mention any names. We met last Saturday night when you dropped in to pay a visit. Remember?"

"Oh, yeah, sure, I remember. How ya doin'?"

"I'm just fine. Tony, does that offer still hold about helping me out?"

"Name it."

"I shouldn't on the phone. Can you meet me for a few minutes? I'm just around the corner at the Cumberland in the café."

"Five minutes."

I had barely got a muddy coffee started when he arrived. We shook hands, and he patted his head with a grin.

"Concussion. I shouldn't be working, but you know how it is. What can I do for you?"

"There are three American pilots doing some work over here on an experimental British aircraft. I've written down their names. There's probably nothing to tie them in to anything that's going on, but I'd appreciate some background on each one. If I tried it officially too many people would know I've asked. Can you help?"

"Nothin' to it. If they're over here officially, we'll have it all on file." He looked at the names, then back at me. "What's up? This has nothin' to do with the Fletchers, does it?"

"Nope. Shall we say I'm just helping someone out with a quiet unofficial enquiry. If nothing turns up, that's the end of it. If there's a connection I'll let you know, and you can decide if anything should be done from your end."

"'Sgood enough for me. I'll call you."

"Be careful what you say on my phone. It's bugged, and that's entirely because of the Fletchers. Someone really wants that list. Have you had any luck?"

"Not worth a shit. An' I gotta be careful, 'cause we been told by 'the man' to lay off. I never knew an ambassador to pull so much clout."

"I have to go, Tony. Thanks."

We shook hands again. He looked at me with narrowed eyes.

"As my old Milanese grandmother would say, slightly paraphrased and translated, 'There's more to thee than the eye can see'. Lemme in on it sometime, David. Maybe it'll help us both."

I paid my bill as Tony exited. I thought about what he said, but I wasn't sure how much he should know. Not yet, anyway.

I was late getting to Marijke, but not much. It surprised me when she came flying out her door, ran to the car and jumped in.

"David," she said breathlessly, "something happens tonight. It is about an airplane. I talk to one of the men who comes back from Moscow. He is always trying to impress me, and he brags that they 'get lucky' tonight with their operation. I try to get more, but he won't tell me. What can you do?"

I was already wheeling the Jag away at a clip.

"The man I should tell is having dinner at the place where we pick up House. We'll be there in a few minutes."

I tore through back streets to avoid lights.

"You have no idea what they are going to try or the time?"

"No, I am sorry. But he calls me one hour ago and is not in a hurry. I am guessing it will be very late. This is the usual time for their tricks."

We squealed left onto King's Road then a hard right, screeching to a halt at the gate. The sentry approached and saluted. I flashed my card.

"Major Baird! This is an emergency! Move it!"

"Yessir!" And he moved it.

I pulled up. "Stay here, love. I'll be quick."

I ran into the mess, catching a glimpse of House as I hurtled by toward the dining room.

"David! What the hell?"

I waved and kept going, slowing briefly at the door. Hammond was seated at a table on the left with three others. I ignored the looks of the stewards and went straight to him. They were startled as I approached, Hammond looking surprised—the others showed annoyance at the intrusion.

"Sorry Colonel Hammond. It's extremely urgent that I speak with you in private."

He said nothing, rose from the table and indicated an anteroom.

"What's wrong?"

"It's tonight, sir. And an aircraft is involved. It must be the P1127. But I don't know what they're planning."

He picked up a telephone.

"This is Colonel Hammond! Get me the Commanding Officer of the 1st battalion of the Parachute Regiment in Aldershot! Priority red, operator! I'm at extension 26!"

He dropped the phone in its cradle.

"Do you know anything else, David? Anything at all?"

"No, sir, there's nothing more. Do you want me to do anything—go down there, perhaps?"

"Not at all. You've done your bit. Now it's up to the security people and the Paras. If anyone shows up tonight they'll get a real shock, believe me. Away with you, now."

The phone rang as I departed and I heard him bark his name. So be it, I thought. House was standing outside the dining room. He shook his head as I came out.

"What next, old son? Aden? Northern Ireland? I'm sure there are some other trouble spots you could clean up by teatime tomorrow. They'll be writing scripts about you. I can hear it now: Look! Up in the sky! It's a turd! It's a pain! It's Superband! One tune from him and it's all over, folks! Can I be your agent, please? God! I'll be rich! Rich! Beyond my wildest dreams!" He came down. "What are you standing there for? Aren't you ready to go?" And he strode out the door.

I laughed as I followed him. He was just what I needed to bring me back to earth. To hell with it all tonight!

Marijke looked at me anxiously, then glanced at House, not knowing if she should say anything.

"Everything's under control," I smiled, then leaned over and kissed her. "Now forget about it. Tonight is ours."

"Desist, lovebirds, desist, I say," intoned House. "Off to the fair Nicki's abode. Oh, David, she wants to know if you can arrange a car chase through the streets of London tonight. You know, something to spice up the evening."

* * *

By the time we had reached Ronnie Scott's Jazz Club it was nearly 10:00pm. Located on Frith Street in the heart of Soho, it had recently opened to a lot of good press and much support from the jazz fans. I had phoned for a table, which was just as well, for the place fills up fast. Ronnie spotted us as we came in and came straight over. A fine tenor sax player, he had been with Ted Heath's band for years, then decided to open his club.

"David! How are you, mate? How's the show coming?"

"Rehearsals in a couple of weeks. Ronnie, I've got a thing coming up on the BBC in the fall. I want to talk to you about it when you've got some time."

"Just call me, mate. Will you sing a few tonight?"

"Depends on the group. Who's taking over at 10:30?"

"It's a surprise evening. Nobody knows until the intro."

"Come on, Ronnie! Fill me in!"

He whispered in my ear and my face lit up.

"Okay, okay! So I'll sing a few!"

He showed us to our table, and I invited him to join us later for a drink.

"Who is it, David?" pleaded Nicki. "I must know."

"Sorry. Mum's the word. I promised. But you'll love it!"

They badgered, but I wouldn't give in. We ordered steaks with a variety of vegetables, and a couple of bottles of wine. We ate as we listened to the group on the stand. They were good, but not spectacular. Around 10:25 they finished their last set, leaving to a pleasant smattering of applause.

A new drummer and bass player appeared. The drummer had a lot of rearranging to do—each has a personal set-up. Even the angles of the 'toms' matter, and the clutch clearance on the high-hat.

"David, that's Kenny Clare on drums and Johnny Hawksworth on bass," said a surprised House. "Must be someone special playing for them to sit in."

"Wait and see," I smiled enigmatically.

Ronnie himself went on the stand, picking up the microphone.

"Ladies and gentlemen! It gives me great pleasure to present one of the rising stars of British jazz! Currently appearing at the Fortune Theatre in *Beyond the Fringe*, the greatest comedy revue to ever hit the London stage, here is DUDLEY MOORE!"

The audience went berserk as a beaming face appeared from the doorway at the left, and then all 5′2" of this remarkable young comedian/entertainer/jazz pianist bounced onto the stand, sat at the grand and went into a sequence of Duke Ellington tunes. The crowd was suddenly hushed—they knew why they were there. An electric tension filled the club with excitement.

The next two hours went by like a whirlwind. Dudley's improvisations and dry wit held everyone spellbound, and when he introduced me I grooved into the mood and couldn't do anything wrong. I sang my songs with an abandon I could rarely use in a studio or broadcast, and the audience sensed something special.

Dudley and Ronnie Scott came to sit with us for a while and have a drink, and Nicki was just about beside herself with excitement. Dudley gave her and Marijke his autograph with a personal greeting, and the ladies were thrilled.

"I've seen you in *Beyond the Fringe* twice," said Nicki. "I think your sketches are marvellous."

"Had I learned to draw instead of play the piano they'd be even better," quipped Dudley. "Sketches. . . draw? Did you get that? Shall I flutter my eyelids? Would that help?"

While everyone was distracted by Dudley, Marijke leaned over casually with her mouth close to my ear.

"David, there is a man at the bar I see at the embassy today. He is second from this end."

I took a casual look, masking it by signalling the waiter. Thin, with a cadaverous face, he wore an ill-fitting dark suit. Not exactly a jazz regular.

"Did he see you at the embassy?"

"No, he is outside. I see him from my window talking to one of third secretaries."

"Have you seen him before?"

"No, he is not with embassy staff."

"Could be just a coincidence."

I said it but I didn't believe it. I didn't want Marijke to panic, but I would watch this man.

After another round of drinks Dudley and House got into a Goon Show routine which not only broke us up, it entertained everyone in the club. They were hilarious together, and were both obviously keen students of the Goons.

"House," said Dudley, "If Peter Cook is ever unavailable, you come and fill in. Forget about all those bearskins and bandsmen! What d'you say?"

For the first time in his life House was speechless!

It was nearly 1:00am when we left, still full of the fun we had shared. Dudley had kissed the ladies good night, and Nicki was in seventh heaven.

"Do you know," she said as we drove off, "he's as funny in real life as he is on the stage."

"The mark of a true genius," replied House. "You don't have to act it—you are it."

We dropped House and Nicki at her place, then Marijke and I headed back toward the centre of London.

"What now, love?" I asked.

"Can we walk for a few minutes? It's a lovely night."

I headed down Queen Victoria Street and found a place to park near Temple Lane, just past Blackfriars Bridge. We began walking along the embankment, looking at the lights from the river. We passed the four historic ships in their permanent berths, and soon reached the obelisk called Cleopatra's Needle.

We stopped to lean on the abutment, looking up-river toward Big Ben and the Houses of Parliament.

"You sing wonderful tonight, David. I don't know you sing so free. I only hear records, and you are more under control."

I laughed. "Do you mean I was out of control tonight?"

I kissed her to show that I was teasing.

"No, no. . . I only mean that. . . oh, I can't explain it!"

"I know what you mean. When I'm with a group like tonight, it inspires you to take liberties with the songs, to let them swing more. But you need someone like Dudley to light the fire."

"I'm glad to hear you sing like this. Now I think I understand. Music for you is everything, is this so?"

"Yes. And I'm glad you see it. Music is part of me—I can't be without it."

"Sing for me, please, right now."

"Okay, but you'll have to imagine the violins, just like in the movies."

I put my arm around her, thought for a moment, and began to sing the song which seemed to fit the occasion—*"Love of My Life"*.

"The time of endless twilight, when I was without you;
Those lonely days still haunt me, if ever I doubt you;
Before we met my life was just illusion,
So much delusion—a passer-by life;
But now with you beside me, to guide me wherever,
To share each carefree moment, each joyous endeavour;
And in your eyes I see the love, the promise of forever,
You are, to me, the love of my life."

She was pensively quiet when I finished, then turned abruptly and gave me a long, searching kiss.

"I love you. I stay with you tonight. Is this all right?"

"Yes." I hesitated, but had to say it. "Did you know that my phone is tapped by the KGB?"

"Yes. I know this before I meet you. It is about a man named Fletcher. He has your flat before. This is correct?"

"More or less. Do you know what happened to Fletcher?"

"No. I hear he is dead. I don't know how it happens."

"His flight was bombed by the man I met in Paris."

"Szrubek? He did this?"

"Well, not by his own hands. He hired some half-witted baggage handler in Gibralter to do the dirty work."

"I don't know this, David. My job in KGB is not this section. I only can hear things if other people speak too much, or maybe leave piece of paper and I see it. I ask not many questions."

She hesitated. Her English was sometimes better than others, and it seemed to be worse when she was under a degree of stress.

"You don't trust me, David?" she asked, softly.

"I trust you completely. And I love you. I just don't know where this is taking us. Do you?"

"No," she answered quietly. "I know I am happy with you as never I am before. I know I love you. Is this enough?"

"Yes, it's enough."

"Tonight we can be together?"

"Yes, if there are no other listening devices."

"No. Only the telephone."

I drew her close.

"Let's go."

We approached the car. A figure stepped from the shadows, startling us both. I froze, pushing Marijke behind me, wishing I had a weapon. It was the cadaver from the jazz club.

"Please excuse," he said with a heavy accent. "I am wisitor. You can tell me at what time pliz is changing of guard?"

I was about to tell him to go to hell when Marijke launched into Russian. The phrases flew back and forth, then stopped.

"David, it's all right. I must speak with this man. He's from my grandfather. We can drive him to Bayswater road while we talk?"

"You're certain it's okay?"

"Yes."

During the drive I had misgivings. Why this clandestine meeting? Why not at the embassy? What was Dmitrienko up to? They spoke in Russian. I just listened—frustrated.

We dropped him just off Bayswater Road near a small hotel, and I swung back on to Edgeware.

"Do you want to tell me about it?"

I was trying not to sound annoyed.

"I must first tell you of my grandfather."

"You don't have to, Marijke. I know about him."

"Yes, of course. I should guess this." She sat silently, brooding. "And still you trust me and want to be with me?"

"Yes. Now what was this about?"

"A warning from my grandfather. People in Moscow are trying to find who kills Szrubek. My grandfather thinks he knows, and if he does then others may find out. He warns me to avoid this man in case something happens."

I had gone cold.

"Do they think it's me?"

She shook her head.

"No. They think it's House."

TWENTY

Past midnight, Tuesday, June 19, 1962

We arrived at my flat to enter past the knowing smile of the night porter. Think what you like, chum.

On the way I had made two phone calls—the first to Hammond. He was waiting for word from Dunsfold. So far nothing. Were we all being manipulated? Marijke told me the truth, I was certain. Hammond was remarkably patient. Let's see what happens, he said.

I told him the KGB theory about House. Marijke was informed that they didn't know the name of the agent—they were just piecing bits together from various police reports. Hammond felt it unlikely that they'd pursue it much further, but he was going to have House watched, and if anything suspicious ensued he would see that House was put on leave and guarded.

My second call was to House. He thought it was hilarious. I should have known. I told him to be careful. He laughed some more. "Incorrigible bastard," I muttered, and rang off.

I showed Marijke around the flat, not that there was much to see. My decorating and furnishing were Spartan, if tasteful. Much of it I had bought from the Fletchers, and since it was sufficient for my needs I felt no necessity of adding to it. I opened the door and showed her

Kate's apartment.

"Tell me about her, please."

I did, and in more detail than I realized I knew. When I finished Marijke gave me a tiny smile.

"I think maybe you are in love with her sometime?"

I wasn't sure how to respond.

"I love her, Marijke, but I am not in love with her. She's a very dear friend, like a sister. That's why I'm so angry about what's happened to her parents. I want to protect her, and now someone has hurt her and I couldn't prevent it. All I can do is try to get even. It's not rational, but emotions never are."

"Please," she whispered, "let us go to bed and then hold me close to you."

Lying together naked, I sensed that Marijke shivered every now and then, even though it was a warm night. She was tense, and it took her a while to relax. We made love, but it was different this time—almost with desperation.

We both fell into a fitful sleep, and once I awoke to hear Marijke—what? Quietly sobbing. When I touched her she stopped abruptly, not responding to my whispered questions. I couldn't tell whether it had been part of a nightmare, or whether she had been awake and simply didn't wish to discuss whatever was troubling her.

I slept badly, haunted by the spectre of the unknown, and wondering about this beautiful woman, this KGB agent, with whom I was desperately in love.

* * *

We left my flat early. Marijke had to be on duty at 07:30, so I took her straight to the embassy. I put my forage hat, tunic, and belt, in the boot, and wore a civilian jacket, in case I was seen. It would have caused quite a stir in the KGB.

Marijke kept some articles of clothing and toiletries in her office at the administration building for the nights when she was on duty, so it was not necessary to go to her flat.

While we were warm with each other in the morning, I was aware of a growing tension which I couldn't interpret, and she resisted any attempt to discuss it. I hoped it was not something personal. The differences in our nationalities and ideologies I was certain could be overcome, one way or another. Hammond had given me a clue to that. Personal problems, on the other hand, do not resolve that easily.

Marijke said she would get something to eat at the embassy, so I decided to surprise Archie at Kneller Hall on my way to Dunsfold. I knew he breakfasted there at 0800 every morning, and there was always enough to accommodate a visitor.

The day was a bit dull, but the overnight rain had stopped, leaving a high overcast. I hoped the weather would hold for flying. Today was my last opportunity to experience the P1127.

It seemed hard to believe that tomorrow I would be boarding a ship in Southampton and sailing through the Mediterranean to the Black Sea and Odessa. I had promised to call Marijke during the day so she could give me the final details about the cruise. She was unable to see me in the evening because of some meeting or other, and the next time I saw her would be when I was picked up for the drive to Southampton tomorrow morning.

I pulled into a petrol station to tank up, and changed into uniform in the men's room. It would not do to arrive at Kneller Hall partially dressed.

Just after 0800 I was at the School of Music, and a steward showed me into the dining room. Archie was as flabbergasted as House had been, but a trifle more genteel.

"What on earth's going on, David? I never expected to see you in uniform again."

"I thought it might be the only way to get a free breakfast out of you, Archie," I teased.

"Och, sit down, lad, and tell me what you're up to."

I filled him in on the sanitized version of the story, but I could tell it wasn't taken hook, line, and sinker. They say some Scots have the gift of second sight.

"I can't say anything more, Archie, as much as I would like to. This military pilot charade is all finished today, then I'm just a simple singer again. I must say it's been fascinating."

"Whatever you say, David. I only hope you're not getting into some kind of hot water, official or otherwise. And speaking of things in that temperature range, have you seen anything of Miss Templaars since you were here?"

Before I could speak the look on my face gave me away.

"Ye're smitten, lad, aren't ye!" he chuckled. "An' all that prattle about bein' too busy. I knew it! I saw it in your eye last week. Ye daft bugger! What d'ye do now? This'll hae' the Russkies skirlin' in their borscht!"

"I don't know what we're going to do, Archie. Right now it's one day at a time. I can't think of much beyond that."

He walked me out to my car. I knew he wanted to offer encouragement, but his dour Scots nature saw only the reality, and in his eyes that reality was impossible. He said the only thing he could as he grasped my shoulder.

"Mind yourself, lad. Don't do anything foolish."

I saluted my friend Archie and went on my way.

* * *

Arriving at the Dunsfold gate, I knew something was different, and it wasn't just the armed Para who stood behind the security officer. There was a tension in the air that had not been there yesterday, as though the place were on a war alert. I went straight to Bill Bedford's office.

"Have you heard about our excitement last night?"

"No. What happened?"

"Hammond must have had a tip about unexpected visitors, so he sent 40 Paras with full battle equipment down from Aldershot."

"That must have stopped any attempt at sabotage right there."

"That's just it! Hammond got them in under cover in a civil registry Hawker 748. Nothing could have been more natural—a Hawker aircraft landing at a Hawker airfield. Here's the brilliant part. They towed the aircraft into the hangar and shut the doors before the Paras disembarked. The pilots were driven out of the main gate in a shooting-brake, plainly visible."

"A 'shooting-brake'?"

"I think you call it a station wagon. Well, a short while later all the lights were turned off, except for the security lamps. The Paras moved into position inside and outside the hangar, around the communications shack, and of course the design office where the plans are kept."

"Isn't the experimental design office in Kingston?"

"Right. I'll tell you about that presently. Somewhere around 0300 the outer fence was breached in three places. There were six men in groups of two. They were past the inner fence in 45 seconds. One group headed for the design office, one headed for the hangar, and the other kept watch outside. Two groups actually got inside the hangar and design office—they did it in a jiffy.

"As soon as they were in, all the lights on the airfield came on. The Paras told them to throw down their weapons. The two outside tried to shoot it out and got hit in the return fire. One died, the other is critical. With the bursts of machine-gun fire, the chaps on the inside knew the jig was up, and they surrendered."

"Were they Russians?"

"That's the surprise—not a Soviet amongst them. From what I've heard, they're all IRA except one, and he's Algerian."

"What were they after?"

"They were offered a lot of money to get the plans for the P1127, and more if they blew up the two prototypes as well. The two who got into the hangar were carrying enough explosives to flatten it."

"Who hired them?"

"A voice on the telephone. They picked up their instructions with a cash advance at a 'drop', I think they called it. After the job they would have been contacted again and told where to leave the plans and how to get the rest of the money."

"Who filled you in, Bill?"

"Our head of security. He was in on the preliminary questioning. But that's not the end of the story. They broke into the design office in Kingston last night as well."

"Damn, I hadn't thought of that. Bad news?"

"No, thank the Lord. Hammond had called Surrey Constabulary. They put a Flying Squad in place and nabbed the buggers after they breached the fence. Same story—explosives, and one man a known IRA safe cracker. All in all, I'd say it was a good night's work."

I mulled over the events. Something wasn't right.

Bill noticed my concern. "What's wrong?"

"I'm not sure. I've been on the inside of this for a week now, and a few things don't make sense. The trouble is, it *appears* to add up, and I can't help wondering if that's what we're supposed to believe. We got out of it too easily."

"For all our sakes I hope that's the end of it. Does this change your plans now, David? Do you want to carry on today with your familiarization?"

"Absolutely. I don't think that's the last of it, Bill, and the more I know about the P1127 the better. I'll be spending next week with the Soviets. If they're planning something else I want to be as conversant as I can be. Maybe I'm just being paranoid."

Bill went to check on the aircraft, leaving me to change into my flying suit. My mind was working overtime. If these raids were all the KGB was attempting, why had Marijke taken me to that house on the south coast? She'd told me that the house figured in the operation, and if last night was the attempt they were planning, where did the house fit in?

Since I was the only one who knew about the house, and they didn't know I knew, last night's attempt could be a complete set-up, a red herring. I still couldn't tell Hammond about the house. If only six KGB were aware of it, it would be very easy to narrow down the leak. I couldn't take that chance with Marijke's life. The horns of this dilemma were sharp indeed.

Bill collected me and we drove again in his car around the perimeter track past the flight line near the hovergrid.

"We're using 972 today. 831 is primping for night trials."

As we passed the flight line I saw 831 and its ground crew doing pre-flight operations. A tall, red-headed man in a flying suit was talking to one of the engineers.

"Who's that, Bill?"

"Stavic. He's the one who's doing the night trials. I hear he's something of a legend in the U.S. Air Force because of his night-fighter experience—Lightnings and Thunderbolts in World War II and F84 Thunderjets in Korea. I still don't think we're ready for this, so I'm keeping my distance."

"What am I doing today?"

"This morning mainly taxiing on one of the disused runways. I want you to get the feel of the aircraft in a conventional sense. If we're both happy we'll try some touch-and-go's so you can adjust to the landing characteristics. How does that sound?"

"Great. Anything to warn me about?"

"Wait 'til we do our walk-around."

We parked on the perimeter at the most southern part of the airfield. During the days of piston engines, flying fields were generally constructed with a triangle of runways. This was to allow the use of whichever runway was suited to the prevailing wind. With the power and speed of jet engines the wind factor was far less critical, and the main runways were used almost exclusively. Thus, on older airfields, there were often remnants of runways which were allowed to deteriorate. This was not the case at Dunsfold, for though disused for landings and take-offs, they were invaluable for taxi trials, clearing the main runway.

XP972 didn't look any different from XP831. In aircraft, however, as in anything else, looks can be deceiving. Control responses can vary widely, and the feel of each aircraft is unique unto itself. An aircraft, then, develops a personality, and most pilots prefer one aircraft over another. Bill liked XP831.

"Perhaps because she was the first, but she seems to be more responsive, a very friendly airplane. XP836, the second prototype, was a beast. You fought her all the time. The only good thing about my crash last December was that it was 836 and not 831. 972 here is not too bad, but not the lady that 831 is.

"The undercarriage on the P1127 is very different. The main wheels are on a common axle through a single leg, amidships and behind the centre of gravity, and the nosewheel amidships and forward of the CG. This 'zero-track tricycle' might take the weight of the aircraft, but it does nothing for lateral stability on the ground. To achieve this, folding 'outriggers' were placed on the wing-tips.

"At first they had castered wheels on the outriggers, but the shimmy created by the castering sometimes caused them to snap. Now the wheels are rigid with a shear pin in place, and they work well," commented Bill. "When you're taxiing, you have to tap the pedals to change the nosewheel direction rather than use continuous pressure."

Bill went on to explain that lessening the weight was the main reason for this unusual undercarriage, and gave me advice on controlling the aircraft while taxiing. Just before I climbed in, 831 did a conventional take-off from the main runway with Stavic at the controls. He was off the ground in very little distance.

"How did he get up so quickly, Bill?"

"He rotated the nozzles downward about 50 degrees after reaching

100 knots. The wing lift plus the jet lift at that speed gives you a very short take-off. Right. In you go."

For most of the morning I taxied 972 up and down the southeast runway, achieving greater speeds while learning how to control the nosewheel. Eventually I was lifting off, then setting down immediately, gradually getting the feel of the bird.

With barely 1200 feet of runway there wasn't much room to spare for this manoeuvre, and once I nearly ended up in a copse at the south end of the runway. I streamed the tail parachute just in time and stayed on the tarmac. Bill called a halt to the proceedings before noon, and we drove back to his office. As we changed we talked about the remainder of the day.

"How do you feel about really flying her this afternoon?"

"Good, I think, but I'm not too sure about a conventional landing from flying speed and height. I worry about control in the vertical axis as speed decreases."

"She does have a tendency to yaw at slower speeds. I think it has something to do with the way the jet exhaust hits the tail surfaces. But you can do a conventional take-off and a vertical landing. I'd like to get you to the jet-assisted short take-off before you finish today, if we have time. That way you've experienced most of the parameters of the P1127, even if you haven't experienced the complete flight envelope."

"How long do visiting pilots usually spend doing the whole flight envelope?"

"Test-pilots like our American friends stay for a month." His eyes crinkled. "I've taken a few short-cuts for you."

"I appreciate what you've done for me, Bill. I'll go away from here with a good working knowledge of vertical flight and the P1127. I can't tell whether it will play a critical role, but at least I know what I'm looking for and how to interpret it."

"Let's get over to the Compasses, if you're ready."

"Why don't you go ahead? I have some calls I must make. I'll drive over and join you."

"Fine. I'll try to save you a seat, but don't count on it!"

With a wave and a grin he departed. I sat and called Marijke at the embassy. The tone of her voice told me something was wrong. It had a lifeless quality I'd never heard before.

"Oh, David. Thank you for calling. I just look at the details for tomorrow. We pick you up at 07:00am. When we reach Southampton we board. There is breakfast on the ship, if you like to wait."

"Did you find out about the band?"

"Yes. It is the regular ship's band which is on this ship all of the time. They are from England. Mr. Nalishkin knew you must have a band like this, so he hires them. Is this satisfactory?"

"I think so. How many are in the band?"

"Five, but I do not know what instruments. I'm sorry."

"I can make a pretty good guess, so it doesn't matter. At least I know which arrangements to bring."

There was silence. I didn't know what was safe on this line into the Soviet embassy, and there was so much I wanted to say.

"Are you feeling alright, Marijke? You don't sound very well. Perhaps you are getting a virus or something."

"I think I am just tired. I rest on the ship tomorrow."

I chose my next words carefully.

"I'll be moving around a lot this afternoon, but if you want to reach me, I'll leave a number with Nicki. Call me if you have any free time. Okay?"

"Yes. . . yes, that is fine. I see you tomorrow, David."

I wondered if she understood. I looked up the number for the *Daily Express* and called through to Nicki.

"Hello, David. This is a surprise. Don't tell me. You're trying to find House. Right?"

"Not this time Nicki."

"Just as well, because he's probably ogling the girls in some strip club in Soho right about now, and you'd never drag him out. What can I do for you?"

"If Marijke calls you, will you give her this number to reach me? It's very awkward calling her at the embassy, because you can never be sure who's listening. The number is Guildford 7349."

"Certainly. It's no problem at all. By the bye, thanks for last night. You're a terrific singer. I'm thinking of letting you share my heart with Dudley."

"What about House?"

"That's not one of the bits he's interested in, I'm afraid."

I laughed. "Nicki, can you do me one more favour?"

"It'll cost you a song."

"For a place in your heart it's worth it."

"What do you need, love?"

"Can you dig out a biography of Dwight Vandenberg for me?"

"The American ambassador? Piece of cake. How soon?"

"How about taking it home with you? I'll call when I get back to London this evening, and if it's okay I'll come and get it."

"That's fine. You might even see your pal. He's supposed to come by later on."

"Great. I'll see you then, Nicki. Thanks."

I wanted to call Hammond, but I decided to leave the phone alone for a few minutes in case Marijke called. I stood to stretch as it rang.

"Hello?"

"David, it's me."

"Where are you calling from?"

"The ladies room in a restaurant on Kensington High Street. I know they have a phone, and I am safe to call you from here."

"Give me the number and I'll call you right back. Otherwise you'll have to keep putting coins in."

"It's fine. Kensington 3362."

"Don't go away."

"I don't."

I waited a few seconds and put the call through. Marijke answered on the first ring.

"David?"

"Yes. I was afraid to talk to you at the embassy. I didn't know what to say. I thought someone might be listening."

"Today they monitor all calls. Something goes very wrong last night. They are very angry."

"I know all about it. Are you in any kind of trouble? Do they suspect you?"

"No, I don't think so. The one who brags to me is too stupid to know I understand what he tells me. He thinks I am only a woman, and women have no brains. They are only for sleeping with."

"Then what's wrong, Marijke? I felt it last night—I felt it this morning—I felt it when I called you just now. Have I done something wrong?"

"No, David. It is because of me, because of my life. It never matters to me before what I do and what happens to me. I have a mission—a duty—and that is all that I care. Now I meet you. And this makes me hate what I do. But it is too late to stop."

She fought to control the emotion.

"It's can't be too late, Marijke. There are ways, believe me! We will talk about it on the ship! Can't you get out of this meeting tonight?"

Her control disintegrated.

"No. I cannot. I cause much trouble. Much trouble. And not for me. For others. I let them down. I have no choice. I don't can change it. I am trapped." Her voice dropped to a whisper. "And now I hate what I do, and I hate what I am."

I hesitated. "Marijke," I said softly, "Perhaps I can help."

"No. You don't can understand. There is much about Soviet Union not for explanation. Some things have roots deep into the earth, and we are born to follow a tradition which places everything above one person. We have worth only because we serve this purpose, and we bring honour to our family when we sacrifice ourselves. And it remains secret, or it destroys us."

"I don't understand, Marijke. Surely anything can be changed. You just have to want it enough and decide not to quit until you make it happen." I hesitated. "I'm the problem, aren't I? I've caused all this trouble in your life."

"No, David, I'm glad I meet you. It brings me love, and this is something I think I never know. But with this love I see everything else different, and this brings much pain. Now I must live with this pain. I must go. I see you tomorrow."

Before I could speak she was gone. I sat there with the dead receiver in my hand, numbed. What had I done to her? What was so terrible that she couldn't tell me? What traditions and loyalties was she talking about? Why wouldn't I understand? Was I so obtuse? God! what was I going to do about it?

Even in the midst of this confusion I knew I had to reach Hammond. I followed procedure, but this time I had to wait.

"Hello, Minstrel. I'm sure you've heard about last night."

"Yes, sir, but somehow I don't think it's over."

The voice was suddenly sharp. "Why? What else do you know?"

"Nothing tangible. It's just a feeling about last night. There were no Soviets involved. Is this normal for them?"

"Very much. The four we caught have been through a pretty hard grilling, and they have no obvious connection with the Soviets at all. If we hadn't tied it to your warning and your source, we mightn't even suspect the Soviets—it could have been purely IRA. Can you give me anything to back up your intuition?"

"Remember I said that the four Soviets who were out of the country were supposed to be involved? Look at last night. How were they involved? The implication was that they would be in an active role. We only know about one voice on a telephone. Sorry, sir. It's just a gut reaction, but it doesn't fit."

"Then to be on the safe side, Minstrel, I'm going to leave the Paras in place for a couple of days, and I have a security team in Kingston which will do the same. Are you departing as planned tomorrow?"

"Yes. Everything seems to be normal as far as the cruise is concerned. All I can do is listen and look and maybe do a little snooping if the opportunity occurs."

"Don't stick your neck out, Minstrel. You're just an observer, remember? Leave the James Bond heroics to my friend Fleming, though I don't know where he gets that nonsense. It was certainly nothing he did around here."

I had to say the next bit carefully.

"If it were either necessary or expedient for a Soviet who has helped me to come over, would there be a problem?"

"Probably not, but I'd like some warning if it's on. There are always repercussions, and we try to head them off."

"No guarantees, sir. If it happens, it may be in a hurry."

"Then so be it, Minstrel," he said quietly.

"Thank you. Oh, sir, what about the plastic cap I found?"

"The film container was made in East Germany. It's not sold in the west. There was a badly smudged partial on the cap, not enough for a match. But I think we learned what we had to. I've already sent a team to search the cottage, and steps have been taken to see that it is secured."

"Then I guess I'll see you when I get back from Russia, sir."

"One thing, Minstrel. If you need help, contact any British embassy or consulate. Use the phrase 'Alpha India Tango'. You'll be given all their resources and I'll be notified immediately. Good luck, Minstrel, and *bon voyage*."

As I put down the phone I heard a car's brakes squeal outside. Bill, I thought, looking at my Rolex. Well, so much for lunch. I heard footsteps on the stairs, and then he appeared.

"I assumed you were stuck on the phone. Here's a roast beef sandwich for you, and a Tizer."

"Thanks."

"You didn't miss much. Most of the talk was about last night's break-in. Did you get anything more?" he asked, gesturing toward the phone.

"Not really, Bill," I said through my munching, "The Paras are hanging on for a few days, just in case."

"I shouldn't think they'll try again so soon, especially since they know we're on to them. Now, about this afternoon. You'll take 972 up off the main runway. When you reach 150 knots, which will give you some margin, rotate the nozzles down 50 degrees. You'll be immediately airborne. Stay straight and level. Advance the throttle and climb to 200 feet, then undercarriage up, and ease the nozzle lever forward. I'll be flying chase in a Hunter, so once you're in the air you'll have company."

"How do we coordinate?"

"I'll take off first, then circle at cruising speed about a mile from the flight line. When I hear the tower clear you for take-off, I fly in over the field and tuck in behind you as you get airborne. We rarely send an experimental aircraft up without a chase plane. Merewether is with Stavic today, for instance. This way I can guide you through some manoeuvres, if we're both happy the way things are going."

My nerves returned with a vengeance.

The two aircraft were on the apron in front of the hangar. By comparison to the stubby little P1127, the Hunter looked sleek and fast. It was a two-seater T Mark 7, XL564, in grey aluminum finish.

"We'll start up here, David, and taxi to the flight line. I'll lead. Oh, here's an ordnance survey map of the area in case you should need it. It's unlikely, but clip it on for safety."

We did our pre-flight checks, climbing in at about the same time. Bill started up and the trolley was wheeled over to me. I ran through the sequence from the list clipped on my knee, and the big Pegasus whined and rumbled. I had wondered at the odour in the P1127, and now I recognized it as similar to that of some older piston-engined aircraft—oil and hot metal.

Bill cleared with the tower to taxi on the perimeter, and I did the same, nudging the rudder pedals to steer and hanging on to the brake in case I overshot. We were at the north-east end of the airfield, taking off in a slightly south-westerly direction.

As I listened to Bill on the radio I checked my altimeter and compass. His streamlined craft lifted gracefully into the air, banked left and commenced a turn around the airfield. He began another wide turn at the extreme end of his circuit, then his voice crackled on the radio.

"Hawker X-ray, this is Hawker Alpha. Start your roll."

"Roger, Hawker Alpha. Dunsfold tower, this is Hawker X-ray requesting clearance to take-off on runway 25."

"Hawker X-ray, you are cleared for take-off."

I pushed the throttle, turned onto the runway with a couple of well-placed nudges, applied the brakes to stop, then had a last-minute look at the gauges. Everything looked normal. Nozzle lever fully forward, throttle back.

"Hawker Alpha, this is Hawker X-ray. Rolling now."

I advanced the throttle to maximum, released the brake, and virtually leapt forward. I nudged the left rudder pedal to correct my track, and realized I had passed 150 knots. Gently I eased the nozzle control back to the 50 degree pre-set, and I was airborne.

I didn't want yaw, so I held carefully straight as I increased height. Reaching 200 feet I retracted the undercarriage and eased the nozzle control fully forward. Still flying straight, the altimeter was racing upward, reaching 2000 feet before I noticed the Hunter to my port side and slightly behind me.

"Hawker X-ray, this is Hawker Alpha. I'm going to ask for clearance to 20,000 feet. Is your oxygen plugged in?"

"Roger."

"Dunsfold tower, this is Hawker Alpha requesting clearance to angels 20, two aircraft in flight."

"Hawker Alpha, Hawker flight cleared for angels 20."

"Hawker X-ray, switch to alternate frequency."

"Roger. Switching now."

"That's better. Now we don't have to do all the procedural brouhaha. How was the take-off?"

"Felt fine. I was over the 150 knot line, though. Got there faster than expected."

"No matter. There's a wide margin. Have you done any formation flying, David?"

"No, and I don't think I want to start right now. That's all I'd need—brush wingtips with you and bring down both aircraft. I don't think Sir Sydney would be too happy."

"Message understood. I'll keep my distance. Start increasing altitude. You can take her up at a climb rate of 3000 feet per minute at a speed of 400 knots. She'll climb much faster, but we'll take it easy."

"Roger, Bill."

I adjusted the throttle, pulled back on the stick, and watched the altimeter wind. Bill was about 30 yards off my port wing in the Hunter.

"I don't want to get too far inland, so turn 90 degrees to port."

"Roger. Turning to port." I watched the compass as I brought it around, straightening out as we touched south south-east. Still climbing, we were now above 11,000 feet.

"Now do that again, and we'll start the next leg. Oxygen switched on."

"Roger. Oxygen on. Turning to port."

I repeated the sequence, and 90 degrees later we were flying east north-east. I looked at the altimeter.

"Angels 20, Bill. Levelling out."

"How's your jet-pipe temperature?"

"About 350 degrees centigrade."

"That's fine. How fast have you flown, David?"

"This is it. Nearly 420 knots. Why?"

"You're going for a new record. Advance the throttle, hold her steady, and watch her fly."

Lord. What next?

"Throttle advanced to maximum stop. . . *Jesus!*"

I was pushed back into the seat hard. The acceleration of this aircraft was incredible. I looked to my left. No Hunter. Air speed indicator. 580 knots. Still accelerating.

"Bill? Where are you?"

He laughed in my headset. "A mile behind you. I can't match that acceleration. What's your airspeed?"

"Just over 600 knots."

"Jet-pipe temperature?"

"450 degrees."

"Throttle back to 500 knots and I'll catch up."

"Roger."

I eased it back, and in 15 seconds the Hunter was on my port wing again.

"Well, how was the ride?"

"Incredible! Does she ever move!"

"If you look down, there's the English Channel. We're just south of Southampton. Now, advance the throttle, put her into a shallow dive, then level out in 30 seconds. Got it?"

"Roger."

Throttle ahead full. Nose down slightly, about 30 degrees. Jammed hard back into the seat! Hold her steady! I weighed a ton! Must be 7 G's! Slight judder. Controls feel easier. Speed 680 knots! I glanced at the Mach indicator. Mach 1.2! I was flying above the speed of sound!

"Holy shit!"

"Ease her nose up and throttle back." Bill was laughing.

"Roger."

BANG! An explosion! I nearly crapped my pants!

"What the fuck was that?" I yelled.

"Just the sound barrier, my dear chap," said a calm voice. "Such vulgarity."

"You bugger! You set me up, didn't you?" I started to laugh.

"The drinks are on you, old chap! Can you handle one more?"

"Why not? I'm sitting in something warm and squishy anyway."

"Did you ever roll a Harvard?"

"Nope."

"Probably just as well. Now, this one rolls like a top. One flick of the wrist, she'll go right 'round. Watch your artificial horizon to bring her out. When you're ready."

I pushed the stick hard to port. It rolled over like a puppy-dog. I lost my sense of balance, focused on the artificial horizon and centred the stick. I was through!

"Okay. Let's go home. How did you like it?"

"Fantastic, Bill. Nothing short of fantastic."

"Good. You handled it well. Now, 180 degrees to port."

"Roger. 180 degrees to port, turning now."

I followed the compass through its swing, then straightened.

"Ease throttle, commence descent about 4000 feet per minute. Should set us up for Dunsfold."

"Roger. Starting descent now."

"We're crossing the coast. There's Worthing."

I looked down, but couldn't recognize anything. We were almost to 9000 feet. At 400 knots the 24 miles to Dunsfold would take about 3 minutes.

"Hawker X-ray, switch to tower frequency."

"Roger. Switching."

"Dunsfold tower, this is Hawker Alpha.

"Pass your message Hawker Alpha."

"Request clearance to hover and land for Hawker X-ray. Hawker Alpha requests permission for circuits until Hawker X-ray has landed. ETA one minute."

"Hawker Alpha cleared for circuits. Hawker X-ray cleared for hover landing."

"Hawker X-ray turning on final," I said.

I had a terrible feeling of let-down.

It was over.

TWENTY-ONE

Moscow, U.S.S.R.— the same day

General Dmitrienko leaned back in his chair.

"I think they've done it this time, Bren."

"Sir?"

"They botched an attempt to sabotage an experimental aircraft in England and steal the plans. It's a total disaster, and you know what the Chairman thinks of failure. We may be rid of Rastvorov sooner than I had hoped."

Dunsfold, Surrey—the same day

The landing had been uneventful, for which I was grateful. I didn't need everything to become a drama—there was enough of that in the rest of my life these days.

Bill had walked to my car with me, and we faced that unpleasant task of saying goodbyes with the promises to keep in touch which most people are too busy to honour.

We exchanged phone numbers, shook hands, and I was genuinely sorry that the two days had come to an end. It was hard to put into words.

"Bill, thank you for your patience and tolerance. I'll never forget the experience. I know I had no honest right to be here. I just hope it all pays off somehow."

"We shall see when we get to the end of the road, shan't we? Good luck, David. It's been. . . well. . . different."

He gave me a smile and a wave as I drove off, and it felt like a door closing on a brief chapter of my life.

What to do first? Get out of the uniform. So, straight home.

Moscow, U.S.S.R.— the same day

He snatched the phone as it rang. He had been waiting impatiently.

"Yes?" he barked.

"Scramble."

"Yes, yes." He turned the switch. "Well?"

"Exactly as planned, Comrade General. It was perfect."

"A success?"

"Absolutely."

Rastvorov smiled smugly.

Dmitrienko's days were numbered.

London, England—the same day

Traffic had been light, still it was after 08:30 when I pulled up to the flat. I ran a bath, and was just about to step in when the phone rang. It was Tony Cippola.

"Hi David. I got those books you asked me about. You can have 'em for a few days. Why don't we get together same as last time?"

"Fine. About 09:30 okay?"

"See ya."

I threw on some dark casuals and left just in time to get to the Cumberland. Tony had beaten me to it.

"I'm glad you called. I was going to try to get hold of you. No trouble getting the stuff?"

"Naw. I played it cool, said it was a routine security check. Nobody asked questions. Wanna tell me why you really want this?"

"I'm playing a hunch, Tony. A little bit of cross-checking. I told you—if I turn up anything dirty, it's yours."

"Yeah. Well, I did a little cross-checkin' o' my own. I'm not sure where you're comin' from. On the surface I see a singer. Underneath I find an army officer."

"In music, Tony."

"Yeah, yeah, I know about the band stuff. I couldn't help wonder what would happen I scratch a little deeper and see what pops out. I know you fly a plane—you learned in the army. I know a Major David Baird has been down in Dunsfold for a couple of days flyin' a new jet. I figure it must be two different David Bairds, right? No possible connection."

I had to tell him something, so I used the story I had used in Dunsfold. At least it would check with the American pilots.

"So why are ya sniffin' around our guys?"

He knew a bit about the supposed IRA raid on Dunsfold. I told him the rest, and that it wasn't IRA.

"The trouble is, I don't think it's over. They're determined to get the technology of that plane one way or another. I just wanted to check the wild cards in the deck—the three Yanks—and do it without ruffling any feathers. If I'd asked officially backs would have been up from here to Pennsylvania Avenue. I don't expect to find anything. I just didn't want to leave a loose end lying around."

"Why you and not one of the MI5 guys?"

"You heard about their leaks? Even if they found something the Soviets would know about it in an hour. I figured it was safer for me to check it out, that's all."

"I don't get the army connection."

"Look, it's like in the States. I'm just a National Guard officer doing my two weeks in the summer. I drew that job because I'm part of a reserve unit that flies planes for army co-operation and communications. It's no big deal, Tony. It's routine."

"Yeah, okay, I got it now. I didn't know it was National Guard stuff. That makes sense. I just didn't want to be gettin' our guys inta some kinda shit, ya know what I mean?"

He handed me an envelope.

"It's all there. On all three of them. Just career stuff. I couldn't get any psych profiles or fitness reports or that crap. Woulda caused too much trouble. I got enough as it is. Okay?"

"That's all I need. Thanks."

"See ya. Keep in touch, okay?"

"Count on it, Tony."

After he had gone I waited a few minutes and phoned Nicki at home. She was there, and House was with her. Yes, she had the bio on Dwight Vandenberg. I was on my way.

* * *

Twenty minutes later I knocked on the door of the former alms house. It was in a row of such houses which bordered the green on three sides. Strange how what was suitable for the poor in the 16th century was now only affordable by the affluent.

Nicki answered the door. "Hi, David. Come in."

I stepped into a delightful little house, tastefully decorated and furnished. A lot of care had been taken.

"Nicki, this is beautiful."

"Well, thanks, but I'm only the tenant."

"You've got good taste just to want to live here."

She took me through to the living room. House was sitting in a large comfortable chair with the ever-present sherry.

"As I live and breathe, it's Sir Dancelot—or is it Sir Singalot? I'm always getting you two mixed up. Have you had a busy day rescuing damsels in distress?"

"Slaying a 'Dragon' seems more my style."

"I beg your pardon?"

"I'll explain it some other time, old fruit."

Nicki handed me an envelope. "This is what you wanted."

"No difficulty?"

"None at all."

"What do I owe you for the copy?"

"David, really."

"Exactly, my dear," said House. "When these colonials offer, grab it. You never know when they're going to dump your tea into the harbour, for God's sake. Makes for a dreadfully soggy cuppa."

"Just ignore his ravings, David."

"I usually do."

"Why do you need the bio on Vandenberg?"

Another evasion. "Just some loose ends around Kate's parents. Their paths have crossed over the years. Kate can't recall—she was either too young or not taking any notice."

"When is Kate coming back?" asked House.

"I don't know. I haven't heard from her, and I hate to bother her with details at a time like this. She'll let me know when the time comes. Look, you two, I hate to dash, but I'm off on a sea voyage tomorrow, and I haven't packed anything yet."

"How long are you away with the Russkies?" asked House.

"I'll be back within a week. I'll see you both then."

"Have a lovely time, David," said Nicki.

"Remember what they told Marco Polo as he left for Siberia?"

"No, House, what did they tell Marco Polo?"

"Watch your 'steppes', old son. Maybe there's a lesson in there for you. Good luck."

"You be careful, too, House. I'm sorry I got you into it."

I left them on a serious note. Why were they worried for me? I was going on a cruise for a holiday, and I was going to be with Marijke. Anything else was happenstance.

Marijke. I started thinking about her as I was driving through Admiralty Arch and down the Mall toward Buckingham Palace. I often came home this way. The Mall was quiet at night, and the vista of the palace a reassuring one, like saying goodnight to Mom on the way to bed. The Royal Standard was flying. She was home. 'Night, Mom.' I wished Marijke were with me.

Maybe her meeting was over! On one of those irrational impulses I decided to drive to her flat. Telephone first? I should. No, that would spoil the surprise. The truth was that I had made up my mind to go and nothing could stop me.

I was close, and arrived at Kensington Square in less than ten minutes. I decided to park the car on the square and walk in.

As I entered the mews I heard music again. It was a balmy evening, and most people had their windows open.

The music came from Marijke's flat. She must be home.

Then I heard the laughter. Not one voice laughing, but several voices. Some of them were male. I hesitated. Perhaps the meeting was at her flat and was still going on.

Next I saw the car. The Facel Vega. Herr Kurt Werner of the West German Embassy. I was uncertain of what to do, yet drawn forward as metal to a magnet.

I was perhaps ten feet from the door when a stray gust of wind caught the drawn curtain of the main living room window, holding it out in the night and displaying the interior like a freeze-frame in a film.

In that instant my world stopped moving, the image seared into my brain.

There were five people in the room, all naked. A pale-skinned woman with dark hair was lying on her back on a coffee table, copulating with a short black man. The other woman was on her knees, bent over the table, caressing both of them orally. One man lay under this woman, another was astride her from the rear. They each had an orifice to penetrate.

This woman had long, blonde hair.

She was the one I recognized.

TWENTY-TWO

London, England—the same night

I sat in semi-darkness, unable to face the light. Light would force everything into the open, and I needed to hide.

I couldn't remember driving home. My mind was partially blocked—some form of denial. When I stepped from the car I was bathed in sweat. I should have been seething with anger and betrayal, but I felt nothing. I was numb.

Instinct was trying to get me to bed, to wipe it out completely. Instead I fought this and climbed into a warm bath. Over the next hour I relaxed, dozing off and on in the tub. I got out, dried off, wrapped the towel around me and made some tea. As it was steeping I poured a brandy, then sat to sip them alternately.

I still couldn't face it. I was utterly confused. As yet no anger. I was in shock, protecting myself from breakdown. In fact, I could barely think of Marijke at all. My recollection of her was as in a dream of long ago, and in long ago there is no pain.

I was forcing myself to stay awake until I could deal with it, while my instinct said shut down and sleep. What about the cruise? I couldn't go now. I could barely think of it.

The bios of the Americans. Perhaps if I sorted through them it would start me functioning, and they were far enough away from the problem to give me an objective focus. I threw on a sweatsuit.

I began to read, then to make notes. I didn't know what to expect, but whatever it was I realized I was going to be disappointed. These people were as American as apple pie, and Reeder and Drinkwater were squeaky clean to boot.

Stavic was one better. He was a war hero, a fighter pilot in both World War II and Korea. Decorated 4 times in the first, twice in the second. Shot down and taken prisoner by the North Koreans. A POW for 18 months. Staff jobs after that—the Pentagon, NATO in Brussels, NORAD, and finally Moscow as the air attaché. Retired at his own request.

So much for the pilots. What about the ambassador? I went through the bio, and every few lines I felt as though I had read it before. I laid Stavic's bio out, and began cross-referencing. Vandenberg had been Stavic's squadron commander in WW II, and his group commander in Korea. Both the Pentagon and NATO appointments had been as a staff officer under Vandenberg. But Vandenberg had not been at NORAD, and he was retired from the air force when Stavic had been in Moscow.

No wonder Vandenberg had pushed to get him a job with one of the big aircraft companies, plus his liaison with the P1127. What the hell. That sort of thing happened everywhere. Why should the air force be any different?

I finished reading and realized there was nothing suspicious. I don't know what I had expected to find. It was just a long shot.

I tentatively reached toward my other problem. Could I face it? Not yet. It was a seething cauldron, and I would be badly burned if I ventured in. The phone rang, and I was glad for the distraction. It was Kate, calling from New Hampshire.

"How is everything in Colebrook?"

"It's been pretty good. Gram's wonderful. I think I needed her more than she needed me. She has this wonderful country philosophy toward life, full of acceptance and spiritual belief. It's helped me a lot."

"When are you coming back?"

"I'm not sure. We went to Boston to visit Gram's younger sister for a couple of days. We just got back. We've had a break-in, and Gram's place is a mess."

I had an uneasy feeling. "Is there much missing?"

"So far we can't find anything that's gone. There's more vandalism than anything—drawers dumped, books all over the place, upholstery ripped open. It's awful. We can't stay here tonight so we're going to neighbours."

"Be careful, Kate. I don't like this. Warn the local sheriff to be on the lookout for strangers, and tell him that it may have something to do with some government papers of your father's that are missing. Get him to call the State Department or the FBI."

"Do you really think it's connected?"

"Don't take chances. These are ruthless people. I'm sorry it followed you to your grandmother's."

"I may try to come back on Friday if we can get this mess cleaned up. Will you be around?"

The pendulum swung. Come on—gut reaction. Don't even think. Whatever you feel this instant, go with it. Rationalize it later.

"I'll be away for a week, Kate. I'm singing on a cruise ship, leaving tomorrow. Through the Mediterranean. I'll fill you in when I see you. But I won't be able to meet you."

"That's okay. The embassy will arrange it. I'll see you when you get back. Have a nice time, David. I mean it."

Fat chance of that.

"I'll see you next week. Give my love to your grandmother, and don't forget to see the sheriff."

I put down the phone, wondering what the KGB would make of that conversation, and replaying it in my mind to see if I had inadvertently made reference to anything I shouldn't. In retrospect it seemed to be pretty normal under the circumstances. Maybe my remark about the FBI would help to scare them off.

I was about to consider my immediate problem and the snap decision just reached when there was a tap on my door. What the hell? Who could it be at two in the morning? I looked through the spy hole. No one in sight. I called through the door.

"Who is it?"

"Delivery for Mr. Baird from British-Lion Export and Import,"said a quiet voice which I recognized.

I pulled the door open. "Colonel Hammond? What's up?"

I shut the door quickly as he entered the flat.

"Couldn't use the phone, as you know. Had to tell you before you left tomorrow. One of the P1127's has gone down."

"Down? You mean crashed? Jesus! What happened?"

"They were doing a night trial. Aircraft had some electrical problems, lost all instrumentation. Chase plane lost him in cloud. Went down somewhere in the channel. Air-Sea Rescue are looking for wreckage or the pilot right now. So far, nothing."

"Who was flying?"

"Chap named Stavic. American. There's going to be hell to pay when the American ambassador hears about it."

"Yeah, I know about their connection. Stavic worked for Dwight Vandenberg in several postings during his service."

"Did you meet him in Dunsfold?"

"No. Just saw him from a distance. Is there more?"

"The engineers at Dunsfold are adamant that nothing was amiss with the electrical systems. They're convinced there had to be some outside interference, sabotage of some kind."

The sin of omission hit me like a hammer.

"Interference from a transmitter of some kind?" I asked.

"It's possible." He caught the look on my face. "Do you know something?" He put it together. "Of course. . . that microwave antenna you asked about. You'd better tell me, Minstrel."

I told him about the house, the 'playroom', the film and recording equipment, and the antenna. I didn't tell him about Marijke. Not yet, I thought. I've still got to face that one.

"This is difficult. If the house is legitimate, then we can't enter. It's Soviet territory. We can just watch the place and see who comes and goes. I'll get it checked tomorrow—no, we'll do it tonight. With that aircraft down I can't take chances. The source still protected?"

"Yes."

"Pity."

"That may change soon, Colonel."

"Good, though it may be too late to save the project."

I walked him to the door.

"You've got some real looking and listening to do on that ship. If you can, find out if they brought the aircraft down, and if they did, how. But be on your guard, Minstrel."

He had barely gone and I realized I was thinking about the Soviets, the KGB, and Marijke. Suddenly, I could deal with it. She was on the other side. One of 'them'. The enemy.

Suppressed rage surged through me, tinged with disgust, loathing, and betrayal.

Now, for what had happened to Kate, the Fletchers, the P1127, and to me—now I could deal with it.

I wanted to get even.

I wanted revenge.

I started to pack.

TWENTY-THREE

London, England—Wednesday, June 20, 1962

I was up early. My clothes were already packed, and I was organizing the case of 'charts', the musical arrangements I was taking for the trip. I wondered how this was all going to fit into one car if there were others travelling as well. I made sure of my passport. It wouldn't do to find myself in Odessa with no way off the ship.

It was not quite seven when Wicks buzzed to say that the car had arrived for me. Though I felt prepared for this initial encounter with Marijke, I realized it was not going to be easy. My throat was dry, my palms moist, and my heart rate increased. It was like opening night. I hoped I could bring off the performance. She was waiting beside the car.

"Good morning, David," she smiled. "It is good to see you. I am so looking forward to this wonderful trip. Are you well?"

"I'm fine thanks. Will we get all our luggage in? I have a case with music to bring along."

I could hardly look at her. I couldn't smile. Some actor you are, I fumed. She didn't seem to notice.

"We have the van behind us for luggage. There are things from the embassy which we take, so there is no problem."

The driver of the van put my cases in, and I walked to the car, a large

Mercedes limousine. Nalishkin was there with one other lady besides Marijke.

Nalishkin was in an ebullient mood. "It's wonderful to see you on such a lovely day, my friend." He turned to the lady. "Tatania, may I present David Baird of the beautiful voice who will sing for us on the cruise. David, this is Tatania Voronin, First Minister of Culture in the Supreme Soviet."

We shook hands, exchanged pleasantries, and I took stock of this very smooth, cultured lady in her forties who had risen to such an elevated position in the Soviet government. Behind that elegant facade there was probably an iron lady.

"David, you will sit in the back with Tatania and me. That way we can talk easily. I'm sure Marijke won't mind."

Nalishkin was expansive, positively beaming. Why, I wondered. The cat who ate the canary? The downed P1127? Very possibly.

Marijke caught my eye as we got in the car, looking for a smile. I gave her a pale imitation.

The next two hours were difficult. I hate small talk at the best of times, and that's exactly what occurred all the way to Southampton. For the most part the conversation focused on comparing Soviet cultural institutions with those in the western world. Needless to say the opinions were loaded.

While I was conscious of Marijke throughout the drive, we hardly spoke at all, and there was little eye contact because of our respective positions in the car. It was just as well, for despite my resolve I was not in control of my emotions. I hoped that would improve.

* * *

The *Empress of Britain* was a fairly new ship of over 27,000 tons. Launched in 1955 by Her Majesty Queen Elizabeth the Second, she was ideal as a cruise ship, for she was completely air-conditioned, yet with considerable open deck space for sports and games, much of it enclosable in case of inclement weather. She could carry 150 first-class passengers and 896 tourist-class with a crew of 465. The Soviets had really wanted her sister ship, the *Empress of Canada*, brand new and with a complete cruise-class potential, but Canadian Pacific were reluctant to part with their flagship. Normally berthed at Liverpool when in the UK, it was unusual for any of the *Empresses* to be docked in Southampton.

The driver wasted no time getting us to gate number 4, the Main Gate of the Southampton Docks. The ship was at the Ocean Dock, and we could see her straight ahead as we entered the dock on Central Road. She shone in her white paint with the green ribband extending around the hull at B deck level, her yellow funnel high above the terminal with its red and white checkerboard of CP Steamships. I couldn't help but feel a twinge of excitement even through my personal misery.

Our embarkation was smoothly effected, and in minutes I was standing in a large first-class suite on the port side of A deck, my luggage arriving right behind me. Marijke had a single cabin next to mine on the inside of the ship. I presumed that this was because she was my liaison for the cruise, not because of a suspicion of our involvement.

Involvement? I wondered. Had I been taken for a ride from the beginning? I became depressed as I thought about it, and I was in no mood to talk with her, so I escaped quickly up a few stairways or 'ladders' to the boat deck. Here I could lean on the rail, observe the water traffic in the River Test, and watch a tall smokestack belching on the far side of the river.

I squinted up at the halyards and saw that we were flying the Blue Peter, the 'P' flag, blue with a centre white square. This was to indicate that we were about to sail. Of course, I thought, our carload from London were the only additional passengers—the rest had come across the Atlantic.

As I watched, another flag was hoisted, white over red horizontally. The pilot was on board to guide us out of harbour. There was a blast from the ship's horn, the gangway was hauled aboard, and one by one the lines were cast off, the Blue Peter being struck as the last line was let go. We were underway. Tugs backed us out into the harbour, but once we turned they let go their hawsers, and we were under our own power, sailing at manoeuvring speed in the deep channel of Southampton Water.

We followed the channel down to The Solent, the strait between the Isle of Wight and the mainland. Soon we passed Portsmouth with its large naval base, then I was jolted back to reality when I saw Bracklesham Bay, the site of that forbidding house with the 'playroom'.

It was enough to make my head pound as I thought of Marijke in the context of everything I now knew.

I forced myself away from those depressing intrusions, looking up at the rigging and the flags. Abruptly I was carried right back to that awful house, for overhead there was an antenna identical to the one I had seen in Bracklesham Bay. They must be more common than I had realized.

We came to a full stop after a few more minutes, and, seeing nothing on the port side, I went across to the starboard. Off our bow stood the pilot boat, waiting for the pilot to be delivered from our ship. I saw the tender pull away with the pilot aboard, and immediately we were making headway again.

I knew I couldn't stay hidden for the whole voyage, and I was getting hungry, so I made my way down to the first-class dining room on C deck. I sat alone at a table for two and ordered a breakfast of Eggs Benedict and coffee.

The dining room was not too large, but very well appointed. If it hadn't been for the feeling of motion, one could have been in a fine restaurant in any major city. Elegant in wood, rose and grey leather, the room sparkled with mirrors and cut glass, reflecting the gleaming white tablecloths and sterling silver.

I was about half through my breakfast when I felt a presence nearby. I looked up to see Marijke. My heart began pounding and my face flushed as I struggled to my feet.

"Oh, hello. Won't you sit down?" I said, with little enthusiasm.

I held the chair for her then resumed my seat. We looked at each other. Strange looks, without smiles. Marijke spoke first.

"I wait for you, then I look for you, but I can't find you. Something is wrong, David. I see this in your eyes, in your face. If I make you angry, don't you tell me about this?"

I'd stopped eating. My appetite was gone. I'd intended to say nothing—just keep up the pretence and wait for revenge. Now I knew I couldn't carry it off. My love for her made it impossible, and as I looked at her I knew I loved her still. The hurt of the night before was tearing me apart. I was shaking.

"Since you've asked me, I'll tell you, because I can't go on like this."

My voice was hushed and trembling, and I knew I was on the verge of tears.

"Last night I came to your flat. It was nearly eleven o'clock. I needed you. I wanted to talk with you. I took a chance that you might be home from your meeting. I heard voices and music, so I held back."

I was having a hard time continuing. There was a look of growing horror on her face.

"As I stood there wondering what to do the wind caught your curtain and blew it aside. I wish to God I'd gone blind before I saw what I did."

Tears were stinging my eyes. My hands were trembling. Marijke was looking down at the table. She was very still. I continued.

"What was it you said to me? 'You are the first man I give myself to from the heart.' Well, maybe so, but from what I saw last night that must be the only part left that hasn't had a cock in it. You must be quite a hit with the Red Army Chorus."

My eyes were brimming with tears. I wanted to hurt her, and I had been vicious. Marijke had turned pale. With a sob she stood and ran from the dining room. I sat for some time, grateful that the waiter had discreetly stayed away. After I had calmed down, I went back to my suite, locked the door, and lay on the bed, tears staining the pillow, grateful for the soothing motion of the ship on the swells.

Moscow, U.S.S.R.— the same day

There was a discreet knock at the door, then it was opened by a KGB major who walked smoothly into the office.

"Comrade General, a cable from the ship."

"Read it."

"It says, 'We have sailed. Mission accomplished. Nalishkin.'"

Rastvorov's laughter echoed down the corridors.

Cherbourg, France—the same day

I must have slept. I checked my Rolex GMT-Master. It was four o'clock. Something was different. The deep-water surge had stopped. I got up to look outside. My suite was one of the few with windows, rather than portholes, so I had a good view.

I was surprised to see docks. Had we gone back to Southampton for some reason? It was far too soon to have reached any Mediterranean port. I splashed my face with water, reached for a jacket, and went out to the purser's office in the entrance hall. There was a man standing near the end of the gangplank, which was down to the dock. He didn't look Russian.

"Pardon me, but do you speak English?"

"I 'ope to tell you, mate. What can I do for you?"

"Answer a stupid question, I hope. Where the hell are we? I took a nap, thought we'd be somewhere on the high seas, and we're in port somewhere, and I don't know where."

"We're in Cherbourg, mate. Last minute decision. They got permission to dock just as we left Southampton, so they decided to give our Soviet comrades a look at France for the day. They made some announcements, but some people missed 'em."

I offered my hand.

"I'm David Baird."

"Right—the singer. I'm in the band, mate. It's you we've got to thank for this cruise. They was going to give us two weeks off, like the rest of the crew, and then they offered us double to make the trip. We all thought it was great. Beats to and fro on the Atlantic run, I can tell you."

"When can we get together to run the tunes?"

"'Ow about tomorrow morning at ten? We'll be underway by then. In the Empress Room."

"That sounds fine. How long are we staying in Cherbourg?"

"They said we'd sail about eight in the mo'ning. Gives the comrades a night on the town, such as it is. I expect they'll get roaring drunk on that French wine, the 'ole bleedin' lot of 'em."

"Well, I'll see you tomorrow. Oh, what's your name?"

"Hicks—Albert Hicks, I play the clarinet and sax so everybody calls me 'Benny' or 'Ben'."

I debated what to do. I didn't expect to see much of Marijke. I'd effectively burned that bridge. Or she had. Or we both had. I didn't know anymore. I went up the ladderway and out on the boat deck. There was no one around—probably all ashore. I walked to the stern and stood looking at the city of Cherbourg.

On the deck below there was a large tarpaulin stretched out on a frame and lashed securely down. The boat deck didn't extend to the stern of the ship, but the one below us did. The tarp was where I would have expected a swimming pool to be, but on the North Atlantic run it wouldn't get much use. Perhaps it was under construction. Pity. Still, there was always the indoor pool.

The harbour was full of odours, as all harbours are, and I caught a whiff of one which was familiar but which I couldn't place. Probably something from my childhood in Canada's Maritime Provinces.

I decided to go ashore. A walk would do me good, and I didn't want company. I went below to my stateroom, grabbed my passport, and headed for the gangplank.

With very little formality from passport control, I obtained a small guide to Cherbourg and headed away from the trans-Atlantic terminal. It was a pleasant walk through the waterfront area. The café terraces were alive with the hustle and bustle of patrons, all eating and drinking to the entertainment of the water traffic.

I realized how hungry I had become. I had barely started my breakfast when Marijke had appeared, and it was now nearly six in France. While many of the cafés on the terrace looked interesting, I wanted something off the beaten track where I would stand less chance of seeing anyone, especially Marijke.

I stayed on Quai de Caligny as it rounded a bend past two lovely sheltered beaches. There were quite a few people swimming and sunbathing, as it was still hot and sultry. Eventually I came to Rue de l'Abbaye, and, debating which way to turn, saw a sign for Auberge de la Bigottiere and headed straight for it. A charming place, it was decorated in a rural style with wooden beams. There was a charcoal fire in the center of the room on which the chef was grilling and *flambéeing*.

Since this was not wine territory I ordered an excellent cider and *agneau vert pré*, a dish of area-raised roast lamb. When I commented on its incomparable flavour I was told that it was the result of grazing on the salt marshes. I finished with Camembert cheese to find that in its home it is a far cry from the packaged variety of the supermarket, and I had coffee and Calvados with the cheese, the latter being a potent apple spirit.

As I sipped my potables, the door opened and Marijke came in. She came straight to my table. I stood, but I could find no words to say until I mumbled for her to sit down. She did, and when I asked if she wanted anything she chose only coffee.

I could only stare at her.

"I follow you from the ship."

"You've been outside all that time? Why?"

"I don't spoil your dinner. I already spoil your breakfast."

"I don't know what there is to say, Marijke."

"I know this. I think about this the whole day. I want I tell you a story. I have hope you allow this. When I finish, I go away. I tell Nalishkin that I don't be your liaison. I change my cabin away from you. Then we don't see or speak again. Is it permissible with you?"

"Yes. . . as you wish." My heart was heavy.

She looked undecided, uncertain, then sighed and began.

"It is the year 1916. A boy named Josef and a girl named Maria have become in love. But there is a problem. Maria's mother is a cousin to Grand Duke Sergius, the brother of Czar Alexander. Josef is only son of cook and stable master. One day Maria will be at the court of Czar. Josef will only be stable master after his father.

"They live outside Moscow at the estate of Grand Duke Sergius. It is called Ilyinskoe. All their childhood Maria and Josef play together. He is very clever and bright, she is beautiful and happy. When Josef is ten he becomes a stable boy, and when he is fourteen he becomes a groom. When Maria goes riding, Josef rides too, as groom. Many times they stop and sit. Maria teaches Josef to read and to write, Josef teaches Maria about nature and animals.

"Now they are sixteen, and they are in love. They must hide this from everyone, or they will be separated. Riding becomes the only way of being together and alone, and they stay away for many hours every day it is possible. On one of these days they begin to make love, and very soon Maria becomes with child.

"Soon they are found out, and they must confess what has happened. There is much anger, but the Grand Duke says after she has baby it must be given to Josef's family. She will continue her training and forget about Josef and the child. Marriage is not permissible.

"A baby girl is born in January, 1917. She is named Alix. She is taken away immediately to Josef's family, and Maria is never to see them. But secretly, she visits them all the time, for her love for them is greater than anything else. They plan to run away to Germany, and then to America.

"But the revolution begins in March, and it is too dangerous for travel, especially with the baby. For a year they wait, but the revolution grows stronger. Then in March, 1918, soldiers of the Red Army come to Ilyinskoe and place the family of Grand Duke Sergius under arrest. They cannot leave the main house, and there are guards inside and outside all the time. Maria and Josef pass messages with Josef's mother, who comes to cook, but they do not see each other.

"In the night of July 17, there are many gunshots from the house. Orders come from leaders of revolution to execute family of Grand Duke Sergius. They kill everyone—Maria, too, who is only distant cousin.

"Josef swears he gets revenge, if it takes all his life.

"Maria was my grandmother. Josef is my grandfather. The baby Alix becomes my mother."

I couldn't help but comment.

"But isn't your grandfather a very powerful man in the communist party?"

She sighed.

"Yes. It is part of plan which begins the day Maria is murdered. Then he can do nothing. He will be murdered like Maria. So he pretends to believe, and joins party. He will fight against them from inside. For many years he works to get higher positions, and then, in 1937, he meets my father, Bren Templaars, who is with the Netherlands embassy. They have many meetings, they become friends, and one day Josef tells my father about Maria and his secret plan.

"My father talks to someone in the Dutch government. It is arranged for my father to be contact. My grandfather will never meet with anyone else. Only one man in the Dutch government will know about this, and he is very high so there is no danger. Only information is passed, so my grandfather stays protected.

"Then my father meets Josef's daughter Alix, and they are married. This is now perfect, for no one can question my grandfather being with his son-in-law. The liaison has begun. From then until now everything has been carefully planned to continue the fight against the communist regime."

I had to mention what Hammond had told me.

"Was your father not expelled from Holland for spying?"

"It is all arranged so my father can come to Russia again after the war. It is pretence for giving him credibility with Soviets. The Dutch official knows everything.

"My father is still the only contact. He works through Dutch embassy. My grandfather must be careful what he gives away in case it is traced back to him, but he passes much. My father hears that many NATO countries get this information, but they don't know how it gets out of Russia.

"If ever they are caught, they will be tortured, and they die in a terrible way. It might happen to my mother and to me, too. But we all work to end communist regime and for memory of Maria, my grandmother."

There were still many unanswered questions.

"Why are you telling me this?"

"When I am in school in Holland I am told by my father about this. He tells me so I will not believe what they say in public that he is traitor. Later, when we are in Russia, I hear all the story. I know how much it affects our family, and I know what risks they take. I decide to help—to be a part of this. This is the best way I can use my life."

"Did your grandfather help get you a job with the KGB?"

"No. It is harder because of him. No one believes I want to do real work. They think I am looking for easy job because of my grandfather. I find out only way to prove I want real job is to do something most cannot or will not do. There are very few chances for this, coming from outside KGB.

"I hear about school where are trained people for using in sex traps. Not many can do this. Females are mainly prostitutes who earn extra money. For volunteer from outside who has university there are many opportunities, and it is a way to learn many secrets of KGB.

"I talk this over with my parents and grandfather. They don't like it. But I make them see this is my sacrifice for what they believe. They give their lives if they are caught. I give nothing comparing to this. Finally they agree. They know that if I do this I am accepted by KGB.

"But my grandfather has warnings for me. He cannot make my life easier if I do this. If he interferes they dismiss me. They will think I am not serious. He also warns me that his rivals in KGB will make my training even harder. They will try to make granddaughter of Josef Dmitrienko run away, and say I am too soft for work like this.

"He is right. My first night at school two men come to my room.

They ask me am I able to do this, or do I run to my grandfather. I tell them I don't complain. They tell me to take off my clothes. Then they touch me and make me do things to them. They use me for sex all night. They don't care I am virgin."

I was disgusted, and yet fascinated. I had heard about this school where they trained females called 'swallows' and males called 'ravens', but I had thought it was hearsay until now. Though my conscious mind was affronted by these revelations, there was something dark inside me which wanted to wallow in the depravity. It was a frightening revelation.

"How did you stand it?"

"I close off my mind. I have a purpose. I must survive for this purpose. If I am there for fun, like some women, or for money, like some others, then I am so disgusted I will leave. But I am there for other reason, and they cannot break my will. Even when they tell us it is necessary to break down all. . . inhibitions? I think is the word, and that we must expect sex at any time, in front of any persons, and with many people, male and female. They tell us if we can't do this, we must leave.

"Many leave after one week. We are made to have sex in classroom in front of class, sometimes with people from class, sometimes with strangers who come in. Many who think they have strength for this do not. This is what KGB wants. Only the strongest can survive this.

"I force myself to do this, like athlete who trains for Olympics. I become a sex athlete—I train my body for sex, but my mind is another place. I am not involved with the sex, only with using my body. I know I work for something more. My body—for me it is a tool.

"We learn to seduce men. We go to hotels for assignment, pretend to be prostitutes. We pick-up men, make them want sex, and make them pay as much as we can get. This is how they mark our success, how much we make the men pay. We keep money—they think it makes us work harder.

"We learn to find out sexual desires of men, then to tease, and then give them what they want. This way we control them, make them give us things, even secrets. We learn about sex instruments, about. . . bondage? About wearing some kinds of sex garments, and how to use pain with sex, allowing men to beat us. There is nothing we are not taught and made to practice."

I was shaking, both inside and out. It was nerves, but there was an element of shock as well.

"And you could do this, submit to all of it?"

"It is hard for me with large groups. With one or two it finishes soon enough. With groups it is maybe hours. Then I am full of disgust for everything.

"Twice I nearly leave after group sex. But I hold on. I am told it is not so bad when really working as in school. I think some instructors at school do this because they like strange sex, and because they rape if they want. They control us. I don't think so much sex is necessary at the school, and often it is made horrible."

"How long were you at the school?"

"Eight months. Then I am given first assignment in Moscow. I meet men from foreign embassies and use everything I learn to trap them. Sometimes it takes many weeks to do it carefully. When I am successful, KGB shows them photographs and threatens them. Then most of them pass information to KGB and become informants."

"I don't see how this is a help to your father and grandfather."

"If foreign diplomat becomes trapped and passes information to the Soviets, I tell who it is to my father. This man's country is told through Netherlands government and NATO, and he is left alone if he agrees to become double agent, passing only what he is told to pass. If he does not co-operate he is arrested. In this way I give names of seven people, four from me and three I know about from others."

I was quiet, and looking at this beautiful woman my mind was a torment of emotion. I knew I had to know it all. I had to reach bottom before I could even face this demon.

"Is there more, Marijke?"

"I don't like to tell you this. You will have more disgust and hate than now."

"You've told me this much. Finish it, please." She stared at the table silently, then continued, though she didn't want to.

"Sometimes we put on sex shows for people to watch. Whatever they want. This way we get information too."

"Like in the 'playroom'?"

"Yes."

"You have been in the 'playroom'?"

"Yes. Three times."

We were both silent. I wasn't sure that I wanted to hear more, and she seemed uncertain, but she took a breath and went on.

"Twice was only play-acting, pretending to hurt with instruments and whips. The sex is real, pain is not. But once. . . once I am there with beast. Only the foreigner and beast are in house.

"It begins in normal way, so I am not prepared. I am tied, but too tight. I should know from this. He beats me, but very hard, and does perversions on my body for foreigner who watches. Then they use me for sex and do things on me I can't say it is so bad. They talk about disgusting ways to hurt me even more. I think beast wants to use a knife, but someone comes and it stops. This is worst for me."

I was shaking. "Who was this 'beast'?"

"Szrubek. The man you kill in Paris. I was two weeks in hospital. I almost stop. I refuse to go to 'playroom' again. I don't care what they say."

Again I was quiet, emotions mixed with shock, disgust, and yet a perverse satisfaction that I had killed Szrubek. I couldn't sort anything out, let alone see anything clearly.

"And now, Marijke?" I asked, softly.

"I can do this no more. My mind is not able to separate from my body. When I don't think I will love someone, it doesn't matter. Now that I feel love, I cannot. When I give myself to you, for the first time with love, it changes my life."

"Then explain last night."

"About last night, I am trapped. This man from West German embassy, he is about to give many things to Soviets. He will do this if he and friends can have orgy with me. He has obsession. I try to avoid this. I don't want to do it anymore. They plan for Monday, but I change it to be with you. He tells Nalishkin he won't wait until after cruise, and he says no one else takes my place. This is his price.

"Nalishkin tells me that I will be traitor, that I must do this for my country. If I don't, it becomes bad for my grandfather. They send me back to Moscow and I become charged for refusing to obey order. I will be arrested. Nalishkin looks bad for failure with the German, so he threatens. I give in. I do it."

I sat still, staring at my glass. I couldn't look Marijke in the eye, nor could I find words to say. Eventually she rose from her chair and started to leave, but stopped and turned back.

"Now you have life and death over my family. I tell you this so no more secrets. I want that you know I trust you. I am sorry I am not the person you think. And I am sorry I hurt you so much. I never want this. Goodbye."

She left quickly without looking back.

I stared at my empty glass for a very long time.

TWENTY-FOUR

Back aboard the ship I was restless. I'd walked blindly through Cherbourg, and now I paced the boat deck. Most of the Soviets were still ashore, so I was quite alone. Occasionally I stopped to lean on the rail and stare at the water or a passing boat with unseeing eyes, or idly count the lifeboats in their davits over my head. My mind was a turmoil.

During one of the 'stop and lean' phases I was on the after part of the deck, staring absently at the tarpaulin-covered framework on the dark-shrouded promenade below at the stern. I caught that smell again, this time stronger, and with a jolt I knew what it was. It was as if someone had thrown a switch. One moment I was absorbed with my own emotions, everything else blocked out, and in an instant of recognition I had swept my problems aside. The enormity of my suspicions had to be checked out immediately.

The two sets of stairs down to the tourist promenade with the tarpaulin were blocked off by metal grills chained in place, so I went below to the enclosed promenade deck and walked aft.

There was a closed door preventing me from continuing to the stern, with a sign in Russian which I couldn't read. I began to fumble with the latch when a rating in uniform appeared to bark a challenge, which I also couldn't understand. But I did comprehend the Vz61 Skorpion machine pistol pointing at me.

"Sorry, sorry," I stammered, "I didn't understand the sign."

"*Entrance forbidden!*" he shouted in English.

I backed off in a hurry. Going below to the purser's office in the entrance hall on A deck, I sought out the junior officer on duty and asked him where I could find Mr. Hicks, from the band. He looked at his crew accommodation list.

"His cabin C26. You must have permission for enter crew quarters. Why you go there?"

"I must talk with him about the concert. I'm David Baird, the singer. Check with Mr. Nalishkin if you don't believe me."

"No. Is no problem. I have your name on list. I give you badge for visit crew quarters."

I stuck it on my jacket and made my way down to the crew accommodations. I knocked on the door marked C26. Ben opened it.

"Well, well, guv'nor, wot brings you down to the slave quarters? Come in, then, and 'ave a drink."

He poured me a generous scotch, neat. The curse of shipboard musicians.

"Cheers," in chorus.

"Ben, did anything unusual happen on the way across the Atlantic this time? Anything that sticks in your mind?"

He thought back.

"Naow, guv, nuffing coming across."

That idea was dashed. Oh, well.

"But there was sumfing a little strange when we was in the channel last night."

"Tell me about it."

"Well, we was makin' for Southampton, but we must 'ave been a bloody 'ell of a ways off shore. I went out on deck an' couldn't see a bleedin' light. Then the word goes 'round that they're 'avin' a bit o' trouble with the steerin', so they 'ave to stop an' fix it. We was dead in the water.

"While we're stopped, they tell us they've got an order to fumigate the 'ole bloody ship—that some sort of bug was picked up when the ship was in the West Indies, and we can't dock in Britain until it's been taken care of."

"What did they do?"

"We 'ad to stay below until we was given the all clear."

"Do you remember the time?"

"Not 'alf. We was sent down about 2100, and they didn't give the all clear until after 2300. About the same time as we got under way again. And I was right about the distance from land. We steamed near two hours before we got into the bleedin' Solent."

I considered this information carefully.

"Did you see or hear anything?"

"One 'ell of a racket from the stern. Sounded like the biggest 'oover in the world. They said it was a spray blower."

"What can you tell me about the tarpaulin over the frame on the tourist promenade at the stern of the promenade deck?"

"It wasn't there until this morning. I asked about it and they said it was because of the fumigation. They had to keep a concentration of the DDT until it was clear. We was all told to keep well away so we didn't get any fumes. We've all noticed a strange smell since last night, like kerosene. What's up, David? Why the questions?"

"I'm just curious about something, that's all. Sort of an amateur detective trying to put some pieces of a puzzle together. Nothing serious. But thanks for your help. I'll see you tomorrow in the Empress Room at ten. Goodnight, Ben."

I went back to my own stateroom and sat down to think. I needed some help, but I needed it on the inside. There was only one place to turn. I went to the cabin next door and knocked. I had to wait a few minutes, but the door was opened a crack, and Marijke looked out.

"Oh! David! I. . . I don't expect to see you!"

"I'm sorry to bother you. I need your help. May I come in?"

She stepped back to hold the door open, then shut it quickly.

I caught her eye, held a finger to my lips, then mimed the word 'microphone'.

"No, none. I check everytime I come in. Please, sit down. You have a problem?"

I sat, carefully weighing my words before I spoke.

"First, let me say that what I said to you in the dining room this morning was unforgivable. I apologize for my terrible behaviour and my despicable words."

"No, don't say this. I understand how you feel."

"About the rest of it, Marijke. I'm having a hard time with what you've told me. I feel that the wind has been knocked out of me. I have no right to judge you, or what you do, or your reasons for doing them—none at all. At this moment I only know that I am very confused.

"Canadians live a simple kind of life—almost puritanical in some ways. We don't know what it's like to live under oppression or fear—to have a government which is able to imprison, torture and murder whenever it wishes. We can't imagine your struggle and your sacrifices. When you tell me what you do, and why, my mind can understand, but my emotions are having a hard time keeping up."

"I am glad that you speak with me. I think you never want to see me again. I will understand."

"Marijke, I have never felt love for anyone as I feel for you, but it's not easy for me. Can you be patient with me?"

"Oh. . . yes!"

We sat looking at each other with a new awareness. I loved her still, but could I ever accept what her allegiances had led her to? Little did I know how quickly I'd find out.

"David, you say you need help. What is wrong?"

"There's something strange going on aboard the ship. Have you heard anything?"

"Only laughter about some 'big joke' against British. I don't hear what it is."

"I've got to find out what's under a tarpaulin cover on the promenade deck. Do you know where I mean?"

"Yes, I try to go there but the sign says it is forbidden. Maybe you can go when it is dark and look?"

"No. There's an armed guard there and no way to get past him. I was hoping you might know what the canvas is covering."

"No, I don't. And I must be careful asking questions."

She was obviously thinking about something.

"This is important, David?"

"It may be very important. But I can't be sure until I know what's under the cover."

"How many guard this?"

"I only saw one."

"Is there another way to get on this deck?"

"There are stairs from the boat deck and A deck, but I'll bet they're all blocked. I might be able to climb up over the rail if there's no one on A deck, but if the guard hears me or sees me I'd get shot for sure."

Marijke was quiet.

"You must know this very badly?"

"Yes, I think very badly."

"I can help you."

"How?"

"I go talk to the guard by the door. You climb up and look."

"He'll hear me."

She gave me a strange look. "I make sure he doesn't hear. When you want to do this?"

"As soon as possible. It's ten now, and the passengers will return by midnight, I should think."

"Yes, that is the time they must be back on the ship. They are in trouble if they are late."

"Then the sooner the better."

"I get dressed and make myself look agreeable."

"I'll go and see how it looks from A deck, then I'll change my clothes and come back for you."

With that I left, went down to A deck, and strolled nonchalantly out to the stern. I was right. The stairwell had a steel grid strung across and clamped down. There was no way to get through it. But by standing on the stairway rail and getting a foothold on the air-conditioning units, I was quite certain I could reach the bottom of the rail above and pull myself up. I went back down to my stateroom to change.

I had a dark blue sweatsuit which seemed about right for this, and some blue canvas deck shoes with rubber soles. I rummaged around in my case and found the penlight I often used backstage to catch a cue or check a line. I hoped it was all I'd need. I went next door and knocked softly. Marijke opened it.

I was almost stunned by her appearance. She was wearing more make-up than I had ever seen, giving her a sultry, seductive look. Her long blonde tresses were pulled to one side, held by an expensive clip. Her stylish white blouse was cut in a V-front, nearly to the waist. The slopes of her breasts were visible, and it was obvious there was no bra. The skirt, in panels of white and navy, was slit up both sides. She was the ultimate in provocative. I had a twinge of foreboding.

"Why are you dressed like that?"

"I know these guards. It takes much to distract them. It must be his idea for me to stay. If I try to make it happen, he becomes suspicious. His eyes must keep looking, hoping for something more. I know about this, David. I embarrass you?"

"No. I'm realizing there is much I have to learn. My simple Canadian upbringing left me very unprepared."

I knew where she had acquired this technique, but I didn't want to think about it.

"David, you still think this is important?"

"More than ever. And time is critical if I have to sneak off to send a message before we sail."

"Then we do it. Whatever is necessary. This I learn from my father when the world calls him traitor."

"One thing. How will I know if it's safe to climb up?"

"Stay somewhere behind me. If I go through door and he close it, then you are safe. How much time you need?"

"Ten minutes, maybe more. I don't want to leave any sign that anyone has been there. When I am out, I will stay on the deck below and whistle a tune. Do you know the "Waltz of the Flowers?"

"From the *Nutcracker* by Tchaikowsky? Yes, I know it. When I hear this, I know you are clear. Please be careful. I don't want something to happen."

"You be careful, too."

I took her hand briefly, squeezing it. She looked at me, gave me a kiss on the cheek, and left. I waited a full minute, then left quietly. Since our cabins were on A deck, I had to walk up one deck. Marijke would be on the starboard side, so I went aft on the port side in the enclosed promenade, then toward the starboard at the rear of the cinema, finding a niche in the bulkhead to hide in. Leaning out, I could just see Marijke at the door, and I heard her try the latch noisily. The door opened.

I listened carefully. First a male voice, admonishing. Then Marijke, laughing, flirting. The male, less brusque. She, about to depart, still teasing. He, entreating, then begging. She, hesitant, then considering. He, cajoling, holding the door open. She, uncertain, leaning against it. He, convinced, pulling her through. She, laughing, entering 'reluctantly'. The door closed.

I wheeled around, heading for a ladder down. Making my way to the open promenade at the stern, I found myself alone, but waited a minute to make sure. Grasping the stair rail I pulled myself up as high as I could, got a foot on the air-conditioning, and by stretching reached the lower part of the rail on the deck above. I swung my right leg a couple of times, then lodged it on the decking. With that support I pulled my body up, then easily went over the rail to land on the deck. With a clatter!

Shit! I stood still, ready to leap over if anyone appeared. Nothing happened. I didn't know if this was good or bad, for mixed reasons. I felt the deck. A steel mesh over sheets of steel. Aha! I thought, the plot thickens. Over to the tarp. At this end there was a tie-down, lashed to a ring on the deck. I looked at the knot with the aid of my penlight. A bowline. Thank you, 8th Moncton Troop, Boy Scouts of Canada. I undid the knot, lifted the tarp and slid underneath. The smell I had noticed before was strong. Why not? It was jet aviation fuel, and in the glow of my penlight I saw the stencilled registration number XP831. I had just found the 'crashed' P1127!

I made my way forward, as quietly as I could under the tarp. I didn't want to keep the light on, but I was afraid of tripping on a line, so I was extremely cautious. The aircraft was facing forward on the ship, and I was on the port side of both. As I came to the engine nacelle, I felt tubes coming out of the starter insert. They must have it ready to fly off in an emergency, I reasoned. Sure enough, there was a rope ladder hooked over the side of the cockpit, and the canopy was open.

I wanted to look in the cockpit, Should I take the chance? I was afraid of making a noise and ending it all right there. I kept still and listened.

I must have been ten feet from Marijke and the guard. The sounds I heard were unmistakable, even in Russian. I felt a visceral nausea to my core. I had asked her to help, and I knew instinctively what I was asking, yet I had let her go. In that instant I knew I was no different from her.

She was giving me the chance, so I took it. Up the rope ladder, very carefully, and look in with the penlight. The helmets were sitting on the seat. The aircraft could be lifted off in little over a minute in case of an emergency. Who would fly it? What had happened to Stavic?

Time to clear out. I went down the ladder, but my foot slipped and hit the side of the fuselage. I froze. There was silence from the other side of the tarp, then a male voice—no, two male voices! Jesus Christ! What had I done? Marijke's voice, teasing, laughing, cajoling—then muffled. I wanted to puke.

Down the ladder, quietly to the back of the aircraft, and out from under the tarp. I tied the same knot in the line, looked carefully below, swung down, and dropped, just as a man and a woman came out onto the deck.

I did a couple of spring ups, some running on the spot, then jogged off down the deck with a cheery "Lovely evening, isn't it?" As quickly as I could I ran around and back out on deck, jogged noisily toward the rail, and stopped to whistle the *Waltz of the Flowers*. I stayed until I heard a commotion and voices, then ran off down the deck as though I didn't have a care in the world.

I went straight down to my stateroom and left the door ajar as I waited for Marijke. It took her ten minutes. The wait was unbearable. She saw me, and I motioned to her to come to my cabin. She shook her head, and said, "Not yet," and went into her own. I left my door open and sat down to wait.

She arrived in different clothes. I beckoned her in, and she shut the door, standing quite still and without speaking. I went to her, gently taking her in my arms and just holding her. She smelled of toothpaste, combined with other masculine odours which I wanted to eradicate. I began to undress her, and she stood there, passively, while I removed every stitch, then stripped my own clothes off.

Gently, I took her hand and led her into the bathroom. Still not a word had been spoken. I reached into the large marble shower stall, adjusted the water to warm, then entered and drew Marijke in behind me. As the water cascaded over us I held her close to me, wrapping my arms around her, and she let go with a sigh, clutching me frantically. I kissed her eyes, her cheeks, her throat, her nose, and her mouth, probing into it with my tongue.

I was already erect, and she dropped to her knees in front of me to take me in her mouth and caress me. I waited, accepting her ministrations, then lifted her up and knelt in a similar position in front of her. Gently I probed with my tongue. She spread her legs wide to give me better access, holding my head as I caressed.

Raising my head to look me in the eye, she drew me up to her, kissing me passionately on the mouth and pressing her body to mine. Placing my hands on her buttocks, I lifted her up. She brought one hand down to my penis, directing it into her as she slid downward, wrapping her legs and arms around me, then clutching me tightly.

I could only hold her. We stayed like that for nearly ten minutes, until spasms made her shudder. I was still erect, but I had no desire to orgasm. This was for her, not for me. I had to tell her something, and there were no words in any language which could have conveyed the message.

We dried off, and, wrapped in towels, went into the sitting room. A generous supply of alcohol had been set out for me, and I poured a snifter of Remy Martin for each of us. We touched glasses and drank, then I set them down to draw her to me once more. Only then were the first words spoken.

"The room is clean," she whispered. "You find out what you need to know?"

"Yes. It was what I guessed."

"Then it was worth it, yes?"

"I think so. But sometimes you realize the price you pay is too high. When I knew what was happening I had my doubts."

"I am a soldier, and this is my training. You know this."

"I knew it, but it was hard to admit to myself that I had sent you for that purpose."

"We use what weapons we have to fight them. That is how I always feel, until now."

"Why did you agree, now that you see it differently?"

"Because it is for you. If you send me, then you accept me. You start to understand."

"I have much still to learn about myself and the ways of the world."

I kissed her, and looked her in the eyes.

"You're not angry that I sent you there?"

She pulled back to smile a little.

"No. Only why you don't tell me there are two? One is easy. Two makes me work very hard. They are boys, no experience. I have to slow them down to give you time. Now you owe me debt!"

"What's the payment?"

"This." She dropped her towel, then pulled mine off. "But only with love. My other life is over."

And we began our new life together.

* * *

Eventually we drifted off to sleep. I knew it would be a light one for me, there was so much on my mind. When I awoke I looked at my Rolex. Nearly 01:00am. Marijke was curled to me, lying in the crook of my arm.

I thought of how far I had come, in both understanding and acceptance. The present mattered, not the past. And yet I knew that sometimes there were sacrifices which had to be made. But now I felt able to comprehend what these meant to those who sacrificed. And I also knew that I would use whatever means necessary if I believed that it was for that greater good.

My mind shifted. The P1127. I would wait a couple of hours, slip off the ship and call Hammond. He could have a team here in an hour, and if he used the SDECE it would even be quicker. How did the Soviets do it? It had to be landed vertically on the ship. That required experience.

Of course! Stavic! Either they bought him or blackmailed him. I thought about his background. A POW in North Korea. Then the tour of duty in Moscow. One way or the other they got to him. They must have offered him a bundle to pull this off.

I began putting the pieces together. The ship was already in place when Stavic took XP831 up for his night trials. The house in Bracklesham Bay? Probably monitoring the Dunsfold tower frequency on a communications set, then beaming a direct signal to the ship on microwave transmission that the operation was a 'go'. The passengers were all below decks because of the 'fumigation', and they had obviously been ready with a makeshift landing grid to protect the deck. The frame with the tarpaulin cover was easy.

I couldn't help but admire the audacity. Once they had stolen the aircraft, they brought it right back into a British port where it sat for 12 hours, under the very noses of the people who were searching for it in the channel. No wonder they were laughing about the 'big joke' on the British. Well, the tables were about to be turned.

The raids on Dunsfold and Kingston were nothing but a smokescreen, intended to lull the Brits into a false sense of 'it's all over'. Now it would be, and I could get on with my life.

I looked at the face in the crook of my arm. Somehow, I wanted to include her in all my future plans. Maybe when we got back to London we could work it out. I began to feel content, lying there half asleep, Marijke in my arms, fantasizing, and being lulled by the motion of the ship.

What? Motion of the ship?

"Shit!" I yelled, jumping up and running through the double doors into the sitting room to look out the windows.

Marijke sat up, startled.

"David! What's wrong?" she called.

"We're under way! Moving! We weren't supposed to do this until morning! What the hell's happened?"

The jigsaw puzzle had just fallen on the floor.

And what had been the final piece was useless in my hand.

TWENTY-FIVE

The English Channel—after midnight, Thursday, June 21, 1962

Marijke jumped out of bed, pulling on her clothes.

"I go find out."

Glancing briefly in the mirror, she headed for the door.

"I try to hurry."

I fumed as I waited, berating myself for not going ashore earlier and placing the call. I thought I was being clever and cautious so I wouldn't be seen, and now I'd ruined it completely. Shit! Shit! Shit!

Marijke was back in ten minutes, out of breath.

"What happened?"

"They tell everyone we must leave the dock for another ship to come in. This is a lie. Political officer hears someone tries to defect. If this happens cruise ship project is finished. They don't want this, so they sail without warning."

"Now what do I do?"

"Can you tell me about this?"

"Let's get some fresh air."

We went up to the boat deck. The lights of Cherbourg were but a glow on the horizon. I considered trying to reach the pilot before he disembarked, but secret messages about a stolen airplane and spies would sound like the ravings of a lunatic. It wouldn't work, and

Marijke and I would be arrested and locked up. From the beginning, I told her everything, nothing omitted. It took a long time, and she listened without asking questions. She knew how agitated I was about my miscalculation.

"David, now we sleep. Tomorrow we think of what to do. There will be something."

Marijke slept, I tossed and turned. My mind churned over how to get a message to Hammond before the ship had gone too far to be stopped. Running out of those possibilities, I considered others, but calm eluded me until I had the simplest solution.

How do you recover a stolen airplane? Why, steal it back, of course. How? Details, just details. 'Sufficient unto the day', et cetera.

Then I went to sleep, smiling.

What fools we mortals be.

Portsmouth, England—the same day

Colonel Hammond glared at the Squadron Leader.

"What do you mean, nothing?"

"That's the truth, sir, nothing. Not a scrap of debris that could be remotely connected to an aircraft."

Hammond shifted to the naval officer.

"And you share this opinion, Commander?"

"Yes, sir. Sorry. We've covered every inch of the area. There's nothing to be found. It's as if a UFO had snatched it out of the air, because there's nothing left of it down here."

"Now that's a thought, isn't it?" murmured Hammond.

"Sir?"

"A UFO. Or something."

The Atlantic Ocean—the next morning

We were down in the dining room early, the first to arrive for breakfast. I wanted to explore all the options, if indeed there were any, before I told Marijke of my hare-brained scheme. We breakfasted lightly—continental style—with rolls and croissants, butter, jam, and lots of hot coffee.

"Do you know if they intend to call at any other port on the way to Odessa?"

Marijke shook her head. "No, they don't tell us about any. If they are afraid somebody defects, they don't stop again."

"I'm pretty sure the radio room is on the bridge. There's no way I'd get at it with the ship's officers around."

She thought about this.

"Do you want I should help again?" she said quietly.

"No. It wouldn't work on the bridge. It's not isolated like the deck where the plane is. And even if I got in there, I wouldn't know what frequency to use or even whether the message was being transmitted. It could be a complete disaster, and we'd probably get caught. And you're retired now, remember?"

"Whatever we must do, David."

I couldn't think of an alternative to my plan. I had to tell her. I knew she wouldn't like it.

"Marijke, I can think of only one way out of this. I've got to fly it off the ship myself."

"You're crazy! You can't do this! They stop you! Maybe you are killed!"

"Calm down, love. There's a lot to consider. If I don't think I can do it we'll find some way of destroying it. We can't let them get away with this."

"I know this. But I don't want you dead."

"I promise I won't take an unnecessary risk. The odds must be 50-50 or better. Even if I get it off I'd have to have somewhere to go. It won't fly very far, and I'd just as soon not end up having a bath in the Atlantic."

"When you will do this if you try?"

"It's got to be soon. Every hour means another 20 knots distance from Britain."

"Why not wait until we go close to Gibralter? This is British, yes? Maybe it's possible to get a message there, or fly the plane there. Isn't this a better chance?"

"It might be, but only if the aircraft stays on the ship until then. When I was under the tarpaulin last night, I discovered that it could be airborne in minutes. They may fly it off to a friendly country or a Soviet aircraft-carrier. The longer I wait the greater the risk of losing it completely."

"The Soviet Navy does not have these aircraft carriers."

"I didn't know that. I just know it's ready to take off."

"Who will fly it for them?"

"Probably Stavic, the American pilot. He must be on the ship. He's probably defected, or he's been working for them for years. They must be paying him a lot of money for this."

"What he is look like?"

"Tall, red hair. I've only seen him from a distance, but I'd know him again. Have you seen anyone like that?"

"No, I don't see him. I can watch."

"Let's go out on the deck above the aircraft. I want to see something. I can use your help."

She smiled. "I retire, remember?"

I smiled. "Not that kind of help. There are other ways, you know." I really was growing up.

We went up to the boat deck, stood briefly on the sun deck abaft the bridge, then casually walked aft toward the stern.

"When we get there, I'm going to lean with my back to the rail and look toward the bow of the ship. You lean on the rail and look to the stern. We'll cuddle close, then I'll ask you some questions and you look for the answers."

"All right."

We arrived at the rail and took the positions I had suggested. I put my arms around Marijke, and we just tried to look like lovers for a few minutes. It wasn't hard. Then the questions.

"On the left side of the aircraft, that'll be your right as you face it, do you see anything that looks like hoses, black rubber tubes, coming out under the canvas?"

She studied the scene casually.

"Yes, I think so. More to front, yes?"

"Yes, that would be correct. Now, where do those tubes go?"

"Across deck, and come to two tanks for holding some kind of gas. This is right?"

"Yes. Now, look very carefully. Anywhere near those tanks, is there anything which looks like a large electrical switch?"

She took her time.

"I don't know. Fastened to the rail is box with handle on the side. Is all I see."

"That's got to be it. Okay, that's enough for now. I don't want anyone getting suspicious. We'll go somewhere else for a few minutes, then I must get my music for the rehearsal."

"Is it permissible that I come to rehearsal?"

I kissed her. "Yes, it is permissible. I want you there."

We kissed again, went below to my stateroom, and nearly didn't get to the rehearsal.

* * *

The Empress Room, on the promenade deck, was the nightclub of the ship. Modern in concept, it was designed around a circular ceiling, bowed windows to port and starboard, with a dais on each side surrounding the circular oak parquet dance floor. We were a few minutes late, arriving to hear the band playing a swing version of "La Vie En Rose". They were quite good, and I didn't foresee any problem with my material. Ben saw us and came over. I introduced him to Marijke.

"Come on and meet the blokes. We're all looking forward to this, David. Now then, this is Taffy on guitar, Dusty on drums, Lofty on the bass, and Choppy on the piano."

I laughed. "Two more and you could hire Snow White as your vocalist."

"Unfortunately," said Choppy, "Disney picked up her option."

I shook hands all round, and introduced Marijke as my liaison with the Soviets. There were some knowing glances.

"'Ere, if I knew Russian ladies looked like 'er, I'd be giggin' in bleedin' Moscow," said Dusty, bringing chuckles to the band, Marijke and me.

"With nicknames like those around me, gentlemen, it sounds like I'm back in Kneller Hall."

"Kneller Hall? You went to Kneller Hall? Look you, Bach, I thought they were all British there like our place in Deal," said Taffy with a decidedly Welsh lilt.

"Then you must have been Royal Marines."

"Four of us were," said Ben, "but Choppy was in the navy as a blinkin' lieutenant-commander. Then we rescued 'im from all that snotty-nosed bullroar. And where do we end up? Right back on a bleedin' boat!"

I laughed. "Choppy? That's a new one on me, and I thought I'd heard 'em all."

"Pater's fault, actually. Loved classical music, wanted me to be a concert pianist. Jumped the gun a bit by naming me Chopin. I expect I'm something of a disappointment to him."

His smile showed how much he cared.

"Well, you must all feel quite at home with that painting behind you," I said, indicating the oil of Queen Elizabeth behind the bandstand.

"Blimey," said Lofty, "when I've 'ad a few, I keep thinking I'm back on the *Brittania* with 'Ma'am' looking over me shoulder."

"Well, let's try some of these," I said, handing out the folders. "We won't have to go through everything, just the tricky bits and some of the intros and finishes. Everything should be in there in the order I'll do them, so let's work down from the top."

For nearly an hour and a half we worked through the songs, re-doing anything that needed polish, and making sure that they knew where the segues were for those that didn't get a spoken introduction. We spent a little extra time on the ballads, simply because they need care in both the singing and the accompaniment. The sound system was good, and I was surprised that there was a wireless microphone for me to use. This would allow me much more freedom of movement, and I could work to the crowd better.

The last song I rehearsed was my finale, "You Are Here". I had begun to use it in clubs as an intimate finish, rather than end with a more boisterous tune. It seemed to work well, and it had almost become my closing theme. I sang it directly to Marijke, and she listened with sad and serious eyes.

When we had finished, I quietly asked Marijke if she would go back to her cabin so I could speak to the band privately for a few minutes. I told her I'd explain later. There was no one else around in the Empress Room, so the six of us put a couple of tables together and sat down.

"What's up, guv?" said Ben. "Something up your sleeve, then?"

"Gentlemen, I'm going to let you in on something which is dangerous to know about, so if any of you have fears for your own safety you should leave now so you can plead ignorance."

"No bloody fear, boyo," said Taffy. "We were all Royal Marines, except for Choppy, and he was close enough. We may have been in the bands, but when we all joined in '43 we were in a Commando unit. I smell a rat, and if there's any hunting to do I want to be in on it."

"Then here it is. Underneath that tarp at the stern on the promenade deck there's a stolen British experimental jet fighter."

There were exclamations of surprise and disbelief, but I told them most of the story, leaving out any reference to Marijke, and only necessary bits of my involvement with intelligence. I explained how they had gotten the plane aboard, and they started to tie the pieces together.

"That whooshing sound two nights ago. I thought it was part of the fumigation. Now that I know about this, I realize it was a jet engine," said Choppy.

"In Montreal I saw them putting steel plates and rolled-up mesh down number 6 cargo hatch. I'd seen the mesh before—it's the same kind of stuff used for landing strips in the bush. One big tank went down as well—possibly the jet fuel," said Lofty.

"Wot do you want us to do, guv?" asked Ben.

"I'm going to try to fly it off the ship, but I can't do it alone. There are two guards on at night, armed with machine pistols. I'll need help getting some tools to get the tarp out of there. The aircraft is probably tied down, so a bolt cutter may be needed to cut the anchoring cables. Then I need someone to throw the breaker for the starter bottles which are lashed to the rail when I give the signal from the cockpit. And 35 seconds later, I lift off and fly away."

The stunned silence was broken by Taffy with his Welsh lilt.

"Wouldn't it be easier if you just clicked your red shoes together, picked up Toto, and went back to Kansas?"

The laughter broke the tension.

"When, guv?" asked Ben.

"Tonight. Sunrise is about 0400, so it'll have to start by 0300. I want to grab it in darkness, but I want daylight to fly it by. My navigation is terrible. I figure we'll have been sailing for about 26 hours, and if our speed has been 20 knots we're going to be 520 knots from England. That's more than the plane can do, so I've got to figure out a place to head for, possibly Spain or Portugal."

"I've become quite chummy with a couple of deck officers," offered Choppy. "They know I was in the Royal Navy, so they've taken to bragging a bit about their seamanship. I'm certain I can get exact information from them about our speed and location. And I always carry charts with me aboard ship, so I can give you a map and help with a course."

"I can get tools," said Dusty. "I'm always borrowing them to work on my drums. I'll tell them I'm doing a major overhaul."

"That's perfect," I exclaimed. "Now I don't have to worry about getting my hands on that stuff. What I'd like you to do this afternoon is have a look at the tarp, the aircraft, the starter tubes, the electric box, and anything else that I might have missed. Remember what has to be done: guards out of the picture, tarp and frame clear, tie-downs off or cut, electric switch on, starter hoses unplugged.

"I suggest you stroll around one or two at a time, and don't stare for very long. You decide who should do what. Oh, the guards are my problem, by the way."

"'Ow you gonna do that?" asked Dusty.

"I'm working on it. Think hard about this. You could get hurt by helping me, possibly killed. You could also be arrested by the Soviets. As soon as I'm off, you've got to get out of there to save your skins. If you want to stay out of it I'd certainly understand. But I need to know now."

"We're in, David. Besides, someone's got to look after you Kneller Hall types, and who better than the Royal Marines and the Royal Navy?" commented Choppy.

"Thanks, chaps," I said. "I'll check with you later to see if there are any questions which have come up."

I went up to Marijke's cabin.

"Hi. I'm sorry I had to ask you to leave, but I wanted to talk to them about helping me get that plane off the ship, and I don't want anyone to find out that you even knew about it."

"What did they say?"

"They all said yes. I thought about it while I was rehearsing and it seemed as if it was worth a try. They've all been soldiers or sailors, so they've got a good idea of what we have to do."

"If you do this I want to help."

"No, you can't. There's a good chance that they'll be seen, and if they are they're in trouble. If you were seen, you'd be dead, and your father and grandfather under suspicion. We can't afford that."

I took her by the hand and we walked to my stateroom to sit near the windows. Marijke's cabin was on the inside of the ship, and she didn't even have a porthole to look out. I put my arm around her, holding her tightly, and kissed her. She had a troubled look on her face.

"What's wrong, Marijke?"

"I don't know when I see you again."

"Surely when you get back to England after the cruise."

"I don't know. If I ask for different job, then maybe they don't send me back to England. They only want me there for one reason, and now I don't do it."

I hadn't considered this. Suddenly I realized that this might be the end for us, unless she were able to stay in the West. The idea sent a chill through me.

"Marijke, stay with me. I've already talked to someone who says it can be arranged."

"How I do this? Tonight you fly in airplane."

"Come with me! It'll be a tight fit, but you don't weigh very much. The engine will lift us out. How about it?"

"Yes! I want to do this. But. . . what happens to my family? I must think on this very much today. I don't know how to answer."

"I won't pressure you, Marijke. We can talk about it this afternoon. I love you."

We held each other and kissed, and yet the fear of losing her was a spectre on my shoulder. Suddenly she pulled away.

"Oh, I almost forget. We must have lunch with Vladimir Nalishkin and Tatania Voronov. They wish you to meet some of the people who try to start Soviet cruise project. Is this agreeable?"

"I'd prefer to be with you alone, but I suppose we'd better play the game today. What time?"

"Now!"

Now became later.

* * *

It's difficult to concentrate on other people's interests when you have a major preoccupation of your own. What made lunch even more exasperating was that everything had to be translated back and forth because of me—I was the only one who couldn't speak Russian. Volodya and Tatania were at their charming best. Marijke translated for most of the committee, none of whom knew me from a hole in the Siberian ice.

Still, having heard that I was a 'famous' entertainer, they were very courteous.

I caught Tatania looking at Marijke and me several times, as though she were sensing something between us, and yet we were completely dispassionate during the meal. That worried me, for if I got away with the aircraft it might be hard for Marijke to prove that she knew absolutely nothing about it.

Most of the talk centred around the committee's desire to institute a Soviet cruise line, and I found myself being asked opinions on topics about which I had none, so my answers were vague at best. Toward the end Nalishkin leaned over to speak.

"David, my friend, the captain has asked me to invite you to the bridge. He thought you might be interested."

"Yes, I would be. When?"

"In half an hour. Marijke will accompany you to translate."

At least on the bridge I might pick up some useful information.

* * *

We were escorted to the captain's day room on the bridge by a junior deck officer. We sat while he informed the captain that we were there. He arrived promptly.

"Captain Nicolai Brezovic, Mister David Baird," said the junior officer, and this was about as far as he could go without an interpreter. Marijke was introduced in Russian, and it was easy to see that the good captain had an eye for the ladies. We had our traditional shot of vodka, and then we went up to the wheelhouse on the navigating bridge.

This was certainly no rudimentary sailing ship. We were shown the gyro compasses, the magnetic standard and steering compasses, the Synchrostep electric telegraphs, the steering telemotor transmitters, the Decca 45 radar, the Decca navigator, and the Kelvin Hughes echo sounder. There were special balanced windows, two of which had clear view screens. The wheelhouse was spotless, with a studded rubber floor. My vision of a wheelhouse had always been of *Tugboat Annie.*

The radio room confirmed what I had thought. Right behind the wheelhouse, it would have been impossible for an interloper to get in there and use the radio, even if the operators had been lured away. And the complexity of the equipment was another story. Marconi globespan transmitters and Atlanta receivers, rigged for both telegraphy and radio-telephone communication on three marine bands. All transmitting power could also be linked into the Reliance emergency transmitter. On the right of the radio room was the massive Pye public address and sound reproduction system, the most comprehensive unit ever installed aboard ship. It would have taken an hour just to figure out the right buttons.

I did learn something in the chart room. Casually I asked, through Marijke, what our track was and what speed we were travelling, and our present position was proudly pointed to by the navigating officer. I was surprised and delighted to find we had only been sailing at 15 knots, and our present position was 47 degrees 15 minutes latitude, 8 degrees 6 minutes longitude. From our intended track, provided I could find out our average speed, I'd have a pretty good idea where we were in relation to land. I might have a chance.

Naturally we had another vodka in the captain's day room, and Marijke told me that the captain would be honoured if the two of us would sit at his table for dinner that evening.

"Please tell Captain Brezovic that I accept his kind invitation, and that he does me honour."

We took our leave, making our way back to the sun lounge for a cup of tea and some biscuits to offset the vodka. We were sitting by ourselves, and it was easy to talk.

"You learn something there, David?"

"Yes. We'd never have gotten away with the radio room, for one thing. I know where we are, and I'll be able to get a pretty good fix on where we are at 03:00am in the morning. And I learned that our dear captain couldn't take his eyes off you. I think that's why we're invited to dinner—it's nothing to do with me. If I don't get off the ship, he'd probably have me clapped in irons for the rest of the cruise so he can make advances to you."

She smiled, but I sensed and saw her dilemma.

"03:00am. That's when you go?"

"Yes." I told her why. "Are you still thinking?"

"Yes."

It was after two-thirty, and I did want to meet the band to see what they had come up with. Marijke said she would like to rest for a while, so this seemed like a good time. I left her at my stateroom—she wanted to sit by the windows—and checked in at the Empress lounge.

Dusty, the drummer, was doing some maintenance.

"I thought I better make it look good after all the kit I borrowed," he muttered. "Look at this lot—bolt cutter, wire cutters, utility knife, pliers, hammer, screwdriver set, and wrench set."

"That's great, Dusty. Where are the others? We should have a little conference."

"I'll chase them up. We'll 'ave to jaw someplace else. This room'll be crawling with stewards setting up and cleaning. Why don't we meet in the first class library on the prom deck? We'll bring some 'dots' to make it official, and since all the books are in English it's not very likely they'll 'ave much activity."

"Okay, sounds good. 20 minutes?"

I filled the time in by strolling past the rail where the aircraft was situated, pausing for a moment to see if anything had changed or if there was any unusual activity. Everything was quiet, nothing seemed different, so I kept going rather more quickly than I would have liked. I didn't want to be obvious.

The library was on the promenade deck between the Empress Room and the drawing room, at the head of the main companionway to the entrance way. It was panelled, book-lined, and set up as a reading room as well. Dusty had been right, and there was no one there. The Soviets seemed mainly interested in the rooms where there was food and drink at all hours, in the swimming pool on E deck, and in taking the sun. The band had taken over the library, putting a 'closed' sign on the door, and spreading music sheets out on two tables pushed together.

"Well, how did you make out?" I asked, taking a seat.

"We've got some ideas," offered Ben. "First of all the tarpaulin. Lofty's pretty sure it's the same kind they use in England for a portable garage. If it is, then the 'ole thing goes together like an accordion."

"You're pretty sure, Lofty?"

"As near as can be without going right up to it. From what I can see the release is on the bow end, which'll be the nose of the aircraft. Two of us should be able to undo the rope, then pull it, and the thing should fold up—canvas, frame, the lot. Shouldn't take more than a minute once we've found the release. Failing that we'll cut the rope and it'll work the same way."

"Will you look after that part?"

"Yeah, sure, and Taffy'll take the other side with me."

"Good. What about the aircraft restraints?"

"We can't see much 'til the bleedin' tarps off," said Ben. "'Ow many do you think there'll be?"

"I'd guess no more than four—nose and tail on the fuselage and one on each wing. My other guess is that they've got this thing rigged for a quick get-away. That means the restraints are probably clips, but we can't be sure."

"No matter, guv," said Ben. "Dusty an' I'll 'andle 'em. He'll take the tail and the starboard wing, I'll 'andle the nose and port wing. If we can't unclip 'em, we'll cut 'em off."

"If you have to cut them, cut as close to the aircraft as you can. I don't want any dangling wires to foul the undercarriage or catch on anything. And by the way, we should all have electric torches. Is that possible?"

"Right. I know where they keep a supply on the boat deck for emergencies. I'll borrow a few. Now, that just leaves Choppy."

The pianist didn't look happy.

"I'm afraid I didn't get much about the position. The chap I know isn't on duty until 1700, so I won't know until later."

"It's okay. I've been up in the chart room. I knew our position just after 1400, and I have a pretty good idea of the track. If we can find out our speed for the rest of the day, we should be able to come pretty close to our exact position at 0300 tomorrow."

"I'll find that out later from Yuri. Now, my job will be to control the external starter. I've spent some time aboard carriers, so I'm not totally at a loss. What exactly do you need?"

"I'm presuming that throwing the switch will activate the compressed air. You must make sure that the valves are open on the tanks, and that there's no other mechanism in the system. On my thumbs up, throw the switch. After another signal to switch off, immediately disconnect from the aircraft end. Then get out of the way. In fact, all of you, once you've done your job, clear out quickly. The engine intake is very powerful, and you could get sucked toward it. The jet exhausts are hot, and they're going to be bouncing all over that deck. And once the engine has started, there's nothing more you can do for me. I'm on my own."

There was a pregnant silence in the library, and Ben voiced what we were all thinking.

"What if there's no power to that breaker box, guv, or the engine doesn't start for some other reason? What then?"

"Then we'll try to push it over the side, or put a rag in the fuel filler and light it. We're not letting them get it. I don't know where that leaves us, probably right in the shit, but that's the way I feel. If any of you wants to stay out of this, no hard feelings—I mean it."

"No fear, guv," said Ben. "We was all talkin' about it, between ourselves, like, an' we're in this all the way. Whatever it takes, mate, we're with you."

I shook hands with each one. It was all the thanks I could give them. We agreed that if anything transpired between then and the concert, we'd get in touch, otherwise we'd have a final meeting after the concert was over.

I went down to my stateroom by the stairway. I hadn't used the elevators since I'd been aboard.

Marijke was sitting near the windows, staring out at the sea.

"Did you sleep?"

"No. I cannot. I have too many thoughts."

I sat beside her, taking her hand in mine, then tapped my ear. Microphones? Bugs? She shook her head.

"Do you want to talk about your thoughts, or are they private?"

"I am in confusion about what I do."

"Then let's look at everything carefully. If you don't come with me tonight, what will happen to you?"

"They will be very angry with me because I am close to you, and I don't find out what you do. Some will say I help you. They can't prove this, but they will think it. Others will say I know nothing, but they will be angry that I fail with you. I don't trap you, no pictures, no blackmail. Then I will say no more work with sex, and they are more angry. I might be finished in KGB, or I get punishment assignment."

"What does that mean?"

"I am sent to bad place—maybe in north, maybe assignment to prison camp. Whatever is not good."

A chill pierced me. I was appalled. "For how long?"

"One year, perhaps, I don't know. It depends how angry they are, and who decides."

"What you are telling me is that if you stay on the ship, you and I may never see each other again," I said, hushed and stunned.

"I think this is true." Her eyes were tearing.

"What happens if you come with me?"

"Then I am happy for me. I have something I don't think I ever have all my life—love, and freedom."

I didn't want to ask the next question.

"And what happens at home to your father and grandfather?"

"First it looks bad for them that I do this. They are embarrassed, and they lose respect with the politburo. Then some rival says there must be investigation to find out if they are traitors to state, too. Maybe they find something, maybe not. But they make enough for suspicion, just to punish because of me. Somehow they arrange so KGB throws them out. If they find anything for treason, they are both shot, and maybe my mother is accused, too. This is for punish me. Doesn't matter right or wrong."

"What do you think is most likely? What are the chances of something giving them away?"

"I don't know. They do this for more than twenty years and there is no suspicion. But I cause suspicion, and twenty years is looked at by enemies of my grandfather. Even if they find nothing for trouble they will lie just to get him."

We held hands, watching the whitecaps as they rolled by the ship, isolated for a moment from the burdens of responsibility. We both knew what had to be done, and that we would do it, but for an instant of eternity we suspended thought, decision, duty.

Even the carefree waves were objects of envy.

TWENTY-SIX

Moscow, U.S.S.R.— the same day

Admiral Arseniy Grigoryevich Golovco, First Deputy Commander-in-Chief of the Soviet Navy, was uncomfortable. Together with most serving officers of the Soviet Armed Forces, he resented the power and interference which the KGB exercised over them.

Quiet resentment, of course. One never knew who was planted by the KGB to spy on senior officers who might make an offhand remark, and live to regret it.

Being summoned as he had by this upstart Rastvorov was particularly nauseating. Even though the admiral was senior in rank, the KGB general was always to be treated with respect and civility. One never knew what they had in their secret files.

"So, my dear Admiral, what steps have you taken to ensure the safe passage of our little cruise ship?"

"Yesterday, Comrade General, elements of our Black Sea Fleet went through the Dardanelles into the Mediterranean, ostensibly on exercises. Fourteen ships in all, with the heavy cruisers *Admiral Nakhimov* and *Dzerzhinski as* the command vessels. They will steam west to meet your *Empress* and escort her to Odessa."

"How many submarines are on station?"

"I'm sorry, Comrade, I'm not allowed to disclose the number or positions of our submarine fleet. You would need a request from the KGB chairman directly to the politburo for this information."

The admiral stifled a smug smile.

"No matter. I'm sure they are there if we need them. Have you arranged air cover as I requested?"

"Of course. Long-range fighters with tanker support are even now monitoring our fleet and very soon your little ship. But I will feel better when it has passed Gibralter and comes within our scope. Until then it is like a sheep away from the fold."

The Atlantic Ocean—the same day

Dinner at the captain's table is the highest honour which can be bestowed aboard ship. It is, unfortunately, a mixed blessing. Because of its formality guests are usually not at ease, and because of protocol the guests are often chosen from those who are influential or wealthy. As one junior officer has put it: 'The very, very rich, and the very, very dull'.

Since I was certainly not in the first group, and, I hoped to God not in the second, I wondered what on earth I was doing there. I came to the conclusion that both Marijke and I were dressing the table, she for her beauty, and me because of her.

The captain made sure that Marijke was at his left, and I was mixed in around the table between two older Russian ladies who spoke no English and rarely in their own language. Now and then I was offered a comment in English from Nalishkin or the captain, but most of the time I sat quietly with my Beef Wellington.

We had dined earlier—7:30 instead of the usual 8:00—mainly because of my concert. I was glad when the captain stood to leave at nine o'clock, since the guests are imprisoned until the captain makes a move. Marijke came to me immediately.

"You don't have a good time at dinner."

"Not really. Those two ladies next to me hardly said 'pass the salt', and I didn't understand when they did. The captain only had eyes for you, and I was on the opposite side of the table so I couldn't even enjoy being with you. And because I'm singing I couldn't eat much. Apart from that it was wonderful."

Marijke laughed. "I'm sorry, David. I don't enjoy it much either. The captain tries to impress me. I don't like this man."

We had walked from the dining room to the foyer, decided to use the lift this time, and went up to the boat deck for some air. Even with the air-conditioning on it felt stuffy at times, so it was good to get outside. We leaned on the rail, watching a passing ship on our port side.

"When you must go to Empress Room?"

"About half-an-hour. Ben said he'd have a table for us arranged near the band. I'm going to start my show from there."

"Oh, I don't know this, and the captain asks me to sit at his table for your show."

"That's tough for the captain, then. It was his dinner, so he called the shots, but this is my show, and I call them for this. I hope you don't mind."

"No, I don't. I tell him when we go to Empress Room."

Neither of us had said anything about later, probably because it was still part of a fantasy—the hero on his white horse saving the beautiful damsel and the two of them riding off into the sunset to live happily ever after. Reality suggested a different plot. It was just as well. I could be left with my illusions 'til after the concert.

We stopped by the stateroom to freshen up. I sucked on a Fisherman's Friend to keep my throat open and moist.

She held me for a few minutes, and I caressed her back. I could have remained there happily.

"I wish you good luck, David. I know it will be wonderful."

"You're not supposed to say that."

"Please?"

"It's a theatrical tradition that you wish performers the opposite of what you really want for them. This way the perverse gods are fooled, and they grant what is really wanted. People most often say 'break a leg'."

She laughed. "This is crazy. Okay. I do it. I make my own. I hope your pants fall down."

"Well, that's a new one," I said, chuckling, and giving her a kiss. I held her close. "I love you."

"I know," she whispered. "And I love you."

We went to the Empress Room and were shown to a table at stage right of the band, on the dais. I had easy access to the floor from here, and Marijke was close enough for me to see her. The captain and his guests were seated much farther back, and I was glad Marijke wasn't there. We had stopped to thank him for his courtesy. He smiled, reminding us of the reception after the show. I didn't want to go, but I still had to keep up appearances.

The band was already playing—they had started about an hour before to play for dancing and as an audience warm-up. They stopped for a break just after 09:45, and Ben came over to the table to check on details and join us for a drink.

"All set, guv?" he queried.

"I think so. I've got my drambuie and my coffee here on the table, my Fisherman's Friends in my pocket, and the lady of my dreams here to sing to. What more could I ask?"

"I gave your lighting cue sheet to the bloke who runs the lights. It's pretty simple stuff, but there's a follow spot, some overheads, and he can get some colours up behind us for effect."

"Sounds fine. You know I'm starting from the table?"

"Yeah. We've got it ready. The Russian MC will do 'is bit and we're off. Got to go. See you on the floor. Break a leg, guv."

Marijke laughed at that, leaned over and whispered, "I hope your pants fall down."

I squeezed her hand, the house lights went down as there was a drum roll, and the Russian MC introduced me over the band's repeated vamping of the first two bars of the intro. The only thing I understood was "David Baird!" The spot hit me as I sang the opening lines from my table:

"Let's take a boat to Bermuda,
Let's take a plane to St. Paul,
Let's grab a kayak to Quincy or Nyack,
Let's get away from it all. . ."

I stood, still singing, and walked to the centre, the spot with me, and then I did a circle of the room, singing a line here and there to individuals, ending up at my table. I sang the last line, the spot went out, and I sat down. The spot opened on the applause, but I stayed seated as the band played the next intro. The first lines were out of tempo:

"Ah . . . I want to fly away—" (if they only knew!)

"Escape the world with you for just one day;"

The band went into Bossa Nova tempo.

"A . . . Brazilian hideaway—

On the golden shore of Guanabara Bay . . ."

I smiled at Marijke, then left the table to continue my show from in front of the band. Standards were my forte, and I interspersed ballads with swing and jazz tunes.

The band was good—tasteful and subtle at times with a nice mellow tenor sax from Ben, and they dug in hard for the up-tempo tunes. I gave each of them solo lines or choruses when it seemed right. I couldn't believe it when the hour was up.

I thanked the audience for the privilege of singing for them, wished them well in their cruise endeavour, and this was translated by the Soviet MC. Then I sang my final song, starting from the floor:

"You are here, closer to my heart,

You are here, though we're far apart . . ."

I moved around the room as I continued the song, arriving at my table and singing the last two lines to Marijke:

"But when I awake , alone with my fear—it's so unclear,

My life won't ever be 'til you are here."

The spot went out, I sat down, and the room erupted with applause. I stood in the spot, went to the floor to bow several times, tried to leave but couldn't—they wouldn't let me. For an encore I did "We'll be Together Again", and the words nearly choked in my throat as I glanced and saw Marijke crying. When I ended I went to the table, reached across and held her hands. I didn't care who saw, but I knew I was being imprudent in the light of what was to follow.

When the band began to play a tune I was besieged by well-wishers, many who simply wished to shake my hand and say thank you. I signed autographs, many on copies of my two LP's. Nalishkin and Tatania Volodin were effusive in their comments, and said they would see me in the club room where the captain was hosting a reception for me. Then Marijke and I escaped from the crowd.

"Is it always like this, David?" she asked as we took the lift to the boat deck.

"Sometimes it's worse—people can get out of control, especially if they've had too much to drink. Worse than that is when there's no one around and you don't know why. It's a strange business."

She rubbed my arm. "You were wonderful, David. The last songs you sing—I know you mean them for me and for you." Marijke hesitated. I feared her next words. "I think you understand what I must say about going with you."

I looked at the sea. "Yes, I know. I wish it could be different."

"I don't try to explain. I say it all before." There was a long pause and she gripped my arm tightly. "Now we go to captain's reception. Then we can be together until you must leave?"

"Yes, for most of the time. I must meet with the band for a few minutes when they finish playing. Marijke, there is one thing I need which none of us can get. I don't know if I should ask you."

"Please, tell me. What is this you need?"

"A gun—an automatic, preferably, with a silencer."

"KGB has them. I get one for you."

"I don't want you to do this. If you can find out where there is one, tell me and we'll do the rest. Don't try to take it. It isn't worth the risk."

"Then I tell you now. Nalishkin has gun with silencer. He doesn't carry it in dinner jacket—I know this from other times. When he travels, he keeps it in pocket in suitcase."

"What's his cabin number?"

"A14."

"Okay. I'll organize something. Let's go to the club room."

We walked one deck down to the promenade, then went forward to the club room. I was glad to see there were quite a few people present—it lessened the amount of serious conversation. The captain spotted us immediately, at least, he spotted Marijke and I happened to be standing beside her.

"Ah, the star of show!" he boomed. "Is wery good sing-er! A toast!"

He rattled something off in Russian. There was a chorus of responses, they drank, then applause. I thanked them in English for their gracious hospitality, and Marijke translated. Then, thankfully, they got on with their own conversations. Nalishkin came over as Marijke was monopolized by the captain.

"You see, David? I was right. I knew you would be success on this cruise. I am grateful. Now you can have holiday for remainder of cruise. I see you are become close friend with Marijke. This is good. She will make sure you have wonderful time. I am sorry I am so busy for two days. But after tomorrow we will find time for talks, yes? Now I must see that my guests have what they wish. You will excuse me?"

"Of course, Volodya." We shook hands.

I looked around for Marijke. The captain was still talking to her, naturally. This was my night. I walked over.

"Ah, Mr. Baird. I think you wery lucky man. Marijke tell me no time for me. Only for you. We change place. I sing, you be captain. I have Marijke. Okay?" He laughed loudly. His vodkas were showing.

"Maybe next trip," I said pleasantly. "I hope you'll excuse us, Captain. I'm a little tired."

Without waiting for a reply I took Marijke's arm and we made our way out, saying good night to people as we passed. We walked down to A deck, and straight to my stateroom.

"I've got to see the band, darling, but I'll hurry."

"It's fine. I bring in some things to your cabin. Don't be long time. We have three hours only."

I kissed her, left, and headed back up to the Empress room. The band was packing up. We grabbed a table which had been vacated and went into a huddle over a drink. It looked good—six musicians having a post-performance recap.

"What's the latest, chaps?" I asked softly.

"I managed to borrow a sextant with some charts and tables from Yuri," said Choppy. "I'll get a fix about 0230. That's even better than trying to guess."

"He won't be suspicious?"

"Not a chance. He knows I was a deck officer aboard a cruiser, so he thinks I just want to keep my hand in."

"That's great. Now, there's something I need from cabin A14. Does anyone have a contact with a master key?"

"What do you need, David?" asked Dusty.

"In Vladimir Nalishkin's suitcase, in a pocket, there's a gun with a silencer. I'm going to need it. If you've got a way to get me in, I've got to take the chance."

"I've got a complete set of keys. One of me mates from the British crew said we'd better 'ave a set along. Figured with all these Russkies about we should 'ave some way of keepin' our eye on things. Leave it to us. We'll get the artillery."

"You sure?" A nod. "Thanks again. You'd better do it soon. Nalishkin is at the captain's reception, but I don't know for how long. Now, here's how I see it. We'll meet in the library at 0245. Lofty, you're going to pretend to be drunk, and fiddle with the door out to the tourist promenade deck. The rest of you be at the rear of the cinema. Lofty—make a big fuss and play it up—act stupid when they try to send you away. This'll give me time to get up from the lower deck. When I've got the guards under control, in you come."

"What're you going to do with 'em, guv?"

"Whatever I have to. Now, can you get hold of some ladies' nylons? You should each pull one over your head just as you come out on the deck. If anyone sees you, you won't be recognized."

"We can pinch some from the crew's laundry room," said Ben. "Anything else?"

"Just make sure we've got some heavy tape—like duct tape. If we have to tie anybody up it's the quickest way."

"Got it already, mate."

"That's it, then. See you at 0245. And by the way, thanks for the accompaniment. It was exceptional. We'll do it again some time, under slightly less demanding circumstances."

"We enjoyed it, guv," said Ben. "Let's 'ope the second 'alf goes as well."

I went back to my stateroom. I felt sure we had a chance to pull it off. I knew the band would give it everything they had. I hoped none of them would get hurt. Oh, damn! I'd meant to ask them to keep my music with theirs, and I could get it in London from them. I hurried back to the Empress Room, but I'd missed them, so I went on down to the crew quarters and Ben's cabin. He was just arriving himself.

"What's up, guv?"

"My music. Can you keep it with yours? Otherwise it'll be gone—I'll never see it again."

"Already sorted that one out, guv," he smiled.

"I should have known. I'll see you later."

Ben gave me a stage wink, and I turned to leave—too hastily. I bumped into someone, looked up at a shock of red hair, and nearly lost my composure right there. Stavic!

"Sorry," I stammered, "my fault," and stepped aside.

He said nothing, but looked at me strangely and kept going. Just my luck, I thought. But he didn't know me, and I hoped he hadn't seen me at Dunsfold. Still, it was nerve-wracking.

Marijke was starting to get worried when I arrived.

"I am afraid something goes wrong."

"No. So far so good. We're going to meet at 02:45. We've done everything we can. Now we have to get lucky. I just saw the American pilot, Stavic. Bumped into him in the crew's quarters. I don't think he knows who I am, but I can't be sure."

Marijke seemed very depressed.

"This plan will work, David?"

"We have a chance."

"If you get away with the plane, where do you go?"

"Spain, Portugal, France. It depends on our exact position when I get off. I might make it to the Channel Islands, but that's not very likely."

"Where will you land? Isn't it dangerous? You might crash."

"This aircraft can land in a parking lot. All I need is a small open space with no trees or wires around, and I'll be fine."

It was my turn to be pensive.

"When will I see you again?"

"I don't know. I try to come back to London, but I don't think they let me. You can come to Soviet Union?"

"I thought about that. After tonight I don't think they're going to be very pleased with me. If I apply for a visa, they'll probably turn it down. I'm sure the KGB will have me on a list of undesirables. What will we do?"

"What we must, my darling. Maybe in one year or two something happens. It matters much, and I can wait. In Soviet Union we must wait for everything. We learn to be patient."

"I have little patience, so I hope it isn't long. What about letters? Can I write to you?"

"This is dangerous. Foreign letters they open very much. If they see letter from England for someone in KGB, they open."

"There must be a way, Marijke. I can't believe we might never see or hear from each other again! What kind of country is this?"

"It is wonderful country, David, full of ordinary people who want to sing and dance and have happy life. What is wrong is not country, it is not people, it is communist system and leaders. Someday we change it. Many people in USSR try. They get arrested, sent to labour camp or Gulag. Sometimes they have trial, sometimes no. Sometimes they are shot by firing squad, sometimes murdered in torture cells. Some survive and come back to tell us. We keep these stories, and we tell them. We grow stronger, and some day we change our country."

We sat, just looking at each other. I had known Marijke for only nine days, yet she had affected my life more than any person had ever done. Losing her was intolerable, but we were seated in separate roller coasters about to careen in different directions, and there was no getting off 'til the ride was over.

"David, we have little time. Please hold me."

I took her hand and led her to the bed. I took off my tux, shirt, and the rest, and I watched Marijke as she did the same. She was so beautiful. We slid under the sheets and held and caressed and kissed. We made love with a feeling of immense longing, as though we were already apart. Then she slept fitfully. I stayed awake, holding her and trying to comfort her, counting down the minutes. All too soon it was time to go.

I eased out of bed and got ready in the bathroom. I had no idea where or when I'd see a toilet next. I dressed in my dark track suit and running shoes, then thought I'd better take a jacket—it might be pretty cold up there. I had my penlight, put a pen and pad in my pocket, then had a bit of inspiration and wrote down the engine start sequence on the pad. I didn't want to be in the aircraft and unable to recall the steps in my panic. I was ready to go. Reluctantly, I awakened Marijke.

"Oh, no, I sleep?" I nodded as she continued. "I don't want to sleep. I want to be awake with you."

"It's all right. I have to say goodbye, darling."

"David, I think about this, I mean to tell you. You must tie me. If you don't, they think I know and help you."

"Marijke. . . !"

"You must. Please. I have adhesive. Put on my mouth. I take strong sedative first, tell them you drug me, when I wake up I am tied, I cannot call for help, and you are gone."

"But you might be like this for hours!"

"No! When plane flies they come here for me. Please! Hurry!"

I hated to do it, but I saw the wisdom. It took a few minutes, but I used two belts and fastened her feet and her hands securely and placed her on the bed. Before I put the plaster on I kissed her gently.

"I'll always love you, Marijke, no matter what happens, and I will never forget you."

"Somehow, we meet again. Be careful, my darling."

I kissed her once again and started to place the tape, but she spoke again, with a tiny smile.

"I hope your pants fall down."

I placed the tape, not too tightly, looked briefly but deeply into her eyes, caressed her cheek, and left quickly. I couldn't look back and see her like that.

Halfway to the library I had an almost uncontrollable urge to run back, free her—and then what? I knew there was no answer. Now I had to shake loose this depression and my thoughts of Marijke or I wouldn't carry this off. I took a deep breath, opened the library door, and there was my team, waiting for me.

"Well, gentlemen, are we ready for this gig?"

There were a few chuckles then Choppy spoke up.

"We've even got a name for it, David. Operation Anacrusis, because this is going to be one hell of a 'pick-up'."

I laughed along with them. I needed that.

Dusty spoke up. "Here's your cannon, David. There was an extra clip and a box of cartridges. I pinched the lot."

I examined it. A 9mm Makarov, very similar to the Walther PP. I screwed the silencer on, checked the clip, chambered a round, put on the safety and shoved it inside my jacket, with the spare clip in one pocket and the box of cartridges in the other.

"Are we ready?"

"We've got the tools, tape, and we've each got a torch and a nylon stocking. We're set."

"Now, listen. As soon as your job is done, get out. Either back along the promenade deck or go over the rail and drop to the tourist promenade aft on A deck."

"We're ahead of you, guv. We dropped two rope ladders from the boat deck. They're 'idden behind the lifeboats. We're goin' up when it's done. We can stay behind the lifeboats until the coast is clear. Less chance of being spotted."

"That's great! Now remember, as soon as you're out, get rid of anything incriminating—tools, torches, nylons—everything."

Choppy's turn. "I took a bearing about 20 minutes ago." He showed me a chart of the European Atlantic Seaboard. "We're just about here, or will be in 20 minutes. That's as close as I can come. Unfortunately we've increased speed to 20 knots—once we'd got clear of Ushant and away from the heavy shipping lanes."

"What's the bad news, Choppy?"

"You're 700 miles from Southampton. What's the kite's range?"

"600 miles at best, depending on the take-off fuel burn. It uses a lot more going up vertically. What are my options?"

"Rather limited, I'm afraid. If you travel 050 degrees northeast you'll cross the Bay of Biscay and hit the coast of Brittany in about 400 miles. If you can last another 200 miles on the same heading you'll make the Channel Islands. Other than that you'd have to head for Cape Finisterre in Spain, heading 110 degrees southeast, and that's about 175 miles. I've put all this down for you, and you can take the chart. What do you think?"

"I'll have to make a final decision in the air when I see the state of the fuel after I'm airborne, but my first preference is Brittany or the Channel Islands. Choppy, thanks. At least I know I've got a chance. Anything else?"

"Yeah, guv, this," said Ben, producing a small packet. "It's an inflatable life jacket—the sort o' thing they use on passenger planes. Just in case you come down in the drink, we wanted you to 'ave a chance to stay afloat 'til 'elp arrives."

"Thanks. I hope to God I don't need it. Choppy, will you keep it with you until I get into the aircraft? You can toss it up to me." I threw it to him. "Let's synchronize the time. I've got 0300 in 17 seconds." We waited for it. "5-4-3-2-1-mark. Okay, everyone in place, Lofty does his act at the door at 0305. See you in England. Drinks are on me."

We shook hands quickly and in silence, then dispersed. I walked down to A deck, went aft on the centre gangway and out to the stern promenade. I tried to be careful with the doors, but aboard ship there is always the sound of the sea and the hum of machinery to mask most extraneous noises.

The deck was empty, and I made preparation to repeat my performance of the night before. One minute to go. My heart was beating rapidly and my palms started to sweat. Not good. I didn't want to slip on the rail. I wiped them on my jacket as I heard the first noises from above.

"Hey! Whassa matter? Why don't you open the door?" And then a banging and pounding began.

I swung myself up as the noise continued, being careful not to land on the mesh as hard as I had before. Both guards were now at the door trying to calm Lofty down and convince him to go away. I had the

Makarov out, safety off, and crept toward them from behind. Lofty was facing me, but not even a flicker of his eyes took any notice as I got closer.

"Okay, okay, I'm going," he roared, starting to turn away. "What a bunch of rotten sods you are."

The guards were convinced he was leaving. They were totally unprepared for me.

"Put your hands up and don't turn around!" I challenged, and one did and one didn't. The Markarov coughed once, hitting the guard on my left in the right arm. Still he turned, and the Skorpion was swinging toward me. I squeezed twice more and caught him in the chest. He went down. My team poured through the door.

Not a word was said as one figure stopped behind the standing guard and hit him hard at the base of the neck with a wrench. He went down like a tree.

"Tape them both, eyes, ears and mouth as well as hands and feet," came a hoarse whisper.

Two had gone straight to the tarp—Taffy and Lofty, who had reappeared with his face covered by black nylon. The other three trussed up the guards, though one was probably dead. Two of my team, most likely Ben and Dusty, held on to the Skorpions.

The tarp was moving easily back, frame and all. Thank God! Ben and Dusty had moved to the restraints with their tools, Choppy was at the starting cylinders. The canopy was clear and I moved to the ladder to climb in.

There was a roar from behind me, powerful hands caught my arms and I was flung to the rail. I dropped the Makarov.

"*You prick!*" yelled Stavic. "I thought I recognized you!"

He came at me as the others ran to my aid. I feinted to the left, grabbing his right arm and pivoting, using his speed and weight to whip him around. His height was his downfall. He hit the rail as I snapped his body, and he went right over into the sea, screaming. For a moment we were stunned. Then I moved.

"Quick! There may be others coming!"

I grabbed the Makarov, shoved it in my jacket and clambered up and into the cockpit, pulled on the cloth helmet, fastened the harness and looked out as Choppy tossed the life jacket to me.

"Clear, guv!" called Ben, as I jammed the 'bone dome' on and pulled the pad out of my pocket.

I clipped it on the instrument panel, shone my penlight on it, and went through the start sequence in a hurry. Choppy was ready for the signal.

I watched the clock anxiously as the whine grew louder, checking that the nozzle control lever was back for vertical. At the first rumble I signalled to Choppy and he pulled the plugs. Another 20 seconds!

I thought I saw movement, then flashes. Christalmighty! Gunfire! Ten seconds! The Soviets were trying to get on deck!

Now! Throttle full ahead! With a tremendous surge I lifted off the deck—but canted at an angle! Quick! Power off! I slammed back down again! Something had caught—another cable?

Ben darted under the aircraft as a hail of bullets followed him. Return fire from two angles hit the Soviet gunner. He went down. Ben appeared, holding his side, gave me a thumbs up and I poured it on again. Straight up! Full power! I felt more than heard some clunks hitting the aircraft as I cleared the top deck, then the stern of the ship passed under me as I kept ascending on full throttle.

I banged up the undercarriage, easing the nozzle control lever forward as I swung to port, my speed increasing dramatically at full throttle. I hauled around to port again, watching the ship below me as I circled at 2000 feet and still climbing.

I wanted to tell them something—to salute those who had helped, to thumb my nose at those who had been foiled. I went around again, 4000 feet now, and a mile ahead of the ship. I headed straight for it, the aircraft in a dive and throttle to full power. Down I hurtled, speed increasing insanely—there! Above Mach 1! I pulled back hard on the stick 100 feet over the ship, starting to climb as the second sonic boom caught up to me.

Those two cracks should shake them up! A futile gesture, perhaps, but nevertheless a gesture. One more circuit, then the ship slid smoothly underneath me as I climbed again, this time with a silent prayer for the band, and for Marijke.

I corrected my course to 050 degrees, checked my instruments, and continued ascending toward the dawning sky.

My prospects were not very good. The odds were against me.

Even so I felt better off than my friends back on the ship.

Compared to them I was in clover.

For the moment.

TWENTY-SEVEN

Bay of Biscay—early morning, Friday, June 22, 1962

I was flying, but I was flying blind. The compass wasn't set for deviation and variation. I didn't know whether there was a wind effect taking me degrees off course. My fuel state was not good—the vertical take-off and the passes over the ship—stupid move—had reduced it drastically. I was on oxygen with the cockpit heat on. At 20,000 feet the temperature falls to –30 degrees Fahrenheit—a bit too cool for comfort.

I'd done as much trimming as I could, and XP831 was flying like the lady Bill Bedford had told me she was, but I knew my chances of reaching France were slender. The higher I flew the better for fuel economy, but I'd freeze to death up there. Even the heat on full would make little difference.

I'd throttled back to 200 knots in an effort to conserve fuel, and after the take-off and 15 minutes cruising at this speed I calculated I had already used nearly half of it. At best I had fuel for another 300 miles, but that would leave me 50 miles short of land, assuming that land would be where I was pointed.

Several times I had tried the radio on various frequencies, but so far no response. I was loath to switch to the emergency frequency and call a Mayday, but that might have to happen yet. Once I got below 20 minutes of fuel I had to call for help. Maybe there would be a ship to ditch near.

The sun was up. It had risen much earlier and more rapidly than usual because of my climb in an easterly direction.

Underlying all this were sickening thoughts—that the band members might have been killed and dumped overboard. Marijke. Was she in the clear? It was hard to worry about my own situation when I had been responsible for involving the others in my escape.

Christ! There's an aircraft just off my port wing! Shit! Another one to starboard! Two jet fighters by the look of them. Talk about luck! If I have to ditch they could direct a rescue helicopter or boat to me, and I had the life-jacket from the band to keep me afloat until help arrived.

One of the pilots was trying to signal me. I couldn't figure out what he meant by his gestures. I kept looking, but he was busy with something in front of him.

I studied the aircraft. They were very large—probably twice as long as XP831. In natural aluminum finish with a long black needle nose, gold numbers under the cockpit, 87 was on my port side and 92 on my starboard, and a large red star on the tailfin.

Large red star?

Fucking hell!

Soviets!

What kind of shit am I in?

This can't be coincidence. They're too far from a land base. They've got to be here with a tanker, probably sent out to shepherd our ship and its cargo only to find the bird had flown the 'poop'. The ship must have directed them to find me. Not hard when they've got radar and I'm only stooging along at 200 knots. But now what?

That was answered in a hurry. The pilot of 87 held up a card. There was a number in black marker. 121.5 I thought, though I wasn't sure. He tapped the side of his helmet. Of course. A radio frequency. I dialled 121.5 Mhz. He was transmitting.

". . . are you receive me?"

"Yes, I am receiving you. What do you want?"

"You steal Soviet property from ship."

"Sorry, chum, it's British property. Take a hike!"

"We go back to ship! You land on ship! You understand?"

"Go fuck yourself, Ivan!"

His voice went up in pitch. "You don't do this, we blow you out of sky!"

I looked under his starboard wing. Two missiles hanging there, that meant two more on the other side. Two planes, ergo: eight missiles. God I was clever! It would only take one of those things to turn me into fish fry, so my odds had dropped from slim to grim.

"English pilot. . . "

Oh, what the hell.

I jammed the throttle fully forward. The big Pegasus engine thundered, and I shot away from them like a bullet from a rifle. I knew they'd catch up shortly—their top speed was probably twice mine, but up to 650 knots at this altitude my acceleration was probably better.

I hit my top speed, swivelled my head around but couldn't see them. A minute later they were coming up on me—they must have been pouring it on. They fell into place again, and I heard 87's voice.

"You stupid! Last chance! We much faster!"

"Ah, yes," I replied. "But can you do this!"

I pulled back both levers in the throttle box and stopped dead in the air, the two Soviets roaring on at nearly 700 knots. I pushed left rudder, swivelled to the opposite direction, and changed to horizontal again, picking up speed to 400 knots.

By the time they turned around to come after me I was miles away in the opposite direction. My fuel was diminishing rapidly. I switched to the emergency frequency.

"*Mayday, Mayday, Mayday!* This is Hawker X-ray Papa eight-three-one British registry, experimental VTOL jet! Estimated position 45 degrees latitude, 11 degrees longitude, heading magnetic 230 degrees at 400 knots and angels 20! Twenty minutes of fuel remaining! I am under attack by two Soviet fighters, type unknown! I have no armament! X-ray Papa 8-3-1! *Mayday, Mayday, Mayday!*"

"X-ray Papa 8-3-1, we are verifying." A voice from the blue in my earphones. Who?

Oh, crap, there are my Russian friends. They were coming at me from behind. As I stretched to look I saw a flash under the wing of one of them. Missile launch! Aw, shit!

I yanked both throttle and nozzle control back all the way. 831 dropped like a rock. The missile screamed over my head. I pushed on power and went to the hover, rotating to find the Soviets. Again they had shot past and were attempting to turn to come at me once more. The radio crackled.

"X-ray Papa 8-3-1, this is the United States Navy aircraft-carrier *USS Enterprise!* We have you and your friends on radar. Hang in there, li'l buddy! The cavalry's on its way!"

"Roger, *Enterprise!* Am I glad to hear you! What's your position? Over."

"We are ten nautical miles from you, bearing 275 degrees."

"Roger, *Enterprise*. Changing heading to 275 degrees. Oh God! My company's back!"

"Hang tight, 8-3-1!"

I pulled the throttle back and put the nozzles down about 45 degrees. This brought my speed down to 60 knots and allowed me to descend slightly. The two Soviets were making wide turns around me, deciding how to make the next move. I went to a full hover and pivoted on my axis. I was able to keep them in sight, like a matador in a bullfight, and like the matador I was ready for the next pass. Unfortunately there were two bulls.

They had obviously figured out that a split attack was the way to get me. They had separated by five miles and were lining up for a head-to-head with me as the salami in the sandwich. I couldn't watch them both easily, despite the pivot. If I dived away, one of them would be on me and it was all over. They had closed to one mile radius, two miles separating them. A flash!

Missile incoming! I pivoted. Shit! Two missiles incoming!

I went to horizontal flight on full power. Straight for one of the Soviets! The Pegasus roared to full acceleration. I was closing on him—the missile on me! I yanked the nozzles down at full power, stopped forward motion and rose suddenly straight up! Both missiles missed! The Soviet I was facing made a frantic break right, and suddenly exploded in a fiery ball of red and orange. With my sudden disappearance the missile had locked on to the aircraft which had taken my place in line-of-sight and blew it out of the sky.

I pivoted. The other aircraft was coming at me. If he had guns, I was in trouble.

"*Enterprise,* this is 8-3-1. Where's the . . . "

WHOOOOOSH! I was drowned out by the most massive boom I'd ever heard as a big US Navy jet fighter came diving out of the sun.

He must have been doing Mach 2 plus, the sound was so far behind him!

"Careful, li'l buddy! He's got a lock on you! He launched! God dammit! Your turn, you bastard!"

I watched the burning flare come at me, figuring I had four seconds. In two I dropped again, the heat seeker completely bewildered by my downward facing nozzles. It roared over my head as the large US Navy F-4A Phantom zeroed in on the Soviet.

"How the hell you do that, l'il buddy? You ain't a helicopter. Catcher, Rooster engaging Tu-28P Fiddler. He has fired his weapon. Is hunting season open?"

"Season open, Rooster. No bag limit. Good hunting."

The big Phantom had done a tight turn and was lining up on the Soviet. Suddenly another Phantom joined the hunt—his wingman had arrived! The Soviet was diving at full power, weaving, bouncing, anything to escape. He went into a vertical climb. Wrong move! The Phantom has incredible power. Up they shot, straight up, gaining on him rapidly. The Soviet was in trouble. Losing power in his climb, he was a sitting duck for the Phantoms.

But he was a good pilot. Dropping his speed he wheeled out at the top of his climb, dropping down the same column he had come up. The Phantoms did a starburst and were quickly diving after the Soviet. The starburst was the right move, bringing one of the Phantoms out in a power dive on an intercept with the Soviet. There was a wink under the Phantom's wing, and the Soviet disintegrated into a red mushroom. It was over.

"8-3-1, this is the *Enterprise.* Retune to 94.2 Mhz."

"Roger." I twisted the knob.

"8-3-1, this is the *Enterprise,* call-sign Catcher. Two F-8 Crusaders will fly escort for you and bring you in for a visit."

"Roger, Catcher."

I eased into horizontal flight to save what was left of my fuel. Two grey and white Vought Crusader F-8A's appeared, one on either side of me, 'AF' on their tailfins—numbers 211 and 204.

"Delta One and Delta Two are with you, good buddy. We're gonna call you 'Jumper' for identification. Do you copy?"

"Roger, Delta One. Jumper copies."

"How 'n the hell were you just sittin' there, Jumper? You ain't no whirlybird!"

"It's a secret formula I invented for anti-gravity. Spray it on and you go straight up."

"No shit?"

"Yeah, and Walt Disney's gonna do a movie about it called 'Flubber Flies Again'."

He laughed. "You're puttin' me on, man! Let's get serious. What's your fuel state?"

"Maybe 8 minutes."

"Jumper, follow us. About 3 minutes. Catcher will resume communications with you at that time."

"Roger."

The F-8's went past me and I increased speed just enough to keep pace. We flew for a couple of minutes.

"There she is, Jumper, about 2 o'clock. We're goin' down."

"Roger, I'm with you."

I pushed the stick forward and followed them in a powered dive, then into a circuit around the immense carrier. A huge white 65 was painted on her deck and on the island. The *USS Enterprise.*

"Jumper, this is Catcher. Suggest you ditch about 100 yards off the port bow. We'll pick you up in the chopper."

"Negative, Catcher. I've got just enough gas left to land this puddle-jumper."

"Jumper, do you have deck-landing experience?"

"No, Catcher, but I hear it's a ride worth trying."

"Do you have arrester gear?"

"Not the kind you've ever seen, Catcher. I'm coming around to line up on the deck. Am I cleared?"

"We will rig the net. Watch the Landing Signals Officer, Jumper. If he waves you off go 'round again or abort. Got it?"

"Roger, Catcher. Jumper on final."

A different voice. "Jumper, you are too high! Abort!"

"Sorry, Catcher. This is a different ball game. Coming in!"

I flew over the angled deck with speed reducing to 30 knots, gauging my descent to 20 feet by looking at the island superstructure. When I was in line with the island I drew the speed down to match that of the ship using the nozzle control, then eased the throttle back to sink gracefully onto the deck. The LSO had given up trying to hand signal me down.

I popped the canopy as a ladder was placed, and I was out and down on wobbly legs. I knew they had other aircraft to recover, so they had to move 831 out of the way. A kahki-clad officer with naval commander's rank ran up to me. I pulled off my helmets.

"Welcome aboard. I'm Pete Birkmann, the Air Group Commander, or 'CAG'. Come on with me. Your aircraft'll be well looked after—don't worry."

"I'm Major David Baird, sir, regardless of what I look like. It's a long story."

"We got a bit of it on the radio. The skipper wants to hear the rest, especially as we just splashed a Fiddler and he's gonna have to explain how come the brand new *USS Enterprise*, the world's first nuclear-powered aircraft-carrier, is knocking down a Soviet aircraft on the way to her very first assignment with the 6th Fleet in the Med."

He led me through what appeared to be great confusion on the flight deck—aircraft coming up in the elevators, then pulled off and parked, some on the catapults launching. I was surrounded by Crusaders, Skyhawks, a few Phantoms, and several types I didn't recognize like the two with large enclosed radar dishes on them. The whole place was humming like a beehive.

Recovery of my rescuers and escorts took place on the runway which angled off the port side of the gigantic ship.

I looked back at XP831. She was surrounded by curious pilots, wondering about the nozzles and how she had hovered.

"Skipper's on the bridge," said the CAG. "Follow me up."

We stepped through a doorway into the island superstructure which contained all of the command, control, and communication functions aboard the ship. Clambering quickly upward, we arrived on the top enclosed level and walked onto the bridge. I glanced around, saw the 4 stripes on an older man as he came toward us. The CAG introduced us.

"Captain, this is Major David Baird who has something to do with the British Army, though what the hell he's doing in the middle of the Atlantic still remains to be seen. Major, this is Captain Robert Driscoll, USN, our Commanding Officer."

"Welcome aboard the 'Big E', Major. This is our Operations Officer, Commander Daniels, and the Officer-of-the-Deck, Lieutenant

Paternoster. I think we'll be more comfortable in my quarters. Would you like a coffee?"

"Yes, sir, I would."

He turned to Daniels. "Have some coffee sent up, will you, Ben, and you join us and get Walt Farrugia."

"Aye, aye, sir."

I followed the Captain and CAG, nearly jumping as a loud voice roared out, "Captain's off the bridge!"

In his cabin he indicated his washroom, or 'head', and I accepted with thanks. Coffee, pastries, and other goodies had arrived when I came out, and another commander along with Daniels.

"Major Baird, our Executive Officer, Commander Walt Farrugia."

We shook hands, then we all sat and helped ourselves.

"Well, Major, what the hell is going on?"

"It's a long story, sir. Briefly, the Soviets had stolen that aircraft and were trying to get it to Russia on a civilian ship, the *Empress of Britain,* which they had chartered and staffed with a Soviet crew. I was on the ship to sing a concert, and when I discovered the aircraft there I grabbed it and here I am."

"Sing? I thought you were a military pilot. Fill me in, please, and don't spare the details. I've got a lot of explaining to do, especially about the two Soviet fighters we downed."

CAG spoke up. "Captain, we only splashed one of them. Major Baird got the other."

"I thought you were unarmed."

"I was, sir. I ducked a missile launch and it hit the other Soviet aircraft."

"You ducked a missile launch?"

"Yessir, using the VTOL capability of the P1127."

He started to laugh. "You ducked? And one shot down the other? Well, don't that beat all. You hear that, CAG? Who the hell needs all this expensive hardware? Just fuck with 'em a little, and they do themselves in."

The absurdity of it hit them all, and the cabin roared with laughter. The captain wanted the details, so I told them, beginning to end, about my involvement with the P1127. When I'd done, there was a perplexed silence in the cabin.

"Jesus, that's quite a tale, Major. And you're only a reserve officer, and really a musician. Dammit, CAG, tomorrow the band flies the missions. Maybe they'll do better than the pilots."

He started to laugh again.

"Well now, Major David Baird, what do we do with you? I suppose you'd like to get that crate home?"

"I would, sir, but I don't have the range for the flight. I was probably going to ditch until you showed up."

"Lucky for you we came on the northern track. Lemme think. CAG, you wanted some flying time before we took up station, didn't you?"

"Aye, sir."

"And Walt, the US Navy band has all its instruments?"

"Aye, Skipper."

"Then I'm going to suggest a little diversion. If we come about and steam north for a few hours, we'd put the major close enough to fly to Britain. For the crew let's clear some space on the hangar deck, and ask the band to play a concert. Otherwise we won't hear them play—they leave us in Naples."

He took a good look at me.

"I think you need some shut-eye, Major. We'll organize a cabin for you."

"Thanks, sir. I didn't get any sleep last night, and there's still a lot of today left to go."

"Walt?"

"Aye, skipper. I'll look after it. We need some time to get the hangar deck organized and the band clued in. I'll fix David up with a cabin. It's 0800. Why not make it a lunchtime thing? We can set it for 1200. That gives David a three-hour rest and time to have something to eat before he launches, and it means we steam north for 5 hours—about 150 knots worth."

"Make it so, Commander," said the captain. "CAG, you'll see to the aircraft?"

"Aye, sir. We'll check it out and make sure that all functions are working properly. We don't have manuals, but we'll come pretty damn close to everything."

"What about communicating with Britain, David? Do you want to pass a message?"

"Not yet, sir. I'm so tired I can't think straight. I'll do it later, if that's all right."

"As you wish. Have a good rest. Why don't you join me for lunch around 1100?"

"I'd like that, sir. And thanks for everything you've done. I could never repay you in a million years."

He waved his hand as I left, dismissing my comments as if he had done nothing at all. I grabbed my helmets, and a few minutes later I had been taken to a cabin in the officers' quarters where a young ensign showed me how to pull the bed down. I wasted little time in getting in, my exhaustion having no trouble convincing me to make the most of it. I was out like a light, but thoughts of Marijke were in my subconscious even as I slept, and my concerns for her well-being and those of the band on the *Empress* would not allow me the peace of mind necessary for an untroubled rest.

Lisbon, Portugal—the same morning

Nalishkin sat in the shielded cipher room of the Soviet embassy in Lisbon. He was alone, waiting for the phone link to be established.

His hands were sweating. This was not going to be pleasant. He had been threatened already when he had reported to Moscow by radio-telephone back on the *Empress*. Now he was to be told what his future would be, if indeed he had a future.

The whole thing had fallen apart. It was Baird's fault. How did he know about the aircraft? How could he fly it?

The telephone rang.

The Atlantic Ocean—the same morning

The light went on. I thought I'd been asleep for about five minutes. I looked at CAG through bleary eyes and mumbled "Already?"

"Sorry, Major. Rise and shine. Just after 1200. The skipper's expecting you for lunch as soon as you can make it. There's a marine corporal outside who'll be your escort. It's easy to get lost in a ship this size. Oh, here are some kahkis for you, if you want to change from the sweatsuit. They should fit. Sorry we don't have any British rank badges."

I got up, had a quick shower, and used the toilet materials laid out for me—even a little electric shaver. Fifteen minutes later, dressed in USN kahki, I was escorted into the senior officers' wardroom and seated for a lunch of bacon, eggs, home fries, and grits, with coffee and rolls. I was hungry.

"How are you now, David?" asked the captain.

"Better, sir, thank you, but reveille came too soon."

"I gave you an extra hour, but we've got to put her about before 1400 in order to meet our schedule. If you launch at 1330 you'll be about 450 miles from Guildford in England, and that's the home base for this aircraft if I'm right."

"Yes, sir, 10 miles away."

"Your aircraft's range is 600 miles?"

"We think so—no one's ever tested it, but given the factors that's the theory. That also depends on the take-off. Vertically you use a pile of fuel. What's the overall deck length, sir?"

CAG answered. "1123 feet. What d'you need to get airborne?"

"Under a thousand, and if the carrier's headed into the wind and we're travelling at 30 knots it'll be a lot less."

"What if we can rig you for a catapult launch?"

"I'd be worried about the undercarriage, especially the outriggers. They mightn't handle the strain. I think we'll be fine with a short take-off, and that'll leave me lots of fuel. I went through the short take-off drill at Dunsfold."

"Okay," said the captain, "that's how we'll play it."

CAG carried on. "We're going to send two escorts with you. We've got four F-4A Phantoms with us from our RAG doing carrier trials. They've got lots of range—over 1500 miles on internal fuel alone. But we're going to arm them to prevent anyone taking a pot shot at you again, so we'll put external tanks on them to give them lots of margin. What'd you say the name of the airfield is?"

"Dunsfold Aerodrome. It's an old wartime field."

"We'll have it on our charts. They'll lay in a course to take you right over it."

"Gentlemen, may I say thank you on behalf of Her Majesty's government and Hawker aviation. And as for me, if any of you get to London I insist you look me up, and the night's on me."

The captain stood up.

"David, wherever the *Enterprise* is you'll always be welcome aboard. You may be an entertainer, but we know you as a flyer. You've been in action, you've deck-landed—you're one of us. We'd like you to have these souvenirs from the United States Navy."

So saying, the captain, CAG and the exec came up to me, pinned silver oak leaves on my collar and gold metal wings on my shirt. They stepped back as the operations officer put a naval hat on my head. Then they saluted as the captain spoke. "Welcome aboard, Commander Baird."

I returned the salute, but I was so choked I couldn't speak as they each shook my hand.

"Time to launch, sir," said CAG. "I'll take David down."

"Right. I'll see you off from the bridge."

I saluted, navy style, and the captain returned it as the others stood to attention, and CAG led me out. We went straight to the flight deck.

"I had your other gear brought up and tucked into a sea-bag. You can probably squeeze it behind the seat. And I've got something else for you from the Air Group."

He handed me one of the most prized possessions of a navy flier—a leather squadron flight jacket, and a pair of flight gauntlets.

"Jesus, CAG," I started to say, but he stopped me.

"That's from the pilots. Just accept it."

A pilot in flight gear came over. CAG introduced us.

"David, this is Lt.-Commander Brad Cochrane. He's leading your escort."

He saluted, so I returned it, and we shook hands as he spoke.

"I've plotted our course, Commander. If we're airborne in 15 minutes we'll be right on the money all the way. I've planned on 20,000 feet and a speed of 400 knots. I did some calculations and figure that'll leave you about 40 minutes of fuel when we get to Dunsfold—enough to divert if necessary. You fly lead, but I'll give you the course and corrections. That way you don't have to formate with us, we'll work off you. Any questions, sir?"

"What's our ETA at Dunsfold, Brad? And please call me David."

"1450 GMT, David," he said with a grin.

"CAG, will you contact Tony Cippola, CIA at the US embassy

in London. Tell him to phone Colonel Basil Hammond of British Intelligence. The message to read: '1450 Dunsfold. Be there. Minstrel.' And not another word of explanation. Can do?"

"Consider it done, David. Now, the two Phantoms will launch from the cat. They'll pick you up when you're airborne. We're facing a north wind. That's good for your deck launch—you may need most of it. Brad, start your engines."

"Aye, aye, CAG. See you upstairs, David."

"Come on, David. We'll run to the stern in a mule."

We sat in this little flat tractor that reminded me of a golf cart, and drove to the stern of the ship. There was XP831 waiting for me. She looked small and lonely all by herself on this huge carrier. There was a crew around her, checking her out.

"They patched a few holes in her, David, and straightened a couple of rods that were a little bullet-bent. No serious damage. You've got a full tank of JP5. We had to adapt our starting cart, but everything works fine."

A sailor wearing a headset came over.

"Excuse me, sir, the Phantoms are nearly ready to launch. They want the word from you."

"Tell them to hold a couple of minutes. I'll say when."

"Aye, aye, sir."

"Climb in, David. Here's your seabag."

I rummaged in it, pulling out the helmets, but kept looking.

"I need the engine-start sequence out of my pocket."

Bingo. Cap in, close the bag. The chief offered to take it.

"I'll stow it behind the seat for you, sir." And off he went.

"Thanks a bunch, CAG," I said, saluting. He returned it.

"And thank you, Commander. See you in London."

I climbed up the ladder and into the cockpit, helmets on, and strapped in. The radio was on, and I could hear the traffic.

"CAG to Catcher. Launch escort."

"Roger, CAG. Ready for launch on starboard catapult."

"Stand clear catapult one! F-4A Phantom departing!"

I looked down the deck to see the big fighter hurled down the launch deck and leap into the sky. The procedure was repeated instantly and the second Phantom tore off the port catapult. My turn. I did it out loud. This was my last flight in a P1127.

"Canopy shut." Clunk.

"Oil temp above 0 degrees." Check.

"Master instrumentation switch on." On.

"Booster pumps on." On.

"Magnetic indicators black." Check.

"Throttle/HP cock at idling." Check.

"Starter trolley connected." Thumbs up.

"Ignition time switch turned clockwise, fully on." Check.

"Light-up in nine seconds." I hope.

She whined up, and the Pegasus caught, roaring to life.

"Disconnect starter." Thumbs up.

"Idling speed in 35 seconds." Another thumbs up.

I was ready. And I was nervous. I knew all of the pilots and many of the crew would be watching this rolling take-off—never seen on a modern carrier with catapults. Here goes nothing.

"Catcher, this is Jumper. Request permission to roll."

"Stand clear the flight deck! British jet departing! Jumper, you are clear to roll!"

"Roger, Catcher."

Nozzle lever forward fully. Brakes on. Flight Deck Officer giving me wind up sign. Throttle ahead. The salute. Returned. The 'go' signal! Brakes off. Rolling! Nudge the pedals! Keep it straight! Passing the island. 150 knots! Nozzles down 50 degrees. Airborne! Keep it straight. Climb. Undercarriage up. Level off, 100 feet. Swing to starboard. Tight turn. Along the ship, past. Tight turn to starboard. Airspeed 400 knots. Approaching port side of the *Enterprise.*

"Catcher, this is Jumper. Requesting flyby."

"Jumper, you are cleared for flyby."

I pushed the throttle to full as I neared the stern, waggled my wings as I passed the island, then snapped the stick to port and barrel-rolled as I cleared the bows and the big '65' on the deck. Nose up, climbing, and the two Phantoms took up station on either side of me.

"Jumper, this is Rooster, your escort leader. Nice pass. Ease to starboard and course heading 045 degrees."

"Roger. Turning now."

Not far to turn, only 20 degrees. Cockpit heat on, gloves on, thank God for the jacket. Still climbing. Oxygen on. Up we go.

"Jumper, this is Rooster. Angels 20. Level flight."

"Roger. Levelling at Angels 20."

It hadn't even been twelve hours since I'd escaped from the *Empress of Britain*. I wondered where they were, what had happened to the band, what had happened to Marijke. How would I find out? I didn't know.

What they had done was worth it.

I was taking XP831 home.

TWENTY-EIGHT

The English Channel—the same day

"Jumper, this is Rooster. How's your fuel holdin' out?"

I checked the gauge. "Over half full, Rooster. Where are we?"

"We're gonna overfly the Isle of Wight in a couple of minutes. I've already logged our flight with Air Defence Command, and we're cleared right to Dunsfold. There's gonna be a lot of folks wonderin' what we're up to, but I'm not spillin' the beans."

"Thanks, Rooster. I want it to be a surprise party."

"Jumper, make a slight course correction and fly 042 degrees. That should lay us right over Dunsfold."

"Roger, course correction to 042 degrees, turning now."

Hardly took a lean. I looked down. The Isle of Wight.

"ETA Dunsfold in 8 minutes. Start powered descent, Jumper, 3000 feet per minute, level out at 1000 feet."

"Roger. Descent commencing now."

I moved the stick forward, the nose dropped and we started down, the airspeed increasing to 450 knots.

"Rooster, this is Jumper. Shall I reduce airspeed?"

"Negative, Jumper. Let's roll downhill."

"Rooster, suggest we switch to Dunsfold tower frequency. 92.5 Mhz. I'll call them up, with your permission."

"Commander, it's your game. We just had to get you here."

"Understood, Rooster. My call-sign at Dunsfold is Hawker X-ray. Switching channels now."

I took a deep breath.

"Dunsfold tower, this is Hawker X-ray."

Surprise! Surprise!

"*Hawker X-ray? What the...* ah... sorry... this is Dunsfold tower. Pass your message, Hawker X-ray."

"Requesting clearance for flyby. Three aircraft. Two US Navy Phantoms and one Lost Sheep. Over."

"Hawker X-ray, standby."

There was silence. I could imagine the consternation and speculation that was taking place in Dunsfold.

"Hawker X-ray, this is Dunsfold tower. You are cleared for flyby above 500 feet."

"Roger, Dunsfold. Did you copy, Rooster?"

"Roger, Jumper—sorry, X-ray!"

"No sweat, Rooster. Descending to 500 feet. I have Dunsfold Aerodrome in visual. Estimating four miles. Turning to starboard."

"Roger, X-ray."

I held XP831 steady, lined up on the runway, and the three aircraft roared over Dunsfold at 400 knots, west to east.

"Rooster, a 180 to port. We'll make a slower pass, and I'll go to hover as you flyby. Stay clear of my tail."

"Roger, X-ray."

"Dunsfold tower, this is Hawker X-ray requesting permission to hover and land."

"Hawker X-ray, you are cleared and more than welcome!"

We completed the 180.

"Rooster, I'm reducing speed to 200 knots."

"Roger, X-ray."

We came in over the runway again. This time I pulled the nozzle control lever back as I approached the tower. 831 came to a nose-up halt in the air, and the two Phantoms hurtled by.

"Gentlemen of the US Navy, thank you for the escort."

"Our pleasure, Commander. See you in London. Rooster out."

I'd been reducing power and 831 was settling to the ground. Gently, gently—don't spoil it now. I touched, breathed a sigh of relief, and shut down. The ladder had appeared, and I popped the canopy to a burst of applause and cheering! The whole station must have been there. Unstrapped and unplugged, I climbed out.

At the foot of the steps—Bill Bedford.

"Good God, David! What a shock! What on earth is going on? You're supposed to be away on a cruise, 831 is at the bottom of the channel, and literally you both drop in out of the blue!"

"I'll tell you all about it, Bill, but in private."

The Hawker people were crowding around, shaking my hand, plying me with questions, but I ducked the answers. I didn't know what the official version would be. I felt a hand on my shoulder.

"Colonel Hammond! You received my message, I see. One misplaced aircraft returned, sir!"

I grinned at him, and for the first time he actually broke into a smile.

"Well, David, I take one look at you in the uniform of a Commander/Flying in the US Navy, and immediately I have the feeling that 'therin lies a tale.' I can't wait to hear it. Bill, can we go somewhere?"

"Use my office, Colonel."

"Come with us, old chap. You should be in on this, too."

Just then there was a fantastic whoosh, and the two Phantoms did a flyby at near Mach 1. They waggled their wings, did a vertical climb, and then they were gone.

We pushed through the crowd, leaving XP831 in the best of hands, and made our way to the relative quiet of Bill's office.

"Well, David? Where did you find it?"

"On the *Empress of Britain*, sir."

"What? But how?"

"Stavic, sir. He faked the whole thing. It was extremely well-planned. The ship effected a breakdown in the channel at night. The Soviets monitored the air-to-ground transmissions between Stavic and the tower, and when they knew it was a go they used that microwave beam to transmit to the ship—there's a similar antenna aboard. They had a landing space prepared on the after deck, and all the passengers belowdecks on a false pretence. Then they put a tarpaulin on a frame over it, and bold as brass steamed into Southampton."

"Why would they do that? Why take the chance? Why not high-tail it for Odessa?"

"I've thought about it, sir. The last place anyone is going to look for a missing jet is on a cruise ship in Southampton. But I also think they came in to give themselves another shot if the first one failed. They could have stretched their visit by a couple of days and sailed when Stavic was going to try again. It wasn't necessary, but they came in anyway to avoid suspicion."

"How did you guess?"

"The smell of the aviation jet fuel gave it away, and I had a sneaking look on Wednesday night to make sure."

"You actually got near it?"

"I had help, sir."

I couldn't mention Marijke.

"The band, sir—the musicians on the *Empress*. They helped me get away. If it hadn't been for them I couldn't have done it. I left them under fire on the deck, and I don't know if they've survived. You've got to rescue them if they're still alive."

"I'll do what I can, David. It's going to be tricky. Leave it with me. We've been monitoring the *Empress* since you sailed. I think she's off Portugal right now. I'll get an update."

Bill was flabbergasted.

"David, there isn't enough range in a P1127 to fly that far."

I related my escape, the Soviet fighters, the Mayday, the *USS Enterprise*, and the subsequent events. They were dumbfounded.

"What would you have done if the *Enterprise* hadn't been there, David?"

"In the drink, I guess. Better than leaving 831 in the hands of the Soviets."

"You might have drowned or died from exposure."

"It was a calculated risk. I would have aimed for a ship to ditch near, and since I was over the Bay of Biscay I figured there'd be a fair number of fishing boats about. What I didn't bank on were the Tupolevs."

"You actually caused one of them to shoot down the other?"

"I ducked."

They broke up. The same reaction as on the *Enterprise*. Why was that so funny?

"David," said Bill, "I'd like you to write a summary of your experiences for us at Hawker's, if you will—I mean the flying, of course.

There's a lot to be studied there, and you've actually landed on a carrier with no previous experience."

"Be careful what you say, Bill," warned Hammond. "There's going to be some political fallout over this, I can assure you. We won't know the official version of the story for some days, perhaps weeks. They may say none of this ever happened, rather than cause embarrassment. You never know with politicians. So please, not a word for a while."

"As you wish, Colonel."

"May I use your phone, Bill? I must put a couple of things in motion," said the colonel.

"Go ahead, Colonel. I'll leave you to it."

He started to go, and I thought I'd step out, too.

"I've got to collect my bag from 831, Bill. Can we go get it while the colonel uses the phone?"

"Certainly. Come on."

We went out into the cooler air. It was good to be in Britain and in one piece, but I was very concerned about the mess I had left on the ship. I hoped Hammond could do something.

"Well, lad, you've had quite an adventure, haven't you?"

"I have, Bill. I don't know whether I believe that it all happened. It's like some sort of strange fantasy that I saw in a movie. This doesn't happen to me, at least it's not supposed to."

We reached the hangar. 831 was being checked out thoroughly.

I went up the ladder, retrieved the seabag, then remembered something and rooted about in the cockpit. I found the Makarov which I had stowed when I flew off the *Empress*, and stuffed it into the seabag. I climbed down as one of the technicians approached us.

"We've counted eight holes in the skin. Looks like the bullet-holes I patched as a fitter in the RAF during the war."

"Couldn't be," I said. "Hailstones. Some really bad weather."

"Hailstones? In June? On the undersurfaces?"

"Sure," I said. "I was up very high. Never know what the weather's like up there."

He was walking away. "Hailstones?"

"Yeah," I muttered, "made of lead."

We collected my bag and walked back to the office. Hammond was coming out.

"Well, the *Empress* is making for Lisbon. She's asked permission to dock, claims there's a rudder malfunction. We're going to monitor. I have an idea, if I can pull the right strings. David, I'm off to London. Can I drop you?"

"Yes, sir, I'd be grateful for a lift. Bill, I'll call you."

"I'll be waiting, old chap. Once again, thank you."

We shook hands, and then Hammond and I were away in his Rover. He quizzed me in detail all the way back to London, wanting a step-by-step account of events as they unfolded aboard the ship and during the escape. I had to be careful. As much as I trusted him, I had to protect the confidentiality of Marijke and her family. If only one other person knew in the Dutch government, I didn't want any possible reference made which could put them in jeopardy. Other than that, I faithfully recounted the details of the entire episode. It took the whole journey back to my flat. There, Hammond stepped out and took my hand.

"It was a fortunate day which brought you to my attention, Minstrel. I hope you have no regrets over the events."

"I have some regrets, sir, but not over my involvement in the operation. They're more personal."

His eyes pierced mine.

"Something to tell me, Minstrel?"

"Not now, sir. Maybe not ever. We'll wait and see."

He was gone in a hurry. I went in, said hello to Wicks, and laughed at the expression when he saw me in the US Navy uniform. I had remembered my keys from the *Empress*, which was just as well. I stepped through the door of my flat, let it close behind me, and felt a weight lift off my shoulders. It was over. Except for Marijke, of course, and there was nothing I could do about that, at least for the moment. I started to relax. The phone rang.

"Lords 0-5-8-2," I answered wearily.

There was silence on the line, but I knew someone was there. Then a quiet, menacing voice.

"Well, my friend, my very good friend, you are full of surprises for a singer of songs, aren't you?"

I turned to ice. Nalishkin! I struggled to remain calm.

"Well, Volodya, I thought you'd be basking in the Mediterranean sun by now. Sorry I had to leave without saying thanks and goodbye and all that, but you know how it is."

"Yes, my friend, I know how it is. But you and I have now a score to settle, and it has nothing to do with music. You have caused me much censure from my superiors. They have given me one chance to make amends for what you have done. You are going to pay dearly, and my revenge will cause you to suffer for the rest of your days."

"Where are you, Nalishkin?"

"Here in London, my friend, thanks to a helicopter and *Transportes Aeros Portugueses*. I am actually surprised to find that you are here and that you are safe. This way will be much sweeter, my friend, much sweeter than having you in 60 fathoms of salt water.

"But I must admonish you. That was not a very nice way to leave Marijke Templaars. I thought you had more class than that, my friend. She was very angry when we rescued her. It is amusing. We thought she was deceiving you, and all the time you were deceiving her. Now I must say farewell.

"By the way, to show you that we are honourable people, your cheque is in the mail. Isn't that how you phrase it? I hope you will enjoy spending the money. Just remember what each penny has cost you. Goodbye, my friend."

I stood there with the dead receiver in my hand. My complacency was shattered. What did he mean? How was he intending to hurt me? He implied that I would be around to regret it. Who was he going to hurt? Not Marijke, from the sound of things. We'd pulled that off. Who then? I had no one that close to me in Europe, except for Kate.

Kate?

Kate!

Dear God! She was coming back today! This is Friday, isn't it? I'd lost track. . . yes, it's Friday.

I racked my brain. I couldn't remember her telling me the flight she was on. No, she didn't. She assumed I wouldn't be here. Now what? Phone her grandmother. Maybe that'll work. I clicked for a dial tone and asked for an overseas operator, then directory for Colebrook, New Hampshire. I didn't know the first name, but how many Fletchers would there be in Colebrook?

I was given the number and placed the call. It rang for several seconds.

"Hello?"

"Mrs. Fletcher?"

"Yes, who is this?"

"It's Kate's friend David Baird calling from England."

"Oh, Kate's not here, David. She's gone back to London. I was sorry to see her go, but I knew it was best for her."

"Mrs. Fletcher, do you remember the flight number or the time she said she'd arrive in London? I want to meet her."

"Oh, let me see. I didn't pay much attention. No. . . no, I can't remember any numbers. I'm sorry."

"What time did she leave your house, Mrs. Fletcher?"

"It was about half-past-six this morning. Does that help?"

"Yes, that helps. And she flew from Montreal, didn't she?"

"Yes, the car from the consulate picked her up."

"Thanks, Mrs. Fletcher. I've got to go, but I hope to meet you sometime."

"Goodbye, David. Look out for her, won't you?"

"Yes, m'am, that's why I'm calling. Goodbye for now."

Let's see. Allow 2 hours to the airport. 08:30. Check in at least 1 hour ahead. The flight should have departed between 09:30 and 10:00. How many could there be? I phoned BOAC and asked.

"Yes, sir, we had one flight departing at 1000 hours Eastern Daylight Savings Time. Flight BA 62, arriving London/Heathrow at 2200 hours GMT."

I thanked her and hung up. 2200 hours. 10 o'clock tonight. It was already after 5. That meant she was in the air—on the way. I'd meet her. I'd check on the flight's progress and arrive at Heathrow half-an-hour early. Leaving myself 45 minutes for the drive, I should be on my way by 08:45. I had a little over 3 hours before I should go.

A bath, a short sleep, and grab some food at the airport while I waited for the flight.

I got to the first two.

Lisbon, Portugal—the same day

The two men stood well out of sight, watching the ship tie up to the dock. One was in uniform, the other in civilian clothes.

"You are certain that these men are wanted in the United Kingdom?" asked the one in uniform.

"Absolutely, Major. I couldn't be more certain of anything. I have cabled copies of the warrants for their arrest. They have been using their positions as musicians to cover their smuggling activities, and now we have the evidence we need."

"Why not wait until the ship returns to Britain?"

"We think they might decide to defect and stay in the Soviet Union, and so avoid arrest. The Soviets would make it political and use it publicly, despite the fact that they are criminals."

"Then we will make sure they do not have the opportunity."

"Will it be difficult?"

"I don't think so. The ship will be impounded until they release these criminals into our custody. If they wish to sail from Lisbon they will have no alternative. We are not after Soviet nationals. There should be no problem. So, I go get your smugglers for you."

He winked, smiling broadly at the Englishman.

London, England—the same day

Once again I felt cheated of my rest. I arose, dressing darkly to fit my mood. I was about to leave when I decided to take a precaution. I pulled open the cord on the seabag and took out the Makarov with the silencer. The cartridges and the spare magazine were still in the jacket which had been stuffed in the seabag for me. I left them in the jacket, put the gun and silencer in a pocket, and took it with me.

I made good time to the Chiswick roundabout, and from there it was an easy run out the Great West Road to Heathrow.

I was just coming out of the roundabout at Cranford when a great hulking lorry cut right across my path. I jammed on the brakes, pulled hard to the left, and went over the shoulder and down the embankment. The Jag came to rest wedged across the ditch. I jumped out, ran up to the road fuming and cursing, but, of course, the lorry was nowhere to be seen.

I went back to the car, started the engine, but it wasn't going to budge—I was stuck tight. Back to the road. There was an AA call box near the roundabout. I used my key and called in. Twenty minutes, they said. I was going to be late.

That was a generous estimate. By the time they arrived, hooked me up, and winched me out, nearly an hour had gone by. It was 20 past 10. The car seemed undamaged, but the AA Road Serviceman suggested I should have the steering checked. I thanked him, signed the chit, and decided to try Heathrow anyway.

As I pulled away I heard the klaxon of an ambulance behind me, so I pulled in to let him pass. He turned into the airport lane, and then the clamour of police cars and flashing blue lights came up on me, and I had to let them pass.

I began feeling uneasy. Surely if there'd been a crash I would have heard it from the road. The police and emergency vehicles were all in front of the main international terminal, and my foreboding increased. I had a hard time parking in all the confusion, finally leaving the car with its wheels up on the pavement in an illegal area. I didn't care. I had to get inside. There were police everywhere. I saw an inspector.

"Excuse me, Inspector. What's happened?"

"Nothing to concern you, sir."

He hurried off, and I saw one of the airport security guards. Try again. Change the approach.

"Bit of excitement tonight for a change?"

"Not 'alf, mate."

"What's up? Flasher in the VIP lounge?" I grinned at him.

"More like a body in the loo, mate, stuck wiv a shiv."

He answered a call on his walkie-talkie, leaving me in a cold sweat. I feared the answers to my questions.

I felt worse when I saw Tony Cippola with a couple of other obvious Americans. They looked very serious. I caught Tony's eye and he came right over.

"What're ya' doin' here? I thought ya' were off somewhere."

"Plans changed, Tony. What's happened here?"

"One of our guys got knifed. He's dead. Found in a locked stall in the men's room."

I felt relief. "Why was he here?"

"He was supposed to meet... Oh, Jesus! I know why you're here. He was gonna meet Kate Fletcher. She was comin' in from Montreal— but you know, doncha?"

"Yes. Where is she?"

"We can't find her. She came through immigration but nobody remembers seein' her after that. We've made announcements, scoured the terminal, checked the taxis, but nothin's come up."

I felt sick. Nalishkin's words echoed in my brain.

"Any speculations, Tony?"

"Our guy's wallet and identification are gone. The embassy car's missing. Somebody wanted Kate Fletcher to go with them without causin' a fuss. We've got the Constabularies alerted in several counties as well as the Metropolitan Police, and we've given them descriptions of the car as well as Kate."

There was a flurry as two uniformed police officers came running in. Tony hurried over to see what was going on. He returned quickly.

"They found the car. Abandoned on a side road near the airport. Nobody in it. They must've had another one waiting for the transfer. They're checking it now for any clues. I don't think they're gonna find anything."

"Tony, it's got to be the Soviets."

"Why?"

"I think Nalishkin is getting back at me for something."

"More two-week National Guard stuff, right?"

"Not exactly. I was in the right place at the right time and put a nasty crimp in their plans. Nalishkin is in trouble because of it. He's really pissed off at me. He knows how close I am with Kate, and I think he's grabbed her."

A wheeled stretcher went by with a zippered bag on it, the police clearing the way and holding back the gawkers.

"We're gonna get this out to our people and see what shakes loose. I get anything at all I call you." He was off at a run.

Hammond! I found a phone, ran the sequence, but he wasn't available. Damn! I didn't know anyone else in the organization. I left a message for him to call me at home, and I'd try him again when I got there. I took off in a hurry.

Approaching the roundabout where I'd been forced off the road, I had a flash of intuition. It hadn't been an accident! They'd deliberately kept me from the airport! They knew my intentions from monitoring my calls! God dammit! Why had I thought it didn't matter anymore? My mind raged with anger. If I could storm their embassy or blow up that hell-hole in Bracklesham Bay, I'd—wait!

Oh God!

Bracklesham Bay!

The 'playroom'!

That's where they'd taken Kate!

TWENTY-NINE

Cranford, Middlesex—the same evening

I hammered down the A30. Terrible visions of the 'playroom' and its toys flashed through my mind, with an even greater horror of what had happened to Marijke in that very room.

What if I were wrong and Kate wasn't there? Well, so be it. But if I were right, would I be in time?

I pushed the pedal down and shot up to 110MPH. Keeping to country roads at this hour meant little traffic and I maintained my speed for most of the run. Ironically, it was one of the few times I would have welcomed a police car, and not one appeared.

It took me 40 minutes to reach Bracklesham Bay.

I parked the car off the road on a side lane, reached into the jacket for the Makarov, the silencer, and the magazine, checked the load, screwed on the silencer, and got out to walk. I kept on the grass verge as I got closer to the house.

Reaching the end of the property I stopped to crouch in the bushes for a cautious look. The fence was too high. I looked around for something to stand on. An oak tree across the street. Quietly I went to the tree, managing to hoist myself up to stand on the lowest limb. I could see over the fence.

There was a car inside in the driveway. A large one. I waited, taking stock. A glow in the dark. A cigarette. Someone was sitting on the steps to the entrance. A guard. Was there another? I waited, listening intently. No conversation, no movement, just the steady glowing of the solitary cigarette.

Now what? Any attempt to go over the fence or the gate would bring that fellow down on me before I hit the ground. But since he was at the front, why not try it from the beach?

I slid carefully out of the tree, went the long way around, and came up to the property from the water side. No cover here. Makes it hard. Anyone looking, I'm cooked. I hoped there was only one guard. Why not? They didn't know Marijke had told me about this place—they thought it was still secure.

Now, the fence. What's around? Driftwood! There's a big piece—at least eight feet long. I dragged it over, propped it against the wall, then tried a cat-walk shinny up the front. Branch stubs gave my feet traction and my hands something to grasp. Near the top I straightened quickly and just caught the cap of the fence before I lost my balance. Carefully inching my feet up, I pulled myself to the top of the wall, narrowly missing getting cut to ribbons on the broken glass embedded there. I stepped across it gingerly, then let myself down the other side, dropping the last six feet and rolling to break the fall and the noise. I was in.

Next, the guard. Very gently I eased along the side of the house, taking care not to allow any twig snaps to warn him of my presence. Every few seconds I'd pause to listen, then keep going. Beside a shuttered basement window I heard a muffled moan, then a cry. A female voice. I had to bite my lip to hang on. I wanted to rush in screaming, but that wasn't the way. Inching forward to the corner of the house, I peeked around.

He was still sitting, just lighting another cigarette. I drew the gun from my belt, slipped off the safety, and stepped out.

"Good evening," I said, and shot him in the head. He fell over without a sound. I ran to him, checked for a pulse, then went through his pockets.

Keys. Two sets. One for a car, the other for a house. That one. Up to the door, select a key, try it in the lock. No good. Next one. Nope. Third time lucky. It opened with a clunk. I froze, gun ready. Nothing happened. I eased the door open and stepped into the dimly lit hall. No one appeared. Whoever was here was down in the 'playroom'.

I crossed over past the living room as quietly as I could. Marijke had indicated the door, and as I grasped the handle I hoped it wouldn't creak. I turned it a little at a time, and when the catch had released I eased it open gradually. Again nothing happened, and I started down. As in many large, older houses, the cellar was very deep and the flight of stairs long.

I had no idea how many were down here, or whether they were all in the same room. I knew there was a room for the voyeurs, probably with one-way glass, and there was a control room on the upper floor. Was there another control room down here? I didn't know how many were in the 'playroom' or the viewing room, and I didn't know if they were armed, though it was a safe bet. I was just another fool rushing in, and there certainly weren't any angels treading here.

I was down. One door straight ahead had no light escaping, while the other, on my right, showed light inside. It seemed to be the far larger room—I guessed the 'playroom'. Voices tended to confirm it. I took a chance on the viewing room. Opening the door carefully, I peered inside, ready to shoot if I were challenged. No one. I crept in.

Instead of one large glass there were three small ones, each separated by a cubicle. Privacy for the viewers while they got their jollies watching. I checked each cubicle—empty. Speakers carried the sound into the viewing room, but they were turned off. I couldn't hear, but now I could see inside.

Kate was stretched on a table of sorts. I guessed it was a rack because of the apparatus at the ends. She was naked. Her arms were held over her head in leather restraints. Her feet were fastened, too, but the table was hinged and her legs were spread apart and bent down, leaving her exposed.

The classic beginning—humiliation.

One man stood beside her, naked. His penis was lying on her right breast. He was semi-erect. As I watched he began to rub his penis on her nipple while the other hand squeezed and prodded her left breast. Another man, clothed, appeared in my view. He stood between Kate's knees and began to massage her genitals. The first man began to rub his penis on Kate's face, trying to reach her mouth. She turned her head away, but the second man, prompted by the first, came to her head, unzipped himself, and, continuing to stroke between her legs with his left hand, assaulted her face with his penis. She had no way to escape, and though she held her eyes and mouth tightly closed they were able to touch her face however they wished with their erections.

Step two—degradation.

I gritted my teeth, trembling from frustration and rage. I could crash in, but would Kate be killed in the process? What was waiting for me? How many were in the room? I found a knob on the wall, turned it slightly, and heard Nalishkin's voice, though he was out of my field of vision.

"... and you have the opportunity of ending this unpleasantness any time you wish, Miss Fletcher. All you must do is give me the list your father left. Tell me where it is, and we will release you."

Kate spoke, but her words were slightly slurred. They must have drugged her.

"No list... I don't know about it... please let me go... don't let them do this... I don't have the list... please don't hurt me."

"Hurt you, Miss Fletcher? Not yet. No, no, no. Not for a while, at least. You see, these gentlemen here are first to receive their little perquisites. Eventually they will torture you and then you will not be a pretty sight. But before this happens, and while your body is still lovely and intact, they will do whatever they wish with you. A little reward for their expertise. In a few minutes you will be fully awake, and they will begin. I assure you it will not be pleasant."

Step three—the fear of sexual assault.

"Have you ever had anal intercourse, Miss Fletcher? I think you'll find it most painful, for they are not gentle. When they are done there will not be one opening which hasn't received their attention, and undoubtedly both at once. Do you wish this to proceed, Miss Fletcher, or shall we end here?"

The two men stepped back, allowing Kate to speak. She was more in control. She was also terrified.

"Please, whoever you are, I don't have my father's list! We've tried to find it but it hasn't turned up! Please, please, let me go! Don't do this to me! I beg you!"

Nalishkin's voice droned on as though he hadn't heard her.

"And then the real pain will begin, Miss Fletcher. Your fingers will be bent back until they crack, one by one. Your toes will be crushed, and then digital amputations will begin. Should you lose consciousness we will revive you with drugs. And then we will get serious, Miss Fletcher. That lovely face of yours will be branded with white-hot irons, and those pretty nipples will be burned off with sulfuric acid."

Mlodzic here has a real treat for you—a little specialty which he learned in the Middle East. He will pop out one of your eyes—just one, mind you, so you will still be able to watch the entertainment with the other.

"And then it gets unpleasant and messy. You will be cut with knives and razors—a little at first, then deeper and deeper, until, finally, those meathooks over your head will be skewered through what is left of your breasts and you will be hung up and butchered, a little at a time. You will see your own entrails drawn out of your gut and sliced like sausage, and you will pray for death, Miss Fletcher. I can promise you that, yes indeed."

Step four—the fear of mutilation and excruciating pain.

The naked ape smiled toward the corner. He said nothing, but I guessed he was looking at Nalishkin. Who else? Were there only three of them? What do I do?

If they were serious about this, they had to prove they weren't bluffing. Or were they? Was it all just to scare her? Kate had said nothing. She wasn't crying or whimpering despite the terror she must have felt. The drug must still be working.

But I knew what they were capable of if Kate did not. I'd seen a sample in Paris. I couldn't allow this to begin. It would be better if she died quickly. I steeled myself.

If I went in I had two choices and a split-second to decide. Neutralize them, or kill Kate. In which case I would die, too. It depended on what happened in the next few moments.

"It's decision time, Miss Fletcher. I think a little demonstration is in order to prove what we say is true. This is all very real, as you are about to learn."

The one with clothes on reached up above him and brought two coiled wires down from an assortment of apparati above the table. There were strong metal clamps on each wire. He looked to the corner, then proceeded to place the clamps on the aureolae of Kate's breasts. She cried out from the pain.

"When the current is turned on this will hurt you terribly, Miss Fletcher. We are not bluffing. Do you have anything to tell me? This is your last chance."

"Please, please, believe me! I'm not a fool! I want this to stop! If I had that list I'd give it to you! Why can't you believe me? Why do you want to do this?"

"Why, my dear?" said Nalishkin softly. "Because I enjoy it."

One of the thugs must have received the go-ahead. He reached up to a switch as I steadied the gun on the back of his head. Before he could flip it I squeezed the trigger. Nothing happened! The gun jammed! There was an arcing sound from the other room and Kate screamed, her body jumping from the table. Frantically I worked the clip out and replaced the round.

"That was nothing at all, Miss Fletcher. Very low voltage. You'll get a real lift from the next one."

The other bastard was readjusting one clamp which had come loose, while his crony was turning up a dial. As he reached for the switch I fired through the glass twice, then slammed open the connecting door and rolled in on the floor. I came up to face the corner with the gun aimed at Kate.

I nearly shot her. Just in time I realized that Nalishkin was the only other one in the room. He was stunned.

The ape with clothes had a hole through his head back to front. Mlodzic was on his knees, holding his gut. I stood, slowly, and shot him in the head. He fell back and lay still. I held the gun on Nalishkin. Kate had lost consciousness. Nalishkin quickly regained his composure.

"Well, well, my good friend David Baird—singer, test-pilot, now marksman. And I should say 'pathfinder' as well—for here you are in the one place I thought was inviolable. What do we do now, my friend? Are you about to rescue the fair damsel, is that it? It will be temporary, my friend, for I will get her again—you can't stop me. You can't protect her every minute of every day."

"I can stop it, Volodya. Right now. I can kill you. That's what I should do." I was trembling. I hoped he couldn't see it.

"No, no, my friend. You won't kill me. Scum like these creatures on the floor, yes, but you are too sophisticated to kill a cultured man in cold blood. It is against everything you believe in. I am unarmed. I offer no resistance. Go ahead, free her. Leave. You win this round, my friend, that is all. But I am puzzled. How do you know of this place?"

I thought. And reached a decision.

"Marijke told me, Volodya. In fact, she brought me here. She told me many things about you, your operation, your sex-traps. In fact, her father and grandfather both work against your communist regime. In time they'll change it—they and others like them."

"Ah. . . I've wondered, many, many times, but no proof."

"You still can't prove it."

"But I will move to stop them now."

"Perhaps I lie, Volodya. Maybe I want you to believe this so I can have my revenge on Marijke."

"Ah, my friend, that is excellent. Now you are thinking like an expert—subtlety of deception in a manner worthy of a Soviet spymaster. You are learning, my friend. Soon you will be a worthy opponent in the game. It is fascinating to watch you develop."

"Game? Is that what all this is to you?"

"Of course, my friend. I bear you no ill will, nor Miss Fletcher. It is all move and countermove. You take my pawn, I take yours—you take my bishop, I take your queen. It is a game, a game of chess, but in this game the pieces are real. Now it's a stalemate. You and I, we will play again, my friend."

"I don't think so, Volodya. If this is a game, then bad luck for you. You lose. It's check, and mate."

I shot him in the heart. He slid off the chair, his eyes staring at me, and fell across Mlodzic. I went to him, felt for a pulse. There was none.

Quickly I turned to Kate, undoing the clamps and unbuckling the straps which held her. Her clothes had been thrown on a chair, and I grabbed them in a bundle. Gently I lifted her head, and called her name.

"Kate. . . Kate. . . everything's all right, love. Come on, wake up. . . it's David."

Her eyes flew open.

"David? *David!* Oh, God, it must have been real! Look at me! Those men, where are they? Are they coming back? Oh, God, David, help me! Help me!"

"Sshh, it's over. They're gone. Come on, let's get you out of here.

"I stood between her and the bodies, and helped get her off the table facing away from them. We moved quickly to the stairs.

"How did you find me? The last thing I remember clearly is being made to get into another car, and then they stuck me with a needle. When I started to wake up I was tied down—I couldn't move. Then the questions, the list, about you, about Mom and Dad, but mostly the list—that damned list."

She ranted, almost delirious, as we climbed the stairs and went into the living room. She stood there, trying to talk, still unashamedly naked.

"Kate, put your clothes on. We've got to go."

"I'll try. I can't lift my arms. Help me, please."

"Here, put these on first."

I handed her her panties. She started to pull them up, then lost her balance. I caught her as she fell against me.

"Sorry."

"It's okay."

We got her panties on, and I handed her the bra.

"You'll have to help. I can't reach behind me."

"Forget it, Kate! Just get your slacks and sweatshirt on!"

I was getting exasperated.

"Kate, I know this isn't your fault, but we've got to get out of here. Come on!"

We got the rest of her clothes on in a hurry. I took her by the arm and led her to the door, ushered her through, then closed it behind me. I steered her away from the body on the steps, and we walked toward the gate, passing the Mercedes.

"My suitcase and my carry-on are in the car, David."

I still had the keys from the guard. We retrieved her bags. At the gate I fumbled keys again, found the right one, and relocked after we passed through. Heading up the lane Kate suddenly slumped against me, walking unsteadily. It was hitting her again.

I looked ahead. Dimly, in the light of a streetlamp, I saw a man apparently out for a stroll. He was smoking a pipe, and sauntering away from us. We were catching up. I couldn't see his face in the shadows as we walked by. I kept my hand on the gun.

A quiet voice said "Good evening, Minstrel."

I jumped, the gun was in my hand, and I caught myself.

"Jesus, Colonel, I could have shot you! How did you find me?"

"Two and two made four. The message from you, Miss Fletcher's disappearance—and we've had a watcher on this place since you told us about it. He rang and described your car. We came straightaway. Heard you talking to Nalishkin. Felt you had it under control. You made the prudent move, all things considered. Now, what have you left for us back there?"

"Four dead. One outside, three in the cellar."

"What did you use?"

"This." I pulled out the Makarov.

"Where'd you get this?"

"On the ship. It's Nalishkin's."

"You shot them with Nalishkin's own gun? Bloody marvellous!"

"What do you mean, Colonel?"

"When the Soviets find this little homosexual love nest of murder and suicide, they're going to want to keep the lid on it tightly. Nalishkin's own gun. That makes it easy!"

I handed it over, bullets, magazine, everything.

"Do you have a gun I can use, Colonel? Under the circumstances I wouldn't want to be unprotected."

He reached in his jacket and handed me a 9mm Browning.

"I shouldn't think you'll need it."

I took out both sets of the guard's keys.

"The keys, sir. The gates, the house, and the Mercedes."

"Anything else?"

"No, sir. I've got to take Kate home. They used a drug to get her here quietly. Coupled with the trauma, it's affecting her strangely."

He looked more closely at her. She was out of it.

"They shouldn't have used a drug—it minimizes the reality. Not thought out. Hurriedly organized. She'll throw it off, David. We use this sort of thing from time to time. There are no lasting effects, but some lose all their inhibitions when they come down."

"That's what's happened. We're going, sir."

"Forget about this, David. Leave it to us. It probably won't even make the papers. The Soviets will make it vanish."

"Colonel." This was hard for me to face. "I shot Nalishkin in cold blood. I needn't have. I was judge, jury, and executioner. My voice broke. "I don't know who I am anymore."

"David," he said gently, "it had become personal with him. If you hadn't finished it tonight it would have gone on. It's over. Go away and forget it."

"No, I may learn to live with it, but I'll never forget it. For me it wasn't a game. Good night, sir."

I held Kate 'til we got to the car, and placed her in the passenger seat. She was still very groggy. I drove off, filled with disturbing thoughts. Gradually I sifted through them and reached a conclusion—the only one which helped my peace of mind.

This time it was really over.

Colonel Hammond had said so.

THIRTY

After midnight, Saturday, June 23, 1962

We were somewhere near Staines when Kate seemed to snap out of it and sit up. It was almost 01:00am.

"David," she whispered, "my mouth is parched. I need some water, and I have to pee badly. I'm sorry."

"Don't be. I'll find something."

The only thing I was sure of at that hour was the airport—the coffee shop is open all night. We were close to it, so I took a short-cut to the west of Heathrow which put us on the approach road and into the parking lot.

"Can you walk, Kate?"

"Yes, I think so. Just hold on to me. I'm not very steady."

She was trembling. We went inside, then straight to the ladies' room. I stood outside and waited. I wasn't taking chances in this place. When she appeared I was relieved.

We made our way slowly to the coffee shop and sat at a small booth for two. I ordered coffee, Kate asked for two glasses of orange juice and two glasses of water. When the water came she downed both glasses immediately, then sipped the juice.

To this point we'd hardly spoken. I felt I had to wait until she was ready. It came, haltingly.

"It's partly my own fault. The picture on the ID didn't really look like the guy who met me. I should've been more careful, especially after what happened in Colebrook. But I just stupidly went along with him."

"If you hadn't they would have jabbed you in the airport and pretended you were sick. They weren't taking 'no' for an answer."

"What happened to the real guy from the embassy?"

"They killed him. He was found in the men's room."

She shuddered. "Oh, God."

There was a silence as she collected her thoughts.

"How did you find me? Why was it you and not the police or the CIA? And with a gun? I don't understand."

"It's a long story, Kate, and eventually I'll tell you the whole thing. You deserve to know, considering what you've been through. Very simply, I stumbled into some nasty people who were searching for your dad's list."

"The damned list. I wish I'd never heard of it. I don't think it exists, that's how tragic this is. People dying, and for what?"

"There's something strange about the list, Kate. Official statements say there's no such thing, but there are still people desperately trying to find it."

"These guys never said who they were. I guessed Russian."

"Yup. KGB."

"And you're mixed up with them?"

"Like I said, it's a long story."

"How long has this been a part of your life? I feel like I don't know who you are."

"Since the day you told me about *Antigone*. I was approached and asked to help because I was going to sing at the Soviet embassy. Before I knew it I was in shit right up to my neck."

There was another introspective silence.

"David, I remember what was going on in that cellar, but it doesn't seem real. I can see it, but it's not me—it was like watching someone else."

"It's probably because of the drug they used on you, and because our minds try to cope with bad situations by masking them to make them less-threatening."

"Did you hear any of the horrible things they said they were going to do?"

"Most of them. I thought at first it might be a bluff to scare you, but it nearly got out of control."

She pondered again.

"They meant it, didn't they?"

"Yes. The electrodes convinced me."

"Where were you?"

"In an area they use for voyeurs with one-way glass. They couldn't see me, but I could see you. I couldn't tell how many there were. If there'd been others with guns we'd both be dead."

"That close?"

"It was that close."

Another silence.

"You killed them, didn't you? The three in the room with me."

I nodded.

"I'm sorry. . . no. . . I'm glad. . . God. . . I don't know."

"I had no choice, Kate. In the past two weeks I've learned a lot about myself. Some of it scares me."

She recollected again.

"I seem to remember standing in front of you naked and thinking some pretty stupid thoughts."

"The after-effects of the drug. It released all your inhibitions. You weren't in control, so don't think about it."

"Aren't inhibitions just the barriers we create to hold back our desires? God, if that was any indication of what I really want I'm surprised I haven't attacked you in the night."

I smiled. "I think inhibitions mask our fantasies, too, and we all have them. It doesn't mean we either intend or want to make them real. Fantasies are just the speculation of the imagination. Never-never land."

Another think.

"What's happening with the new lady in your life?"

I considered my reply. "I may never see her again. It's another part of the long story. It's very involved. You can't imagine what's happened to me since you left last Friday."

"If tonight was a sample I'd believe anything."

I hesitated before bringing the next subject up.

"Kate, we should face up to a couple of unpleasant things."

"Like what?"

"You were abused tonight, both psychologically and physically. Do you want to go to a hospital, or see a doctor?"

"I thought about it in the car. My thoughts were vague, but this is what I feel. It was like a nightmare. Now I'm awake, it's over, and it's fading away. If you hadn't arrived and they'd hurt me it would have been a different story. Maybe my mind would have come apart. It's really like it happened to somebody else.

"I sit here calmly, I can talk about it, and I thank God that I got out of it. I don't know how I'll be tomorrow or even in a few days, but if I have any problems we'll deal with them. Okay?"

"Okay."

"Now let's go home."

As we drove Kate kept up her chatter, mainly about her visit with her grandmother, seeing friends and relatives, the flight, and all the minor details and variations. It told me that however much she protested, the ordeal was taking its toll on her. Still, if this was the way she had to handle it, so be it—I'd help her play it out.

Even back at the flat she didn't want to stop talking, let alone go off to bed. I made some tea, and we sat down at the table in our habitual seats and carried on with whatever came into her head. Through the circuitous process of random conversation we ended up where we had started—her father's list.

"Why is it so important, David?"

I told her what I knew.

"Then you think the Soviets want it to kill the people who worked with my father?"

"Perhaps. Certainly to neutralize their influence."

"And the Americans want it to try to get those people to work with someone else."

"They'll have a stab at it. From what I understand, your father's credibility and honesty were the only reasons so many of these people co-operated. Without him I doubt it'll work no matter who tries to pick up the pieces."

I hated to rub salt in the wound, but it seemed like the right time to try the question.

"Kate, you have no ideas at all about the list? Tell me to shut up if you don't want to talk about it."

"No, it's okay. I've gone over everything I can think of, and I can't come up with a single clue. If I had anything at all, I'd have told those creeps anything they wanted to know."

"After your parents died, is there anything connected to them that you didn't have or weren't aware of beforehand?"

She considered this at length.

"No. Nothing. I've been through this before, and apart from the letter from Dad there's absolutely nothing."

"Do you still have it?"

"I have a copy of it. They kept the original at the embassy because they wanted to analyze it for codes or microdots or something. They said I could have it back in a couple of weeks."

"I bet your dad wouldn't have been so obvious. May I see it?"

She returned in a few minutes with a photostat. It was only one page, neatly written in longhand.

"May I read it, Kate?"

"You don't even have to ask."

It was undated, and read:

"My dear daughter Kate,

"If you are reading this it means that something has happened to me. I chose the life that I lead, and it does have elements of danger. I wouldn't change it, because I think I've made a worthwhile contribution.

"What I wanted to leave you with is that you have been the best child that I could ever have wished for. I've loved you from the moment I saw you squealing in the hospital, and that never diminished an iota as you grew into a precocious tot, a scatterbrained adolescent, and a beautiful young lady.

"I hope you'll remember our holidays in Colebrook, the excitement of world travel, the talks we shared, the plays I never got to see (well, I made a few of them!), and that you'll think of me whenever you hear a Sousa march.

"Remember how proud I am of you, and carry that with you whatever you end up doing, and that it doesn't matter what you do as long as you do it well and you're happy.

"If there is one thing I am sure about it is that I respect your judgement in all things. I know this will see you through the perplexing decisions you will face in life.

"My love will always be with you.

"Dad."

It was hard to read it without a sense of great loss and deep sadness. Kate had a tear in her eye just watching me.

"I'm sure you've been asked this many times, Kate. Is there anything here that isn't normal? Anything that stands out?"

"That's just it, it's completely natural—there's nothing there that's forced in. I'd have known."

"What about a hidden meaning? Is there any way that something here could jog your memory about an incident or a place that wouldn't be seen on the surface?"

"I've done this, too, and it hasn't worked."

I looked at the letter.

"The hospital you were born in. Anything?"

"No. And not only was I too young to remember, Mom and Dad never talked about anything significant that was connected to it."

"Colebrook?"

"We were there so often, and yet I can't think of a single thing that disrupts the pattern. I thought about this when I was there, and Gram and I even talked about it. Nothing."

"World travel?"

"I've been to Europe with them, Central and South America, and all over the States and Canada. If he wanted to leave a clue there I think it would have been more specific. Sorry."

"Talks? Did he ever say anything to you about something you should do in case he were to die? A hidden envelope, a place where he'd put things?"

"No. Never anything like that. It was always positive, always sharing, always encouragement. We talked all the time, so it's impossible to single out one thing from years of conversation."

"Plays you were in?"

"David, I've been in plays since I could walk. It's been my passion. There were dozens."

"What about his reference to the few plays he got to see?"

She considered this.

"He saw *Oklahoma!* when I was in tenth grade, and two or three things from Sunday school and grade school. I don't even remember them."

"Anything from *Oklahoma!* that stands out, or that you and he talked about?"

"Nothing at all. We talked about the various actors, the singers, the music, the set—but it's all normal."

We seemed to be getting nowhere.

"What's the reference to Sousa?"

"He liked band music, and Sousa marches were his favourites."

"Is there any one in particular?"

"The 'Stars and Stripes Forever', I think. I don't know the names of any others."

"Does that title mean anything different?"

"Nothing at all."

"Why don't I name some Sousa marches, and you tell me if anything jars your memory."

"Okay, but I don't think we'll find anything."

"Take your time, and think about each title."

"Go ahead."

"The Thunderer."

Pause. "No."

"High School Cadets."

Pause. "There was this boy I liked. He was a cadet."

"Anything that connects him to your dad?"

"No."

"Okay. Next one: El Capitan."

Longer pause. "I was trying to see if there was anything from our trip to South America, but there isn't any connection."

"Semper Fidelis."

"What does that mean?"

"Always faithful."

"Nope."

"King Cotton."

"No."

"Manhattan Beach."

She took her time with this one. "We spent some time in New York, and we got out to the beaches a couple of times, but never one called Manhattan Beach. Sorry."

"The Washington Post."

"What?"

"The Washington Post."

"I thought it was a newspaper."

"It is. Sousa named the march after the paper. Anything significant?"

Kate hesitated. "Well. . . probably not."

"Tell me anyway."

"When we lived in Washington I was quite small. I liked to come in to their bedroom and play on their bed. It was a big old fashioned one. I had an idea that I could fasten a rope to one of the posts and make a swing. I didn't know that the post wouldn't support my weight, and it snapped off. I thought I was in big trouble, but dad just laughed, and they called in a furniture repair man. I remember he had to drill and put a rod inside it and glue it back. When it was done Dad said that wherever we moved we'd always have our own 'Washington Post' with us. That's it."

"Where's that bed now?"

"They sold it before we came to Britain."

"End of story," I sighed.

"No, there's a bit more. They liked that bed so well they bought one here that's almost identical. That's the bed you bought from them—the one you sleep in."

I had a sense of growing excitement.

"Kate, do you remember which post you broke?"

"I'll never forget it. As you face the head from the foot it'd be the one on the right."

"Show me."

We rushed into the bedroom. Kate went to the head of the bed at the side nearest the door.

"This one. But these posts are thicker than the one we had in the States. These wouldn't have broken."

I examined it carefully. Nothing seemed obvious. I ran to get a flashlight and a magnifying glass.

"Now, let's have a closer look."

I used the light and the magnifier, peering carefully at the one, and, for comparison, at the other.

"You have a look. Kate. Tell me if you see any difference."

She went through the same procedure I had.

"What d'ya think?"

"I'm not sure, but I think there's a line on the 'Washington Post' that isn't on the other."

"That's what I thought. Let's see if it moves. I don't want to break it."

"Then it would become the 'London Post'."

We laughed. I took hold of it, gently at first, then with increasing force tried to lift it off. It didn't budge. I knocked it with my hand a few times and tried again. No movement.

"I've got a feeling it's solid wood glued firmly in place. I'll try unscrewing it."

Again with increasing force I tried to turn it counterclockwise. It didn't budge.

"Are you turning it the right way?"

"Clockwise on, counterclockwise off. That's the rule."

She considered that.

"Dad changed the rules a lot, David."

I tried again, this time clockwise. Harder and harder I twisted, then suddenly, with a loud screech, the top of the post came free, and as I continued unscrewing wooden threads appeared on a thick dowell. The post came off to reveal that the dowell was hollow. Inside was a rolled piece of heavy vellum. I drew it out with shaking fingers, and handed it to Kate.

"Here. You have a look. Tell me what it is."

She unrolled it carefully. Her fingers were shaking, too.

"A list," she said, hushed. "A list of names."

"Read one or two."

"Ihab El-Khatie. Alexandria 3-5684. Abdul Khadirhashi. Bahrain 6-8859." She looked up. "This is it, isn't it?"

"It must be. How many names, Kate?"

She counted. "18. One or two seem to be in the same city."

We sat in silence, looking at the list.

"What do we do, David? Who do we give it to?"

"I don't know. Maybe we shouldn't give it to anyone, Kate. Look at the trouble it's already caused. If it got into the wrong hands some of those people could end up dead, and everyone of them placed their trust in your father. I don't know what's best."

"Can't we give it to Dwight Vandenberg? He was a friend of my father's, and he knows how important the list is."

"That's probably best. If we don't hand it over you're still a target for any crazy who thinks he can pump it out of you. If we give it to Dwight Vandenberg we've got to make sure the Soviets know about it."

"How do you do that?"

"Simple. Make one call on my phone. The Soviets have both mine and yours tapped."

"Jesus. I don't like this at all. It gives me the creeps."

"How well did your family know the Vandenbergs?"

"Really well. When Dwight was in the air force a couple of his postings coincided with Dad's, and the friendship sort of grew. When Dwight and Barbara were in Moscow they met us in Berlin and we spent a holiday together in West Germany."

"I didn't know he'd been in Moscow."

"It wasn't an embassy job. He'd just come out of the air force, and he led an American aerospace trade mission to Moscow. It was only for a month and wasn't very high profile."

Well, well, well. Another piece of the puzzle.

Kate started to yawn.

"I think I'll have a bath and turn in. What about you?"

"I have some thinking to do. I may want to talk to you before you go to bed."

"Sure."

When she'd left, I sat in a quandry. I had to do something about this thing, and it had to be in a hurry. I looked at various possibilities, and one began to emerge as the most logical. Getting a pen and paper, I set about making another list, returning the original to its 'Washington Post'. Kate came out looking pink and fresh, wrapped in a fluffy white housecoat.

"Have you decided anything?"

"Yes. I'm going to call Dwight Vandenberg right now. Then the ball's in his court. Do you have a private number for him?"

"Yeah, I'll get it."

She was back immediately.

"Are you sure this is the way to do it, David?"

"No. But I'll know after I talk to the ambassador."

"It's four in the morning. Isn't that a little late?"

"I'll know after I talk to him. If he tells me to get lost I'll know I made a mistake."

I went to the phone and dialled the ambassador's private line. The phone rang twice, and then I heard the unmistakable tones of the man himself.

"Yes?"

"Mr. Ambassador, it's David Baird. I know it's late, but I thought you'd want to know immediately that I've got the list."

"What? You've really got it? There's no mistake?"

"I'm certain of it, sir. Through a process of deduction we finally figured it out."

"We, David? Who knows about this?"

"Just Kate and me, sir."

"Kate? What the hell's going on? I was called to say she was missing and one of our people had been killed at the airport."

"They found her, sir, and she's fine. I'm not sure of the details. The authorities will probably tell you about it tomorrow. Shall I bring the list to the embassy in the morning?"

"Not wise. There are certain people who shouldn't even know it's been found. Do you realize how dangerous it is?"

"Only too well, sir."

"Are you willing to meet me right now?"

"Whatever you say, sir. Shall I bring it to the residence?"

"No, too risky. It's watched all the time. Do you know the Chiswick Bridge over the Thames?"

"That's the one near Mortlake. I know it, sir."

"Coming from Chiswick, just before you get to the bridge there's a turnoff on the left which leads to a lane along the river bank. It's right beside Duke's Meadows Sports Ground. Can you find it?"

"I know it exactly, sir. How soon?"

"Half an hour." He paused. "Will Kate be with you?"

"No, sir, she's exhausted. I'll see you there."

He hung up. Kate looked at me curiously.

"He wants you to meet him now, at this hour?"

"I thought he might. It's very important to him. I'll be back as soon as I can. Make sure the door is locked."

"I really don't want to be alone. Do you have to do this?"

"Yes. I want it over and done with, once and for all."

I grabbed my jacket, putting the list in an inner pocket.

"'Bye, love."

Kate threw her arms around me, kissing me on the cheek. I did the same, then left, waiting to hear the lock click. I had to hurry. I ran to the car, raced down Edgeware Road and stopped at the first call-box I saw. I made two calls, then drove off toward Chiswick.

Now I took my time.

I had every intention of being late.

* * *

If you didn't know where to turn off the road, you'd miss it. The spot was popular with lovers—secluded, dark, romantic because it's right on the river, and lonely, because of the immense sports field which backs it. I drove in carefully until I saw a car. It wasn't the ambassador's, yet there he was, standing and waiting. I pulled up on top of the dike beside him, stopped, and got out, leaving the door open.

"I was afraid you'd gotten lost."

"Took longer than I thought. Kate was a little nervous about being on her own."

"Did you bring it?"

"Yes, its here."

"May I see it?"

I handed it over. He pulled a flashlight out and scanned it. I stuffed my hands in my pockets.

"Did you look at it. David?"

"Yes, just to see if it really was the mystery list. It seemed to be the right one. Can you tell?"

"I have no doubt at all. That's what we've been looking for."

He pulled something from his pocket.

"In a way I'm sorry you found it, David. As long as it was missing things could remain unchanged. Now that it's shown up I must see that it reaches the right people. Officially the list will still be lost. Unfortunately, as in ancient Greece, the bearer of the bad tidings must be put to death. I regret this."

He slipped the safety off his old service pistol.

"I think you'd better wait, Dwight," I said, calmly. "Did you think I'd be so gullible that I'd meet you on a deserted riverbank in the middle of the night with a list that must be worth a pile of money to somebody? It's a phony."

He dragged it from his pocket. "You're bluffing. That's the list. It must be the list."

"Look at the fourth name, Dwight. Singhiz Lalkaka. Right out of the Goon Show. Look at the sixth name. Abdul Abulbul Amir. From an old 78rpm record. And to make sure, Dwight, look at the last phone number. Recognize it?"

"My office! You fuck! What the hell are you up to?"

"It finally clicked that giving it to you might be handing it to the KGB, so I set up this little test. You failed, Dwight. How long have you worked for them? I know about Stavic. Who went first? My guess is that he did in Korea, and then he made you an offer you couldn't refuse. Probably in Moscow. Is that it?"

"What the fuck do you know about anything, you son-of-a-bitch? I was promised a crack at the vice-president's slot on the ticket. Then they changed their minds. This ambassador thing was their way of buying me off. Then what do I do? Stavic set it up, and now I have enough to live in style."

"But you had to deliver, didn't you, Dwight? The Kremlin boys want quid pro quo. And that list of Cal Fletcher's was part of the price, wasn't it? Were you in on his death too, Dwight? Did you set him up? Nice way to treat a friend. Now what? No list, and I have it, safe and sound."

"How much do you want for it," he rasped. "Name your price. Whatever you want."

"That sounds desperate, Dwight. No deal. I'm not for sale. But I'll make you an offer. You resign tomorrow—call it ill health, if you like—and I won't say anything. Stay out of aerospace and politics, live a quiet life somewhere, and I'll leave you alone.

"But if I hear you're involved in anything sensitive, then the Justice Department gets everything I have on you and Stavic. What do you say, Dwight?"

"You bastard. You had to come along and fuck it up, didn't you? Well you can go to hell. I'll kill you, and then I'll tear that apartment of yours apart. You haven't had time to get rid of the list, and Kate knows about it. She'll tell us. I've sent some people to get her. You're finished, Baird."

He squeezed the trigger. Nothing happened.

"You have to chamber a round and cock it, Dwight."

Feverishly he worked the slide as I pulled the Browning from my pocket and pointed it at him.

"Drop it, Dwight!"

He pulled the hammer back and jerked the gun toward me.

I fired, hitting him high on the right shoulder. The gun fell from his hand, and he went down on his knees. There was the sound of running feet, and Tony Cippola with two other men came full tilt down the lane.

"Jesus, Tony! I was afraid you weren't going to make it. I stalled as long as I could. A few more seconds and he'd have been potting at me."

"Sorry, David. We got lost. Did ya get it all?"

"I think so. I ran a wire recorder on the car battery, and the microphone was wedged in the quarter-light."

"The what?"

"No-draft to you."

"Hey, I'm from Brooklyn."

The other two were attending to the ambassador. I rewound the spool, then put it on play.

"I was afraid you'd gotten lost."

"Took longer than I thought. . . . "

"That's what we're gonna need, David. We can count on your co-operation?"

"Anyway you want it. That's why I called you. . . it's your turf. But that shot of mine will probably bring the law, so I think I'll cut out. Better have a story ready."

"Whadaya think we are, amachoors?"

He gave me a good-natured pat on the back, and I got away in the nick of time. Three 'Black Marias' were belting down the road.

* * *

I wasted no time in getting home. My other telephone call had been in the nature of insurance, and I wanted to make sure that the policy was in force. Deliberately I parked around the corner on Hamilton Close and walked to the block of flats. The tall figure was waiting on the corner, smoking a pipe.

"Good evening again, Minstrel."

"Colonel. How are things here?"

"Under control. They arrived within 20 minutes. We let them commit themselves, then moved in and picked them up."

"Get anyone worthwhile?"

"Much to our surprise we nabbed a Soviet. That helps. He'll be expelled, and the other three will be sent down."

"Is Kate all right?"

"Of course. It was quiet, and we had them out of there in the blink of an eye. Now, I have some good news for you. We convinced the authorities in Lisbon that there were five British people aboard the *Empress of Britain* who were wanted for drug-smuggling. We got them off. Home in a day or so."

"Are they all right?"

"Two have bullet wounds, and they were all a bit roughed up, but our sources say they're being well looked after and they're in good spirits."

"Thank God for that. Without them I'd never have made it."

"I think this about wraps it up, doesn't it?"

"Not quite. I still have that list we found. I don't know what to do with it. The Americans want it, the Soviets want it, and they're both desperate. The thing is like a loose cannon on deck—its going to roll around wreaking havoc until it goes off. Then a lot more are going to be hurt."

"It's nothing to do with us, David. I'm afraid it's a matter of conscience, for both you and Kate. I'm off now. I'll be in touch. Cheerio."

And away he sauntered. I went in quietly. The night man was back at his post, giving me a strange look as I passed. I went into the flat, considered going to sleep, but there was too much on my mind. Kate was in my bed, so I left her there in the security of her parents' presence.

I made tea, and I sat, sipping, and was still sitting long after it had gone cold and a dreary day had dawned on London. Kate found me like this in the morning—gazing into space, almost in a trance. She had to touch me to bring me out of it.

"David. . . what's wrong?"

"Oh!. . . oh, nothing. I'm just trying to reconcile the person I used to be with the person I've become."

"Any success?"

"Not much. I'm going to take some getting used to."

"What happened last night with Dwight?"

As carefully and as gently as I could I told her the truth about Vandenberg. I expected this to be the final straw—that it would tear her apart. I was wrong. She listened with icy calm.

"Where is it?"

I told her. She left the room and returned with the list from the bedpost.

"I know my father, David. The reason this list was not known to anyone was because he wanted to protect the people who trusted him. If I found it, he'd want me to do what I thought was best. He told me, didn't he?"

We went into the kitchen. Kate turned a burner on in the gas stove, held the sheet of vellum in it until it caught fire, then threw it in the sink where we watched it burn into black fragments. She washed the residue down the drain.

"Ashes to ashes," I murmured, not knowing why.

Kate responded. "That's strange, David. I almost feel better, as if I'd been given a chance to bury them."

I held her hand as we stared into the sink.

We had celebrated a requiem for Cal and Betty Fletcher.

* * *

Kate went out later to the Royal Academy. Her reality was returning.

Mine, on the other hand, was eluding me. I made more tea, resuming my seat to stare out at the greyness which seemed to invade my mind. I considered my two previous weeks. . . no, it was only eleven days. Could that be possible? I felt the weight of a lifetime on me from the intensity of my involvement, and, while I was glad it was over, there was a part of me which was going to miss the unexpected challenges. I had been taken to my extremes, and I knew I would never be the same again. How this would eventually affect my life I couldn't even imagine, but without doubt it would leave its mark.

Marijke. I couldn't think of her without feeling the pain of loss. The most depressing aspect was not the distance between us, but the void of communication. Any attempt at contact by either of us could endanger her and her family—it was unthinkable.

But for how long?

A lifetime?

A lifetime of loneliness.

EPILOGUE

London, England—July to September, 1962

The papers reported Dwight Vandenberg's 'breakdown' from overwork. He went back to the States into a 'secluded sanatorium'. Privately Tony Cippola told me they'd given him immunity from prosecution in return for every detail of his and Stavic's espionage. The FBI and CIA together put fourteen people in prison or out of office because of his confession. The government was happy, Vandenberg was neutralized, and scandal was avoided.

Both the British and the Soviets agreed that the theft of the P1127 never happened. The Soviets claimed that it had been a rogue faction within the KGB acting without orders, and that the leaders had been disciplined. No one believed any of it except the part about the leaders being disciplined. Little doubt about that.

Vandenberg's 'illness' undoubtedly led the Soviets to believe that Cal Fletcher's list had been intercepted by the CIA. I told Tony the truth. They weren't happy, but that was the end of it.

Kate was a sensation in *Antigone*. Olivier himself singled her out for praise, and she had several offers to choose from. She had arrived. Her only regret that her parents had not lived to see it. I filled in as best I could, and we remained close, with a bond that transcended that of spouse or lover—ours was unswerving and permanent.

Luggage arrived at my flat one day, amazingly, everything I had taken aboard the *Empress of Britain*. The band had managed to get it together with their equipment, and when they had been 'arrested', it all came off the ship with them. Patiently I sifted through it, looking in every nook and cranny for some message from Marijke, but to no avail.

Nothing at all appeared in the press about Nalishkin or Bracklesham Bay. The Soviets kept an airtight lid on the whole thing, and Hammond told me that they had taken the mess away by launch. No ambulances or hearses had appeared to attract the curious, and since it was Soviet territory no report was made to British authorities. Hammond's team had had a field day setting up their scenario, and the ridicule which would have ensued did not bear consideration.

When my cheque arrived from the Soviet embassy I got my own back by donating the whole thing to Amnesty International's fund for Soviet political prisoners.

I managed to see the Bedfords a couple of times, and Bill kept me up-to-date on the progress of the P1127—the 4th and 5th prototypes were flying. With heightened British interest more funds were made available, and there were feelers from the U.S. Marines. Its future seemed fairly secure.

Through July and August I was totally involved in *Curtain Call*—rehearsals, costume fittings, publicity, et cetera, and suddenly, before we knew it, we were ready for our pre-run in Brighton. It went well, and with minor changes to a couple of production numbers we headed for London and the West End stage. When I could, while we were in Brighton, I drove to Seaford and walked out on the cliffs to sit and look at the Seven Sisters. I felt Marijke here, and I missed her so much that I clung to every tangible link to bring her closer.

Nicki phoned the Soviet embassy from time to time to ask for her. For a few weeks they said that she had not returned from Russia, then they changed it to say that she had been 'reassigned'. I shuddered at the ambiguity.

On opening night in early September, Kate, Nicki and House were with me in my dressing room before the show, helping keep track of the phone calls, flowers, cards, gifts, and telegrams which arrived. Despite the excitement and anticipation, I was inwardly depressed that Marijke wasn't to share this moment with me. I tried not to let the cast see my sadness, but on this night it was extremely difficult to keep the mask in place.

My mood changed abruptly from forced good humour to exuberance when House, who had been reading the telegrams out loud, began chuckling to himself.

"I say, chaps, here's a new one for you. It reads: 'David Baird, Victoria Palace Theatre, etc. (stop) I hope your pants fall down (stop)'. It's unsigned."

I jumped up. "Give that to me!"

I read it , my heart pounding. Origin: Amsterdam. Somehow, she had done it. It was the finest gift I could have received. I went out that night with an exhilaration that infected the cast, and the show caught fire.

I did the closing 'curtain call' section with an introspection reaching deep inside me. I knew I was a different person because of my eleven days in June, and I was only gradually finding out how it had affected me. This night was one of the revelations. The audience sensed it, and there was an electricity in the air which charged the hushed gathering. I sang my last song clearly and effortlessly, but with unashamed tears.

> "You are here, closer to my heart,
> You are here, though we're far apart;
> I can't understand,
> I reach for your hand—it's not there,
> But, in my dreams,
> I feel your touch, and so it seems
> Here you are—walking by my side,
> Never far—love can't be denied;
> But when I awake, alone with my fear—
> It's so unclear;
> My life won't ever be 'til you are here."

And now there was a glimmer of hope.

THE END